THE NIGHT ALIVE

and Other Plays

Other Books by Conor McPherson published by TCG

A Dublin Carol

Port Authority

The Seafarer

Shining City

The Weir and Other Plays
  Also includes:
  St. Nicholas
  This Lime Tree Bower
  The Good Thief
  Rum and Vodka

THE NIGHT ALIVE

and Other Plays

Conor McPherson

THEATRE COMMUNICATIONS GROUP
NEW YORK
2016

The publication of *The Night Alive and Other Plays* by Conor McPherson, through TCG's Book Program, is made possible in part by the New York State Council on the Arts with the support of Governor Andrew Cuomo and the New York State Legislature.

TCG books are exclusively distributed to the book trade by Consortium Book Sales and Distribution.

Library of Congress Cataloging-in-Publication Data

McPherson, Conor, 1971–
McPherson, Conor, 1971–Bird. McPherson, Conor, 1971–Veil.
The night alive : and other plays / Conor McPherson.
ISBN 978-1-55936-473-7 (softcover)
Subjects: BISAC: DRAMA: English, Irish, Scottish, Welsh. FICTION: Occult and Supernatural. BODY, MIND AND SPIRIT: Unexplained Phenomena.
PR6063.C73 A6   2016
822/.914—dc23   2015049194

Cover art by AKA for the original Donmar Warehouse production of *The Night Alive*
Cover photo by Adrian Samson/GettyImages

First Edition, February 2016

For my wife and daughter with love always

Contents

Introduction

The best plays come in a flash. An image, a feeling, and that's it. You know these ideas because they are the undeniable ones that won't let go. They pull you in and compel you to start scribbling notes. If you are a playwright and you have one of these on the go, you know you have a responsibility. To what? Something that doesn't exist? But the good ideas feel like they do exist. They're just beyond view, and you're trying to capture them with glimpses that may or may not be accurate.

So many things can go wrong along the way between the vision and its presentation on stage – missed beats in the writing (or too many beats), the wrong cast, wrong director, wrong theatre or just the wrong time. Any and all of these may consign your hard work to the 'Who Cares?' file. And you know you are playing Russian roulette – it all comes down to those couple of hours on opening night. But you keep the faith and you pull the trigger. What else can you do?

You start scribbling. Worry, issues of control, and even, ironically, a sense of longing to be free of the process, all propel you to write your first draft. Subsequent drafts can never quite fix all the problems, yet neither can they prompt the same exhilaration. Many playwrights I've talked with agree that the best moments are often those tentative notes when the ghosts first present themselves in your mind. They are so insubstantial, yet bear their complete mysterious history within. This is when playwriting is at its most private and, paradoxically, when the play is at its most beautiful. The more real you make it the less magic it retains. You are aware of this but what can you do? You keep going. Always writing at the very edge of your limitations. And your limitations are not necessarily a bad thing. Your limitations are in fact what give you your unique voice. But it's hard to view your limitations in a warm light when you've just read over your work and it makes you embarrassed.

The truth is nobody really knows how to write a good play. You just do your best to avoid writing a bad one. The rest falls to fate. Joe Penhall once said to me, 'Who knows if the magic is there and – even if it is – will the bastards see it?', which I think sums up the car crash of hope, despair and paranoia that accompanies artistic creation.

And the enemy of art is not the pram in the hallway, it is self-consciousness. When you are young you know nothing, least of all yourself. You write plays quickly, perhaps in a matter of days. As you grow older – and if you've managed to survive some decades of playwriting – you may gain a little wisdom. But you lose your recklessness. Why? Because, like the ageing stuntman, you know exactly what's at stake each time you do it. Further, you are no longer new. Everyone knows what you can do and they have certain expectations. So you go the long way round, trying to surprise everyone. But going the long way round kills spontaneity.

And what's wrong with that? Well, Neil Young's late producer, David Briggs, said that the best way to record music is the simplest way. You get the mic as close to the sound as you possibly can and just record it as it is. 'The more you think, the more you stink' was his mantra. Neil Young's albums are full of first takes – often the very first time the band have ever played the song – because that's where the magic is. Neil Young calls it 'the spook'. In other words you've got to be careful not to perfect what you are doing to the extent it has no soul left. Perfect is not best. Okay, so he's talking about rock 'n' roll, but there's something in that for playwriting too.

And if there's anything I can see that's worth passing on it's this: it's as important to *forget* what you've learned as it is to learn.

The short story *The Birds* by Daphne Du Maurier was presented to me by the inimitable producer David Pugh. I had no flash of inspiration, just a desire to write it and to explore the female psyche (i.e. it has self-consciousness written all over it!). People have said it's their favourite play of mine, but I suspect there are many others who felt I should stick to my more well-trodden ground. For myself, I like it because it really feels like someone else wrote it, and that's a rare enough relief for any playwright watching their work on stage. I want to thank Joe Dowling at the Guthrie Theater in Minneapolis and Henry Wishcamper, who directed the American premiere. Their belief in the play has undoubtedly ensured its continued life in the United States, where it's regularly being produced. Whatever I was working out in that play continues to draw directors and actors – and that's everything.

David Hare was once asked what advice he'd give to young playwrights, and he said: to enjoy the moment if your first play or two
finds an audience. People are interested and you're confident – because you have lots of ideas you haven't tried yet. But, he cautioned,
you must remember that sustaining that for thirty or forty years, fighting through the sheer incomprehension that may greet your efforts to
develop your craft, is no picnic.

Bearing this in mind, I recognise that, in some quarters, a certain incomprehension greeted *The Veil*. It was a play written out of the disgust and panic at how my country had managed to almost destroy
itself over the previous ten years. And personally I was also in thrall
to the world of eighteenth- and nineteenth-century German transcendental philosophy, not to mention an obsession with James Joyce's
concept of time in *Finnegans Wake*. Talk about a heady brew! I think
we presented a beautiful show (incredible design by Rae Smith and
lighting by Neil Austin), and every performance was top notch,
but when all the moments were strung along together, maybe some
people – certainly more than usual anyway! – emerged wondering
what all the ideas had to do with each other. And yet something tells
me this play will be back in my life at some point, and that I may
even begin to see it as one of my favourites some day because,
strangely, it's the tricky ones you end up most proud of.

And then, out of nowhere, August Strindberg walked into my life,
kicked me up the arse, and reminded me what it's all about. Josie
Rourke who had just taken over at the Donmar Warehouse asked me
to consider adapting *The Dance of Death* for their young directors'
programme. And Strindberg just took me right back to the beginning:
i.e. it doesn't matter what's happening on stage as long as it has
energy and emotion. Ideas flow from the energy, not the other way
round. And we ended up with a cracking little production directed by
Titas Halder starring Kevin McNally, Indira Varma and Daniel La
Paine that really blew people away. The U.S. premiere of the adaptation at Writers Theatre in Chicago was also a joy, with Larry Yando,
Shannon Cochran and Philip Earl Johnson. It was a source of great
personal satisfaction that their production won the premier Chicago
theatre prize, the Joseph Jefferson Equity Award for Best Production,
and that Larry and Shannon won the awards for Best Actor and Best
Actress respectively.

Instructive for me were how Strindberg's plays seemed so free dra-
matically. Where most plays turned left, he went right, and vice versa.

He was truly original in this regard and I could see all the writers he'd broken a path for – Samuel Beckett, Harold Pinter, Edward Albee and so on. And I decided that my next play would have no 'ideas' (if that's possible), only feelings. And it came in a flash one day while I was pushing my daughter on the swing in the park. And when I went home I started scribbling.

The play which emerged was *The Night Alive*. Bringing it to the stage was one of the most pleasurable experiences I've yet had in the theatre. I'm not saying this is because I brought anything to the table which I didn't have before, but probably because I was simply a different person.

I was beginning to understand that for a new play to come, the playwright has to be renewed also. By this I mean part of you has to die, and part of you has to be born. Every few years we change. I don't know if we change for the better or for the worse, and that's not even important. Our circumstances change, perhaps even subtly. You move home. A relationship ends. A child arrives. Someone passes away. All of these normal events rebuild your world and demand a new understanding.

The writer seeks to place order, indeed beauty, on the chaos of experience. Whether this impulse is innate or conscious cannot be known. The writer writes because this is how they function. Without it the writer will lose their mental health. The question of free will versus determinism is interesting within this context. Does one choose a subject (or an 'idea') or are we compelled to write about the only subject we *can* write about at that time? I suspect it's the latter. And this is of course a paradox: How can you be creative if you do not freely 'choose' your subject?

The answer lies somewhere in the middle. The writer does not truly create. They merely interpret. Their skill as an interpreter affects the success of the project, but in a sense all writing is really only an adaptation of an already questionable and unstable reality.

But of course, the playwright is also required to be a collaborator and my accomplices in this case, Ciarán Hinds, Jim Norton, Michael McElhatton, Caoilfhionn Dunne and Brian Gleeson, could not have more perfect. There was a tremendous balance in the cast. While all were very different, each performer complimented and augmented the strengths of the others. This was especially useful considering our sole guiding principle was to stay ahead of the audience. We shifted mood and tone as often and as stealthily as we could, allowing the substance of the play to exist beneath the surface, in between the lines, in the space between the characters' needs, histories and motivations.

And what was that substance? Well, we never discussed it. We never regarded the text of the play as the most important thing. We did no 'table work' (i.e. sitting round table discussing the script). From the first day of rehearsal we were on our feet, digging into every moment, mining for the hidden details underneath, indeed beyond, the play.

All I can say is that the particular chaos at the heart of *The Night Alive* seems to be specifically that of broken families. No parent is with their child, no family is intact, almost no one has a home. And yet, like a nativity play, shelter is found, alongside love, redemption and rebirth.

When we presented the play in London at the Donmar Warehouse some critics struggled with the uplifting outcome, comparing it unfavourably with earlier, gloomier, work. And yet when we presented the exact same production in New York at the Atlantic Theatre, the play received the best reviews I've ever had, and the New York Drama Critics' Circle presented me with their award for Best New Play of the year. A pat on the head from critics may not sit well with the rebellious self-image of most playwrights, but the truth is, we'll take the love.

Whereas in the past I had shunned opportunities to see new productions of my plays, for some reason with *The Night Alive*, I felt compelled to attend to help with productions at Steppenwolf in Chicago and at The Geffen Playhouse in LA. There was still something in the nebulous heart of the play I could never quite grasp, but which always drew my attention.

To have your play accepted so unconditionally is the kind of playwriting equivalent of a climber reaching a summit. You get a good clear view of your journey to this point, but at the same time you are drawn towards other mountains – now shrouded in the mist.

All you know is that you have to go right back down if you're ever going to get up there again.

—Conor McPherson

THE NIGHT ALIVE

The Night Alive was first performed at the Donmar Warehouse, London, on 19 June 2013 (previews from 13 June), with the following cast:

MAURICE	Jim Norton
TOMMY	Ciarán Hinds
AIMEE	Caoilfhionn Dunne
DOC	Michael McElhatton
KENNETH	Brian Gleeson

Director	Conor McPherson
Designer	Soutra Gilmour
Lighting Designer	Neil Austin
Sound Designer	Gregory Clarke
Casting Director	Alastair Coomer CDG

'When they saw the star they rejoiced. They went into the house and they saw Mary and her child. And falling to their knees they offered their gifts of gold and frankincense and myrrh.'

Matthew 2:11–12

Characters

MAURICE, *seventies*
TOMMY, *fifties*
AIMEE, *late twenties*
DOC, *forties*
KENNETH, *thirties*

Dialogue in square brackets [ ] is unspoken.

Setting

An Edwardian house near the Phoenix Park in Dublin.
Autumn. The present.

*The first-floor drawing room of an Edwardian house near the
Phoenix Park in Dublin. High double doors lead to a small metal balcony with steps down to the rear garden. The room is now a bedsit. It
is cluttered and messy. Boxes of knick-knacks, old newspapers and
magazines are piled into corners, spilling out on to a single bed on
one side of the room and a camp bed on the other. There is a battered
old armchair, a 1970s stereo, a foldaway chair or two. A door leads
to a little toilet that has been built in one corner. Another door leads
to the landing and the rest of the house.*

*There is a little gas hob and a sink with dirty dishes and saucepans
piled into it. There is a framed poster of Steve McQueen on his motorbike from the movie* The Great Escape, *a framed poster of Marvin
Gaye's album cover,* What's Going On, *and two posters advertising
Finland as a holiday destination.*

*As the play begins, moonlight pours in through the double doors from
the balcony. The door to the hallway is open and electric light spills
in from the landing. An elderly gentleman,* MAURICE, *is standing in
the room looking out at the garden. He wears pyjamas and a dressing
gown and carries a walking stick. He stands still for a moment until
distant church bells and a dog barking somewhere stir him from his
reverie. He looks about the room in disgust. He lifts a garment or two
with his stick, wondering how anyone can live like this. We hear*
TOMMY'*s voice coming up the stairs to the balcony from the garden.
As* MAURICE *hears voices approaching he hurries quietly off
through the landing.*

TOMMY (*off*). Now, that's it. Yeah. This is it. Up the stairs. Are you
alright? That's it. Head back. Nice and easy. Around here now.
This is us.

We see TOMMY *leading* AIMEE *in. He is in his fifties, well built
but well worn. She is in her twenties, skinny and also well worn.
She holds her head back, pressing* TOMMY'*s Dublin Gaelic football tracksuit top to her face. It is covered in blood. She stands
there while* TOMMY *goes and switches on the main light. An
overhead light comes on.*

Come in we'll sit you down and we can have a look.

The light blinks off again.

Ah balls! Hold on. You don't have a euro, do you? That's alright. I'll jimmy the lock.

He goes to a few drawers and roots noisily around and finds a hammer amid the detritus. He takes a chair and stands on it to reach an electric coin meter. He bangs the side of the meter, jimmies the lock, and pulls out the coin drawer. He takes a coin from the drawer and sticks it back in the slot. He turns the dial and the lamp pops back on again. The stereo erupts into life too, blasting out some music. TOMMY *quickly shuts it off.*

This place is a fucking madhouse. Now. That's it. Come here till we have a look at you. Sit down here. There we go.

He shifts a pile of crap off the armchair and sits AIMEE *down.*

AIMEE. Your jacket is wrecked.

TOMMY. Don't mind that, I'll bang that in the washing machine. Show me.

AIMEE *lets* TOMMY *gently pull the tracksuit top away from her face. Her nose has bled down her chin and on to her clothes.* TOMMY *adjusts her head so he can see.*

TOMMY. Well, the bleeding has stopped.

AIMEE. Is it broken?

TOMMY. I don't know, love – it looks swollen.

AIMEE. I have a big nose anyway.

TOMMY. Like very big?

AIMEE. Big enough.

TOMMY. Was it always crooked?

AIMEE. Yeah, a bit.

TOMMY. Crooked to the left or the right?

AIMEE. The left.

TOMMY. To my left?

AIMEE. Yeah.

TOMMY. Okay. Then I don't think he broke it.

TOMMY *goes rooting through a cupboard near the sink. He finds a little plastic bowl and a tea towel.* Do you think you might get sick again?

AIMEE. No.

He runs some water and wets the towel, bringing the bowl to AIMEE.

TOMMY. You can use this if you are.

AIMEE. Thanks.

She holds the bowl on her lap.

TOMMY. Up to me, love, we wipe this up a bit.

She raises her face to him and winces while he wipes the blood.

Wup, sorry too hard. That alright?

AIMEE *gives a tiny nod.* TOMMY *cleans her face. She watches him from time to time.*

God, I wonder should we ring an ambulance.

AIMEE. No.

TOMMY. No?

AIMEE. No, it'll be alright.

TOMMY. I could run you down to the hospital.

AIMEE. No, they'll ring the guards.

TOMMY. The police?

AIMEE. Yeah, they'll think it was you.

TOMMY. They'd think it was me?!

AIMEE. Probably.

TOMMY. Well look... I certainly don't need that, so...

AIMEE. I don't want the police.

TOMMY. No, you don't want the bleeding guards in all over it. (*He looks at her face.*) Well, now I'm not an expert, but in my [opinion]... I would say, that it's probably going to be [alright]... You see, I've no ice! I've no fridge!

He throws his eye ineffectually around the room for something that might substitute for ice.

AIMEE. Can I use your bathroom?

TOMMY. Yeah! (*Indicating the door in the corner of the room.*) There's a little toilet in there, or there's a bigger, proper bathroom down the landing out there.

AIMEE. No that's fine.

AIMEE *gets up.*

TOMMY. Wait, hold on.

TOMMY *bolts towards the little loo. He switches the light on and goes in. We hear the toilet flush.* TOMMY *bangs around trying to make it presentable.* AIMEE *stands waiting, gingerly touching her nose. She goes to a little mirror above the sink and has a look.* TOMMY *comes out, grabs a two-pack of toilet rolls, smiles apologetically at* AIMEE, *holding them up, and disappears inside the loo again, and emerges, wiping his hands.*

There you go.

AIMEE. Thanks.

TOMMY. Do you want a cup of tea?

AIMEE (*uncertainly*). Em…

TOMMY. It's no problem. I'm having one.

AIMEE. Okay. Thanks.

She goes into the loo and shuts the door. TOMMY *checks the kettle and flicks the switch. He looks for some mugs. There are no clean ones. He picks one up from the floor and sniffs it, it seems acceptable. He rinses their mugs in the sink and throws two teabags into them. He quickly shoves some used takeaway containers and dirty work clothes away. He tidies up to make some space as best he can. He piles newspapers on top of other piles of newspapers. He tries unsuccessfully to fit an enormous empty pizza box in a bin bag. At a loss, he kicks it in under the bed.* AIMEE *comes out.*

TOMMY. Okay?

AIMEE *nods.*

I'm sorry about that loo. It's just one that I use. The one on the landing is for the whole house but it's always freezing.

AIMEE. Is there many people?

TOMMY. No, only my Uncle Maurice. It's his house. He lives upstairs.

AIMEE *reaches for a tissue.* TOMMY *thinks she's looking at his books.*

Do you like reading cowboy books? You can have all of them. I've been meaning to drop them up to the Vincent de Paul but I'm just so busy. Do you take sugar?

AIMEE. Thanks.

TOMMY *brings* AIMEE's *tea and a bag of sugar to her, finding something to put it down on.*

TOMMY. Sit down. Spoon's in the bag. Bag's in the cup.

AIMEE. Thanks.

TOMMY (*indicating a plastic bag full of individual UHT milk servings*). There's milks.

TOMMY *gets his tea and watches her spoon a few spoonfuls into her cup. They are silent for a moment.*

I'll tell you one thing. You were extremely lucky.

AIMEE. Yeah?

TOMMY. Yeah, I was starving. I'd been promising myself a bag of chips, so… (*He signals with his thumb: 'I left'.*) Only for that I wouldn't even have seen what happened you.

AIMEE. Yeah, well…

TOMMY. Yeah! Split second timing. (*Pause.*) And I dropped my bleeding chips. In the end. (*Short pause.*) Somewhere.

AIMEE. I'm sorry.

TOMMY. Who was he? Boyfriend?

AIMEE. No.

TOMMY (*unconvinced*). Yeah?

AIMEE. Just someone giving me a lift.

TOMMY. Do you know him well?

AIMEE. No.

TOMMY. Well this is it. There you go. You can't just get in a car with
fellas you don't know. You know? I mean, unfortunately, that's...
but there you are.

AIMEE. I don't know you and I'm in your flat.

Short pause.

TOMMY. But that's different.

AIMEE. How is it different?

TOMMY. It's different because I'm different.

AIMEE. Different to what?

TOMMY. What do you mean different to what? Different to fellas
like him.

AIMEE. Yeah?

TOMMY. Yeah! Listen. I've never hit a woman in my whole life –
ever. And listen, believe me there was times I had good reason to.
Very good reason to. Maybe I fucking should have!

AIMEE. Okay.

Pause.

TOMMY. Yeah. (*Short pause.*) I can't believe you'd compare me to
someone like him.

AIMEE. I never said that.

TOMMY. Do you want a biscuit?

AIMEE. No thanks.

TOMMY. I'm starving.

TOMMY *takes a box of dog biscuits. He takes one and starts
munching on it.*

Why did he hit you?

AIMEE. I don't know, 'cause I was trying to make a phone call I think.

TOMMY. A phone call?

AIMEE. Yeah, he grabbed my phone and he pulled over. I thought he was just gonna let me out but...

TOMMY. Yeah I saw him! Only he heard me shouting... I mean... (*He shakes his head, indicating how much worse it could have been.*) I got his reg. number 09 D something something.

AIMEE. It's just a phone.

TOMMY. Yeah, I suppose. Do you need to call anyone? Unfortunately I have no credit but Uncle Maurice would probably let us use his landline, if you want me to wake him.

AIMEE. No it's alright.

TOMMY. Are you sure?

AIMEE. Yeah, it's okay, really. Thanks.

TOMMY (*laughs ruefully*). He might only go mad if I woke him up now anyway.

He looks at AIMEE, *watching her stare into her cup.*

Do you want to stay here?

She looks at him. Pause.

AIMEE. Where?

TOMMY. In the camp bed. Or over here and I can kip in the front room, Maurice won't mind. I mean, if that's... if you want to get a taxi, I'd give you the money only I don't... (*He looks at some change from his pocket.*) Or I could drop you somewhere, it's no problem.

AIMEE *looks at the camp bed.*

Or you can sleep there. That other pile of books is all James Bond.

The lights change while music/sound fades up. When the change is complete, AIMEE *is gone.* TOMMY *stands, one side of his face covered in shaving foam, razor in hand, while he talks on his mobile phone. He is in his shirt, underwear and socks. The music fades into a little transistor radio. Morning light reveals the room's true squalor. It is the next day.*

Well I don't know what happened to it then. It was in a little yellow envelope. Doc stuck it in the letter box. (*Pause.*) Yeah. Three

hundred euros. Suzanne, give me some credit will you? (*Pause.*)
Well one of the kids must have picked it up. Ask them. (*Pause.*)
Michelle? What about her? Yeah, of course I'll meet her. Listen,
I went to meet her the last time she didn't even show up I was left
standing there freezing my arse off on North Earl Street. (*Pause.*)
Well that might be what she says but it was her who stood me up.
(*Pause.*) Oh? (*Pause.*) What does her teacher say? (*Pause.*) Well if
she's better off out of school, well then, that's… What do you
mean? I do care! Of course I care! I will, I'll text her now if you
get off the bleeding phone. Yeah, I'll meet up with her. Listen I'm
happy to talk to her if she'll talk to me…

TOMMY *is startled by a noise. He turns to see a man in his for-*
ties come through the double doors from the garden balcony. He
wears a sweater and filthy looking trousers. This is TOMMY*'s*
friend and business associate, DOC. *He is carrying a dirty sack.*

I have to go. I'll call you later. Okay. I will! Bye. (*He hangs up.*)
For Jaysus' sake, Doc!

DOC (*his usual greeting*). Aye aye.

TOMMY *goes to resume shaving over at the little mirror above*
the sink.

TOMMY. Why do you always have to come in the bleeding window?
Giving me a heart attack.

DOC. 'Cause then I wouldn't have got all of these out of Maurice's
vegetable patch.

TOMMY (*rounds on him*). I told you not to be doing that! He thinks
it's me!

DOC (*pulling a turnip out of the sack*). Yeah, but look at that turnip –
look at it! You're not looking at it!

TOMMY. You're a fucking turnip! You're getting muck all over the
floor!

DOC (*producing more vegetables*). And the potatoes are absolutely
perfect. He'll just let them all rot in the ground!

TOMMY. Well that's his business! And you fucking nicking them in
broad daylight – he'll be straight down in here now in a minute!

DOC. His curtains were closed.

TOMMY. Right…

DOC. You can't see through the hedge, Tommy. Trust me, I know what I'm doing.

TOMMY. What did you do? Climb over the wall?

DOC. Don't have to, the back gate is busted, you just push it.

TOMMY *finds his trousers and gets dressed.*

TOMMY. Yeah, well, as soon as I get my tools out of the lock-up, all that'll be over, mate. And listen, don't you think for a second you're gonna be boiling any of that crap up in here. He'll be down like a bullet.

DOC. We'll just say we bought it, Tommy. Chillax, will you? I'll stick 'em in under here, no one'll be any the wiser. (*He pushes the sack in under some rubbish and pushes some books in around it. He finds a bloody tissue on the bed.*) Hey, did you cut yourself shaving?

TOMMY. What? Yeah. Here stick that in the bin, will you?

DOC *considers all the black plastic bags.*

DOC. Which one's the bin?

TOMMY. Any of them.

DOC (*getting rid of tissue*). So listen, Tommy, my old sausage, any chance of me getting my wages today?

TOMMY. Wages? For what?

DOC. Thirty euros.

TOMMY. Thirty euros?!

DOC. Yeah – for those two days we did last week.

TOMMY. What two days?

DOC. On Monday we picked up all the Peppa Pig potties in County Meath.

TOMMY. What Peppa Pig potties?

DOC. The Peppa Pig piano potties.

TOMMY. Oh the pink Peppa Pig piano potties.

DOC. And last Thursday when we cleaned out the lock-up.

TOMMY. Cleaning out the lock-up doesn't count as a day, Doc, come on.

DOC. It was nearly dark by the time we took everything out – we had to just put it all back because we couldn't see anything!

TOMMY. Yeah, in a whole new system. Though.

DOC. Listen, we didn't get out of there till nearly eight o'clock, Tommy. So two days, fifteen euros a day, thirty euros.

TOMMY. Yeah, but wait, hold on – I bought you your lunch the day we went out to County Meath.

DOC. No you didn't!

TOMMY. I did!

DOC. You didn't! You gave me a half of your banana sandwich when we were sitting in that traffic jam in Mullingar!

TOMMY. Yeah? And?

DOC. Ah come on Tommy…

TOMMY. That was your lunch! What do you want?

DOC. You said we were gonna go to a carvery!

TOMMY. Yeah, well I carved the banana sandwich!

DOC. Don't give me that…

TOMMY. We had no time for a carvery! The traffic was murder, Doc!

DOC. Tommy, you owe me thirty squids. End of. Don't be so stingy.

TOMMY. Hey! Wait a minute. Wait a minute. Wait a minute. Who's stingy? Have I ever let you down?

DOC. No. That's what I'm… that's what I'm saying.

TOMMY. This is just the art of negotiation, Doc. This is how you learn it.

DOC. Yeah I know.

TOMMY. Of course I'm gonna pay you. What do you think I am for Jaysus' sake? And just to show you there's no hard feelings, you know what I'm gonna do?

TOMMY *goes to a pile of crap and digs out three boxes of cigars.*

DOC. Ah, Tommy, not the cigars!

TOMMY. No, no, no wait listen, listen… You know how much these cigars retail for, in any of the fancy shops in town? Seven euros each!

DOC (*simultaneously with* TOMMY). …Seven euros each…

TOMMY. Yes, bang on! Seven euros each. There's twenty cigars in each of these boxes. Do the maths. Go on, do it.

DOC. Eh…

TOMMY. Straight retail? Sixty cigars?

DOC. Yeah…

TOMMY. Yeah, what is it?

DOC (*tone of, 'This is almost too easy to bother computing'*). Yeah, it's…

TOMMY. Seven by twenty, by three.

DOC (*tone of, 'Yeah – I know!'*). …Yeah!

TOMMY. That's right. One-forty, by three, how much is that? Carry the one…

DOC. Yeah – I am!

TOMMY. That's right. Four hundred and twenty euros…

DOC (*with* TOMMY). Euros…

TOMMY. Straight retail, with all your taxes and overheads and all that bollocks all thrown in – but the beauty of this? As a business model? You *have* no overheads, or tax, you just walk into Joyce's lounge on any night of the week – at your leisure – whip these out, a euro a piece, two euros a pop, and you've already doubled your money. Because? Because why?

DOC. Yeah.

TOMMY. Because that's… you're a good businessman. Or are you not a good businessman?

DOC. No, I am a good businessman.

TOMMY. Well there you go. And that's all on me. Whatever profit you make. That's yours. I don't ask for a cent.

DOC. Yeah, but you know these are all out of date…

TOMMY. In what sense?

DOC. The date on the box.

TOMMY. On that? Don't mind that! Cigars never go out of date.

DOC. They do. They dry out.

TOMMY. Drying out only makes them easier to light. Everybody says that.

DOC. Well, even so, look, thanks, Tommy, but I can't sell them in Joyce's, so…

TOMMY. Why not?

DOC. The new lad who works on the door won't let me in anymore.

TOMMY. Why?

DOC. He says I'm not a regular.

TOMMY. You are a regular. You're very regular.

DOC. That's what I said but your man says he doesn't care how regular I say I am, I'm not as regular as the other regulars.

TOMMY. Yes you are!

DOC. Yeah, well, the other regulars are more regular, and he says it doesn't matter how regular I ever become – I'll never be as regular a regular as the other regulars because they're just way more, em….

TOMMY. Frequent.

DOC. Yeah.

TOMMY. Well sell them in the Padraig Pearse!

DOC. I'm barred out of the Padraig Pearse!

TOMMY. Since when?!

DOC. Since I went in trying to sell all that black pudding you gave me! Your man in there whipped out a baseball bat and chased me all out into the car park – I fell down an open manhole and he just broke his shite laughing at me!

TOMMY. So what do you want me to do about it?

DOC. What?

TOMMY. Well, like that's just not my problem, Doc.

DOC. Tommy, listen to me, all I'm saying is, no cigars, no black pudding, no banana sandwiches, you owe me thirty euros, Tommy, end of story, sin scéal eile, that's it!

TOMMY. Alright! Keep your wig on Doc! All you had to do was say that! Jaysus! What do you want – cash or a cheque?

DOC. Yes, cash.

TOMMY. Cash won't be a problem. (*As though* DOC *has behaved completely unreasonably*.) It's alright. Everything's okay...

TOMMY *goes to a loose floorboard and lifts it, taking out a biscuit tin. He opens it and counts out some five euro notes.*

Now, twenty euros, cash, count it.

DOC. Thirty euros.

TOMMY. That's what I mean. Thirty euros. Count it.

DOC. This is only twenty euros.

TOMMY. Count it!

DOC. I am counting it! It's twenty euros.

TOMMY. Exactly! (*Handing over another pair of five euro notes*.) Now count the rest of it.

DOC. And listen, I haven't forgotten my Christmas money you know.

TOMMY. That money is beyond question, Doc. I'm holding it for you right here. I'll have it for you at Christmas, you just say the word. I mean otherwise...

DOC. Yeah, I know, I'm just...

TOMMY. Roll around Christmas, Doc is broke.

DOC. No, I'm just saying it, so our accounts are in order.

TOMMY. Our accounts are in impeccable order, Doc. As you well know, I challenged, I *dared*, the revenue commissioners to come and audit me, you know that. They ran a bleeding mile, so they did, because they were terrified – of our accounts!

TOMMY *is putting the biscuit tin back under the floorboard as* AIMEE *appears in the doorway, holding a towel round her head.* TOMMY *quickly conceals what he is doing.*

You alright?

AIMEE. Does the water just go cold like that?

TOMMY. Oh yeah, you get about five minutes and then... (*Indicating upstairs.*) 'Cause Maurice only ever puts on the small immersion.

AIMEE. I just need to rinse my hair.

TOMMY. If you want to wait for another few minutes then you can...

An awkward silence as TOMMY *goes about his business. He seems like he's going to somehow try and get away with not introducing* DOC *and* AIMEE. *But he finally realises he will have to.*

This is Doc.

DOC. Hello.

AIMEE. Hi.

TOMMY. This is... Shu... (*He can't remember her name.*)

AIMEE. Aimee.

TOMMY. Aimee, Aimee.

DOC *just stares at* AIMEE.

DOC. Hello.

TOMMY. So, look, we're gonna go out. We have to do a few bits and pieces and we'll... We'll be back.

AIMEE. Is there any deodorant I could use?

TOMMY (*looks around*). Deodorant, deodorant. Doc, do you see any deodorant there?

DOC. Deodorant? Deodorant?

TOMMY (*finds some*). Oh look.

AIMEE (*not wanting to be rude*). Oh thanks, Old Spice...

TOMMY (*laughs*). Yeah, well I'm not... I'm hardly gonna have a woman's deodorant, am I? Although... I mean... (*He looks around.*) I might...

TOMMY *goes into the little toilet.* DOC *stands looking at* AIMEE. *Then he takes some overalls from up off the floor. He signals that maybe she should leave while he changes.*

DOC. Do you mind if I...?

AIMEE. Sorry?

DOC. Get dressed?

AIMEE (*going nowhere*). Oh yeah fire away.

DOC *has lost this round. He has to get changed in front of her. He climbs into the overalls.*

Are you some kind of doctor?

DOC. A doctor? No. Why?

AIMEE. He called you Doc.

DOC. No, it's, it's just short for Brian.

AIMEE. How is Doc short for Brian?

DOC. Well I used to be called Bri – short for Brian – but then, em...

AIMEE. But why would you need to make Brian any shorter?

DOC. Ah, it's a bit long.

AIMEE. You can't get much shorter than Brian.

DOC. No, Aimee, I'm afraid that's where you're wrong there, because, you see, you can. Bri is actually two letters shorter. Than Brian.

AIMEE. But it nearly takes longer to say Bri than Brian though, doesn't it?

DOC. Well that's why it got shortened again – to Doc. I mean people don't have all day to be saying your name, you know what I mean?

AIMEE. But how do you get Doc out of Brian?

TOMMY (*sticks his head out the door of the loo*). Doc Martens. (*Disappears inside again.*)

AIMEE. Is your second name Martens?

DOC. No, my name is Brian de Burca, but I used to always wear Doc Martens so...

TOMMY. He has fallen arches.

DOC. Yeah, so people used always call me 'Docs'.

AIMEE. Okay.

DOC. But that was a bit long so...

AIMEE. Right.

DOC. So now it's just – (*He indicates straight ahead.*) Doc.

TOMMY (*comes out of the loo, searching*). Doc works with me and he... he's my associate in our business and he...

DOC. I sometimes sleep in the camp bed.

TOMMY. ...Yeah. The odd time. If we have an early start.

DOC. But I'm basically freelance.

TOMMY. Yeah.

DOC. By definition.

TOMMY. Yeah. We both are. But Doc shouldn't be working at all because technically he's disabled.

DOC *shoots* TOMMY *a look – clearly affronted.*

AIMEE. What's your disability?

DOC (*playing it down*). It's borderline.

TOMMY. Yeah, he's borderline. I mean, the way the doctor put it was like this: apparently no matter how long Doc may have to process unfolding... events at any present given time he will always, *always*, be five to ten minutes behind everybody else.

DOC. Five to seven seconds.

TOMMY. Five to seven seconds, excuse me.

DOC. It's just with new things.

TOMMY. Just new things. That's all.

AIMEE. Right.

TOMMY. Yeah, so...

Pause.

DOC. And how are you?

AIMEE. Yeah, I'm... I'm fine thank you.

TOMMY (*finds a deodorant spray in a box*). Aha! Lynx. That do you?

AIMEE. Yeah, no, that's....

TOMMY. But look I'll tell you what, we're gonna head out and we'll get you some shampoo and anything else, what else do you need?

AIMEE. You don't have to do that.

TOMMY. No, it's no problem. We probably have... we always have a bit of everything at the lock-up.

AIMEE. Well, thanks I'll just... I'll try the water again, 'cause I just need to rinse my hair, so...

TOMMY. Should be some there now. Now, Aimee, there's beans over here. Tea, coffee, crackers. Don't eat them dog biscuits.

DOC. Do you like turnips?

AIMEE. Em...

TOMMY. Doc...

DOC (*conspiratorially*). Listen, there's a bag of turnips in under there.

TOMMY. She's not gonna be boiling up turnips you bleeding dingbat, leave her alone. Now the only thing, Aimee, when you're done, just stay in here. Uncle Maurice can be bit... he's alright, but he can just be a bit... 'Who's in the house?' You know what I mean?

AIMEE. Okay.

TOMMY. Just fucking stay in here we'll be back in an hour and we'll get you sorted out, alright?

AIMEE. Okay. Thanks, Tommy.

AIMEE *goes.* TOMMY *breezily acts as though nothing unusual is happening.*

TOMMY. Right, where's me keys?

DOC. In your hand. Who is that?

TOMMY. Who? Aimee?

DOC. Yeah. I know her.

TOMMY. Yeah? From where?

DOC. I don't know. It'll come back to me.

TOMMY. Yeah, well she's just kipping here for a few nights. She was in a spot of bother.

DOC. She's kipping in here?

TOMMY. She was in the camp bed. I was in the front room.

DOC. And Maurice doesn't know?

TOMMY. Why should he know? This is my place in here, so...

DOC. So where will I kip?

TOMMY. When?

DOC. Tonight?

TOMMY. What are you talking about?

DOC. I told you my sister says I can't keep going back there. She says her boyfriend is going to piss off on her 'cause I'm always in her toilet.

TOMMY. Well, now Doc, that's not really my problem, in fairness now, is it?

DOC. I'll sleep in the front room with you.

TOMMY. There's only the old settee in there, there's nothing else to sleep on.

DOC. I'll bring in the camp bed.

TOMMY. Aimee is in the camp bed.

DOC. But she can sleep in your bed.

TOMMY. Yeah, but that's my bed, Doc, you know what I mean? She's in the camp bed.

DOC. I'll sleep in the van.

TOMMY. Ah come on, Doc.

DOC. No, I like sleeping in the van, you know that.

TOMMY. But that's gonna be a pain in the hole! If the guards twig you're sleeping in the van again they'll go apeshit. Just tell your sister you'll stay out of her way and it's only for a few nights while Aimee is here, 'cause she's afraid to go out.

DOC *is staring out the double doors at the trees in the park.*

Doc. Alright? Doc. (*Pause.*) Doc. Alright? Come on, let's go. (*Pause.*) Alright! Sleep in the fucking van, okay? You can sleep in the van. Alright? (*Pause.*)

DOC. No... I... just remembered. I know where I know her from.

TOMMY. Who, Aimee?

DOC. Yeah. Fintan Mackenacky pointed her out to me one night
down in Joyce's lounge last Christmas. He said she's on the game.

TOMMY. He said that about Aimee?

DOC. Yeah. He said she pulled him off in his back garden for forty
euros on the previous October bank holiday.

TOMMY. In his back garden? Come on...

DOC. No I swear to God.

TOMMY. Listen, Doc, I don't want that kind of talk in here, alright?

DOC. What?

TOMMY. I said I don't like that kind of talk.

DOC. Oh, yeah. Okay. Sorry, Tommy.

Pause.

TOMMY. And that's probably fucking bullshit anyway. I mean what
would Fintan Mackenacky know? The cross-eyed fucking head on
him – can he even see properly? You know what I mean? Fucking –
(*Crosses his eyes and weaves his head around.*) one eye going that
way and the other one kind of coming around trying to fucking...
look at you – you know what I mean?

DOC *bursts out laughing but stops when the door opens.* MAU-
RICE *enters, stick in hand, a white shirt and an old blazer on. He
carries a piece of paper.*

Would you not ever think of not knocking? No?

MAURICE. Why should I?

TOMMY. Because this is where I live!

MAURICE. Yeah, in my house!

TOMMY. And this is my flat!

MAURICE. You call this a flat?

TOMMY. What would you call it?

MAURICE. A room in my house.

TOMMY. That I pay rent in.

MAURICE. Yeah, chance would be a fine thing! And where's my paper?

TOMMY *goes towards the toilet to get it.*

TOMMY. I was just bringing it up you.

MAURICE. Yeah well you can just leave it where it lands on the doormat in future, thanks, I can get it myself. And there's the other genius.

DOC. There I am. Well, Maurice. What think ye of Christ?

MAURICE. What?

DOC. How's it going?

MAURICE. Yeah.

DOC. You're looking well anyway. Is someone else doing your hair for you these days?

MAURICE. Would you go away out of that and don't be annoying me.

TOMMY (*bringing the extremely read-looking paper out from the toilet to* MAURICE). Here, I was saving your legs for you.

MAURICE (*unimpressed*). Yeah, sure... Look at it!

Behind MAURICE*'s back,* TOMMY *signals to* DOC *that they should go.*

And here, who's used all the hot water?

TOMMY. I was using it to have a shave. Is that alright?

MAURICE. What were you shaving? A dog? There's no water left!

TOMMY. Well if you're only gonna put the immersion on for two minutes a day, Maurice, you can hardly expect...

MAURICE. What in the name of God would you know about the immersion, or what it costs for that matter?

TOMMY. Listen mate, that meter up there is chock-a-block full of money I have to keep putting in – and all I ever use is (*Pointing.*) that kettle for a cup of tea or (*Pointing.*) them two lamps so I'm not sitting in here in the dark! Now if you will please excuse us, we have work to do, actually, alright?

At TOMMY*'s signal,* TOMMY *and* DOC *start to go.*

MAURICE. The guards were looking for you.

TOMMY. What?

MAURICE. The police.

TOMMY. When?

MAURICE. Yesterday afternoon. Two detectives called saying your van was caught on CCTV when you drove off without paying for petrol at a station in Enfield in County Kildare last week.

TOMMY. Last week?

MAURICE. Yep.

TOMMY. *Last* week? Well I am flummoxed by this 'cause that can't have been, em...

MAURICE. They gave me a picture. It's your van with your registration.

MAURICE *hands* TOMMY *a printout of the picture.*

TOMMY (*a sickened laugh*). You know what that was?

MAURICE. What?

TOMMY. Doc, do you remember? You were gonna... and I was gonna... and then you had gone back in for a Twix or something and I thought... (*Signalling to* MAURICE *that* DOC *is useless.*)

DOC. Yeah. I went back in for a Twix.

TOMMY (*with sudden volume, startling* DOC). You're a fucking eejit!

MAURICE. Well that's fine then, isn't it?

TOMMY. Yeah! We'll get that sorted out. (*Short pause.*) Right, well look, do you want a lift to the shops?

MAURICE. No, I've been to the shops.

TOMMY. Oh, okay. Well. I might lock-up here actually, so...

MAURICE. Well if you don't mind I was actually going to do a land-lord's inspection actually.

TOMMY. A what?

MAURICE. You think I could face looking through all this crap? No, I just wanted to remind you about Maura's anniversary mass on Saturday.

TOMMY. Oh yeah.

MAURICE. You're going to it.

TOMMY. Oh yeah, no that's...

MAURICE. Ten o'clock.

TOMMY. Yeah.

MAURICE. Set your alarm. Alright, well I'll see you later.

TOMMY. Right.

> MAURICE *stays where he is giving no indication he might leave.*
> TOMMY *loiters at the door for a moment wondering if he should*
> *just bite the bullet and tell* MAURICE *about* AIMEE. *He comes*
> *back in.*

Listen Maurice...

MAURICE (*irritated*). What.

Pause.

TOMMY. Don't let yourself get too cold. (*Pause.*) Okay well... I'll
see you later.

MAURICE. Mind how you go.

> TOMMY *and* DOC *leave, going off down the stairs. We hear the*
> *front door slam.* MAURICE *stands there, lost in thought. After a*
> *few moments he calls out.*

You can come in. You don't have to hide out there in the hallway.

Pause. AIMEE *appears in the doorway.*

And you are...?

AIMEE. Aimee Clement. You Uncle Maurice?

MAURICE. The very same. (*He roots in his pocket.*) Come here,
Aimee Clement, I want you to climb up there to that box for me.

> MAURICE *holds a little key out to her.*

AIMEE. What do I do?

MAURICE. You open it and pull out the drawer.

> AIMEE *climbs up on a chair and opens the electricity meter.*

MAURICE. You didn't see anyone bringing any fresh vegetables up through here, did you?

AIMEE. What?

MAURICE. Never mind, show me that.

AIMEE hands him down the drawer. He takes out a single coin.

Now what would you make of this?

AIMEE. I'd say someone is just putting the same coin in it over and over.

MAURICE (*ironically*). Oh, you think? Here, put it back.

He throws the coin back in the drawer and AIMEE *slides it back to the meter.*

How long have you been here?

AIMEE. Since last night.

MAURICE. How long are you staying?

AIMEE. I don't know. Not long.

MAURICE. So, what, you're a friend of Tommy's?

AIMEE. I suppose.

MAURICE. You know he's married?

AIMEE. He told me he's been living here for two years so I don't know how married that makes him.

MAURICE. Married is married.

AIMEE. You married?

MAURICE. My wife slipped on the ice outside the gate there, three years ago this week, got a clot on the brain that no one detected. Passed ten days later.

Pause.

AIMEE. Do you have kids?

MAURICE (*shakes his head*). We used to look after Tommy, you see. And now I'm still bleeding looking after him!

AIMEE smiles.

Yeah! (*Pause.*) So... You gonna tell me anything about yourself?

AIMEE. Nothing to tell.

MAURICE. I doubt that somehow. You married?

AIMEE. No.

MAURICE. Kids?

AIMEE (*a tiny hesitation*). No.

MAURICE. Do you take drugs?

AIMEE. No.

MAURICE. Yeah? (*Pause.*) I can't have any trouble. And Tommy doesn't need any trouble. (*Pause.*) Alright? (MAURICE *starts to go.*) Nice talking to you. (*He turns on his way out.*) Do you want some breakfast?

AIMEE *looks around at* TOMMY*'s filthy food station.*

AIMEE. Well…

MAURICE. You can't eat in here! Come up to me in ten minutes, you can have a boiled egg that won't give you botulism.

MAURICE *goes.* AIMEE *stands there. The lights change, dusk falling to night until all is dark except for external light through the windows and a little night light from somewhere off in the house. Silence as though no one is there. Then we hear* AIMEE *crying out in the darkness; then* TOMMY*'s voice calling out in startled reaction to hers. He flicks on a lamp. We can see that* TOMMY *and* AIMEE *are in bed together.* AIMEE *is having a nightmare.* TOMMY *shakes her awake.*

TOMMY. Hey! Hey! Hey! It's alright! Suzanne! You're dreaming! You're dreaming…

AIMEE *looks about, unsure where she is for a moment. She sits up. A loud thumping noise comes from upstairs.*

AIMEE. What's that?

TOMMY. It's Maurice. (*He calls out.*) Alright Maurice! It's alright!

The thumping stops.

He hates noise. Are you alright?

He reaches out and looks at his watch.

AIMEE. What time is it?

TOMMY. Eleven. Are you okay?

AIMEE. Yeah.

TOMMY. Here, do you want another drink?

TOMMY gets out of bed, wearing a T-shirt and boxers. He pours some rum into a couple of mugs and brings them to the bed. He hands her one and stands looking down at her. He blows through his lips.

Some dream.

AIMEE. Yeah.

TOMMY. What were you dreaming about?

AIMEE. We were somewhere. We were...

TOMMY. Who?

AIMEE. You and me. We were in here and two men came in and told me I was dead and I had to get up and go with them. And it was like... (*Shudders.*) Uh!

TOMMY. Jaysus, well you nearly gave me a heart attack.

They laugh.

Are you hungry?

AIMEE (*still waking up*). Em...

TOMMY. I'm starving. (*Getting a biscuit.*) I didn't know I'd fallen asleep.

AIMEE. Me neither.

TOMMY. That was... em... That was... (*He points at the bed.*) That was A-one.

AIMEE. Oh. Good.

TOMMY. A-one. Excellent.

AIMEE. Okay.

TOMMY. I mean this... this suits me... (*Getting his trousers and taking some money out.*) Forty right? (*She nods. He puts it on the locker.*) And I'll tell you why – because... in a... in a relationship... you have all this fucking... *negotiation* and everything. Whereas, this way: that's your money. That's... everything is – (*Indicates 'on the level'.*)

AIMEE (*indicates money*). Well look, if you prefer to call that the rent and...

TOMMY. The rent! Don't mind the rent! What are you talking about? That's... (*Indicates money*.) That's... (*Indicates 'yours'*.)

AIMEE. That's all I ever do, okay?

TOMMY. But that's perfect! That's all I would ever... I mean... the full... the full job and all that huffing and puffing, it's so unbecoming. But the hand. The hand is perfect. It's a service, I mean, it's a skill, don't get me wrong. I'd take care of myself only (*He rubs his elbow*.) I have repetitive strain injury. But that was – that was absolutely A-one. Bull's-eye. I must have... I passed out!

AIMEE *smiles. They take a sip from their drinks.*

So look, no bullshit now. The man who hit you. Was that... Was he like... a...

AIMEE. No, he was my boyfriend.

TOMMY. I knew it! Didn't I say that to you?

AIMEE. Well, my ex.

TOMMY. I fucking hope he was your ex! Jaysus!

AIMEE. Yeah.

TOMMY. You're well shot of him.

AIMEE. I know.

TOMMY. Yeah. You're well shot of him now. Okay?

Short pause.

Here. I got you a coat.

He gets an overcoat and brings it to her. It is an old dark grey Crombie.

AIMEE. Thanks.

TOMMY. I don't know if it's for a man or a woman. I don't think it matters...

AIMEE *takes it and tries it on.*

...With that kind of coat.

It looks good on her. TOMMY *nods his approval.*

AIMEE. Thanks, Tommy.

TOMMY. I mean it'll do you, just in the cold, so you're not...

AIMEE. No, it's really cool. Thanks.

TOMMY. I'll get you a few more bits and pieces.

AIMEE *darts to a spot and pulls out a pair of runners wrapped in a towel. She brings them to* TOMMY. *The runners are huge, certainly too big for* TOMMY.

What's this?

AIMEE. I was round in that shopping centre round there.

TOMMY. Yeah?

AIMEE. Yeah, I wanted a pair in my size but... that was all I could get.

TOMMY (*looking at the size*). Size fourteen.

AIMEE. Yeah...

TOMMY. They're nice! I could jam a bit of toilet roll up in the toes.

AIMEE. Yeah?

TOMMY. Yeah. Give it a go anyway. Thanks. Thanks for thinking of me. You didn't get a receipt?

Short pause.

AIMEE. No.

TOMMY. I'll stick a bit of toilet roll up 'em. They're very trendy, aren't they?

TOMMY *starts to try the runners.* AIMEE *gets some tolietries and starts getting ready for bed, brushing her teeth, etc.*

AIMEE. How old are your kids?

TOMMY (*dismissively*). Ah! Sixteen and seventeen.

AIMEE. Boys or girls?

TOMMY. The older one is a girl, the other fella's a boy. (*Pause.*) Their mother has turned them against me you see. Brought my daughter a Connemara pony for her birthday there. But I didn't know them fucking things are half-wild.

AIMEE. Well yeah!

TOMMY. Living out the back garden! It kicked in the coal shed door and knocked down the wall into the fucking neighbours and everything...

AIMEE *laughs*.

Yeah so, no matter what you do, you fucking [mess up somehow]... (*Pause*.) And then I lost my business and [that was the end of it]...

AIMEE. What do you do?

AIMEE *goes into the loo*.

TOMMY. Ah no, I had two outdoor live gig rigs? But they got impounded by the department of the social environment because – even on very calm days – they both kept getting struck by lightning. I bought them in from Belarus. The bank threw the money at me! And now it's all like a legal nightmare and I...

AIMEE *comes out to the sink*.

How can you be with a fella like that? Who hits you and...

Pause.

AIMEE. He changed.

TOMMY (*sceptical, dismissive*). Yeah?

AIMEE. And sometimes... like... if you know that you can kill yourself... (*She shrugs. Pause*.) I know it sounds mad...

Pause. TOMMY *Shrugs*.

TOMMY (*rationally*). Yeah. (*Pause*.) You wouldn't be too scared. To do it.

AIMEE (*getting into the camp bed*). I probably would.

TOMMY. Mm.

AIMEE. It's fucking ridiculous.

TOMMY. Yeah. No, listen. I've thought about it.

AIMEE. Yeah?

TOMMY. I've thought about it a lot.

AIMEE. Yeah?

TOMMY. Yeah. Me? I'd just do it with pills. Just… bang. No need to make a big bleeding point about it. You know? But then you think, 'What about the other people…'

AIMEE. Yeah.

TOMMY. That's the… What if they need you? You know? (*Beat.*) They probably don't! (*He goes and starts brushing his teeth at the sink.*) I got involved in a boxing match one time. When I was younger. I was offered five hundred quid to box a chap over in Wolverhampton. I was never any use, but I thought – hey, I could win this. Outlook, you see?

AIMEE. What happened?

TOMMY. Ah, he fucking destroyed me. But then afterwards, I'm lying on me back in the dressing room. In he walks, this big black lad, to see if I was gonna be alright. And he's wearing a beautiful suit! Shakes my hand, being real nice to me, and all I could I think about was, 'He brought a fucking suit to the boxing match!' I'd thought I'd had a chance – but you don't bring your suit to wear home unless you *know* you're gonna win, you know what I mean? (*They laugh. He gets into bed.*) Outlook. That's… It's all about your outlook. Goodnight, Aimee.

He switches off the lamp. They are in semi-darkness.

AIMEE. Goodnight, Tommy.

TOMMY. Although – you know, someone told me later it was probably a fix.

They are startled by the double doors from the balcony rattling and opening with a thump. DOC's head peeps in. He carries a bag from the chip shop. He has a nasty-looking black eye.

DOC. Guten nacht mein schitz.

TOMMY. What are you doing?

DOC. What?

TOMMY (*switching on the light, looking for his trousers, etc.*). What do you mean, 'What?' What are you doing?

DOC. Can I come in?

TOMMY. What do you want?

DOC. I have chips.

TOMMY. Do you know what time it is?

DOC. I thought yous might be hungry.

TOMMY. Are you having me on?

DOC. Oh, were yous asleep?

TOMMY. Yeah, well no actually Aimee was asleep, I only came in to get... a... get some milks, and you're after scaring the living daylights out of her here.

DOC. Oh I'm sorry.

TOMMY. Like, I didn't even have me pants on here, Doc!

DOC. No well, I just saw the light and I...

TOMMY. 'Cause I was on my way to bed, like, you know?

DOC. Sorry.

TOMMY. Close the bleeding door, will you? You have chips do you?

DOC. Yeah.

TOMMY. Well get some plates for fuck's sake.

DOC *goes to the sink, looking for clean plates.*

(*To* AIMEE.) Do you want a few chips?

AIMEE. Yeah.

TOMMY. Get a plate for Aimee. What are you doing? What did you get?

DOC. I got you a battered sausage.

TOMMY. Come here, hold on, what's happened to your face?

DOC (*dismissively*). Ah... Teresa's just pissed off with me staying there.

TOMMY. Did she hit you?

DOC. Nah, her fella gave me a smack. He broke my glasses.

TOMMY. Because you were staying there?

DOC. No, because we were all arguing.

TOMMY. It looks nasty.

DOC. Ah, it was more the way he kind of caught me. The strap of his watch kind of... (*He demonstrates the blow.*)

TOMMY. Are you alright?

DOC. Yeah, I'm just starving. Have you got any Sellotape?

TOMMY. Here, let me do that.

TOMMY *takes over organising the food.* DOC *stands there sheepishly fiddling with his glasses.*

So she threw you out?

DOC. What? Yeah.

TOMMY. This is getting like Jurys Inns here. There you go.

TOMMY *hands* DOC *a plate.*

DOC. Thanks, Tommy.

TOMMY. Is there a single here for Aimee?

DOC. They always throw in the extra scoop – you'd be mad buying another single!

TOMMY *signals to* AIMEE, *'Get this guy.'* TOMMY *brings some food to* AIMEE, *singing.*

TOMMY. Islands in the stream, That is what we are, no one in between, How can we be wrong... Sail away with me...

DOC *is singing too.*

TOMMY and DOC. To another world, And we rely on each other ah ha. From one lover to another ah ha.

TOMMY *stops singing.*

DOC (*singing alone, looking at* TOMMY). Making love to each other ah ha...

TOMMY *glances uncomfortably at* DOC. *They all eat their chips for a moment.*

Here I got you a present.

TOMMY. For me?

DOC (*takes out a CD*). *The Rockin' Sound of the Vuvuzela* – double CD for 2.99!

TOMMY. Oh, thanks, Doc.

DOC. And a book for 1.99. We can share it. *How to Survive Life Threatening Situations.*

TOMMY. Now that's handy!

DOC. Check it out. Chapter One: Surviving a Gun Attack.

AIMEE. A what attack?

DOC. A gun attack. 'If your assailant is firing directly at you...'

TOMMY. Yeah...

DOC. 'Try to move away.'

TOMMY. Okay.

DOC. 'And as soon as you can...'

TOMMY. Yeah?

DOC. 'Turn a corner.'

Pause.

TOMMY. Is that it?

DOC. 'However should you be unable to turn a corner or are not in a built-up area...'

TOMMY. Yeah.

DOC. 'Locate a large object, such as a motorised vehicle...'

TOMMY. Yeah...

DOC. 'And endeavour to keep it between you and your assailant.'

TOMMY. Okay.

DOC. 'However, should you ascertain that your assailant is discharging armour-piercing ammunition...'

TOMMY. Yeah?

DOC. 'A car will provide little cover.'

TOMMY. No shit.

AIMEE. How do you ascertain if your assailant is discharging armour-piercing ammunition?

DOC. What? The bullets will go through the car, Aimee.

TOMMY. You see?

DOC. They will pierce the armour.

AIMEE. So what do you do?

DOC. What do you do, what?

AIMEE. If your assailant is discharging armour-piercing ammunition?

DOC (*looks at the book*). That's it.

AIMEE. That's all it says?

DOC. Well you're running out of options in fairness, Aimee. I mean, be realistic, he's got a gun, you know what I mean? Chapter Two: How to Survive an Attack of Killer Wasps.

TOMMY. Well that's… (*As though he has been there before.*) You do not even want to be *in* that situation!

DOC. No!

TOMMY. Stay out of that one! Do not even get *in* to that one – would be my [advice]…

DOC. Yeah.

They eat their chips for a few moments.

TOMMY. Tell Aimee about your book, Doc.

DOC. It's not a book.

AIMEE. What is it?

DOC. Ah it's just… I write down my dreams and stuff.

TOMMY. Tell Aimee what it's called.

DOC. *The Call of Nature.*

AIMEE *smiles while she eats.*

It's just a few pages of a copybook, it's not a book.

TOMMY. Don't be down on yourself. Doc is very spiritual.

DOC. Don't mind him.

TOMMY. Read out that thing you heard on the radio. Doc hears things on the radio.

DOC. Nah, I'm not reading it out.

TOMMY. Tell Aimee what you heard, about the pope.

DOC. Ah that was... I heard on the news that they were hoping the pope was gonna be able to walk from his funeral in the church down to the graveyard by himself, but then they said that it didn't look like that was gonna be able to happen.

Short pause.

AIMEE. What?

DOC. Yeah and then the next day – on the news – the pope was dead.

TOMMY. What do you make of that?

AIMEE. That's insane.

DOC. Yep. Crazy.

TOMMY. And he's a student of Eastern philosophy.

DOC. I'm not really – I just do my yoga in the back of the van. I used to go to a class but they asked me to stop coming.

AIMEE. Why?

DOC. Because during one class... I actually started to levitate – just a tiny bit – and everyone got a bit freaked out.

AIMEE. What?!

DOC. No, it's true, I went into a trance and I started to – (*Lifts himself up a little to demonstrate levitation.*) and this girl starts screaming.

AIMEE. Were you not just dreaming?

DOC (*affronted*). No. Aimee, there was a time when no one knew what air was.

AIMEE. What what was?

DOC. What air is. No one understood that hearing things was just our perception of sound waves? So I'm saying – what about time waves, you know what I mean?

AIMEE. Not really, no.

DOC. Time waves? Just like sound waves – a day will come when we understand what time is and that we can perceive, you know, time waves, waves in time. Vibrations from another time – like why not?

AIMEE. No, I hear you.

DOC. Yeah!

TOMMY. Fucking… 'Time waves…' Don't ever get into sniffing glue, Aimee. Here, Doc.

TOMMY *holds his cup towards* DOC. DOC *gets them some drinks.*

DOC (*going to pour drinks*). Where are you from, Aimee?

AIMEE. Clare Hall.

DOC. Out in the countryside?

AIMEE. It's not the countryside.

DOC. It used to be.

AIMEE. A long time ago maybe.

DOC. Oh no. It was. It was right out. (*About to take a drink,* TOMMY *stops him.*)

TOMMY. That's Aimee's.

DOC *brings the drink to* AIMEE. *He then wanders back to* TOMMY *and stands beside him, putting his hand casually on* TOMMY*'s shoulder, all the while looking territorially at* AIMEE. TOMMY *shrugs* DOC *away.* DOC *loiters disconsolately for a moment, then:*

DOC. Here Tommy, will I put on *The Midnight Hour*?

TOMMY. Oh, yeah, lash it on there.

DOC *switches on the transistor radio. Marvin Gaye's 'What's Going On?' starts playing.*

Marvin – turn it up.

DOC *turns it up.* TOMMY *gets to his feet and starts grooving around to the music.* DOC *and* AIMEE *laugh.* TOMMY *sings but his grasp of the words is surprisingly rudimentary considering how much the song seems to mean to him. He holds his hand out to* AIMEE, *she takes it and they groove around together.* DOC *also gets up and grooves around on his own. After a couple of minutes they hear* MAURICE *thumping on the ceiling from upstairs.*

(*Calls up.*) Alright! Alright, Maurice! (DOC *turns off the music.*) Old bollocks would give you a pain in your arse. (*He raises his mug to his poster of Marvin Gaye.*) Marvin, you said it there, man. What's goin' on? That is the question. What in the name of Jaysus is goin' on? The man who answers that one will... (*He raises his mug to whoever will answer that question.*)

DOC. What's goin' on?

TOMMY. What the fuck is goin' on? (*Pause.*) Here did you check the lottery numbers?

DOC. Nah, I didn't buy a ticket this week.

TOMMY. What, did you forget?

DOC. Nah, sure it's only two-point-two million. I wouldn't be bothered in my hole playing for two-point-two million...

TOMMY. What?! Well I played it. Here we are, we might all be millionaires and we don't even know! Aimee, you want to nip down with me we can check the lotto?

AIMEE. Is it far?

TOMMY. No, just down to the Eurospar. I have to get dental floss anyway, we can buzz down on my motorbike. Look. You can pick.

He grabs two motorbike helmets, one modern and one old-fashioned, open-faced helmet with goggles.

AIMEE. Well I'm not wearing that one!

TOMMY. I'll wear that one.

AIMEE. Go on then, give me a sec.

AIMEE goes into the little toilet.

DOC. I'm sorry, Tommy.

TOMMY. For what?

DOC. For crashing in on you.

TOMMY. No, it's grand, I just... I didn't want her getting a fright.

DOC. Yeah, I'm...

TOMMY. Do you want to stay here tonight?

DOC. Really?

TOMMY. Yeah, just... just clear out early and...

DOC. Thanks, Tommy.

TOMMY. Yeah, but here, listen, about that other thing. About what you were saying she'll do for forty euros...

DOC. I don't have forty euros.

TOMMY. Yeah but even if you did.

DOC. I don't.

TOMMY. Yeah, but even if you did. I can't have that kind of shenanigans going on with Maurice upstairs, he'd go mental.

DOC. I don't have forty euros!

TOMMY. That's not the point! Listen to me!

DOC. I'm only just gonna go asleep!

TOMMY. Just don't be annoying her!

DOC. Tommy, come on. You know me. I'm a good guy, come on.

TOMMY. Yeah I know, but I'm just saying...!

DOC. Tommy, I'm not even able to get the horn!

Pause. The toilet door opens and AIMEE *emerges.*

TOMMY. Alright?

AIMEE. Yeah.

TOMMY. Okay. We won't be long.

DOC. Yeah, see you later.

TOMMY (*pointing upstairs*). And here. And no noise alright?

DOC. Yeah, I won't.

DOC *accidently knocks a pot full off cutlery onto the floor with an almighty crash.* TOMMY *glares at* DOC*, then* TOMMY *and* AIMEE *leave through the balcony doors.* DOC *starts to tidy up.* KENNETH *steps into the room from the landing. He is slim, but strong looking. He wears a grey/beige suit and fawn-coloured slip-on shoes. He closes the doors and stands there for a moment.* DOC *comes out of the toilet to the sink and continues tidying up for a few moments without noticing* KENNETH.

KENNETH. Tommy?

DOC *jumps, crashing dishes into the sink. He stands looking at* KENNETH, *startled.*

DOC. What?

KENNETH. Where's Tommy?

DOC. He's gone out.

KENNETH. Oh. (*Pause.*) I might just wait then.

Pause.

DOC. Is he expecting you?

KENNETH. I'd say so, yeah.

DOC. Oh, okay.

KENNETH. Is there no one else here?

DOC. No. Just Maurice. (*Pause.*) The man who lives upstairs. (*Pause.*) It's his house. (*Pause.*) He's probably asleep.

Pause.

KENNETH. Okay.

Pause.

DOC. I wouldn't say Tommy will be long. He's just gone to check the Lotto numbers.

KENNETH. Okay, well I'll wait here then.

Pause.

DOC. Do you want a cup of tea?

KENNETH. Nah, you have one.

DOC. I'm alright.

KENNETH *looks out the window.*

KENNETH. Look at that. You can't see a thing out there.

DOC. No.

KENNETH. The park is like a big black hole.

DOC. Yeah, the trees block it out.

KENNETH. Right, yeah. (*Short pause.*)

DOC. Sometimes you can hear the animals. (KENNETH *looks at* DOC.) In the zoo.

KENNETH. Do you ever go down for a look?

DOC. In the park?

KENNETH. Yeah.

DOC. No.

KENNETH. I don't blame you. Look at it. Jaysus, look at that! (*He picks a hammer up from a pile of stuff.*) I wouldn't want to get a smack off of that would you?

DOC. No.

KENNETH. That would smack your fucking head off!

DOC. ...Yeah!

Pause.

KENNETH. You don't be going out there into the park.

DOC. At night-time?

KENNETH. Yeah.

DOC. No.

KENNETH. 'Cause you look like you might. (*He gives a little laugh.*) You know what I mean?

Short pause.

DOC. Not really. No.

KENNETH. No? You do! You look like you'd have no problem wandering in under the trees there.

DOC. No.

KENNETH. Well, there must be something wrong with my eyes then, is there?

DOC. Well, I don't.

Pause. DOC *looks around at the sink.*

KENNETH. Are you alright?

DOC. Yeah, no I was just [wondering if I should do the dishes]...

KENNETH. Do you want to do the dishes?

DOC. No... I can [do it later]...

KENNETH. Come here, did you hear about that fella that took his winkle out? Up there behind the girls' primary school?

DOC. What?

KENNETH. You don't know who it was, do you?

DOC. No.

Pause.

KENNETH. It wasn't you, was it?

DOC. No.

Pause.

KENNETH. You sure?

DOC. Yeah.

KENNETH. He was up around the back of the primary school. He took out his winkle.

DOC. I don't know anything about it.

KENNETH. You seem very sure of yourself.

DOC. No.

KENNETH. You're not sure?

DOC. No, I mean, I'm...

KENNETH. You're not sure if it was you, or...?

DOC. No, I am...

KENNETH. But you just don't remember...

DOC. No, I do.

KENNETH. You do remember?

DOC. No, it wasn't me, is what I'm...

KENNETH. Then who was it? (*Pause.*) Who was it?

DOC. I don't know.

Pause.

KENNETH. Because don't start saying it was me.

DOC. No.

KENNETH. Okay?

DOC. Yeah.

KENNETH. Okay.

Pause.

Do you not know I'm just pulling your peanut?

DOC. What?

KENNETH. I'm just pulling your peanut on you!

DOC. Pulling my what?

KENNETH. Your peanut. I know it wasn't you!

DOC. Oh.

Pause. DOC *gives a little laugh.* KENNETH *smiles.*

KENNETH. You were probably nowhere near the place!

DOC. I know! I wasn't!

KENNETH. You've probably never been up there.

DOC. No!

KENNETH. Sure I'm only jockin' with ya!

DOC. Yeah.

KENNETH. You like wrestling?

DOC. What?

KENNETH. The black eye.

KENNETH *picks up* AIMEE*'s bag and looks through it.*

DOC. Oh yeah… no it was…

KENNETH. It was an accident was it?

DOC. Yeah.

Pause.

Are you… a friend of Tommy's?

KENNETH. Am I a friend of Tommy's?

DOC. Yeah.

KENNETH. Well what would you call a friend?

DOC. Someone who's friendly with him?

KENNETH. Mm-hm, what else?

DOC. What else?

KENNETH. Yeah, what else?

DOC. Well, like, do you know him?

KENNETH. Does anyone really know anyone? Though. You know what I mean? Like what would you call a friend?

DOC. Someone… you want to see?

KENNETH *picks up* AIMEE*'s sweater.*

KENNETH. Did you see a girl in here?

DOC. A girl…?

KENNETH. Yeah. A girl. Is she here?

DOC. No.

KENNETH. Is she gone out with Tommy?

DOC. They're just gone down to check the Lotto.

KENNETH. Yeah, you told me that.

DOC. Oh yeah. (*Short pause.*) And maybe em…

KENNETH. Yeah?

DOC. Get some milk. I think.

KENNETH. And yous are in business?

DOC. Me and Tommy?

KENNETH. Yeah.

DOC. Yeah, I suppose.

KENNETH. So you're partners or…?

DOC. Yeah, partners, you know… Well, like Tommy owns the van. We might clear out somebody's shed or tidy their garden…

KENNETH. Okay.

DOC. Yeah. I don't drive but.

KENNETH. Okay.

DOC. Yeah. Keeping it real, you know.

KENNETH. Are you in business with Aimee?

DOC. Oh no.

KENNETH. You're not.

DOC. No.

KENNETH. But Tommy is.

DOC. No... I don't think so. (*Pause.*) I think she's just staying here.

KENNETH. For work.

DOC. No I don't think so.

KENNETH. But, kind of... it's vague.

DOC. No, I don't... like... I'm...

KENNETH. Do you sleep in here?

Short pause.

DOC. Well, you know. Sometimes.

KENNETH. Where does Aimee sleep?

DOC. I think over there.

KENNETH. Where do you sleep? In there as well?

DOC. No, you see I just sleep here sometimes if we have an early start. I haven't slept here with Aimee here yet.

KENNETH. Not yet, no?

DOC. No.

KENNETH. Is your leg shaking?

DOC. No.

Pause. KENNETH *regards* DOC.

KENNETH. Well, look I'll tell you. Fear is not just one thing. Sometimes you're just worn out by being really scared for days on end, where you actually just want something bad to happen – just to...

DOC. Yeah.

KENNETH. Get it over with. Here, look at this.

KENNETH *takes two rows of jagged fangs from his pocket and puts them in his mouth. He opens his mouth wide, bearing the teeth, standing there looking at* DOC. *Pause.*

DOC. Yeah, that's… They're pretty eh…

KENNETH *growls at* DOC. *Pause.*

(*Unsure.*) Ha ha ha…

KENNETH *advances on* DOC, *growling.*

Ha ha ha.

DOC *instinctively sits on* TOMMY's *bed.* KENNETH *approaches* DOC, *opens his arms over him, and roars down at him. Pause.*

Yeah… they're… pretty good.

KENNETH (*muffled*). They're fucking mad aren't they?!

KENNETH *goes and gets the hammer. He stands over* DOC *again and roars down at him.* DOC *is now frozen in terror. Pause.* KEN-NETH *suddenly hits* DOC *with the hammer.*

DOC. Hey!

KENNETH *hits him again.*

Hey! What the fuck are you doing?

DOC *gets to his feet and backs away.* KENNETH *follows him. He swings the hammer at* DOC *again.*

Get off!

KENNETH *follows him.*

Get off!

KENNETH *follows* DOC *around the room.* DOC *tries to bolt for the door to the hallway but* KENNETH *blocks his way.* DOC *runs into the little toilet and tries to lock the door but* KENNETH *pushes his way in after him. We hear* DOC *crying out as* KEN-NETH *beats him. From above we hear* MAURICE *banging down from upstairs in protest at the noise. After a few moments* DOC *falls silent.* KENNETH *steps back into the room. There is blood on his suit and his face. He stands looking up at the ceiling. The*

thumping stops. The lights change, bringing us to late afternoon a
few days later. TOMMY *is in the middle of packing* DOC'*s clothes*
into a bag while he listens to his phone.

TOMMY. What do you mean burnt? Was the tinfoil itself burnt?
(*Pause.*) Where was it? (*Pause.*) I don't know what people smoke
off tinfoil, probably lots of things. Yeah! I know it's not good! Of
course it's not good! (*Pause.*) What did you say to her? Well why
not? Maybe it's a school project for school or science or
something. I don't know – an experiment! (*Pause.*) Well how
would I know? I left school when I was fourteen! (*Pause.*) Of
course I will – I'm happy to talk to her any time! That's…! Will
she talk to me is the… I *am* gonna ring her! I told you I'd ring her!
Yeah, I'll ring her, I won't text her. Look, Doc is awake. I'm run
off my feet here, Suzanne. He woke up.

The door opens and MAURICE *stands there looking at* TOMMY.
There is a mean look about MAURICE. *He has been drinking*
upstairs by himself for a few hours.

(*Seeing* MAURICE.) Look I have to go. Yeah, I'll tell him. Yeah,
I will, I'll call her tonight. I will! She knows I love her! I do love
her! Jesus Christ…

He hangs up on her.

MAURICE. What haven't you put that woman through?

TOMMY. Oh… Don't you fucking start Maurice.

TOMMY *looks for a bag.*

MAURICE (*drunkenly*). What?

TOMMY. Suzanne is no saint either, okay? (*Pause.*) So…

MAURICE (*amused*). Oh-ho!

TOMMY. Yeah, so… Before you…

MAURICE. Mm-hm…

TOMMY. Maurice. Are you drunk?

MAURICE. Look at the way you live.

During the following TOMMY *starts stuffing some clothes into an*
old Liverpool F.C. sports bag.

Look… at the way you live.

TOMMY. Look at the way you live…

MAURICE. I live alright mate! At least I clean up after myself and I wash myself!

TOMMY. I wash myself Maurice! For Jaysus' sake.

MAURICE. Look at the state of your clothes! What are you doing with them?

TOMMY. These are not my clothes! They're Doc's clothes.

MAURICE. Will you not iron them for him?

TOMMY. I don't have an iron.

MAURICE. I'll iron them, come on.

TOMMY. They'll do him. He's going to his sister's – let her bleeding do them.

MAURICE *watches* TOMMY *getting* DOC*'s clothes together.*

MAURICE. Can I ask you where you were earlier?

TOMMY. Where I always am! Back and forth up to the bleeding hospital, where do you think I was?

MAURICE. Did you forget?

TOMMY. Forget what?

MAURICE. Maura's anniversary mass. (*Short pause.*) At ten o'clock.

Pause.

TOMMY. Yeah. I forgot.

MAURICE. Yep.

TOMMY. Just with the… the circumstances.

Pause.

MAURICE. Yeah.

TOMMY. Oh just give me a break Maurice, will you?

MAURICE. I said that girl was trouble. (*Short pause.*) Didn't I?

Pause.

Tommy.

TOMMY. What.

MAURICE. I said that girl was trouble, didn't I?

TOMMY. Yeah? Well she's gone, so...

MAURICE. Yeah? (*Doubtful she is really gone for good.*) Where?

TOMMY. I don't know.

MAURICE. What?

TOMMY. I don't know!

Pause.

MAURICE. You disgust me, Tommy.

TOMMY. I beg your pardon?

MAURICE. You disgust me.

TOMMY. I disgust you, do I?

MAURICE. I'm disappointed in you! I'm disappointed in you!

TOMMY. Maurice at least I'm not drunk out of my mind at – what is
it? Four o'clock in the afternoon!

Pause.

MAURICE. Do you know how many people were there? Do you
know how many? Eight people, Tommy. Eight people for a whole
life. Is that what it's all for? All the worry and all the battles?
(*With cold bitterness and restraint.*) She wasn't talking to me, you
see, so I didn't offer her my hand and anyway I was already down
the road before I even realised it was icy and I just heard it –
smack. And I turned around and there she was. Do you know what
she said? She said, 'Maurice.' And I never felt so... And so... (*He
gives a short shout of rage, and punches downward. Pause.*) Death
is *real*, Tommy!

TOMMY. Oh for fuck's sake...

MAURICE. Yeah! (*Matter of fact.*) You're just knocking the days
off the calendar. There's even days when mass just takes you
nowhere, just deposits you back on the pavement, just another
invisible man, knowing that the end is sneaking in on you and
knowing it's gonna be the worst part of your life. Looking at the
news every night – for what? I don't even want to see it! What do

I want to see some little girl with half her face hanging off in some bomb in some Arab country for? What can I do about it? And you feel like you have to witness all this fucking crap or else you're not a good person! What can I do about it?! And I look at you. You don't even know how lucky you are. You have two beautiful children and what do you do? You piss off on them! Fuck-arsing around with young ones...

TOMMY. Yeah well, it's not like that, Maurice.

MAURICE. What's it like then? Don't tell me what it's like! I know what it's like! Don't tell me what it's like, you little pup! I reared you, when no one else could cope with you. Maura had to toilet-train you! You were nearly four and a half!

TOMMY. Okay alright, Maurice.

TOMMY *struggles to close the zip on the bag.*

MAURICE. What?

TOMMY. Just go and lie down will you?

MAURICE. And you bring whores in under my roof! Under my roof! A whore!

TOMMY *suddenly throws the bag across the room against the wall. It lands near the door.*

TOMMY. For fuck's sake, Maurice!

Pause. TOMMY *sits disconsolately on the camp bed.*

MAURICE. Evil... has... no meaning. (*Pause.*) All I'm asking – what happened to all that sweetness... is what I want to know.

TOMMY. What sweetness?

MAURICE. When we used to go down the canal, and you holding my hand, and asking me all the questions in the world. And now the country is a shambles and we're crying out for people like you. That can lead us into the light, Tommy.

TOMMY. I'm just a moocher, Maurice.

TOMMY*'s mobile phone rings. He goes to answer it.*

That's all I ever was. Hello? (*Pause.*) Okay. It's alright, calm down. Where are you? (*Pause.*) Well just stay there. No, just sit there. Take it easy! I'm coming! Okay?

TOMMY *hangs up and grabs his coat and his keys.*

MAURICE. Who's that?

TOMMY. Doc. His sister hasn't shown up to collect him and they're kicking him out.

MAURICE. I'll come with you.

TOMMY. No, Maurice, come and lie down, will you?

TOMMY *tries to guide* MAURICE *out by the arm.* MAURICE *pulls his arm away.*

MAURICE. No, I want to go and look at my vegetables.

TOMMY. Ah, suit yourself!

TOMMY *storms out with* DOC's *clothes.* MAURICE *stands there for a moment. He takes a small bottle of Irish whiskey from his pocket and drinks from it. He goes to the double doors and lets himself out to the balcony, going off down to the garden. Time passes. A heavy dusk gathers in the room and raindrops spatter the windows. After a few moments, the door opens and* AIMEE *slips in quietly. She waits a moment, listening, then goes to the loose floorboard and takes out the biscuit tin with* TOMMY's *money. She opens the tin and starts counting money out on to the floor. When she has three thousand euros she puts the rest back, replaces the lid, and puts it back under the floorboard. As she goes to leave,* KENNETH *appears in the doorway.*

AIMEE (*startled*). What are you doing!?

KENNETH. There's nobody here!

AIMEE. Right, come on.

KENNETH. Woah, woah woah. What's that?

AIMEE (*showing him what she has taken*). Three thousand.

KENNETH. Don't mind that.

Pause.

AIMEE. You said three thousand.

KENNETH. Don't mind what I said.

AIMEE. There is no more, that's it.

Pause.

KENNETH. Alright you've made your point. (*He knocks the money to the floor where it scatters.*) You can leave that there. Come on, we'll get a smoke.

AIMEE. No, I'm not doing that. Just take it.

She scrambles to pick it up.

KENNETH. Do you know what's so…? It's not even about any of this. It's not about any of that.

AIMEE. Then what's it about?!

KENNETH. I'm on top of it.

AIMEE. What?

KENNETH. I'm on top of it.

AIMEE. What?

KENNETH. I've got up back on top of it. Alright?

AIMEE. What the fuck are you talking about? You don't want this?

She gestures to the money. He shakes his head. Angrily, she starts putting it back. He suddenly tries to embrace her.

KENNETH. Aimee listen… I'm sorry. I'm just sorry.

She pushes him off her and starts to leave.

Those people wrote to you.

AIMEE. What people?

KENNETH. The people. They wrote you a letter.

Pause.

AIMEE. Where is it?

Pause.

KENNETH. I read it for you.

Pause.

AIMEE. What did it say?

KENNETH. Ah it was just… all this medical stuff.

AIMEE's face crumples.

They'll keep you informed and all this but they're not gonna let you to meet the little one. Because they think it'll only confuse her 'cause she's too young. (*Short pause.*) She's too young!

Pause.

AIMEE. Do you have it?

KENNETH (*shrugs and shakes his head*). Yeah. (*Short pause.*) No.

AIMEE. Did they say what they call her?

He shakes his head. He comes to her, holding her.

KENNETH. Aimee, listen. She's better off and you're better off because unfortunately, you're not right in the fucking head. (*Pause.*) You're not right in the fucking head, unfortunately.

He gently strokes her arm.

Let's go, okay? Come on.

AIMEE *shakes her head. She goes and sits on the bed defiantly.*

(*Warning.*) Aimee…

He advances on her menacingly, about to attack her. TOMMY's voice halts him.

TOMMY (*entering*). What's going on?

KENNETH. Tommy! (*He comes to* TOMMY, *offering his hand.*) How are you?

TOMMY. What are you doing?

KENNETH. I'm not doing anything.

TOMMY. What are you doing with my money?

KENNETH. Tommy. (*Pause.*) We're bereaved.

Pause.

TOMMY. What?

KENNETH. Has Aimee not told you? (*Pause.*) Ah for Jaysus' sake! Ah well look. Well then this is a total misunderstanding! Listen, what's happened is we've had to move in with Aimee's nana in her house to look after her because she was in a virtual coma, or she might as well have been! (*He laughs*.) And then the doctor said that actually she was dead, so Aimee's brother decided to break up the asset without any remuneration towards my... towards my... So Aimee has, if I am correct, decided to reimburse me, and because she's now within your... sphere going round your orbit she's dug in under your floor to borrow your resources to pay me back, with, I believe, Aimee?, the full intention of paying you back. So that's... who I am.

TOMMY. Yeah, I know who you are. Whatever your fucking name is.

KENNETH. That was self-defence Tommy. She scratched me in the eye for Christ's sake! (*He laughs*.) Aimee?

AIMEE *doesn't answer.*

Oh thanks! Listen, Tommy, I know how this looks. This looks fucking pathetic. That's fine then, we'll cut out the middle man. I'll call around here say every Saturday evening, Saturday night around eight o'clock, nine o'clock, we can keep it loose, or even every Sunday after dinner, you just give me an envelope, it's Aimee's instalments, that's fine, straight *i mo phóca*, I don't need a cup of tea, I've already eaten, I have somewhere I have to be, that's fine, see you next week. Ding dong. The week has flown by! That kind of thing.

TOMMY. Well no, I've a better idea. Why don't you just clear off out of here?

KENNETH. Me clear off?

TOMMY. Yeah.

KENNETH. Listen there's no need to fly off the handle. (*Pause*.) You're saying to clear off and not come back?

TOMMY. Yeah.

KENNETH. Yeah come back or yeah not come back.

TOMMY. Not come back.

KENNETH. So just take this [tin] and not come back.

TOMMY. No, leave that.

KENNETH. And not come back?

TOMMY. You're not taking that.

KENNETH. Well then I don't understand what's happening.

TOMMY. I don't give a fuck what you understand. Give me the box.

AIMEE. Tommy...

KENNETH. She says she's paying you back! (*To* AIMEE.) Right?

AIMEE. Tommy. I'm gonna pay you back.

KENNETH. In forty-euro instalments, right?

Pause.

TOMMY. That's not the way it's gonna happen.

KENNETH. Well then will someone please explain to me what is gonna happen?

TOMMY. You give me the box and go. Both of you go.

Pause.

She goes to leave.

KENNETH. No wait, we're talking.

She ignores him. He grabs her.

We're talking!

AIMEE *hits at his arm, trying to free herself.*

TOMMY. Hey now! Hey, hey, hey! Now, listen I don't give a fuck how yous go, together or separately or on your own or together, but you're not taking that box!

KENNETH. Well you're not doing a lot to help the situation, are you?

TOMMY. What the fuck is your problem?!

KENNETH. *My* problem? Oh now *I* have a problem?!

TOMMY. Yeah, I'd say you have a problem! I'd say you have a lot of problems, yeah!

KENNETH. Oh yeah?

KENNETH throws the tin on the bed and advances on TOMMY. *They move round the room,* TOMMY *backing away while* KEN-NETH *pushes and taunts him.*

Well maybe my problem is it's like my eyes have been taken out
and I just can't see what's in front of me like it's always night-
time so when night-time really comes you think it feels like a
relief except I can't sleep so that when it's morning it feels like it's
burning my brain and I drink too much coffee on my own 'cause
you're going around everywhere with a clouded mind trying to
forget a devil lives inside you and you should probably just go
home but you can't do that so you're all the time out and about
and you're getting annoyed with people because they won't listen
and the same old same old is going round and round and round
and round and round and round and round and round and round
and round and round and round and round and round until you
start to fucking think that maybe *that's* your problem!

TOMMY. Look. I'll help anyone out. Same as the next man, but I've
got troubles. I've got my own problems and you're not taking my
money.

TOMMY *picks the tin up off the bed.*

KENNETH. You think she's gonna love you?

TOMMY. What?

KENNETH. You think you can change her? You think you can go up
and down the courts with her and talk to the solicitor about all her
shoplifting charges? And talk to the doctor about the time she
managed to get lost in town.

AIMEE. I'm not staying here for this!

AIMEE *starts to leave.*

KENNETH. We're still talking!

KENNETH *grabs her and they wrestle,* AIMEE *tumbling to the
floor.*

TOMMY. Jesus Christ! What the fuck is wrong with you?

TOMMY *strikes* KENNETH *with the lid of the biscuit tin.* KEN-
NETH *grabs* TOMMY. *The tin drops and they grapple with each
other. Suddenly* AIMEE *is up and grabs a kitchen knife which she
plunges into* KENNETH's *back, leaving the handle protruding.*
KENNETH *stops fighting. His arms drop. He stumbles towards*
AIMEE, *who pushes him away. He stumbles towards* TOMMY.
TOMMY *tries to hold* KENNETH *as he slips to the floor. All is still
and silent for a few moments.* TOMMY *puts a hand to* KENNETH's
neck. He realizes KENNETH *is dead and steps away in shock.*

Pause.

AIMEE. Tommy.

TOMMY. Yeah.

AIMEE. What'll we do?

TOMMY. We'll hide him.

AIMEE. What?

TOMMY. We'll hide him!!

AIMEE. Where? (*Pause.*) Where?

TOMMY *grabs a blanket and throws it over the body.*

TOMMY. What do you mean where? People disappear every day. People just go... (*He gestures.*) Poff! And we can, we can... we can... we can just... We can just... go! Okay?

AIMEE. Go where?

TOMMY. Just go! Who cares? Finland.

AIMEE. Finland?

TOMMY. Finland is a beautiful country, Aimee. The light! You go off up into the forest. No one cares who you are.

Pause.

AIMEE. What about your kids?

TOMMY. They don't [need me]...! They're...

AIMEE *raises her hand to her mouth. Her hand is shaking uncontrollably. Her knees give way and she tumbles to the floor.* TOMMY *goes to her. The door to the landing opens and* MAURICE *stands there, half-undressed. He wears stripy pyjama bottoms and a blazer over his vest. He seems even more inebriated. He stands there for a moment.*

MAURICE. What in the name of sweet fucking Jaysus is going on?

TOMMY. Nothing.

MAURICE. It doesn't fucking sound like nothing!

TOMMY. It's alright, Maurice. Go back to bed.

MAURICE. I'm not in bed!

TOMMY. We had a row, alright?

MAURICE (*sarcastically*). Oh yeah? (*To* AIMEE.) I knew the feather wouldn't blow too far – because there's too much shite on the egg! Hm? Hello to you too. Ha? (*Suddenly starts singing like a crooner.*) Don't ever leave me, Don't ever go, 'Cause if you do, I'll have nowhere to run to...

He looks over at the camp bed where KENNETH*'s body lies curled up.*

What's that?

Silence. MAURICE *starts towards the body.* TOMMY *tries to block his way.* MAURICE *pushes him aside.* MAURICE *walks over to body and peers down in the gloom. But rather than examine the body, he crouches and drags something out from under the detritus. It is a sack of vegetables. He opens it and looks inside.*

I fucking *knew* it! And you and that other gobdaw trying to tell me the crows had dug them up? The crows! What do you think I am? A nincompoop? Well I have you now. Ha? Explain that! Explain it! (*Pause.*) You can't explain it. There is no explanation. A tiny modicum of respect, Tommy. That's all I've ever been talking about – that you might even ask me. (*Pause. To* AIMEE.) I don't even eat them! (*To* TOMMY.) You know that I can't! (*He takes the sack to the door, then turns.*) You know Tommy? Maybe it's time you moved along, okay? I don't think this is working.

MAURICE *leaves.* TOMMY *and* AIMEE *stand there. Then* AIMEE *goes and kneels beside the body. The lights go down and bring us to a bright morning two days later. The body is gone and* DOC *is sitting in the room. His head is bandaged. He has a dressing on his ear and two of his fingers are taped round a splint.* DOC *adjusts his arm in his sling, trying to get more comfortable. He is in considerable pain.* TOMMY *comes in the double doors from the balcony.*

DOC. You just missed Maurice, Tommy.

TOMMY *just nods, bringing a bag from the chemist to* DOC.

TOMMY. Here.

DOC. He was just in here looking for you.

TOMMY. Okay, here you go. (*A little box.*) This is an inhaler, you take that twice a day, morning and evening.

DOC (*pause*). What is it?

TOMMY. You stick it up your nose and you press the button.

DOC. Oh yeah.

TOMMY (*taking out tablets*). If your headache gets really bad, you just take a half of one of these, alright? Otherwise just take two of these, they're paracetamol, and you take one of these (*Another little box.*) every day. Alright?

DOC. Yeah, you can remind me.

TOMMY. Well, just, look it's all written there.

DOC. Yeah but just in case I forget.

TOMMY. But, Doc, I'm not gonna be here, man.

DOC. What do you mean?

TOMMY. No, I'm going away.

DOC. I thought you were just moving.

TOMMY. No, I'm going away.

DOC. Away from Dublin?

TOMMY. I'm going abroad man. I have a... I've an offer of work, so...

DOC (*brightly*). You need me to come with you?

TOMMY. No, I don't think I...

DOC (*hiding any discomfort at this news*). Where is it? Up in the north?

TOMMY. Yeah, up in the north, and maybe in Scotland as well, so you know...

DOC. And you're going now?

TOMMY. Yeah, I'm going now, I'm going this morning.

DOC. Now?

TOMMY. Yeah, now.

Pause.

DOC (*laughing*). What are you talking about?!

TOMMY. What do you mean what am I talking about? Didn't I just say it to you?

DOC. Well I'll come with you if it's just Northern Ireland. I can mind the van.

TOMMY. No, it's gonna be abroad, Doc, so... you know.

DOC. Well do you need me to mind the van here?

TOMMY. I'm taking the van.

DOC. The van's gonna be gone?!

TOMMY. Yeah, the van is gonna be gone and I'm gonna be gone. Okay? Okay?

DOC (*again hiding any discomfort or fear*). Oh.

TOMMY. Yeah so...

DOC (*as though this is all only a little snag as opposed to his world falling apart*). Yeah, no, that's... the only problem is...

TOMMY. What?

DOC. No, it's just, Teresa is saying I can't stay with her, so...

TOMMY. Well what's that got to do with me?

DOC. No I was just...

TOMMY. What?

DOC. No I was just... I was hoping that... you wouldn't mind me staying here until my ear got better.

TOMMY. But I'm not gonna be here.

DOC. Yeah.

Pause.

TOMMY. I'm not gonna be here, Doc.

DOC. Yeah that's... That's the...

TOMMY. You're gonna have to do your own thing.

DOC. Yeah that's...

TOMMY *is throwing his razor and toothbrush, etc., into a little bag.*

TOMMY. You know what I mean?

DOC. Yeah.

TOMMY. You'll have to get yourself sorted out.

DOC. I know.

TOMMY. I mean this is… you know… Maybe it's time you got serious anyway, you know?

DOC. Yeah.

TOMMY. Not fucking around and sleeping here and sleeping there. I mean it's all a bit mad, Doc.

DOC. I know!

TOMMY. You know what I mean?

DOC. I know! It's mad.

TOMMY. It's… you know…

DOC. Listen, you don't have to tell me that. The only problem is I was hoping that I'd be able to… to just… be able to stay here.

TOMMY. You want to stay here? Talk to Maurice.

DOC. What about the rent?

TOMMY. You can get the rent! Go down the social welfare office.

DOC. Just talk to them in there…

TOMMY. Yeah, you go in, and you fucking… say… you know… I don't have any fucking money! Just tell them. The banks are bust, you need your rent, you know…

DOC. Yeah.

Pause.

TOMMY. Yeah? Okay?

DOC. Yeah, no that's…

Pause. DOC exhales heavily.

TOMMY. What?!

DOC. No, just, (*Laughing.*) what am I gonna do?

TOMMY. What are you...? What have we just been talking about?

DOC. I know, but...

TOMMY. It's not up to me, Doc. (*Pause.*) Okay?

DOC. Yeah.

Pause.

TOMMY. Okay?

DOC. Yeah. (*Pause.*) No, it's just...

TOMMY. What.

DOC. Just you go in the hostels and... (*Again smiling to hide his pain and fear.*) I'm just not able for all the fucking people in there, you know...

TOMMY. But you won't be in the hostels! Go down the social welfare. Go down now. Go down this morning.

DOC (*as though these are annoying details rather than scary realities*). Yeah but they say you're not on the books anymore and you need a letter from your previous employer and all this and then in the hostels you get all them, Batman, and Landline and all them fuckers, they take your runners, they take your shower gel...

TOMMY. But that's not [going to happen]...! Look, come here, look. (*He goes and takes some money from a coat pocket.*) Now, look, here we go, there's all your Christmas money. (*Pause.*) And this is... (*From his own pocket.*) Look, take this. That's from me. We'll call that a soft loan.

DOC. For how long?

TOMMY. For what how long?

DOC. For how long the loan...

TOMMY. I'm giving it to you.

DOC. What?

TOMMY. I'm giving it to you, okay?

DOC (*laughing with incomprehension*). What?

TOMMY (*unable to resist laughing with* DOC). There you go. That's... now. Okay?

DOC *stands there looking at the money in his hand while* TOMMY *goes and continues getting his stuff together.*

DOC. Tommy?

TOMMY. Yeah?

Pause.

DOC. Did I tell you Maurice was looking for you?

TOMMY. Yeah you told me.

Pause.

DOC. Tommy…

TOMMY. Yeah? (*Pause.*) What?

Pause.

DOC. No, just em…

TOMMY. What? (*Pause.*) What? What's the matter with you? (*With sudden rage.*) Would you fucking leave me alone will you?! What's the matter with you? You're like a fucking stone brick around my neck every time I turn around you're coming in the fucking window! What's the matter with you?! Ha?

DOC. What?

TOMMY. What's the matter with you? What's wrong with you? What's wrong with you?!

Pause.

DOC. I don't know.

TOMMY. Ha?

DOC. I don't know.

Pause. AIMEE *comes in the door tentatively and stands there.*

I'll see you, Tommy.

DOC *leaves through the balcony doors and is gone.* TOMMY *stands and looks guiltily at* AIMEE. *Then he notices that* DOC *has forgotten his medications. He grabs the bag and goes to the balcony doors.*

TOMMY (*calls*). Doc! Doc! (*To himself.*) Fuck it.

He comes back into the room and throws the bag on the bed.

What are you doing? Where were you?

He goes and closes the door behind her.

AIMEE. I went for a walk.

TOMMY. A walk? Are you fucking mad?

AIMEE. You were asleep.

TOMMY. Well I must have only fell asleep for a few minutes.

AIMEE. I couldn't wake you up.

TOMMY. Did you go and buy drugs?

AIMEE. No.

Pause.

TOMMY. I have it worked out. (*He shows her a piece of paper.*) We drive up to Belfast, get the ferry to Stranraer in Scotland, drive down through England to Harwich, ferry from Harwich to the Hook of Holland, drive up through Denmark to Frederikshavn – ferry to Gothenberg okay? In Sweden get to Kapellskär and ferry – bang – into Marienshaven. In Finland, we're there. It's that easy.

Pause.

AIMEE. That doesn't sound so easy though, Tommy.

TOMMY. Of course it's easy. Why isn't it easy?

AIMEE. Because I don't have a passport.

TOMMY. What? Why not?

AIMEE. I never had one.

TOMMY. Why didn't you tell me that?

AIMEE. I didn't think of it.

TOMMY. When did you not think of it, just now?

AIMEE. I don't know, this morning.

TOMMY. This morning? (*Angrily hissing his rage.*) You couldn't have not thought of that two nights ago and me breaking my bollocks digging a grave in the pitch dark down in the wilds of County fucking Wicklow, no?!

AIMEE. Just go without me.

TOMMY. What? (*Pause*.) Ah don't be ridiculous! Anyway, you don't
need a passport for the ferry.

AIMEE. Someone is bound to want to check somewhere.

TOMMY. Just stay in the back of the van!

AIMEE. You should just go on your own.

TOMMY. I'm not gonna just go on my own, come on!

AIMEE. Why not?

TOMMY. What?

AIMEE. Why not?

TOMMY. Because we're! Because we're...

AIMEE. I did it.

TOMMY. What, do you think I'm gonna just leave you in the lurch?
What kind of person do you [think I am]...? Oh right, maybe it
was just your problem before, but now it's... It's too late for that
now, isn't it?

Pause. AIMEE *shakes her head*.

AIMEE. I'll see you, okay?

TOMMY. But where are you gonna go? You don't have a passport!
Where are you gonna go? Listen, I want to go to Finland!

AIMEE. Well go to Finland. No one's stopping you!

TOMMY (*suddenly changing tack and becoming positive*). Look!
We'll get you a passport! We'll get you one. We'll get it. I mean,
why the panic?! How long does it take to get one? A few days?

AIMEE. It's not going to work, Tommy.

TOMMY. Why is it not gonna work?

AIMEE. It's just not going to work!

TOMMY. What's not going to work?

AIMEE. Everything.

TOMMY. Listen, fuck all that. We say how it works! We did what we
had to do, and we'll... This is... This has... And maybe that's...
(*Pause*.) I love you, Aimee, okay? I love you. Okay?

AIMEE. You don't even know me, Tommy.

TOMMY. I do know you. I do. I've always known you. I've always known you.

AIMEE. You're just lonely.

TOMMY. Lonely?! I'm not lonely!

AIMEE. Tommy, I'm gonna go. Okay?

TOMMY. You think I'm just some... fool? Who doesn't know what's going on inside his own head? Like I don't fucking know what's going on? I know what's going on! I know, okay?

Pause. TOMMY *goes to get her some money.*

AIMEE. Don't give me any money, Tommy.

TOMMY. No, take it.

AIMEE. No.

TOMMY. Take it.

AIMEE. No.

TOMMY. Why not?

AIMEE. Because there's no point.

TOMMY. What do you mean there's no point?

AIMEE. There's no point.

Pause. He realizes she has decided to kill herself.

TOMMY. Don't do that. (*He grabs her.*) Don't you fucking do that!

AIMEE (*recoiling as if from an electric shock*). Just leave me the fuck alone, will ya?!

The door opens and MAURICE *is there in his grey slacks, black shoes, a white shirt, a tie and a blazer. Pause.*

MAURICE (*to* AIMEE). Are you still here?

AIMEE. No.

AIMEE *goes to the door.*

Bye, Tommy.

She goes. Pause.

MAURICE. Well I wanted to em... May I have a word?

TOMMY. What?

MAURICE. May I have a word with you?

TOMMY. What do you want?

MAURICE. I have a... an appointment with my solicitor at four o'clock.

TOMMY. About the rent?

MAURICE. No, not about the rent. I eh... I don't want to end up in a... I... You see, I need to be able to live here right to the... (*He points at* TOMMY *with his open palm and makes a single clicking sound.*) So if you want to stay on, I'll... I'm going to leave you the house. And... (*Pause.*) okay?

TOMMY *nods.*

Okay?

TOMMY (*quietly*). Yeah.

MAURICE. Well don't get too fucking excited about it.

Long pause.

Is she coming back?

TOMMY *shakes his head.*

You're better off. You need a settled woman, Tommy. Someone who's settled in herself.

TOMMY. Yeah.

MAURICE. You only get a few goes, Tommy. At life. You don't get endless goes. Two, three goes maybe. When you hit the right groove you'll click right in there. No drama. That's only for fucking eejits. (*Pause.*) This is it. (*Pause.*) Living in the moment. (*Beat.*) Tommy.

Pause. The balcony doors rattle and DOC's *head appears.*

Oh here he is. The gay caballero.

DOC. There I am. I'm sorry. I forgot my prescription.

TOMMY *goes to get the bag from the chemist.*

MAURICE. You forgot your what?

DOC. My prescription for the chemist.

MAURICE. Is it here?

TOMMY *brings it to* DOC.

DOC. Thanks, Tommy. Sorry I wouldn't have come back, only I knew you'd be gone so... Bye, Maurice.

TOMMY. Here, hang on. You're alright.

DOC. Nah, I won't stay.

TOMMY. You're alright.

Pause.

DOC. What, are you [two having a private conversation]...?

TOMMY. Sit down.

DOC *stands inside the room. All three of them are silent.*

DOC. So, you're moving out later on or...?

TOMMY *shakes his head. Pause.*

MAURICE (*apropos of nothing*). Yeah.

Pause.

DOC. Does anyone... want a cup of coffee?

MAURICE. What kind of coffee?

DOC. Instant.

MAURICE (*as though this is preferable*). Oh instant? Yeah, I will.

DOC *goes to the sink to fill the kettle.* TOMMY *sits.* MAURICE *goes to the double doors and looks out at the garden.*

DOC. You see out there, the hedge and all that, Maurice?

MAURICE. Yeah.

DOC. I was thinking you should pull that all up.

MAURICE. Were you now?

DOC. Yeah, and look, where the sun is now? That's where you want to put down a patio where you go and sit in the morning.

MAURICE. Yeah?

DOC. Yeah, Tommy has paving blocks in the lock-up. Tommy?

TOMMY. Mm?

DOC. Paving slabs.

TOMMY. Yeah.

DOC. Me and Tommy dig it up, bang bang bang, a patio, a few
chairs, put on your coat and your hat and your scarf, you sit out
there in the evening, up the other end, and have your hot whiskey.
Think about things.

MAURICE. Hm...

DOC. The sun going down behind the trees. Whistle up to Tommy.
Hot whiskey please, Tommy!

MAURICE. Yeah, I'd be waiting a long time. I'd be freezing my balls
off.

MAURICE and DOC laugh, but they can't look TOMMY *in the
eye.*

DOC. Don't mind that. And look over all there. Dig all that out, turn
it over, put down your few bulbs. Next thing you know, it's spring
– and boom – all the flowers.

MAURICE. Yeah, I don't know. Maybe. (*Pause. He glances at*
TOMMY.) Come down, show me what you mean.

DOC *and* MAURICE, *uncomfortable with* TOMMY's *withdrawn
demeanour, walk out to the garden together. As they go off:*

Well I'm glad you're on the mend.

DOC. You should see the other fella.

MAURICE. Yeah?

DOC. Yeah, I milled him.

MAURICE. Yeah?

DOC. Yeah, I absolutely brainalised him.

MAURICE (*off*). Yeah?

DOC (*off*). Yeah.

MAURICE (*off*). Fair play to you.

DOC (*off*). Now look. Do you know what decking is Maurice?

A low afternoon sun creeps into the room, catching TOMMY *alone with his head in his hands. Lights and music take us to a winter's evening. The music goes into the radio and we find* DOC *alone in the room fixing the plug on some fairy lights. His bandages are gone. After a few moments* TOMMY *bustles in from the landing with his coat on and a few bags from the shops.*

(*Without looking up.*) Aye aye.

TOMMY. What are you doing?

DOC. Fixing the Christmas lights.

TOMMY. It's only the bleeding tenth of November!

DOC. Yeah I know, but you know, get it done, it's not hanging over you.

TOMMY. Did you clear up all them leaves?

DOC. Yeah. I did that ages ago. I'm just waiting for the rest of them to fall.

TOMMY (*giving up*). Right...

DOC. How did you get on?

TOMMY. Yeah, good.

DOC. How was Michelle?

TOMMY. Yeah, good.

DOC. She talking to you?

TOMMY. Yeah. No, she was. She's having a baby.

DOC. A baby?!

TOMMY. Yeah. Suzanne is going bananas.

DOC. What's she gonna do?

TOMMY. Who? Suzanne?

DOC. No. Michelle.

TOMMY. She's gonna start training to be a hairdresser.

DOC. Never be out of work.

TOMMY. I know.

DOC. Because even bald people get their hair cut.

TOMMY. I know.

DOC. The joke is on them because the sides and back still get all bushy.

TOMMY. Yeah, but I'd say the idea of cutting auld baldy lads' hair is not where she's at.

DOC. No but I mean, if you had to. You can always earn a few bob.

TOMMY. Well, yeah.

DOC. Just watch, she'll be in here cutting all our hair for us. Grandkids will be running all over the house and she'll be trimming all the hair in your ears and your nose and everything.

TOMMY. I doubt it somehow.

DOC (*convinced he is right*). I don't know. There's beans in that pot on the ring.

TOMMY. Is there no sausages?

DOC. Eh... No.

TOMMY. Just as well I got some. Do you want one?

DOC. Yeah. I'll have a few more. Sausage sandwich please, Grandad.

TOMMY (*takes an invitation from his pocket*). Listen I wasn't gonna go but... Michelle's invited us to her eighteenth birthday party.

DOC. Tonight?

TOMMY. Yeah.

DOC. You and me?

TOMMY. Yeah you and me and Maurice.

DOC. Will we go?

TOMMY. Do you want to go?

DOC (*looking at invitation*). Will Suzanne mind us being there?

TOMMY. It's not up to her.

DOC. Maurice is gone down to The Little Nibble to have his dinner.

TOMMY. Do you think he'd want to?

DOC. I'd say he would.

TOMMY. Alright, well... I'll get changed.

DOC plugs in the lights. They come on.

DOC. Here listen, thanks for the runners.

TOMMY. Oh yeah, are they alright?

DOC. Perfect, check it out. (*He comes and stands quite close to* TOMMY.) They give me another half an inch.

TOMMY. Oh yeah.

TOMMY *takes some shirts from a bag from the dry cleaners and starts taking one out of the plastic wrapping.* DOC *goes for his jacket.*

DOC. Oh here, em, Mick Mounfield was in the bookies earlier with those twins, Romulus and...

TOMMY. Remus?

DOC. No Romulus and...

TOMMY. Remus?

DOC. No! What do you keep saying 'Remus' for? Is that even a name? No, what do you call them, the Casey twins, Romulus and... Dwayne Casey.

TOMMY (*does not know them*). Okay...

DOC. Mick Mounfield was in there with them and he told me that he saw... he said he saw... em...

Short pause.

TOMMY. Aimee?

DOC. Yeah, but I don't think he's right. I didn't think he described her right.

TOMMY. Where was she?

DOC. He said he saw her sitting on the steps at the Custom's House but he said he thought she was about fifty years old. So it couldn't...

TOMMY. No.

DOC. ...couldn't have been her. But, you know, I always keep an ear out.

TOMMY. Yeah.

DOC. 'Cause my hunch is that she's alright.

TOMMY. Yeah?

DOC. Yeah.

TOMMY. Yeah.

DOC. Will I tell you the good thing about Christmas? No one can turn you away. You see that light in the window. In you go.

TOMMY. Yeah. But you can't save everybody though, can you? I mean...

DOC. Yeah, I suppose. (*Pause.*) Here, do you know what a black hole is?

TOMMY. A black what?

DOC. A black hole.

TOMMY. In space?

DOC. Yeah. Do you know what it is?

TOMMY. Eh yeah, it's a... What is it?

Pause. DOC has his jacket on. He is near the door. TOMMY is sorting out his clothes. DOC is lost in thought for a moment.

DOC. No, I had a mad dream. Before I woke up. (*Pause.*) I had to write it down.

He goes to the camp bed and takes a piece of notepaper up.

TOMMY. Are you alright?

DOC. Yeah, no, it was just... I woke up and there was an old chap sitting there and do you know who he was?

TOMMY. Who?

DOC. He was one of the three wise men.

TOMMY. What he told you that or...?

DOC. No, you know the way you just know.

TOMMY. Okay.

DOC. And he was looking out the doors there up into the sky. And
I sat up in the camp bed and he saw me and he said that when a
star... dies, okay? It collapses into itself and its gravity is an unbelievable force, right? Not even light is quick enough to escape. He
said that's why it's called a black hole. And he said that the faster
you travel, the slower time goes, okay? And he said that if you
ever came near a black hole you'd be sucked in so fast – faster and
faster and faster – that time would slow down so slowly and it
would take you so long to reach the heart of the dying star that
you would never actually arrive, because at that speed, time, itself,
becomes meaningless. So a black hole is a place, he said, where
there is... no time. And he said that all the stars in our galaxy, and
all... our sun, and all... everything is just spinning round and
round a black hole. And he said that when you consider this fact:
that we are all just going round and round a place where there is
no time, how can any man say there is no God?

Pause.

I had to write it down.

TOMMY. Yeah, well that's a heavy fucking dream right there, man.

DOC. Yeah. (*Pause.*) Well, I'll go and get Maurice.

TOMMY. Yeah.

DOC. I'll see you in about fifteen, twenty minutes.

TOMMY. Yeah. In fifteen or twenty measurements of time.

They smile.

DOC. Yeah in fifteen or twenty units of time. I mean, like, time...
What is it? You know what I mean?

TOMMY. Yeah, I know. Maybe you'll go down to The Little Nibble
and never come back!

DOC. I know!

DOC *is about to go out the balcony doors.*

TOMMY. Doc, use the front door.

TOMMY *disappears into the toilet.*

DOC (*goes out on to the landing*). Oh and he told me to tell you what
heaven is, Tommy.

TOMMY (*off*). Oh yeah?

DOC (*off*). Yeah, apparently, when you die, you won't even know you're dead! It'll just feel like everything has suddenly... come right, in your life. Like everything has just clicked into place and off you go.

TOMMY (*off*). Oh well, that's good, isn't it?

DOC (*off*). Yeah!

DOC leaves. TOMMY reappears and starts to get ready. He turns up the radio. A plaintive song is playing. He quickly washes his face in the sink. He puts on his clean shirt and goes into the little toilet.

For a few moments the room is empty except for the music. Then the balcony doors open and AIMEE silently steps into the room. She looks in good shape. She wears a new leather jacket, jeans and boots. She carries a bag with a strap which she puts down on the floor. She stands there while TOMMY comes back into the room. He does not see her at first. He goes to the mirror and combs his hair. After a few moments he sees AIMEE's reflection and turns.

They stand looking at each other. For a moment he wonders if she is real. Darkness falls.

THE BIRDS

From the short story by Daphne du Maurier

Then the Lord God placed the man in the Garden of Eden to cultivate it and guard it. He said to him, 'You may eat the fruit of any tree in the garden, except the tree that gives knowledge of what is good and what is bad. You must not eat that fruit of that tree; if you do, you will die the same day.'

Genesis 2:16-17

*I am the eye with which the Universe
Beholds itself, and knows it is divine.*

Percy Bysshe Shelley,
Song of Apollo, 1820

The Birds was first performed at the Gate Theatre, Dublin, on 29 September 2009, with the following cast:

DIANE	Sinead Cusack
JULIA	Denise Gough
NAT	Ciarán Hinds
TIERNEY	Owen Roe
Director	Conor McPherson
Designer	Rae Smith
Lighting Designer	Paul Keogan
Sound Designer	Simon Baker

The play received its American premiere at the Guthrie Theater, Minneapolis, on 25 February 2012, with the following cast:

NAT	J.C. Cutler
JULIA	Summer Hagen
DIANE	Angela Timberman
TIERNEY	Stephen Yoakam
Director	Henry Wishcamper
Set Designer	Wilson Chin
Costume Designer	Jenny Mannis
Lighting Designer	Matthew Richards
Sound Designer	Scott W. Edwards

Characters

DIANE, *late forties/fifties*
NAT, *forties/fifties*
JULIA, *twenties*
TIERNEY, *fifties*

Setting

A house in the countryside.

Author's Note

It would be preferable if stage management remained invisible for
this play and the actors make any necessary changes to the set
between scenes themselves. This way we also get an opportunity to
watch them living together.

Scene One

In the darkness we hear DIANE*'s voice through speakers. It should
sound intimate. We hear her thoughts. Lights onstage gradually
reveal an isolated house in the countryside.*

DIANE (*voice-over*). I met the man on the road. We had both
abandoned our cars and decided to take our chances cutting
through the fields. We broke into a house beside the water and
locked ourselves in. The waves of bird attacks continued for the
next two days, punctuated by terrifying hours of inexplicable
silence. The man, who said his name was Nat, was sick. I nursed
him while he slept through a restless delirium. And that night was
the last broadcast we ever heard.

*New England in the near future. It is night. The shutters are
closed. We hear birds rustling outside the house. A fluttering of
wings here and there.* NAT *is asleep.* DIANE *is trying to tune in a
radio. All she gets is static with the odd voice trailing in and out.
She adjusts the dial and begins to pick up a signal as voices fade
in. Throughout the broadcast, random voices and sounds obscure
what's being said. There is chaos in the studio from where the
broadcast is coming.*

VOICE 1. Okay, so centres, aid centres, places where people can feel
safe, somewhere to sleep. They know there's a meal there...

VOICE 2. I never said that. I can't say that.

VOICE 1. Yes, but they can...

VOICE 2. There are people there, they seem organised, maybe it's
safer there, that's what we're...

VOICE 1. We're saying Mountstewart, St Thomas, Port Argus...

VOICE 2. Port Argus won't be able to take the strain.

VOICE 1. Well, Lowtown, Newchurch?

VOICE 2. Well... And Winford, we think, although...

VOICE 3 (*distant, off-mic*). No...

VOICE 1. Sorry, what?

VOICE 3. No, there was no... eh...

VOICE 2. From Winford...

VOICE 1. Don't go to Winford.

VOICE 2. No, what we are saying is what we can't confirm. I'm not trying to tell people where to go. I'm saying that I've been given this advice, that I have received...

VOICE 1 (*to* VOICE 3). What's the situation with Winford?

VOICE 3 (*unintelligible*).

VOICE 2. Because, I wouldn't even have said St Thomas myself.

VOICE 3 (*distant*). There are people there...

VOICE 1. There are people there. One could go to St Thomas...

VOICE 2. So it seems but...

VOICE 1. City Councillor John Little announced today that if he couldn't organise a quorum here tonight in Mountstewart that he will propose a... I can't read this...

VOICE 4. Listen, the situation is...

VOICE 1. Sorry, Dr Brodie, you want to come in there.

VOICE 4. The situation is – (*Interference.*) simply because no one could have prepared for a...

Interference...

VOICE 2. This is what I'm saying, we are all in the same situation, but there's no point in...

VOICE 3 (*distant*). They got into the gym at Cottonhills last night...

VOICE 1. Sorry, what?

VOICE 3. They got into the gym at Cottonhills last night so...

VOICE 4. You see, once they're in...

VOICE 2. We're talking about crows, sea birds, robins, sparrows! I mean, you think a man could... a grown adult can...

VOICE 4. Yes, but your average gull is big! Four or five or six pounds in weight coming straight down out of the sky, easily reaching speeds of forty miles an hour, can cause a tremendous amount of damage to a...

NAT *stirs restlessly.*

NAT. Sarah?

DIANE *switches off the radio.*

Sarah! No! Don't!

DIANE *goes to him, taking a cloth from a bowl of water to soothe his forehead.*

No! Stay away from me!

DIANE. Shh...

NAT *suddenly springs up towards the door.*

NAT. I have to get out!

DIANE *puts her hands on his shoulders.*

DIANE. No, don't do that.

NAT *grabs her roughly, forcing her back across the room.*

NAT. I'll fucking kill you! I mean it...

DIANE. You're just having a dream. It's okay, it's me, it's Diane.

NAT *looks at her, his eyes are wild.*

NAT. It's so cold.

DIANE. Why don't you lie down? Here, come on...

DIANE *goes and holds the blanket for him to get back into his 'bed'. He looks around the room.*

NAT. The baby was here.

DIANE. No. It's okay...

NAT. She was over there. She came in the door. She... (*Goes towards the stairs.*)

DIANE. No, come over here and lie down.

He obediently goes to her and goes to lie down, suddenly springing up.

NAT. I hope she didn't go back out!

DIANE (*gently*). No, no, it's alright. Shh… Just try and rest. Try and
stay warm. I'm here.

*NAT quietens down and we hear birds shuffling around outside,
enlivened by the voices.*

Scene Two

Dusk. DIANE *is at the stove, putting some fuel in. We can hear some
wings flapping outside and scratching or pecking here and there.*
NAT *is awake, watching* DIANE.

NAT. What time is it?

DIANE. Oh, hi. Are you hungry?

NAT. I'd love a drink of water.

DIANE. Yeah.

*She pours him a cup of water from a plastic bottle. He gulps it
down.*

More?

He nods and she pours him another cup.

NAT. Thanks. How long was I asleep?

DIANE. Two days.

NAT. What?

DIANE. Your temperature broke yesterday. It must have been at least
a hundred and three.

NAT. Oh… I'm sorry; did you say your name was Diana?

DIANE. Diane.

NAT. Oh yes, Diane. No sign of the owners, of this place?

DIANE. No.

NAT. Is everything…?

DIANE. Everything's… the same.

NAT. No news or...?

DIANE. Nothing for the last twenty-four hours.

NAT. Right. God... But nothing like, from the Government or...? I mean, how can all the phones all just be out?!

DIANE. I don't know. They think it's the tides.

NAT. What is?

DIANE. The birds go out with the tides. And they come back at high tide. Every six hours.

NAT. Oh.

DIANE. I mean, they don't know why.

NAT. God... I thought maybe it was all a dream.

DIANE. I know. It's high tide now.

Pause. They listen to the birds scrabbling around outside.

NAT. Do you think they know we're in here?

DIANE. Yeah. I do.

Pause.

NAT. Did you say you had a daughter?

DIANE. Yes. But, you know, grown up. Moved away. Et cetera. I was on my way to see her. It was her birthday and I was... going to...

Pause.

NAT. What about your husband?

DIANE. We're separated.

NAT. Right.

DIANE. He lives abroad.

NAT. Is this happening everywhere?

DIANE. It seems to be.

Pause.

NAT. What does he do?

DIANE. Who?

NAT. Your husband.

DIANE. He's a writer. We're both writers.

NAT. Really?

DIANE. Yeah, really.

NAT. What do you write?

DIANE. Books... you know. I haven't written one for a while but...

NAT. Well, I'd say it's tough enough to... to write a book, I mean...

DIANE. Do you have any children?

NAT. Well, I... no, they're my... the children of my ex.

DIANE. Ex-wife?

NAT. ...My... ex-girlfriend – or partner, I suppose. Not wife. We were living together. But not... not recently.

DIANE. Right. (*Short pause.*) Well, you were a family.

NAT. Yeah.

A loud smash somewhere makes them spring up. NAT *grabs a hammer and wields it like a weapon.*

DIANE. How old are they?

NAT. Six and eight. But I haven't seen them in about... ten months, a year.

DIANE. Right. Well, that's hard.

NAT. Yeah. And the break-up was... you know...

DIANE. Mmm...

NAT. It was... (*Looks at the shutters where some wings are heard flapping, birds bang against the glass.*) difficult, so...

DIANE. Yeah. Well, that's...

NAT. Yeah.

Pause

DIANE. Was this Sarah?

Pause.

NAT. Yeah, how do you know?

DIANE. Because you were talking to her.

NAT. What do you mean?

DIANE. You were talking to someone called Sarah. You pushed me right across the room.

NAT. Are you serious?

DIANE *just gives a little wry smile and raises her eyebrows.*

Oh, I'm sorry. Did I hurt you?

DIANE. No – (*Beat.*) just my finger.

NAT. Oh, no. I'm sorry. Is it bad?

DIANE. No, it just got bent right back, you know when that happens.

NAT. Oh God... Listen, I'd never do anything like that. I mean...

DIANE. I know.

NAT. I'm sorry.

DIANE. No, it's okay.

Pause. A concerted effort by a bird to fly repeatedly through a window makes them fall silent. The noise passes.

NAT. I can't believe I did that. She's absolutely crazy. I mean, she had me locked up, you know?

DIANE (*looking at him standing there with a hammer in his hand*). Who?

NAT. Sarah.

DIANE. In your dream?

NAT. No, like really. In real life. She's crazy.

DIANE. What do you mean 'locked up'?

NAT. Not in prison. She signed me into a... hospital. And she's the one who's nuts! That's the... that's the sick... irony.

DIANE....Right. Was this recently or...

NAT (*playing it down*). No... About a year ago?

DIANE....Right.

NAT. I mean, I wasn't well. I'm not saying that I wasn't. I certainly wasn't a hundred per cent. I was just suffering from a... a form of exhaustion really. But the way she decided to... to deal with it was... it was hugely disproportionate.

Pause.

DIANE. Right. (*Pause.*) What... happened, I mean, I'm...

NAT. Oh no, it's nothing to worry about.

DIANE. Right. No. (*Pause.*) You don't mind me asking. I'm just, I don't want to...

NAT. No, no, it's fine. No, just... There were just... a lot of arguments – you know how that... is...

DIANE. Mmm.

NAT. And a lot of criticism, coming my way from her family. About money, about other things... And I'd started getting these headaches and I wasn't able to sleep.

DIANE. Right. (*Pause.*) Do you... still get headaches, or...?

NAT. No. No, not for a long time. Yeah. No, I'm okay. I was always okay, really. There was just a lot of, you know *other* stuff going on there. You know. Certain agendas. But I still... I mean, you worry about people. I mean, I just... that's where I was going when all the... the birds started to happen. Probably a stupid fucking thing to do really.

DIANE. Oh, I don't know. You know what they say.

She gets up, tidying away her cup.

NAT. What?

DIANE. The first cut is the deepest.

NAT. Mmm.

He sits, looking into firelight of the stove.

Scene Three

The lights bring us to daylight. The door is open. The shutters are open, revealing boards up outside the windows. NAT *comes in.*

NAT. Listen, em... I think someone's been outside.

DIANE. What?

NAT. The padlock on the shed door was on the ground out there.

He shows her.

DIANE. Is anything gone?

NAT. I'm not sure. I thought I saw a can of kerosene in there a few days ago. It's not there now. And a shovel, I think, is gone.

DIANE. When do you think it...?

NAT. I think maybe just this morning when we were at the gas station. I mean, it might have even just been while we were down at the lake. I don't know.

DIANE. Just now?

NAT. I don't know!

NAT walks restlessly into the hall, looking around and comes back.

DIANE. Who would it be?

NAT. I think there's someone in that house across the lake.

DIANE. Where?

NAT. On the other side of the lake. I saw him yesterday morning when I was scavenging in the gas station. I think he had a gun, or a shotgun. He stepped back in behind the wall when he saw me.

DIANE. Why didn't you say anything?

He shrugs.

He must be watching us.

NAT. Yeah well, if it was him. If he's still there, I mean... I don't know.

DIANE. Let's go round there. We might see him. We might see smoke coming out of his chimney, I mean, if there's someone else living here we should... I mean, shouldn't we at least... be...

NAT. He's got a fucking gun though, Diane!

She is taken aback by the forcefulness of his outburst. He sees this.

I'm sorry.

DIANE. No. I know.

NAT goes. DIANE stands there.

Scene Four

Night. The room is lit by a candle or two. DIANE is tuning the radio, getting only static. The wind is howling. Occasionally a thump makes her look up as a bird tries to smash its way in. NAT comes down the stairs carrying a toolbox.

NAT. They can't get in.

DIANE. Doesn't it seem louder to you, tonight? I mean it sounds like there's a lot more of them.

NAT. Maybe they see the light. Maybe they hear us.

DIANE wonders if NAT is telling her to shut up. She switches off the radio and sits despondently, perusing a road map. NAT regards DIANE, then reaches into a hiding place and produces a bottle of cheap sherry with a screw top with about half left in it.

Listen, em, I picked this up in the office of the gas station, I don't know if it's... I mean it's a screw top. (*Reading label.*) It says it's wine... or sherry...

DIANE. Oh great...

NAT. I don't know when your birthday is, or was exactly, or was it your daughter's?

DIANE. Ah, Nat! It was Nina. It was her birthday.

NAT. Well, you said something about a birthday… and…

NAT gets two cups…

A birthday's a birthday. So happy birthday to Nina, right?

DIANE. Yeah. God, this is very swanky.

NAT. Well, I wouldn't say that.

He opens the screw top.

Fuck knows what this is like.

He sniffs it and recoils…

Oh Jesus

DIANE. Hit me.

He pours them drinks.

Thank you.

NAT. No cake, but…

DIANE. You can't have everything.

NAT. You can't have anything!

They laugh mordantly.

You could blow out a candle.

DIANE. No, I'm good.

NAT. Good luck.

DIANE. Cheers.

They drink. They both grimace. DIANE proffers her cup anyway.

DIANE (*hoarsely*). That's not too bad.

NAT (*hoarsely*). No!

He pours them another drink.

DIANE. It gives you kind of a nice warm…

NAT. Yeah, when you get it down!

They laugh. They stand near the glow of the fire. DIANE suddenly puts her face in her hand and cries silently. NAT looks at her for a moment, unsure what to say.

DIANE (*regaining her composure*). Sorry.

NAT. No...

DIANE. Thanks, Nat.

NAT. No...

DIANE *goes to get the map, bringing it to* NAT.

DIANE. Listen, I've been looking at this. We could get to St Thomas and back – in six hours.

NAT. Yeah...

DIANE. I mean, there's got to be a supermarket. There's got to be something.

NAT. Diane...

DIANE. We could be there in two, two-and-a-half hours. At the very least we'd have had a good...

NAT. Yeah, but...

DIANE. And even if we... if somehow we got... that we thought it was getting too late, there has to be somewhere that we could... I mean, what do we...

NAT. Shh! (*Holds his hand up to silence her.*)

They hear shouting in the distance. Different voices. Sporadic.

Blow out those candles!

They quickly douse the lights. The voices fall silent. There is a lot of flapping and scratching as the birds become excited coming and going from the roof of the house.

They wait listening. They only hear the birds. Then they hear a church bell off in the distance. Lights fade as they listen.

Scene Five

It is a bright afternoon. All is quiet. A girl of about twenty, JULIA, *comes into the room, rolling a cigarette. She has a dressing over a cut on her head. She is wearing a pair of high-heeled shoes. She finds some matches. A tape is playing in a radio/cassette player. It is someone playing a piano. She smokes, taking a saucer as an ashtray.* DIANE *arrives, a blanket wrapped around her. She throws a cold eye on the scene.* JULIA *gets up and turns down the music.*

JULIA. Sorry.

DIANE. Is that the radio?

JULIA. No, I found a few tapes upstairs in a shoebox.

DIANE. Tapes will wear down the batteries.

JULIA. Okay. Sorry.

> *She switches it off.*

And I found some shoes. They're going to kill me, but they'll have to do.

DIANE. How are you feeling?

JULIA. You have no idea what it means to me to be here, Diane. I can hardly believe it. I haven't felt safe like this for so long.

DIANE. How's your head?

JULIA. It's sore. But I want to start pitching in with all the chores now. When I stop feeling dizzy.

DIANE. Should you be smoking if you feel dizzy?

JULIA. Probably not.

> JULIA *stubs the fag out.*

DIANE. Where did you get the cigarettes?

JULIA. I found some tobacco in a drawer upstairs. It's kind of horrible actually.

DIANE. Is it okay if you don't smoke in the house?

JULIA. Yeah, sorry, I didn't think.

DIANE (*indicating a mattress and blanket on the floor*). Are you finished with your bed?

JULIA. Yeah. Oh sorry.

She goes to help DIANE *tidy it away.*

DIANE. Show me that dressing.

DIANE *goes to* JULIA *and maternally looks at her wound.*

I didn't do a great job. Let me put another one on.

JULIA. Thanks, Diane.

DIANE. Lie up here.

JULIA *lies on the sofa.* DIANE *wipes her hands and gets the first-aid kit. She goes to* JULIA *and carefully removes the dressing.*

What did you say he hit you with?

JULIA. A bell.

DIANE. A bell?

DIANE *gently dabs at the wound with some antiseptic.*

JULIA. I know. He found it in the classroom where we were hiding. And this particular person, he'd been trying to… you know… trying to be with me for a few nights, I woke up and he was trying to, you know, get close to me.

DIANE. Where were the other girls?

JULIA. They were in a different classroom and in the office. I was in a kind of big closet off one of the rooms. I'd been asleep.

DIANE. How many were there?

JULIA. Two other older girls. But I don't think they would have helped me. I had to get out. I ran across a huge football field, he came after me, but he was drunk. The birds got him. I heard him trying to get back into the school, but I don't think he made it. I hope he didn't.

DIANE. The birds didn't come after you?

JULIA. No. I hid in the church for a few hours and then I started walking out down by the road, but because I had no shoes and my legs were really wobbly, I was like... Then when I saw the smoke from your chimney I just thought, God, this is a miracle!

Pause.

DIANE. But why did you leave Port Argus?

JULIA. It was insane there, Diane. The whole place was drunk. There was a fire in the library and everybody had to leave. We had tried to get into Mountstewart. But no one was getting in. They'd closed the whole place down. So we started fucking walking. We slept in a house out in the country like this for a night but it was too crazy. Birds got in.

She winces in pain.

DIANE. Sorry.

JULIA. No it's fine. Then we slept in a factory, but that was horrible. We were in the school then for two nights. They'd found a load of malt liquor in a truck and I was sleeping away from the others 'cause I knew that something was going to happen. Something bad.

DIANE *finishes dressing the wound and starts tidying up.*

Thanks, Diane.

DIANE. You're welcome. It really needs a stitch.

JULIA (*lightly touches the dressing*). Thanks for looking after me.

DIANE. Hey, anyone would do it.

JULIA. I don't know about that! Nat told me you have a daughter. Is that right?

DIANE (*nods*). Mm-hm.

JULIA. How old is she?

DIANE. Older than you.

JULIA. I hope you get to see her again soon.

DIANE. Well. We'll see...

DIANE *is over where they keep their food.*

Julia, there was a can of spaghetti here.

JULIA. What was it?

DIANE. There was a can of SpaghettiOs on top of that box there.

JULIA. I don't know.

DIANE. You didn't see it?

JULIA. No. I only had half a stock cube and some water all day.

DIANE. But it was right there.

JULIA. There's pasta in the other box.

DIANE. I know, but the canned stuff is... I'm always very careful with it, because we can mix it with other things. And we never...

DIANE is searching for it.

JULIA. Maybe Nat will bring some back from the gas station.

DIANE. Yeah, but that's not what I'm talking about.

JULIA. Diane, I swear to God... I was just looking for tobacco. Diane. I didn't eat the spaghetti. I wouldn't do that.

NAT *arrives in the doorway. He carries a few things, not much.*

NAT. What's happened?

JULIA. Some food is gone missing. I was just telling Diane I didn't take it.

DIANE. I didn't say that. It's just, there was a can right here on top of the box and now it's gone.

NAT. I ate it.

DIANE. What?

NAT. I ate it.

DIANE. When?

NAT. Before I left. I had to or I couldn't walk all the way round the lake.

DIANE. Oh. Well. I'm sorry, Julia. I didn't know.

NAT *is taking off his overcoat, hat, belt, etc....*

JULIA. No. That's okay. I know. Do you want a glass of water, Nat?

NAT. What?

JULIA. Do you want a drink of water?

NAT. Hm?

JULIA. Do you want a drink?

NAT. Thanks.

DIANE. Here.

DIANE *pours a drink of water for* NAT. *She hands it to* JULIA *who brings it to him.*

NAT. Listen. (*Pause.*) There's nothing left up there. Your friends cleared it out.

JULIA. I knew they would.

DIANE. What are we going to do? Try St Thomas?

JULIA. We'll have to.

DIANE. What about we just get the fuck out of here?! Try to keep going!

NAT. There's nothing organised out there! You should have seen what they did over at the gas station. We could run into any kind of... (*Indicating* JULIA*'s injuries.*) St Thomas is as far as we could make it.

DIANE. Well, let's do it.

JULIA. We found food in a place about four miles or five miles from here. It was a house with a shop.

NAT. Where exactly?

JULIA. On the way to Port Argus.

DIANE. How long would it take us?

JULIA. Three hours, four, maybe more, depending.

DIANE. We could do it.

JULIA. I could show you where it is.

DIANE. We could take the wheelbarrow. Or the other handcart. Take turns wheeling it through the traffic jams.

NAT. I don't know. I don't like the idea of no one being here.

NAT *begins closing up the house.*

DIANE. Why? Nat. Why?

NAT. I don't know. I just... No reason, I suppose.

JULIA. You and me could go, Nat. I can show you exactly where it is.

NAT. Let me think about it.

JULIA. We'd be quick.

NAT. Yeah, I just think it's crazy not to have checked everywhere around here before we start going miles away.

Pause.

DIANE. Did you get anything?

NAT. I got some candy.

DIANE *takes some rice and considers it.* NAT *starts shutting up the house.*

JULIA. I like candy.

She shuts up immediately when she gets nothing from the others. The sound of birds gradually builds taking us into:

Scene Six

The birds are going crazy outside the house. They are whacking into the boards, scraping, fighting. DIANE, NAT *and* JULIA *all sit huddled in blankets. They have no lights on. They are dark, frightened silhouettes, trying to wait out the onslaught.*

This gradually becomes:

Scene Seven

Silence. It is late afternoon, near dusk. JULIA *is looking out the window, peeping between the boards while* NAT *shaves.*

JULIA. What's the bigger one to the left?

NAT. You don't know what that one is? Have a guess.

JULIA. A sycamore?

NAT. No, those two down there are sycamores. That one there on its own, is that the one you're talking about? That's an oak.

JULIA. Oh, an oak. Do you think it might be related to, em… broccoli.

NAT. Broccoli?

JULIA. Don't you think it looks like a big broccoli?

NAT (*laughs*). I suppose it does!

JULIA. It could be.

NAT. Whoever planted everything out there knew what they were doing. You see where the line of the old ditch meets the wall down there? That's practically prehistoric.

JULIA. Yeah, I mean, you do think that…

NAT. What.

JULIA. That we're safe here?

NAT. We're… pretty… safe here. They can never get through those boards – as long as we're alert, and even if one got in, or more, we'll go in the cellar in the kitchen. Wait for the tide to go out…

JULIA. The tide could change though.

NAT. The tide won't change!

JULIA. How they react to it might change. (*Pause.*) Where's Diane?

NAT (*checking his watch*). I don't know.

JULIA. Nat?

NAT. Yeah?

JULIA. You don't think that maybe Diane feels like… that I'm like…

NAT. Diane is a good person, Julia. She's a great person. We all have to look after each other. And if someone else came here we'd have to look after them too. Right?

JULIA *nods*.

I mean, that's… I mean, this is the new… This is the new way of living. Right? I mean, we're here.

JULIA *nods*.

DIANE *enters wearing a fencing mask. She wears a coat and gloves. She carries a bag with not much in it.*

Jesus, you're cutting it close! Where did you go?

DIANE. Down to the crossroads and into the little post office. I got some candles, oh, and some confetti.

NAT.…Great…

DIANE. I know.

NAT. Anything to eat? (*Throws a look at* JULIA.)

DIANE. Two cans of 7 Up. And a pack of yellow tomato seeds.

NAT. Oh well. We could grow them in here.

DIANE. I know. (*To* JULIA.) Here, I got you a watch.

JULIA. Oh. Thanks, Diane.

DIANE. The time is right. Don't mess with it and I'll show you how to wind it later. Right, we've about one hour, who's going to light the fire?

Pause. NAT *watches* DIANE *put her things away.*

NAT. We're okay for a couple of days, right?

DIANE. Not really. We have some rice. We have prunes.

NAT *looks at* JULIA

NAT. Turn on the light.

DIANE. What?

NAT. Turn on the light.

DIANE. Nat, I'm not in the mood!

NAT. Diane, turn it on.

DIANE. Are you serious?

She goes to a wall switch.

NAT. No, not that one. The lamp.

DIANE. Really?

She goes to a switch. A lamp comes on.

When did the power come back?

NAT. I fixed the generator. It burns a fuck-load of juice but as long as we're careful...

DIANE (*deflated*). And here I thought it was the end of the end of the world...

NAT. We could even rig up a little hotplate, if we can find one.

DIANE. All we need is the food.

JULIA. Diane. We have food.

She produces a big basket of food.

DIANE. Oh my God, where did you go?

NAT. I didn't go anywhere. I was working on the generator. It was Julia.

JULIA. You didn't tell me where you were going. I went after you. You were gone but I found a house with a big cellar in the back.

DIANE. Is it nearby?

JULIA. My arms are killing me! I thought I nearly wasn't going to make it!

NAT. Look, pound cake!

JULIA. Pound cake. Easter eggs. Cans of fruit. Pasta. Cans of soup.

DIANE. Where was it? Is there much left?

JULIA. I think there is. I couldn't look through everywhere properly 'cause I was afraid I was going to run out of time!

DIANE. Well, we can go back tomorrow.

JULIA. I hope I can remember where it is.

NAT. What are you talking about? Of course you'll remember.

JULIA. I nearly got lost coming back.

DIANE. Where did you go?

JULIA. Right, right over, over the other side of the lake. All the way over behind the trees, behind the quarry.

DIANE. What in the name of God were you doing all the way over there?

JULIA. I don't know, I just went for a quick look. And I... I just kept going and I just had this mad thought, 'I bet I can find something.' I knew I would.

DIANE. Julia...!

JULIA. I just thought... I'll have a quick look before I come home. I was so frightened!

DIANE. It's so dangerous going off on your own in a place like that!

JULIA. I knew the tide had gone out at one o'clock – Nat said.

DIANE. I know, but what if...

JULIA. You go off.

DIANE. I never go that far! I'm always...

NAT. Look. Diane's right, Julia, you shouldn't go off like that – without saying or.... What if you ran into the people you were with before – or anything could happen.

JULIA. I didn't mean to go that far! (*Throwing things back in the box.*) I just ended up over on the other side of the lake and I just thought, 'Well, I'm here, I might as well see what I can, you know, see if I can... see if I can contribute.'

NAT. Well, yeah, no, thanks this is great, I mean... (*Looks at* DIANE.) But...

DIANE. No, it's great, but, you know... If this is someone's food and they saw you or...

JULIA. I got four bottles of wine for Nat's birthday! So now we can have a little party and cheer ourselves up, because we can even play tapes now!

JULIA storms off up the stairs. Pause.

DIANE. I didn't know it was your birthday.

NAT. Well... it's around now.

Scene Eight

Night. The piano player's tape is playing on the stereo. Three empty wine bottles stand on the table. They have all dressed up. JULIA wears a wedding dress. NAT stands opening the last bottle. JULIA holds DIANE's hand in hers, reading her palm...

JULIA. Jesus Christ, Diane, there's an awful lot of pain here.

DIANE. Don't say that.

JULIA. No, it's all in your past.

DIANE. Good.

JULIA. All the old pain is going to melt away, Diane.

DIANE. When?

JULIA. It's all going to be gone.

DIANE. When?

JULIA. You won't believe how it can go. But it will.

NAT. Is this the only tape we have?

JULIA. Leave it on. I see so much peace in your future. You're so
    lucky.

DIANE. Is this all true?

JULIA. Yes.

    They laugh.

    Your whole life story is here, Diane, if you could read it you'd
    know.

DIANE. How can you read it? I want to believe you.

JULIA. You want to believe me because you know that it's real.

DIANE. Who showed you how to do it?

JULIA. My mother showed me. She could see a lot more than me
    though. She died when I was twelve.

DIANE (*sympathetic*). Oh...

JULIA. She had a room where she read fortunes up this old windy staircase down a side street in Port Argus. I used to go there after school. She used to make me sit in a big chair facing the wall to do my homework where the people couldn't see me. She had all kinds of people would come. Politicians, rich people, poor people, drunks, people who'd cry.

DIANE. Wow, what a way to grow up.

NAT. Hey, I never had my birthday cake.

JULIA. Get the pound cake, Nat!

NAT. I love pound cake…

NAT *goes to get the cake.*

JULIA. The chemicals they put in make those things last a thousand years I heard one time.

NAT. I fucking love chemicals.

DIANE (*indicating her hand*). Tell me more.

JULIA. That's all I see, all the pain stops, Diane. It's like someone opens a little door here and you step into paradise.

DIANE. That sounds like I'm going to die!

JULIA. No, it's your life, Diane.

DIANE. All the old pain…

JULIA. It's going to melt away.

DIANE. I wish I could believe it.

JULIA. You do believe it. Your body knows. Your mind wants to stop your body.

NAT *is slicing the cake.*

DIANE. Why?

JULIA. Because you're afraid. (*Pause.*) Have you ever read the Bible, Diane?

DIANE. Oh, please…

DIANE *is looking in the cups for her drink.*

JULIA. What do you mean, 'Oh, please…'

NAT *holds up a can with a white label and a distinctive green stripe, but no writing.*

NAT. Hey, Julia, what did you say was in these cans? Fruit?

JULIA. Yeah, it's pears.

NAT. Who wants pears with their cake?

NAT *is opening the can.*

JULIA. We should get a Bible. You should read it, Diane.

DIANE. I don't want to read the Bible, Julia.

JULIA. I know, but…

DIANE *turns way from her.*

DIANE. Where's my drink?

JULIA. Hey, Nat, you're next!

NAT. Next for what?

JULIA. I'll tell you your fortune.

NAT. No way!

JULIA. Why not?

NAT. I don't want to know.

DIANE. Good thinking.

NAT. Tell me something from the Bible. Something nice to cheer me up.

DIANE (*irritated*). Ohh… Nat, you're drunk.

JULIA. Diane's an atheist.

DIANE. I never said that.

NAT. No, but do tell me something. Not my fortune. Tell me something that'll make me feel happy.

JULIA (*spreads her arms a little*). 'Someone who is always thinking about happiness is a fool. A wise person thinks about death.'

Pause. NAT *looks at* DIANE *and back at* JULIA.

NAT. Thanks.

JULIA (*laughs*). No, that's wise words, Nat. Ecclesiastes. Ecclesiastes is so beautiful, Diane. 'Sorrow is better than laughter; it may sadden your face, but it sharpens your understanding.'

NAT. I think I'd prefer to be happy and not understand.

DIANE. Yes.

JULIA. 'When a fool laughs, it is like thorns crackling in a fire. It doesn't mean a thing.'

My mother always said she could see herself in Ecclesiastes. She said it's like a mirror.

NAT. Who wants pears with their pound cake?

JULIA. The Bible's not just about God, you know, Diane. It's about people as well. Real people like you and me.

DIANE. Stupid people like me.

JULIA. You're not a stupid person, Diane! (*Short pause.*) Does anyone else ever feel like there's someone upstairs?

DIANE *and* NAT *do not answer her.*

NAT. Right, who wants pears? I'm having pears. Oh, balls!

JULIA. What's wrong?

NAT. I've just put onions all over my cake!

JULIA. Onions?

NAT. It's not pears, it's onions!

DIANE *and* JULIA *start laughing.*

I've ruined my birthday cake!

JULIA. No, have another slice!

NAT. Whoever heard of canned onions?

DIANE. You moron...

NAT (*looking at the can*). Where does it say it's pears?

JULIA. I don't know... I... I think it must have said 'pears' on the cardboard tray they were in...

NAT. That's a pain in the balls. That's what God gives us now for laughing at him.

NAT *brings his plate to clean it off and get some more cake.*

JULIA. I'm sorry, Nat.

DIANE. Have mine, Nat.

JULIA. Have mine.

NAT. No, it's alright, there's more.

JULIA. Oh, hold on!

JULIA goes and gets a little box of birthday-cake candles.

Put one of these on!

NAT lets her put a candle in his slice of cake. She lights it. They all sit at the table.

(*Sings.*) Happy birthday to you...

NAT. Oh no...!

DIANE joins in...

JULIA *and* DIANE (*singing*). Happy birthday to you, Happy birthday dear Na... at... Happy birthday to you!

They applaud him...

JULIA (*sings*). For he's a jolly good fellow, for he's a jolly good fellow,

NAT. Oh God...

JULIA. For he's a jolly good fe... el... low... Which nobody can deny. Which nobody can deny...

NAT. Please...

JULIA. Make a wish. Wait! Did you make a wish?

Pause. JULIA blows out the candle... They applaud.

DIANE. I hope you made a wish to get us out of here!

NAT stands up unsteadily and raises his drink.

NAT. I just want to say...

JULIA. Speech! Speech!

NAT. I just want to say... I know that this is... I know that this is a... well, a terrible time for all of us. For everybody. But... Be that as it may, I just want to say... to both of you, to all of us. Thank you for giving me a birthday... treat.

DIANE (*claps a little*). Thanks, Julia.

NAT. It's not easy. It's not easy for any of us. But I think that the three of us have done admirably. And I don't know what the future holds. Only Julia knows that...

They laugh.

JULIA. Ah fuck off...

NAT. But while we have been here. And for the time we have left to come, whatever is going to happen, I just want to say that I'm proud of... of both of you, of all of us.

DIANE. Hear, hear...

NAT. Because it's not easy and... Well... Look, we're all different people. We all have different lives and... But you know, as long as there's... (*Pause.*) kindness... there's hope, right? (*Pause.*) Every day, I've been waking up. Wondering if this is my last day alive. So frightened that this is the end, every day. But recently, I mean, just in the past few days I've been... at the end of each day, I've been actually *thankful* for that day. (*Almost starts to cry, but recovers.*) When I was a boy I always dreamt of being in the Army. Of course, they wouldn't fucking have me. But be that as it may, I always felt... safe when I was having those dreams. Because I was ready, I suppose. Ready for any disaster. We were equipped for it. We were ready. Mmm. But I feel that the three of us... we can... We can make it. I know we can. (*Shouts at the windows.*) Fuck them! Fuck you! Fuck you!

There is a flurry of activity from the birds as they hear him shouting.

Yeah, that's it! That's it...

NAT *laughs and goes to the shutters, banging on them to* DIANE *and* JULIA's *alarm. Then he starts to open them in a mad attempt to fight them.* DIANE *and* JULIA *go to him, shouting, 'Stop! Nat, don't!', etc....* DIANE *slaps* NAT *across the face.* NAT *abruptly stops shouting and stares at* DIANE *while* JULIA *quickly closes the shutters.* NAT *goes back to the table. The others follow warily.*

Anyway. Thank you. Thanks. Thank you.

Pause.

JULIA. I always think whoever used to play that piano is still upstairs. (*Pause.*) I let someone die. About four days before I got here. We were in a factory, in the office. Suddenly there was a loud bang and there were hundreds of birds outside. We got under the desk and a tiny little one pecked its beak through one of the windows. I just went through a door and up these stairs, I turned at the top and I looked at this girl and she was holding birds in both her hands and a bird had her eyelid in his beak and he was just pulling and pulling up towards the ceiling. (*Tearfully.*) That's all I saw and I ran upstairs and hid in an oven.

Pause.

NAT. You didn't let her die.

Pause.

DIANE. That's right.

DIANE *embraces* JULIA.

NAT. There was nothing you could do.

Pause.

DIANE (*fixing* JULIA*'s hair*). The last time I saw Nina, my daughter. She had decided to go and visit her father, who lives on the other side of the world with his girlfriend and their young child. A taxi was picking her up to take her to the airport at six o'clock in the morning. I'd been up all night because I'd run out of these sleeping pills I'd been taking – and we had a huge fight. I was just so scared she'd never come back. (*Pause.*) She sent the taxi away, but I told her she was being stupid and I called her another one and she made it. She told me that she never wanted to see me again.

Pause.

JULIA. To kindness.

DIANE. To kindness.

They drink. In the distance they hear dogs howling. With the music gone off they can hear the birds scratching and banging round the house.

JULIA. What is that?

NAT. Dogs.

JULIA. How are they alive?

NAT. They're living up in the caves up there beyond the quarry. They hide in there. It's a full moon tonight.

JULIA. Won't the birds hear them?

Pause.

NAT. People all round here used to worship the moon.

> JULIA *turns the stereo back up. She goes to* NAT *and takes his hand. He dances awkwardly with her at first, in a slightly formal way. They laugh at their inability. But soon the music takes him and* JULIA *holds him closer and they dance slowly, enjoying the closeness.* DIANE *watches, a lonely figure at the table, as the lights fade.*

Scene Nine

It is a hot afternoon. They are all in states of undress, the heat being almost unbearable. JULIA *taps out a few desultory notes on the piano.* NAT *is mending a gear mechanism from a bicycle.* DIANE *writes in a notebook. We hear her voice as she writes.*

DIANE (*voice-over*). Day after day, you know it's not a dream when you wake up into reality's heavy deadness. We've scavenged what we can out of all houses in the area – always avoiding the farmer's house on the other side of the lake. We never see him. Maybe he's dead. For three days in a row we went off to locate the house where Julia found all the goodies, but she'd forgotten which way she went! We got lost and arrived back frustrated and exhausted and barely talking to one another. Nat deals with stress by setting about practical tasks; mending the boards or tinkering with a broken lamp brings him the steady rhythm of meditation, and Julia…

> DIANE *watches* JULIA. JULIA *smiles at* DIANE. DIANE *smiles back and we hear her thoughts without her necessarily writing anything.*

Julia. I can't decide whether she sees us as her parents or if it's something else. She seems so open, but there's something there that I can't see. That she doesn't show. Or just doesn't show me. When Nat gets down, and we all get down, you can feel her anxiousness like a physical vibration in the air. But she never comes to me to share it. I can't help feeling that they communicate something to each other in the silence. But all I get is the silence.

And the strange… hatred that consumes me isn't just for them and their proximity and the claustrophobic pain of never having any privacy – it's a hatred of myself too. Sometimes it grows so great I feel like just picking something up and…

JULIA. You have lovely legs, Diane.

DIANE. What?

JULIA. You have lovely legs. Doesn't she, Nat?

NAT (*working*). Mmm. (*Goes out to the hall.*)

DIANE. Really?

JULIA. Were you ever a dancer?

DIANE. No!

JULIA. No!

DIANE. No. (*Relenting.*) I've always done a lot of walking.

JULIA. And you have lovely feet.

DIANE. Do you think?

JULIA. Yeah, they're in nice proportion. I have fat toes.

DIANE. You have very nice feet.

JULIA. They're nothing like yours. Yours could be in a commercial. For sandals or something.

DIANE *considers her feet.*

What do you write about?

DIANE (*closing her notebook*). Oh, nothing, just… you know, thoughts.

JULIA. Like a diary?

DIANE. I suppose.

JULIA. God, it's so hot…

DIANE. I know.

JULIA. I'm so bored!

DIANE. I know.

JULIA. What time is it?

DIANE. Where's your watch?

JULIA. It's around somewhere.

DIANE. Around or lost?

JULIA. Around, Diane. It's around.

DIANE. Two more hours of high tide.

JULIA. And no birds.

Pause.

DIANE. I know.

They are looking at each other. But not wanting to get their hopes up.

JULIA. And none yesterday.

DIANE. I know. What do you think? Try for St Thomas…?

JULIA. Yeah, just go for it. Do it in the morning. Just even you and me go.

DIANE. Do you think.

JULIA. I'm going out of my fucking mind, Diane.

NAT (*coming in*). What's this? (*Pause.*) We'll find that house.

JULIA (*exasperated*). Oh!

NAT. I mean, it's got to be nearby!

JULIA. But I don't know where that is. I can't remember!

NAT. Come on, how far can it be? If it saves us going all the way to St Thomas. It's definitely worth having another good…

JULIA (*with force*). I told you, I can't remember where it is!

Pause.

DIANE. We have the bikes now, Nat.

NAT. We have two bikes and one of them the gears are jammed.

DIANE. Alright, well then we'll draw straws.

JULIA. Diane and me can go, Nat.

NAT. Aw, get real…

DIANE. We'll draw straws.

DIANE *goes and takes three long matches, snapping one in two.*

NAT. Listen, all I'm saying is why don't we wait until we get another bike and...

DIANE (*simultaneous, overlapping* NAT). Because I'm not going to wait around here starving to death while you go...

NAT. That way if we get stranded, we're not separated, and at least we all know what's happening...

DIANE (*simultaneous, overlapping* NAT)....round the countryside looking for a suitable bike! We're drawing straws, so just draw a straw, because someone's going and if you don't want to go, someone's going, so draw a straw.

NAT. No, I'm not going to draw a straw.

DIANE. Draw a straw.

NAT. No, I'm not doing this.

JULIA. Nat.

DIANE. Draw a straw.

NAT. No.

DIANE. Draw one.

NAT. No.

JULIA. We're all doing it.

DIANE. Just draw one!

NAT *reluctantly draws a straw. It looks long.* DIANE *offers the straws to* JULIA. *She draws one. It looks about the same length at* NAT*'s. They look expectantly at* DIANE, *who reveals that she has the short straw.*

NAT. Happy?

JULIA. Okay?

Pause. NAT *just goes back into the hall.*

DIANE. Right. (*Pause.*) Okay.

JULIA. You can go the next time.

DIANE. Yeah.

Scene Ten

Morning. A grey sky. The door is closed over. DIANE *is alone, doing some sit-ups. All is quiet. Then a figure passes the door.* DIANE *looks up, wondering did she see something. No one is there. A shadow appears in the doorway, a key turns in the lock and the door is gently opened.* DIANE *can only watch the door in horror. A big, heavyset man in his fifties has come in, carrying a plastic bag and a shotgun. He is filthy. He has what looks like a bamboo waste-paper basket with eye holes cut out over his head.* DIANE *stares at him, as though she can't believe this is happening. He takes his 'helmet' off.*

TIERNEY. All on your own?

DIANE. No.

TIERNEY. No, you are, that was rhetorical. I'm your neighbour.

DIANE. What do you want?

TIERNEY. I brought you a few gifts. To say hello. I was wondering why you didn't go off with the other pair this morning. Where are they gone? St Thomas? (*Pause.*) There's nothing there. I could've told you, but you're never sociable.

DIANE. They're only down at the lake. They'll be back in a few minutes.

TIERNEY. I saw them going off up the road more than two hours ago towing a wheelbarrow. They're not at the lake.

DIANE. What do you want?

TIERNEY. This is my sister's house. I grew up here.

Short pause.

DIANE. Well, I'm sure you understand that all bets are off. I mean, we don't want to be here either, but we don't have a choice. Just take whatever you want and...

TIERNEY (*gives a little laugh*). All bets are off, I like that. (*Produces a bottle of brandy from his bag.*) Have a drink with me.

DIANE. No, I'm... I'm fine, thank you.

TIERNEY. Mind if I grab a cup?

DIANE. Do I have a choice?

TIERNEY. Of course you do. Hey, welcome to reality – where anything is possible, right?

TIERNEY takes two cups and pours them both a drink.

Seen anyone else about?

DIANE. No. (*Short pause.*) Have you?

TIERNEY. Not for weeks. Nothing on the radio any more. Nothing on the TV. Nothing nowhere. (*Drinks.*) What do you think? Are we the last people left in the world?

DIANE. I don't know.

TIERNEY. They never saw this one coming, ha? No one ever thought nature was just going to eat us. (*Pause.*) Mm? (*Short pause.*) Jesus Christ, it's so *quiet*! (*Pause.*) Sometimes I wonder if I'm going insane! (*Laughs grimly.*) Probably lost it long ago. Here.

He offers her an open envelope.

DIANE. What is it?

TIERNEY (*shakes it a little*). Pills. Tablets. All the kids from Port Argus and Mountstewart used to take them. I got them out of a pharmacy. They're a controlled substance you might say. If you take them with a drink they make the time pass quicker.

DIANE. No, I'm alright.

TIERNEY. They kill pain.

DIANE. No thanks.

TIERNEY. Okay. (*Pops a pill and shudders.*) I have to stop taking them. (*Pause. Regards DIANE.*) Why do you look so familiar?

DIANE. I don't know.

Pause.

TIERNEY. Look. I got food. I got drink. I got medicine. I got the lot. I've got a whole lock-up. I can get by for years. I've seen you going around with Romeo. But the girl's with him now. Your days are numbered.

DIANE. What do you mean?

TIERNEY. You're crowding them out. The girl wants him to herself. What good are you to her?

DIANE. What are you talking about?

TIERNEY. Ah, wake up, will you? You're on the final countdown here, baby.

DIANE. No. Look, I think you've... You see, the three of us. We don't want to be trespassers but we're just trying to...

TIERNEY. Do me a favour and don't be stupid, will you? You think that girl was out there surviving by her wits and her charm? Anyone who's left out there is an animal! The people she was with ransacked the whole place over at the crossroads. They killed a woman who'd been hiding in the house up behind the gas station. I saw the body. Her mouth was wide open, like this – (*Does the dead woman's face.*) screaming into the floor.

DIANE. That wasn't Julia, she was with some bad people for a while but...

TIERNEY. Use your brain, missus, she's out for herself. I know!

DIANE. How would you know?

TIERNEY. Because... I've lived like that. I was one of the armies of the road. In the eighties, the nineties. Living on the streets over in Wolchurch – and Birhaven. Years, I lived like that before I came back. To look after my mother. You go from morning to night, morning to night, that's all you know about. That's all you know. I can see it in her. I know exactly who she is. It's not her fault, but she'll have to get rid of you.

DIANE. No, you don't know her.

TIERNEY. So you say.

DIANE. Well, I don't agree.

TIERNEY. Well... Hey, be a Christian. Watch where it gets you. (*Pause.*) Look. What I'm saying is... If you... if you want to... you can come with me. (*Short pause.*) You can be safe. (*Pause.*) It's not easy for me to come here like this. I never even meant to. I never would have... But as time goes on... (*Drinks.*) When I lie down at night and... it's so dark. For some reason I see your face and I know I could... take care of you. And we could...

DIANE. Look…

TIERNEY (*suddenly shouts*). I'm a gentleman, missus! But any plant, be it a weed or beautiful flower, needs the water and the sun!! We're all just the same! It's so cold on the other side of the lake. Don't you see what a waste it's gonna be when she gets her way? The two of them will be nice and cosy on their own here. And the wind will just blow across the water. (*Pause*.) Bluejays killed my dog. Maybe just as well.

Pause.

DIANE. I can't go with you. I'm sorry.

Short pause.

TIERNEY. Hey, I know who you are. Your photo was on those books my mother used to read. I read one. Am I right?

DIANE. I don't know.

TIERNEY. That's it. I knew I'd seen you. You wrote that book about the woman with the wart on her face, right?

DIANE. A long time ago.

TIERNEY. Well, I'll be damned. What about that? It's good to meet you.

Pause.

He takes some cans from his bag. They are white with a distinctive green stripe on them, but no writing.

No hard feelings. Here, these are pears. I'll leave them here.

DIANE. Thank you.

TIERNEY. And here. (*Leaves the envelope of pills on the table*.) I have millions.

TIERNEY *goes to the door. He stops and turns to* DIANE.

What am I gonna do?

DIANE *has no answer for him. He leaves.* DIANE *waits a moment then bolts the door. Turning, she considers the cans. She grabs the can opener and opens one of them. She sniffs it and puts it down on the table.*

Scene Eleven

Night. NAT *sits drinking a glass of whiskey. A box with more whiskey bottles sits nearby.* JULIA *is reading a book.* DIANE *is staring at the fire. Outside a wind blows softly. A bird flits from a branch to the roof. The atmosphere is solemn. They are all oppressed by boredom. Nothing happens. They even seem oblivious to the sounds of birds scratching or thumping at the house outside.* JULIA *wanders to the radio, switches it on and spins the dial. She only gets white noise and high-frequency whining. She switches it off.*

JULIA. Don't drink too much, Nat. You'll get a hangover.

NAT. Yeah...

Pause. JULIA *regards* DIANE.

JULIA. Getting all that rice wasn't bad, right, Diane?

DIANE. Hm?

JULIA. Just saying, all that rice we got.

DIANE. Yes, no, that's... that's fantastic.

JULIA. And there just wasn't a huge amount of time. (*Pause.*) I mean, even if we don't drink all the whiskey, we could...

NAT. What?

JULIA. Well, if we ever met anyone else we could trade it.

NAT. For what?

JULIA. I don't know. If they had something we needed.

NAT. With who?

JULIA. I don't know.

DIANE. If we have any left.

NAT. Hey, I carried it back... Have a drink, Diane.

DIANE. Whiskey was never my drink.

NAT. Mix it with something.

DIANE. With what?

NAT. Tomato juice.

DIANE. I'll leave it thanks.

JULIA. I'm going to use the bucket.

She takes a bucket and goes upstairs.

NAT. Look, I'm sorry we didn't do better, Diane. Jesus Christ, it was so creepy in St Thomas. I thought we'd never get back. I was just waiting for someone to jump out of a doorway and...

DIANE *goes to the stairs and looks up, listening for* JULIA. *She goes to* NAT.

DIANE. Nat. Listen. The farmer who's over on the other side of the lake. He came here today.

NAT. What?

DIANE. The guy who we've seen on the other side of the lake. He was here. He said this is his sister's house.

NAT. You're joking.

DIANE. No, he was here.

NAT. What did he want?

DIANE. Company. He says he has food and medicine.

NAT (*loudly*). Why didn't you tell me? What did he say?!

DIANE *puts her finger to her lips and gets one of the white cans with the green stripe. She brings it to* NAT.

DIANE. He gave us this.

NAT. Yeah...?

DIANE. He said it was pears. But I opened one. It's onions.

NAT. Yeah, we know these are onions.

DIANE. But why did Julia think they were pears? She said they were pears too. (*Pause.*) How come she could never find that house again – where she got all the stuff?

NAT. She said she got lost.

DIANE. No. What if he gave her all that stuff?

NAT. She would have told us! (*Pause.*) Why wouldn't she have told us?

DIANE. I don't know. (*Pause.*) Listen, Nat. I know you probably don't want to tell me, and I can understand but...

JULIA comes back down the stairs. DIANE and NAT fall silent. JULIA goes to where she was sitting and picks up her book, sensing a strange vibe.

JULIA. It's gone very quiet in here.

DIANE. We've run out of things to talk about.

JULIA (*holds up her book*). It won't be long then before we have you reading the Bible, Diane. We can have a book club.

DIANE. Yeah... You didn't find any other books?

JULIA. There were other books there, there were loads of books about farming and tractors but I didn't see anything you'd like, I mean, I didn't know what kind of books you're in to.

DIANE. Oh, anything...

JULIA. Yeah but we were really looking for food, Diane. We didn't want to get stuck out after dark.

DIANE. Yeah, I know.

JULIA. We'll go back. We'll get you some books.

DIANE. It's okay.

JULIA. I'm sorry.

DIANE. No. It's okay.

The three of them sit there thoughtfully, the wind blowing. JULIA gets her bedding and starts to bed down. DIANE opens her notebook. As the lights dim to black, we hear her voice...

(*Voice-over.*) They say people who've killed someone think about it like no other event in their lives. And they say that to taste it and walk away unpunished is worse than being caught and confessing. The universe seems indifferent to your act – people die every day and the cold Earth doesn't care how they go. But you, the killer, return to it over and over in your mind. No drug can induce its giddy exhilaration. No agitation can match its tantalising meaninglessness. Once you have killed, it calls to you again and again. So they say.

Scene Twelve

Night. Darkness. The wind is howling. Lightning illuminates JULIA
and NAT *standing in a corner, discussing something quietly and
urgently. A thunderclap wakes* DIANE. *She sits up and shines her
flashlight at* NAT *and* JULIA.

DIANE (*lighting a candle*). Is everything alright?

JULIA (*returning to her bed*). Just stay out of it, Diane, alright?

DIANE. What's going on?

JULIA. Why do we all have to sleep in this one fucking room?

DIANE. What?

JULIA. We've no privacy! Why can't we be alone to even talk?

DIANE. Sleep where you want! Am I in the way here?

NAT. No. We were... We were just talking...

   NAT *reaches for the whiskey bottle.*

JULIA. Nat! Stop drinking.

NAT. My head is fucking killing me!

JULIA. Well, that'll only make it worse! (*Beat.*) Tell her, Nat.

   Pause.

DIANE. What.

NAT. We'll talk about it in the morning.

   JULIA *picks up her bedding.*

JULIA. I'm sleeping upstairs.

NAT. It's not safe – they got in up there before.

JULIA. I'll take my chances. Thanks, Diane.

DIANE. For what?

JULIA. Don't act all innocent. You needn't bother.

DIANE. What? What did I do?

JULIA (*on her way up the stairs*). Oh spare me, Diane, the lies have to stop somewhere.

JULIA *is gone.* DIANE *looks at* NAT, *who cradles his drink, down by his mattress.*

DIANE. Will she be okay up there?

NAT. The tide's gone out.

DIANE *gets a cup and comes to the table. She pours a drink and sips it. She grimaces.*

DIANE. Are you lovers?

NAT (*rubs his face*). She's pregnant.

DIANE. What?

NAT. She's pregnant.

DIANE. How long?

NAT. I don't know. She said a few weeks.

DIANE. A few weeks?

NAT. We were going to tell you but...

DIANE. Am I that bad?

NAT. No, of course not!

DIANE *goes to a window and opens the shutters, looking out. The first brush of dawn is in the sky.*

DIANE. Look, don't worry.

NAT. How can I not worry? We can't bring a child into... into this.

DIANE. We'll pull together.

NAT. Jesus, the last thing I wanted to do was to cause any trouble... You have to know that, Diane, I... The first time, it was... It was the night we had my birthday.

DIANE. Yeah, okay, Nat...

NAT. I was dreaming and then, there she was beside me. I thought she was frightened. I thought I was protecting her.

DIANE. Society's gone, Nat. No one's keeping score. So you can do whatever you want...

NAT. Yeah, well, all that is fine when you're writing your novels, Diane. But this is bigger than that! This is... A child is...

DIANE. How do you know it's yours?

NAT. Because I asked her. I had to.

DIANE. Is that what you were whispering about?

NAT. I just asked her.

DIANE. What...

NAT. I asked her if she was with him for the food...

DIANE. What did she say?

NAT. She said no.

DIANE (*unconvinced*). Mmm.

NAT. She said no, Diane. I didn't even know she was pregnant. She only told me yesterday. All the way to St Thomas she kept trying to hold my hand. But God forgive me, I just wished she'd fuck off.

DIANE. Sweetie, who knows where she was before she got here? Who knows what happened out there? She could easily have been pregnant before you even met her. If she is pregnant. (*Notices that* NAT *is holding his head, wincing.*)

NAT. Oh, I haven't had a headache like this in so long.

DIANE. Come on. Sit down over here.

He goes to her and they sit on the sofa.

It'll be okay.

NAT. I'm sorry.

DIANE. I know.

From her pocket she takes the envelope TIERNEY *gave her with the pills. She considers it.*

Let me get you some water.

Scene Thirteen

Late afternoon. DIANE *is alone. She is reading* JULIA*'s Bible. It is grey and still.* JULIA *steps into the room from outside.* DIANE *closes the book.*

JULIA. It's okay, Diane, you can read it. I wouldn't stop you.

DIANE. I know.

JULIA. Where's Nat?

DIANE. He's gone for a walk.

JULIA. Is he feeling better?

DIANE. I think he just wanted to get some fresh air. While there's time.

JULIA. Right.

JULIA stands there awkwardly.

I wasn't sure if you were talking to me.

DIANE. I wasn't sure you were talking to me!

JULIA. Of course I am.

DIANE. You weren't too happy with me last night.

JULIA. I just couldn't believe that you'd say something like that to Nat. About me.

DIANE (*goes to* JULIA *and takes her hand*). I'm sorry if I offended you, that's not what I meant to do.

JULIA. Okay.

Pause. DIANE *goes to get their dinner ready.*

DIANE. You know you could have come to me any time and told me about… what's happened.

JULIA. I just… I've always been a bit too… afraid to talk with you about… certain things, Diane.

DIANE. Why?

JULIA. I don't know. I sometimes think that you always think I came here and wrecked it for you and Nat and that's not...

DIANE. Julia, everyone in the world is dead. We've no food and we can't go anywhere because we'll all be killed. Believe me, I have bigger things to worry about.

JULIA. It's just that Nat's been really hurt.

DIANE. In what way?

JULIA. Well, you've made him question whether he's the father of our baby.

DIANE. Jesus Christ, Julia! Who knows who the father is?

JULIA. I know!

DIANE. Oh, please...

JULIA. That's the problem with you, Diane, it's always 'Oh, please... Oh, please...'

Oh, please what?

DIANE. Julia...

JULIA. I've read your diary, Diane.

Pause.

DIANE. Ohh... how could you?

JULIA. I had to! And I was right to, because now I know what's really been going on around here.

DIANE. Julia...

JULIA. If Nat knew half the things you say in there about him...

DIANE. But that's not, I mean, it's not what you think.

JULIA. I know what the word 'love' means, Diane.

DIANE. I don't mean it in that way. I'd have feelings like that for anyone I care about or worry about...

JULIA. Love is love, Diane. That's the whole problem, isn't it? That's why you're against me.

DIANE. Don't be so stupid.

JULIA. What's stupid about it?

Fishes DIANE's *diary out from under the cushion and throws it on the floor at* DIANE's *feet.*

You even say it yourself. You wrote it down – that no one has ever loved you and your daughter hates you.

DIANE (*going and grabbing a can*). Look, when some... man comes in here with those cans that you came in here with and says they're pears, but they're not, and starts offering me food for... for... whatever, I have to ask where you got it.

JULIA. What does it matter where I got it? You ate it, didn't you? It's kept you alive. What does it matter where I got it?

DIANE. It matters because Nat is upset and worried about it. And he's right to be, because you lied to us.

JULIA. I didn't lie. I got that food fair and square.

DIANE. Really...

JULIA. Yes, really... You know what your problem is, Diane, you think everyone else is like you. Sneaking around, writing in our little notebooks, scribbling down all your horrible blackness and then turning around and being all sweetness and light to everybody.

DIANE. Right...

JULIA. Yeah.

DIANE. Well, maybe you should look at your own behaviour, Julia, crawling across the floor in the middle of the night. Waiting until we're all asleep to make your sordid little advances, sticking your nose into my private thoughts where it doesn't belong.

JULIA. That's bullshit. You don't even have a clue what you're talking about. Myself and Nat have discussed this together. The human race has to continue, Diane.

DIANE. The human race!

JULIA. People can still love each other. We all need to take responsibility! You just don't see it that way because nobody loves you!

DIANE. Are you fucking nuts? What are you trying to bring a baby into the world for? You think it's all going to be a fairy tale? That

there's going to be a coach and horses for the fairy princess to take
you off, with your precious young ovaries in a little jewellery box
on your lap? Look around you, child!!

JULIA. You're just jealous.

DIANE. Oh, please.

JULIA. 'Oh, please...'

DIANE. Yes! You know, if you like I can sort this all out in a
heartbeat.

JULIA. Oh yeah, how?

DIANE. All I have to do is walk over to that farmer and ask him
exactly what you did for all that chocolate. (*Beat.*) And the wine.

Pause.

JULIA. Well, do then!

DIANE. I will.

JULIA. Well, go on then!

DIANE. I'll go when I fucking well like!

JULIA. Well, do go, because when you know you're wrong, you'll
know the truth.

DIANE. Fair enough, and if that's the case I'll apologise. Now are
you going to sit there all day? Look at this place. It's like a
fucking pigsty!

DIANE *goes to the stove and begins to put wood in.* JULIA *starts
to tidy up. She looks at an axe that is nearby. She walks to it and
picks it up. She looks at* DIANE *kneeling at the stove. She
approaches* DIANE *from behind and stands there getting ready to
hit* DIANE.

JULIA. Hey, Diane...

DIANE (*without looking round*). What.

JULIA *realises she can't do it. She turns away, stifling her tears of
frustration.*

JULIA. Nothing... (*Puts the axe down and looks outside. Pause.*) It's
getting dark.

DIANE. Mmm.

Pause.

JULIA. You don't think anything has happened to Nat, do you?

DIANE. I hope not.

JULIA. I mean, the tides going to turn. Where did he go?

DIANE. I don't know. To the lake I think.

JULIA. You don't think he might have fallen asleep?

DIANE. I know he hasn't been well, but surely he wouldn't fall asleep out there?

JULIA. How long do we have?

DIANE. I guess a half-hour.

Pause.

JULIA. I better go. I'll just be a minute.

DIANE. Well, don't be long.

JULIA. No, I'll be quick.

JULIA *is about to go. But she turns to* DIANE.

I never meant for any of this, Diane. I'm sorry I read your diary. But I had to.

JULIA *runs out of the house.* DIANE *goes to the door. She looks out, watching* JULIA, *then steps back inside. She shuts the door and bolts it, putting up whatever wood they use to block it, locking* JULIA *out. She closes the shutters. She comes back to the chair by the fire and sits there. The room is very dark. We hear* DIANE's *voice...*

DIANE (*voice-over*). When you do kill someone, the first thing you think is, 'That was easy. What's all the fuss about?' The peaceful silence that descends when you've done it fills you with such relief. But it's more than that. It's the power that you get. You get that person's power. They are so completely subdued and obliterated. They have bent to your will completely and they are just... gone. You thank God for the strength and you wonder why you didn't use it long before.

The room darkens as night falls…

But then as time goes on, you realise that you not only have that person's power. Something else has happened. You have their soul inside you. And it's impossible not to feel their pain, their rage and their embarrassing frailty, which joins with your own. You get it all.

As dusk gathers outside, we hear the first flapping wings of the night.

Scene Fourteen

Morning. DIANE *is in the chair as the lights come up. It is just past dawn.* NAT *comes down the stairs. He is naked from the waist up. He has a blanket wrapped around his lower half. He gingerly makes his way down, squinting.*

NAT. What time is it?

DIANE. Just after six-thirty.

NAT. Six-thirty what? In the morning?

DIANE. You slept for twenty-four hours.

NAT. Where's Julia?

DIANE. She's gone.

NAT. Gone where?

DIANE. I don't know.

NAT. What do you mean she's 'gone'?

DIANE. She left last night.

NAT. She left?

DIANE. Before it got dark.

NAT. But where did she go?

DIANE. I don't know.

NAT. What happened, Diane?

DIANE. Nothing happened.

NAT. Well, what did she say?

DIANE (*taking up the Bible*). She told me that I was to tell you that Ecclesiastes says…

NAT. Are you fucking serious?

DIANE. She said I was to tell you that – (*Finding passage.*) 'I found something more bitter than death – the woman who is like a trap. The love she offers you will catch you like a net; and her arms round you will hold you like a chain.'

NAT. Is that it?

DIANE. That's it.

NAT. What does that mean?

DIANE. How would I know?

NAT. But she'll die out there!

He goes to the door and peeps out through the boards.

DIANE. Maybe she had somewhere she could go. I tried to stop her. I'm sorry, Nat.

NAT. There's something you're not telling me, Diane.

DIANE. I swear to God. She said I was to show you that bit from Ecclesiastes. I told her she was being crazy. I tried to make her stay.

NAT. Read it again.

DIANE. She was too strong for me, Nat.

NAT. Read it again!

DIANE. Oh, for God's sake! 'I found something more bitter than death – the woman who is like a trap. The love she offers you will catch you like a net; and her arms round you will hold you like a chain.'

NAT. I don't get it.

DIANE. Do you think she's saying she's… set you free? (*Pause.*) Go to bed, Nat.

NAT goes to walk up the stairs.

NAT. I have to look for her. I mean maybe she's…

He stops, hearing a flutter of birds outside.

How long have the birds been out?

DIANE. Only an hour.

NAT *comes back, unsure what to do.*

NAT. Gimme that.

DIANE *hands him the Bible. He looks at* DIANE. *He takes it upstairs.*

Scene Fifteen

Night. The wind is howling outside. NAT *sits at the table.* DIANE *brings two bowls to the table. They both sit, despondently.*

NAT. What is this?

DIANE. Onions. (*As* NAT *pushes it away.*) Do you want some ketchup? There's rice.

NAT *puts his fork down.*

Try and eat, Nat. Do you want some curry powder?

NAT. No.

DIANE (*gets up*). I'll get us some food. Look, if nothing else, I'll go over to the farmer. Maybe Julia's there.

NAT. Julia's not there.

DIANE. Maybe I can talk to him.

NAT. He's dead. I saw his body in the rushes two days ago.

DIANE. We can get his food.

NAT. There's nothing there. (*Gets up and moves away.*) Listen. When I was up under the eaves fixing the boards, I could see that the birds have been laying eggs.

DIANE. Are there birds up there?

NAT. No birds. Just their eggs. I can get in with a stick and smash some of them up, but to get them all – they're in between the floor, the insulation and the ceiling, if I get in to get them all, then the whole roof is exposed up there, it won't be safe.

DIANE. Nat, if the birds aren't sitting on the eggs, they can't hatch, they'll be too cold.

NAT. Well, I don't know! I don't like it! I mean, what if they do hatch? What if hundreds of birds suddenly get their way down through the plaster and down and in here?

DIANE. Surely we could... Couldn't we board it up?

NAT. Look, I just don't feel good about it. I think we should just go. I can't sleep.

DIANE. Do you want to take a painkiller?

NAT. I don't want to take anything.

Pause.

DIANE. Where will we go?

NAT. I don't know. Find somewhere else. Start again?

Pause.

DIANE. Okay.

NAT *gets up and goes to the fire.* DIANE *stays near the table alone.*

Scene Sixteen

Dark grey daylight. Forbidding black clouds. The wind howls.
DIANE *and* NAT *are packing up, making some final arrangements.*

DIANE (*voice-over*). Today we leave and wander into the wilderness.
I lay awake all night. Nat's right. Anything would be better than
the cold ghost of the girl – and her child – blowing round here in
the evenings. We're finally going to St Thomas. Together, if we're
careful, maybe we can we make it for another year or two, or
longer, who knows?

She picks up her notebook and reads to herself. NAT *goes to the*
door and looks out up into the treetops and the sky.

And then what? If only I could give him a child. My genes will
never make it past me now. We'll all be extinct soon. All my life
I've always thought, 'What's so precious about the human race
anyway?' When there were loads of us all clogging up the planet I
always thought, 'How disgusting.' But now that there's so few of us
left, I think – (*Looks up – out at us.*) 'Wait a minute, in all the cold
eternal expanse of the cosmos, what if we are the only life anywhere
in the vastness of time that can actually think, and knows that it
exists, and that knows that it will die? And I realise that God is real.
Because I am God. But I never realised before how helpless God
is – in the face of reality and eternity. And how alone God is.

NAT *approaches* DIANE. *He is ready for the road. An old coat is*
tied by a piece of string across his belly. He holds a stick like a
pilgrim.

NAT. Are you ready?

DIANE *nods and puts her book down, leaving it on the table. She*
takes her bag and puts it on her back.

Do you not want your book?

DIANE. No.

Pause.

NAT. Okay?

DIANE *nods*.

DIANE. Let's go.

They leave, closing the door firmly behind them as they walk out into the wind.

Lights down.

End.

THE VEIL

For Fionnuala and Sumati

The Veil was first performed in the Lyttelton auditorium of the National Theatre, London, on 4 October 2011 (previews from 27 September), with the following cast:

MRS GOULDING	Bríd Brennan
CLARE WALLACE	Caoilfhionn Dunne
MARIA LAMBROKE	Ursula Jones
MR FINGAL	Peter McDonald
REVEREND BERKELEY	Jim Norton
CHARLES AUDELLE	Adrian Schiller
HANNAH LAMBROKE	Emily Taaffe
MADELEINE LAMBROKE	Fenella Woolgar

Director	Conor McPherson
Designer	Rae Smith
Lighting Designer	Neil Austin
Sound Designer	Paul Arditti
Music	Stephen Warbeck

Characters

LADY MADELEINE LAMBROKE, *a widow*
HANNAH LAMBROKE, *her daughter*
MARIA LAMBROKE, *known as 'Grandie', Madeleine's grandmother*
THE REVEREND BERKELEY, *a defrocked Anglican minister*
MR CHARLES AUDELLE, *a philosopher*
MRS GOULDING, *a housekeeper and nurse*
MR FINGAL, *an estate manager*
CLARE WALLACE, *a housemaid*

Setting

A fine old house in the Irish Countryside. Early summer, 1822.

ACT ONE

Evening of Wednesday May 15th, 1822. Late in the evening – after 11 p.m.

The spacious drawing room of a big house in the countryside in Ireland. The room is gloomily lit by one or two candles. There are large windows, beyond which are mature trees with rich foliage, but for now they are unseen in the darkness. Heavy raindrops are heard falling out in the night.

There is a mantelpiece, stage right, with a large mirror above it. Some dark old portraits and landscapes grace the walls. The effect should be that the house has seen better days and needs some care. This room was once a versatile social space for receptions and dancing, now it looks bare. What chairs are here are lined against the walls, the only exceptions being one near the fireplace and one near a piano.

Among the entrances are a main door to the hallway, stage left, and high double doors in the back wall, leading to a conservatory with steps to the garden.

A man, MR FINGAL, *stands in the room, perhaps peering out the window, lost in thought. He wears dirty boots and a shabby-looking coat which is wet and torn. An old horse blanket is draped round his shoulders. While he may be younger, he looks at least forty. He is broad-shouldered and strong but looks tired. He hears a door slam out in the hallway and looks up. Light spills in as* MRS GOULDING *approaches, carrying a lamp and a bucket. She stops in the doorway. She is about sixty, small and wiry with a lined, intelligent face.*

MRS GOULDING. Mr Fingal!

FINGAL. Mrs Goulding.

MRS GOULDING. I might have known it was your muddy boots!

FINGAL. What?

MRS GOULDING. You have dirt and mud and whatever else all across the floor out here.

FINGAL. Oh, I'm sorry.

MRS GOULDING. What way did you come up?

FINGAL. I came up through the scullery.

MRS GOULDING. The scullery!

FINGAL. Clare let me in…

MRS GOULDING. I don't believe this! Could you not look at what you were doing?

FINGAL. I couldn't see! Sure there's hardly a candle lit in the place!

MRS GOULDING. Do not dare rebuke me, sir! Where have you been?

FINGAL. I was abroad – almost up as far as Queensfort! – looking for Miss Hannah.

MRS GOULDING. Yes, well, her ladyship found her herself.

MRS GOULDING *crosses to the coal scuttle near the fireplace and, using a rag, takes some pieces of coal, which she puts in her bucket.*

FINGAL. Where was she?

MRS GOULDING. Down in the glen. We're heating water for her bath.

FINGAL. What happened?

MRS GOULDING. I don't know. They had an argument.

FINGAL. Were you not here?

MRS GOULDING. No. I had the evening off.

FINGAL. Well, that's nice…

MRS GOULDING. I had the evening off to go to my niece's house. Nearly every child in the parish has scarlet fever, and her baby got it.

FINGAL (*chastened*). Oh, well…

MRS GOULDING. Yah. We were waiting for a woman from Clonturk who was supposed to have the cure. She arrived full of poitín and nearly fell into the fire, the bloody tinker.

FINGAL. How is the child?

MRS GOULDING. My niece's child?

FINGAL. Yes.

MRS GOULDING. She won't last the night. (*Wipes her hands.*)
Where's the boy? We need turf brought in.

FINGAL. I sent him home. I'll bring turf in.

MRS GOULDING. No, I'll get it. We were heating some stew for
Miss Hannah. It'll be nearly warm if you want.

FINGAL. I'm alright. I'm just waiting for her ladyship.

MRS GOULDING. You can give me those boots now.

*She pulls the horse blanket from his shoulders and throws it on the
floor.*

FINGAL. Hah?

MRS GOULDING. Stand on that. Here.

She moves a chair for him to sit on. He starts to unlace his boots.

I'll kill that young one for letting you walk all up here like that.

FINGAL. It wasn't her fault.

MRS GOULDING. Not a brain between yous.

FINGAL. It was dark, she didn't see.

MRS GOULDING. I'll rip her bloody ear off for her. (*Tugs at his
torn sleeve.*) Where's your good coat?

FINGAL. It got wet in the rain.

MRS GOULDING. You didn't lose it playing cards down in
Jamestown, no?

FINGAL. No.

MRS GOULDING. No?

FINGAL. No!

MRS GOULDING. You were always a bad liar, Mr Fingal. Which is
why you shouldn't play cards.

FINGAL. Yes, well, I don't.

MRS GOULDING. Yah, right you don't. Down in that kip. With
them animals. Sure look at you! You're not able for them, man.
The dark rings under your eyes. What are we going to do with
you? And no good coat to present yourself tomorrow.

FINGAL. What's tomorrow?

MRS GOULDING. Thursday.

FINGAL. I know what day it is. I mean why do I have to present myself?

MRS GOULDING. Has no one told you?

FINGAL. No.

MRS GOULDING. Her ladyship's cousin, the Reverend Berkeley, is arriving from London.

FINGAL. What!

MRS GOULDING. He's bringing a companion and they'll want to go grousing, I've no doubt, so you better see about them horses. Madam is fit to be tied – both horses lame and she going out to look for Miss Hannah earlier.

FINGAL. The both of them?

MRS GOULDING. They're both lame. Mike Wallace had to hitch up his old grey mare to the buggy and she could hardly pull it! Madam is not the least bit happy, I can tell you. And listen, we'll need to stir a churn of milk out of somewhere for tomorrow.

She takes up his boots.

FINGAL. Why?

MRS GOULDING. Because the cows are all huddled up the far end of the field under the trees and won't be shifted. (*Indicates the rifle.*) What's that rifle doing in here?

FINGAL. Some young lads were throwing stones at us earlier.

MADELEINE LAMBROKE, *the lady of the house, appears at the door to the hallway. She is in her early forties. She is attractive and sombrely dressed. She looks worn out from worry.* MRS GOULDING *looks at her.*

MRS GOULDING. I'll have your boots down at the door. I'll give you a can of stew for the boy's supper on the way out.

FINGAL. Thank you.

MRS GOULDING. Madam.

MADELEINE. Thank you, Mrs Goulding.

MRS GOULDING. Yes, madam.

MRS GOULDING *leaves, taking the boots and bucket with her.* MADELEINE *and* FINGAL *stand there for a moment.*

FINGAL. I trust Miss Hannah is alright.

MADELEINE. Yes, thank you.

FINGAL. We went looking for her up towards Queensfort. There are some new foals up there. I thought she might have gone for a look.

MADELEINE. No. She was sitting down by the brook in the glen. A place her father used to take her.

FINGAL. I see.

MADELEINE. Well, thank you for looking.

FINGAL. Of course.

Pause.

MADELEINE. Well?

FINGAL (*producing some coins*). Of the householders I could find and speak to, four holdings have paid quarterlies. Thirty-seven have withheld all payment.

MADELEINE. Thirty-seven?

FINGAL. They have organised themselves into one body formally requesting they might delay payment until their crops are renewed in the autumn.

MADELEINE. And you have accepted these terms?

FINGAL. I have accepted nothing. If you agree, I will go to the magistrate in the morning. Perhaps he could have a constable down here by the end of the week.

MADELEINE. Huh! That's exactly what happened before and here we are again.

FINGAL. They have not the means, madam.

MADELEINE. Yes, well, neither do I! Think how different it would be if there was a man in charge here.

FINGAL *looks down.*

Water is pouring in the gable end of the upstairs landing.

FINGAL. I will take a look at first light.

MADELEINE. It needs a roofer, Mr Fingal.

FINGAL. Yes, madam.

MADELEINE. Did you call on Colonel Bennett?

FINGAL. Yes, madam. He is happy to extend further credit if and when your estate should require. And he has also reiterated his offer to buy the houses you own in Jamestown. And he has suggested again he is willing to make an offer for the entire estate if...

MADELEINE (*impatiently*). Yes, I am well aware of the Colonel's addiction to acquiring property. Look, the reason I wanted to see you, Mr Fingal...

FINGAL. You received my letter...

MADELEINE. Yes, I received your letter, but that is not the reason I wanted to see you.

She holds an unopened letter to him.

FINGAL. You have not opened it.

MADELEINE. No I have not. Is it of a personal nature? (*Pause.*) Is it of a personal nature?

Pause. He takes it.

FINGAL. Yes.

MADELEINE. Then I will not read it. I want no more of these letters, Mr Fingal. While I appreciate your offers of... friendship, understand that such is impossible. I cannot reciprocate on any level. My status as a widow is one I bear without regret. Entirely.

FINGAL. Yes, madam.

MADELEINE. So kindly desist. While matters remain cordial.

FINGAL. Yes, madam.

MADELEINE. But thank you.

FINGAL. Yes, madam.

MADELEINE. The reason I wanted to see you is that my cousin, the Reverend Berkeley, arrives here from London tomorrow. He will accompany Hannah to Northamptonshire where she will be married in six weeks' time.

FINGAL. Married?

MADELEINE. Yes. (*Short pause*.) Her fiancé is the Marquis of Newbury, the eldest son of Lord Ashby, whose seat is outside Northampton.

FINGAL. I see.

MADELEINE. My cousin being a trusted spiritual advisor to Lord Ashby, has kindly agreed to chaperone Hannah to Northampton while I settle my affairs here. These matters have been undertaken with great delicacy and as such I have not been at liberty to disclose anything to you or the household before now.

FINGAL. I understand.

MADELEINE. It is my intention to travel to England for the wedding.

FINGAL. Of course.

MADELEINE. And I will remain there.

Short pause.

FINGAL. For how long?

MADELEINE. Indefinitely.

FINGAL. I see.

MADELEINE. I am mindful you have not received your salary for...?

FINGAL. Thirteen months, madam.

MADELEINE. Yes. Well, Hannah's forthcoming union will release a good deal of revenue towards this estate and all outstanding debts will be satisfied.

FINGAL. Thank you, madam.

MADELEINE. Despite the problems we have been beset with here, Mr Fingal, I hope you will remain as estate manager in my absence. Things have been run tolerably well and I expect may be maintained to a satisfactory degree under your charge.

FINGAL. Yes, madam.

MADELEINE. While I have been advised to sell the estate, and indeed I may have to, I am disinclined at present. This is our home. I regard those we know here as our friends.

FINGAL. Of course.

MADELEINE. I know how all of this must appear disruptive,
Mr Fingal...

FINGAL. No...

MADELEINE. But one must act in the interests of the estate.

FINGAL. Naturally.

MADELEINE. And Hannah's best interests obviously.

FINGAL. Obviously. You will forgive me for seeming forward... but
I had heard...

MADELEINE (*softens towards him*). Heard what?

FINGAL. That Miss Hannah was... That an old complaint had...
returned.

MADELEINE. Who told you?

FINGAL. Only those that are within the house.

MADELEINE. Who? Clare? (*Pause.*) Yes well, I'm sure half of
Jamestown knows so you may as well tell me. What have you
heard?

FINGAL. I have heard that Miss Hannah says she has been hearing
voices here again.

Pause.

MADELEINE. Yes, well, so she says.

FINGAL. Do you think this is an appropriate time for her to be
married?

MADELEINE. You are too forward, Mr Fingal.

FINGAL. Yes, madam.

MADELEINE (*dismissively*). She used to always claim that while she
played the piano, she could hear someone... singing. Or crying. I
forget which. She always said that.

FINGAL. Yes, I remember.

MADELEINE (*playing it down*). So... (*Pause. Considers him,
unable to stop herself from opening up.*) Now she says she heard
some man shouting in here on Sunday evening. She ran down to
the kitchen and sat with Clare until I came back from the
Colonel's dinner. You weren't calling out to the boy outside or...?

FINGAL. On Sunday we had our dinner in Jamestown. There was no noise or shouting here to my knowledge. I mean, it might have been...

MADELEINE (*interrupting him*). Yes, well, I am sure there is some explanation. In any case, a change of environment will do her the world of good.

FINGAL. As you say.

MADELEINE. Now, when I went to fetch her today I wanted to take the buggy but both our horses were lame, Mr Fingal.

FINGAL. I only just found out myself...

MADELEINE. Mike Wallace had to loan me his senile old mare. Only with great good fortune did I guess where Hannah had gone and luckily I found her before the cold and the rain had quite chilled her. You will see to the horses, Mr Fingal. How can such a thing have happened?

FINGAL. I don't know.

MADELEINE. Are the horses not your responsibility?

FINGAL. They are the boy's responsibility.

MADELEINE. Well, you will have to put him before his responsibilities.

FINGAL. Yes, madam.

MADELEINE. Our guests will no doubt want to ride abroad in the days they are here, so please see to it.

FINGAL. Yes, madam.

MADELEINE. This is not good enough.

FINGAL. I know.

MADELEINE *goes towards the door, but pauses near him before she leaves.*

MADELEINE. I want you to know that the gate lodge will continue to be at your disposal, for you and the boy, Mr Fingal, no matter what happens.

FINGAL. Thank you, madam.

MADELEINE. I believe Mrs Goulding has some warm stew. You will take some home for your supper.

FINGAL. Yes, madam.

MADELEINE leaves. FINGAL stands there for a moment, then takes up his rifle and the horse blanket and exits. The lights change to a bright fresh morning. Birdsong is heard outside. CLARE, a young housemaid of about twenty or so, comes into the room carrying a tray with a silver teapot and cups and saucers which she places on the table. She is a local girl. She is quick-witted and understands the nuances of everything that goes on about her, but has the intelligence never to let on. The REVEREND BERKELEY follows her in, absent-mindedly reading a newspaper. He is about sixty and wears the black garb of a vicar. While he is jovial and likable for the most part, he is very serious when it comes to things he cares about. In these matters he brooks no contention and displays the confidence of a man who entirely believes in the uniqueness of his vocation. It is two days later, 10.20 a.m. Friday May 17th.

BERKELEY. Thank you, Clare, for a delicious breakfast.

CLARE. You're welcome, sir.

BERKELEY. Oh, Clare, here…

CLARE stands waiting awkwardly while BERKELEY roots in his waistcoat and trouser pockets for a coin he can't find.

I'm sorry, Clare, I seem to have…

CLARE. No, sir.

BERKELEY. Will you remind me later to give you a coin?

CLARE. I'm sure I won't, sir!

She goes about her work setting the room up.

BERKELEY. Then I'll just have to remember myself. And I will!

CLARE. There is no need, sir, honestly.

BERKELEY. Little Clare Wallace! I scarcely believe the last time I saw you, you were this high. Do you remember me?

CLARE. Of course I do, sir.

BERKELEY. I have changed terribly, no doubt.

CLARE. No, sir.

BERKELEY. Whilst lying is always a sin, 'In certain lies there is but kindness.' Do you know who said that?

CLARE. No, sir.

BERKELEY. That's one of mine.

CLARE. Oh, very good, sir...

CHARLES AUDELLE *enters. He is in his mid-forties. He is striking-looking, somewhat intense, his eyes always searching for hidden depths.*

BERKELEY. Ah, Mr Audelle, you rise. And you have missed a delicious breakfast.

CLARE. Would you like me to bring you some up, sir?

AUDELLE. Please, don't go to any trouble. Is that tea?

CLARE. Yes, sir.

AUDELLE. Tea is fine.

BERKELEY. Slice of soda bread, Audelle?

CLARE. A slice of toast, sir?

AUDELLE (*without enthusiasm*). Em...

BERKELEY. Bring him some toast and some butter, Clare, should you be so kind.

CLARE. Yes, sir.

BERKELEY. Thank you, dear.

She exits.

(*Ominously.*) Well, sir, how did you sleep?

AUDELLE. Not well. And when I did drop away it was only to play host to some terrific nightmares.

BERKELEY. I thought as much.

AUDELLE. And you?

BERKELEY. I must confess, this place being something of a childhood home for me allied to the considerable relief to have arrived after such a turbulent journey, I had a passably comfortable night – but tell me, of what did you dream?

AUDELLE. I dreamt of a presence.

BERKELEY *pours some tea, watching* AUDELLE *take in the room.*

This is the room.

BERKELEY. This is the room. He hung the rope from a brace above the mirror, stepped off the mantelpiece and hung there until young Hannah had found him.

AUDELLE. The heart of the house. How old was she?

BERKELEY. Eight or nine. Yes. However, having heard the stories that have seeped under the door down the years, it is my belief that rather than stepping into oblivion he has found himself trapped here in an endless bad dream. Somehow caught between this world and the next. One of time's own prisoners.

AUDELLE. And Hannah has heard him...

BERKELEY. She has heard something.

AUDELLE. It is quite uncomfortable here, Berkeley.

BERKELEY. Is it bearable?

AUDELLE (*brusquely, advancing on the tea things*). Yes, it's bearable, but I suggest here is where we begin. When you begin.

BERKELEY. These occasions require a subtlety you might best leave to me, Charles.

AUDELLE. Oh, I intend to!

BERKELEY. For now, we are merely here to escort Hannah to Northamptonshire...

AUDELLE. Of course...

BERKELEY. However, when the household is more relaxed and we have gained a certain confidence, we may encourage such shadows that dwell here to make themselves manifest, which once apprehended... Ah!

He breaks off seeing that MRS GOULDING *has appeared in the doorway. Beside her is a little elderly lady known as* GRANDIE. *She has Alzheimer's disease; while she makes eye contact and smiles from time to time, she rarely speaks.*

MRS GOULDING. Reverend!

BERKELEY. Mrs Goulding! Why, you have not changed one bit! And Grandie!

BERKELEY *gives* MRS GOULDING *a kiss.*

MRS GOULDING. Oh, you say so…

BERKELEY. But it's true. It is true. You are radiant. And Grandie, how are you, my dear?

He offers her his hand.

MRS GOULDING. You remember the Reverend, Grandie. Will you shake hands?

GRANDIE *smiles vaguely, but does not shake hands.*

She'll be alright. Sometimes new people confuse her a bit. Sit down, Grandie, and we'll get you a slice of cake in a minute. That's right.

GRANDIE *does not sit, but places herself with her hand on the back of a chair, watching them.*

BERKELEY. Mrs Goulding, may I present my travelling companion, Mr Audelle?

MRS GOULDING (*shaking hands with* AUDELLE). You are welcome, sir. And anything we can do to make your stay more comfortable, you will tell us.

AUDELLE. I cannot see how that could be necessary.

BERKELEY. And this is Grandie, grandmother to the lady of the house. Quite a beauty in her day, Mrs Goulding.

MRS GOULDING. Oh, they all got their looks from her! Didn't they, Grandie? We'll get you a slice of cake now in a minute. You are looking hale and hearty, Reverend. And but I had no idea of the nature of your trip, sir! Is it true you will accompany Miss Hannah to England!

BERKELEY. For her wedding!

MRS GOULDING. Well, I am overcome. With joy, of course, but with sorrow too.

BERKELEY. Mrs Goulding has been almost a second mother to Hannah, Audelle.

MRS GOULDING. To both Hannah and her mother. I am like another grandmother to this house, I have been here so long.

BERKELEY. We used to call Mrs Goulding our 'maid mother'. And you are keeping well yourself, Mrs Goulding?

MRS GOULDING. I am middling well, thank God. What more can we ask? I'm sorry, your grace, and I'm sorry to you, sir. It's just… to suddenly see yourself again after so long, Reverend. Suddenly all the time that seems to have just…

She wipes her eyes.

BERKELEY (*puts an arm round her*). No, no, come now, we are all happy. These feelings are as natural as a leaf falling to the earth. To know a little sadness on account of past joys is surely a cause for gratitude.

MRS GOULDING. You are right, sir.

MADELEINE enters, holding the door for CLARE, who carries a tray in with more tea, cups and some slices of toast under a napkin. MRS GOULDING supervises CLARE at the table, and they pour tea for all during the following.

BERKELEY. Madeleine!

MADELEINE. Berkeley.

BERKELEY. I have longed for this embrace.

He comes to her and embraces her. She allows him to kiss her cheek.

You cannot be eating well, Madeleine. Where have you gone? Ha ha ha! Oh, but you make me feel old. Finally I may introduce you. Lady Madeleine Lambroke, eternal succour to all in her protectorate; Mr Charles Audelle, gentleman of letters, philosophy and higher learning.

AUDELLE (*takes her hand*). Madam, such pleasure at last.

MADELEINE. We did not want to disturb you, Mr Audelle.

AUDELLE. With embarrassment, I must assure you I do not normally sleep on past seven o'clock, but we have not had comfort such as your wholesome dwelling provides for some nights now, and I am afraid I could not stir myself.

MADELEINE. I would have preferred to greet you last night, but the hour had grown so late, I had assumed you would not arrive until today.

BERKELEY. The bridge was half destroyed by so-called revolutionaries.

MRS GOULDING. Oh no!

BERKELEY. Yes! So we had to wait for the ferry, but the waters had risen so in the deluge, the pilot wouldn't go! We were loath to turn back and face our depressing lodgings at Jamestown so it was our good luck that a fisherman, who was determined to get home, took us across for two shillings. And thank you again, Clare, for admitting us so late. It was almost gone two o'clock!

MRS GOULDING. She is a well-mannered girl, is she not?

BERKELEY. Most decidedly!

MRS GOULDING. Say thank you, Clare.

CLARE. Thank you, sir.

MRS GOULDING. And Mr Audelle.

CLARE. Thank you, sir.

AUDELLE. No, thank you, Clare.

CLARE. Thank you, sir.

BERKELEY. Thank you, Clare.

MADELEINE. Yes... You will have noticed the deterioration of Jamestown, Berkeley.

BERKELEY. To an extent I had scarcely suspected, Madeleine. Our coach stopped near what we now realise was the workhouse.

MRS GOULDING. Oh, yes.

BERKELEY. Desperate men and women suddenly descended upon our coach. So numerous were the pale hands outstretched towards us, it was only later I understood that an insensible infant thrust before me by a cadaverous wild-eyed woman must surely have been deceased...

MADELEINE. Oh, Berkeley...

BERKELEY. Yes.

AUDELLE. I'm afraid it was so.

MRS GOULDING. Clare, why don't you run along and tell Miss Hannah there is tea in the drawing room.

CLARE. Yes, Mrs Goulding.

She goes.

MADELEINE. Times are hard here, Berkeley, there is no doubt. The meagre crop has failed again. But we have sought to assist those we can, have we not, Mrs Goulding?

MRS GOULDING. We have indeed, madam. Those as we can, God help us.

BERKELEY. Well, of course.

Pause.

MADELEINE. And you reside with the Reverend at present, Mr Audelle?

AUDELLE. I do, which is perhaps another reason I slept so late – I am not accustomed to the silent pleasures of a room of one's own. I am sorry to say the poor Reverend's snoring vibrates the slim walls of our modest apartment in Highgate at the best of times, but to share a room with him as I have these past few nights on our way down here, is to have one's very teeth shaken out of one's head!

They laugh.

BERKELEY. And I am blissfully unaware of it! More's the irritation! But we make good company, do we not?

AUDELLE. Oh, yes!

MRS GOULDING. Madam has always cried out in her sleep.

MADELEINE. Oh, not for a long time.

MRS GOULDING. And loud enough to wake me and I on the floor below.

BERKELEY. Oh dear! There is little so disturbing as the cry that reefs you to the surface!

MRS GOULDING. Now you said it!

MADELEINE. I haven't done that for a long, long time, Mrs Goulding.

MRS GOULDING. I wouldn't know – my hearing is not what it was.

Pause.

BERKELEY. You know, it occurs to me that each of us here in this room has been widowed.

MADELEINE. Oh, well, my sympathies, Mr Audelle.

AUDELLE. And mine to you, all.

MADELEINE. I have always envied Berkeley's faith in trying times. I must admit, I was never overly concerned for your welfare when Alice passed away – I knew your belief would hold strong. Certainly stronger than mine!

BERKELEY. My faith didn't protect me, Madeleine. It was my congregation who protected me. But only because Alice was beloved by all. Only when the Bishop took my lodgings away did I feel a loneliness that came and gutted me like a knife. That first winter I moved to London alone was… well, it was wretched.

MADELEINE. Your letters never betrayed that, Berkeley.

BERKELEY. Well. (*Short pause.*) But happily, on my travels – (*Touches* AUDELLE'S *shoulder.*) I met Mr Audelle, whose intellect and curiosity have given me great joy in our evenings together at home in Highgate. And in return he bears the burden of my company. Snoring and all!

CLARE *enters and holds the door open.* HANNAH *enters. She is seventeen and slender, alert with a keen perceptiveness of her situation and that of others. She wears spectacles and has a bandage on her right hand. She regards the room somewhat coolly.*

Can this be Hannah?

MADELEINE. This is Hannah.

BERKELEY. My word, the ten years that have passed since I was here had seemed but ten hours until now. Time itself has conjured a beautiful young lady where moments ago was a child. Do you recall me, cousin?

HANNAH. The last time I saw you we carved our names in the fairy tree near the gallops. Your initials are still there.

BERKELEY. That's right!

HANNAH. And you told me of a hanging you witnessed at Leitrim Gaol where the man called out to the Virgin Mary over and over after they put the sack on his head.

Short pause.

BERKELEY. Ha ha ha... And now we have come to take you away to be wedded to your love. Can it be so?

HANNAH. It certainly appears to be so.

BERKELEY. And I see, Madeleine, that my old sparring partner, the Bishop of Solsbury himself has been engaged to perform the ceremony. He may be a notoriously insufferable old bore, but one cannot fault him in matters of canon law. When you are married by him, it will be like an iron lock closing for ever in the eyes of God! (*Laughs.*) Permit me to introduce Mr Charles Audelle, Hannah, who has been so kind as to accompany me on my pleasant task. I trust you will find his company most instructive. Here... (*Produces a slim volume.*) is a copy of his book!

MRS GOULDING. His book!

HANNAH. Thank you.

HANNAH *takes it.* AUDELLE *offers her his hand. She presents him with her left, unbandaged, hand.*

AUDELLE. Pray, what has happened to your hand? Nothing serious, I hope.

HANNAH. I pierced it grabbing hold of some brambles the day before yesterday.

AUDELLE. I see.

BERKELEY. Mr Audelle is considered to be – especially by many young people, Hannah – one of the finest writers of the age in London. His mind is as delicate as any in his generation.

AUDELLE. Now please, Reverend.

HANNAH. I have heard of this book, sir. Weren't you recently accused of plagiarism?

AUDELLE. Well...

MADELEINE. Hannah...

BERKELEY. That was a misunderstanding...

MADELEINE. That's not a nice thing to say, Hannah.

AUDELLE. No, it's true, there was an... accusation...

HANNAH. I merely wanted to ask whom he was *accused* of plagiarising, Mother.

MRS GOULDING. What's plagiarise?

HANNAH. When you steal someone else's ideas and pass them off as your own.

MADELEINE. Hannah, that is not a kind thing to say.

AUDELLE. No, no, I'm afraid it has already been said, madam. Hannah is merely asking about something many already believe.

HANNAH. Who did you plagiarise?

MADELEINE. Hannah, you mean, who do they... say... he plagiarised...

HANNAH. Yes.

AUDELLE. Oh, some Germanic philosopher who was merely thinking along the same lines as myself. And while I allow he had already published some ideas similar to my own – they remained untranslated... and I was to all intents and purposes, unaware of them in their most recent form.

HANNAH. What was his name?

AUDELLE. Oh, I can barely pronounce it. Or bring myself to utter it.

HANNAH. You don't speak German?

AUDELLE. Certainly not well enough to dissect the latest in up-to-the-minute Prussian transcendental philosophy. No.

MADELEINE. Well, what a misfortune...

BERKELEY. The greater misfortune is that the bear pit of critical appraisal in London tends to be a hundred times more savage than the most animalistic assault in the wild.

MRS GOULDING. Dear God.

HANNAH. They had no case against you?

AUDELLE. Well, you see, some years ago I had the pleasure of visiting the universities of Tübingen and Jena. While my grasp of the language was rudimentary, like many, I was intoxicated by the potency of the lectures there. Certain ideas were... hung in the ether, like unplucked fruit upon an overripened vine, and while I had mistakenly assumed I was the first to give their utterance...

HANNAH. You were in fact not.

Pause.

AUDELLE. No.

BERKELEY. Such a thing can easily happen.

HANNAH. And you do not tire of philosophers inventing worlds where nobody lives?

AUDELLE. I, personally, have no need to invent a world to argue about – since the one I find myself in already confounds me quite enough.

HANNAH. But isn't every world an invention?

MADELEINE (*interrupts*). Oh, it is surely far too early in the day for such discussion, is it not? The sun is finally peeping out to beckon us to the garden.

BERKELEY. Precisely, Madeleine, the magic gardens call me here yet. We arrived in darkness and Mr Audelle has no idea of the beauty and wildness that surround us.

MADELEINE. There are plenty of old boots down by the kitchen door. You must spare your shoes after the rain. Mrs Goulding, will you show the gentlemen?

MRS GOULDING. Certainly, madam.

MADELEINE. Perhaps Grandie would like some air. Clare, you may leave the tea tray. Hannah and I will take a cup before we join you.

BERKELEY. Capital.

CLARE. Would you like some freshly brewed, madam?

MADELEINE. No thank you, I'm sure it's fine. We will join you presently.

AUDELLE. Thank you, Lady Lambroke. May I say what a pleasure it is to have finally met you, Miss Lambroke.

MADELEINE. You are welcome, sir.

MRS GOULDING *offers her arm to* GRANDIE *who takes it.*

MRS GOULDING. Now, Grandie.

GRANDIE *suddenly goes and kisses* HANNAH *on the cheek.*

Now, there's a lovely kiss. Let's go and get some nice cake.

BERKELEY *leaves, followed by* AUDELLE, CLARE *and* MRS GOULDING, *who helps* GRANDIE *out. From the hall we hear* BERKELEY.

BERKELEY (*off*). Now, you see that painting above the fireplace?

AUDELLE (*off*). Oh yes, I saw that.

BERKELEY (*off*). That's the very view one is furnished with as we approach the gazebo.

MRS GOULDING (*off*). Come down this way, Mr Audelle.

AUDELLE (*off*). Yes, thank you, I'm coming.

MADELEINE. I see your temper has yet to abate.

HANNAH. Yes, well, I'm sorry, Mother. But to actually walk in and meet the men who are to take me away filled me with such anxiety I had spoken before I knew it.

MADELEINE. And must you articulate your anxiety with such bad manners? Do you know what Lady Fitz-Morris said.

HANNAH. What.

MADELEINE. She said a marriage such as you have before you would be the envy of any English girl, let alone an Irish girl who lives where the prospect of a decent match is remote.

HANNAH. Really?

MADELEINE. Oh, so what would you prefer? One of the Colonel's cockeyed twits, with not an idea in his head that doesn't pertain to beagles or billiards? In England you may reside three or four months of each year in London. Can you imagine I had but a month there in my whole life? I was presented to women and men of such nobility my limbs were positively liquid in uncontrollable acknowledgement of their position. And you will meet them as an equal!

HANNAH. With a husband who bears me no love.

MADELEINE. Of course he will love you.

HANNAH. It is his father who is attached to me. Surely you have seen that.

MADELEINE. Oh, nonsense. He admires you.

HANNAH. All the time we were there the old man's eyes followed me like black holes of insensible longing, while the Marquis spoke to me only of dogs and guns. When he deigned to actually ask me anything my answers were greeted with a decidedly unenthusiastic silence.

MADELEINE. So what, you will you remain here at Mount Prospect with its endless debts, enduring the hatred of those who rent your holdings, until you too are finally turfed out? You will be alone for ever – stigmatised as a bumpkin from the colonies whose only dowry is the odour of our failure!

HANNAH. Yes, I know about dowries. You have bought your way out of this place with whatever you could get for me!

MADELEINE (*slaps* HANNAH). How dare you! You are not too old to be spanked, my girl.

HANNAH. Hit me then! If you must! Your marriage was arranged for you and look how that ended!

HANNAH *goes to the door.*

MADELEINE. Hannah, come back here!

MADELEINE *gets there first and blocks her way.*

HANNAH. Get off me!

MADELEINE. Yes, my marriage was arranged. What could I know at nineteen years of age about husbands and how the world works? What happened to your father was due to… what he bore within him, before we ever even met. As such it was unavoidable yet impossible to foresee. (*Pause.*) Please understand how worried I have become. I undertake none of this lightly. I know how you like the solitude of your room and your books and your fire and your walks. But now you will always have those things! And have them where you are safe and well – within yourself. Where these sudden… voices cannot distress you.

HANNAH. Yes, well, I wish I had never said anything about that now.

MADELEINE. What would you have me do? Take Dr Henry's advice and put you in a hospital in Dublin?

HANNAH. What if they are trying to tell me something?

MADELEINE. Who?

HANNAH. The voices.

MADELEINE. Oh, Hannah! I cannot imagine they have anything good to say.

HANNAH. Perhaps they are warning me against the very plans you have made.

MADELEINE. Oh, come now.

HANNAH. Well, why not?

MADELEINE. Because the voices cannot love you like I do. I will help you in your new life, with your new family.

HANNAH. You would come also?

MADELEINE. Well, of course.

HANNAH. No.

MADELEINE. What do you mean, no?

HANNAH. I would forbid it, is what I mean.

MADELEINE. And go alone?

HANNAH. Why not? You have already arranged my chaperones.

MADELEINE. Hannah, I know you don't mean it.

HANNAH. No – I will endure Hell there with him or Hell here with you, but I will not endure both.

MADELEINE. Hannah!

HANNAH. And if I must be sold, I will sell myself into personal sovereignty. And you, madam, may do as you wish.

MADELEINE. And you would leave me here? Where will I go?

HANNAH. Why, Mother, but you are putting me out!

BERKELEY *appears in the doorway holding a stick.*

BERKELEY. Ladies! The sky is burst through with sunlight behind the blackest clouds you have ever seen. Mr Audelle has described it as an aspect of the sublime! Please say you will join us as we walk down to the old pond.

MADELEINE. Of course.

BERKELEY. And I almost forgot to mention it! I have a letter from Hannah's prospective father-in-law.

MADELEINE. A letter?

BERKELEY *puts his stick down, takes an envelope from his inside pocket.*

BERKELEY. A letter he has asked me to read aloud before our assembled company after dinner one of these evenings. I must say I have rarely seen him so satisfied, Hannah. You will be a queen among his household.

MADELEINE. Let us walk then. Hannah. You will take my hand?

BERKELEY *examines the envelope as he goes out into the hallway.* HANNAH *regards* MADELEINE *for a moment, then steps forward and takes her hand.* MADELEINE *holds it tightly, grateful for the affection.* HANNAH *looks down.* MADELEINE *kisses* HANNAH's *hair. They regard each other in a moment of reconciliation, and leave.*

(*Off.*) You may lead the way, Berkeley.

BERKELEY (*off*). Yes, oh, just let me find my stick. The damp air gets me in my hip, I'm afraid.

BERKELEY *returns for his stick. He stands for a moment looking up at the brace above the mirror by the mantelpiece then follows them out. The lights change, bringing us to evening, two nights later, Sunday May 19th. It is about 9 p.m. There is still a trace of dusk in the sky.* FINGAL *helps* CLARE *light one or two oil lamps in the room.* FINGAL *then stands looking at a chessboard.* CLARE *stands as though waiting for his attention, but leaves when* AUDELLE *comes in, carrying a candle and a glass of red wine.*

AUDELLE. Ah, Fingal… You see what I've done there.

FINGAL. You certainly know how to use those rooks.

AUDELLE (*seeing some decanters with liquor*). Brandy! Thank God… (*Knocks back his wine and advances on the spirits.*) Care for a drop?

FINGAL. Em… Maybe later.

AUDELLE. I don't think you can escape.

FINGAL. I think you may be right. (*Knocks over his king on the board.*) You win, sir.

AUDELLE. A good game. Set them up again and you can be white. Good God, did you see those poor wretches who came into the yard for soup earlier on?

FINGAL (*setting up the pieces*). I did.

AUDELLE. I had no idea things were so bad.

FINGAL. Yes, they're bad from time to time.

AUDELLE. To my shame I had not the confidence to approach them. Would they have spoken to me?

FINGAL. Ah, yes. They are a curious people; they would show you great interest and courtesy, no doubt.

AUDELLE. I will greet them the next time.

FINGAL. Oh yes, they are always keen to learn English, sir.

AUDELLE (*savouring a large gulp of brandy*). Well, I have no doubt, in the future, the Irishman will be beholden to no one and walk amid the spirit of his age with pride.

FINGAL (*uncertainly*). Mm.

AUDELLE. No doubt. You were born near here, Mr Fingal?

FINGAL. I was.

AUDELLE. How do you all get on?

FINGAL. Who?

AUDELLE. You and the locals.

FINGAL. Ah, I'm neither one thing nor the other any more. Each side rejects you and everyone is suspicious.

AUDELLE. How unpleasant.

FINGAL. My father always said it suits the nature of a contrarian, Mr Audelle.

AUDELLE (*laughs*). Yes, it must rather. But this house is generous, is it not?

FINGAL. As generous as it may afford to be. Against the advice of many, her ladyship took in an orphan a few years ago. A boy who resides with me down at the gate lodge. He was given the name James Furay.

AUDELLE. Oh yes, I have seen him. I attempted to exchange
greetings with him out on the steps this morning but he just looked
at the earth.

FINGAL. He means no discourtesy. He's often silent in himself, but
he's conscious of his great debt to the house in ways others I may
mention are not. Here, sir.

FINGAL *holds out a coin to* AUDELLE.

AUDELLE. What's this?

FINGAL. Our wager, for the chess game.

AUDELLE. Oh no, sir, I will not accept your money.

FINGAL. A wager is a wager.

AUDELLE. No, no, come now.

FINGAL. I insist or we cannot play again.

AUDELLE. I was warned about you Irish. I'll tell you what, keep
your money, but perhaps you might do me a small favour. (*Taking
a piece of paper from his pocket.*) I have a doctor's script for some
pain-relieving tincture which I was accustomed to buying in
London. You see, I have a permanent jabbing in my lower back,
sustained in a fall from a window some years ago. I had a small
bottle with me, but unfortunately it cracked when we took our
bags down from the coach in some haste in Jamestown the other
evening. I asked the girl. Is her name Clare?

FINGAL. Yes.

AUDELLE. Yes, I asked her if she might take this and procure me
some during her errands in town, but she returned it to me this
morning saying Mrs Goulding forbade her to make the purchase!
Can you believe that!

FINGAL. What's in it, sir?

AUDELLE. Nothing harmful!

FINGAL *takes the script, reading it…*

Medicinal herbs…

FINGAL. I see. Mrs Goulding has some firm ideas, I'm afraid.

AUDELLE. And you, sir?

FINGAL. Less so.

AUDELLE. You're a good man, Fingal.

FINGAL. I always pay my debts.

AUDELLE. Debts! Why, it's a little wager over a game of chess, not a bank loan, man. Only as long as it's no trouble.

FINGAL. It's no trouble, sir.

AUDELLE. I knew I could count on you. Goodness, this brandy evaporates so swiftly! Can I pour you one?

FINGAL. A… very small one only then, sir, to be social. Please allow me.

AUDELLE. Not at all. (*Pours them both quite large drinks.*) Have you eaten? We had some excellent trout earlier, at table with the curious young Hannah. Does she ever eat?

FINGAL. I assume she must.

AUDELLE. Our conversation ventured to an old tomb nearby which her mother seemed uneasy talking about. Do you know of it?

FINGAL. Up at Knocknashee?

AUDELLE. That's it.

FINGAL. It's just an old hole in the ground.

AUDELLE. What do they call it? The Queen's Tomb?

FINGAL. Some do. Others will not speak of it.

AUDELLE. What do you think it is?

FINGAL. I couldn't say. A doctor came over from Oxford when I was a boy. He said there's a passage underneath that's maybe been there for thousands of years.

AUDELLE. I'd love to see it.

FINGAL. Don't go up there on your own, sir.

AUDELLE. Is it frightening?

FINGAL. No, it's not frightening, but there are gangs of boys, and men, in that locality who would have certain perceived grievances with anyone they see wandering up from out of here. Up around the cottages at Knockmullen.

AUDELLE. I see.

FINGAL. If there's time I'll bring you up in the buggy maybe some morning, but please do not wander up there on your own, or at night.

AUDELLE. Understood.

FINGAL. The Reverend would know more about it than me.

AUDELLE. He knew much that he has forgotten.

FINGAL. He has indeed aged since I saw him.

AUDELLE. Well, that's what the Church of England has done.

FINGAL. Can I ask why he was he expelled, if that's not an impertinent question?

AUDELLE. Not at all. Perhaps you might ask him yourself if you have a spare hour or two to withstand his account.

FINGAL. You are not religious then, I take it.

AUDELLE. My religion is philosophy, sir. Do you pray?

FINGAL. No.

AUDELLE. Never?

FINGAL. Maybe in the night. I don't know.

AUDELLE. In the night.

FINGAL. Mmm.

> *Pause.* FINGAL *looks down.* AUDELLE *regards him. The door opens and* HANNAH *enters. The men stand. She shuts the door.*

HANNAH. Am I disturbing you?

AUDELLE. Not at all. We were just talking about you. Please, sit by the fire. I was just sipping some brandy for my cold whereas Fingal is just drinking. I'm joking. Come. Join us.

> HANNAH *comes into the room and stands looking into the fire, her hand on the back of a chair.*

FINGAL. I meant to tell you, miss; Liam O'Leary's mare had two beautiful foals. I thought you'd probably want to go and have a look before you leave.

HANNAH. Twins?

FINGAL. Yes.

HANNAH. Oh, I will.

Pause.

AUDELLE. How nice it is to sit here at your fire. Three nights ago
we were at a ghastly inn at Jamestown. You must know it. We
dined in the front parlour with a fire which, no matter how much
coal the old pot boy shuffled on, never seemed to penetrate the
damp chill of the room. The handful of diners as were present ate
with their coats on. Nothing stirred in the street outside. The only
sound was the hollow ticking of a clock in the hallway. Dear Lord.
After a few restless, frozen hours in a narrow bed beside your
kicking cousin, the Reverend, I went for a dawn walk that burnt
my skin raw. Where the street ended and became countryside was
the brick wall of the workhouse and a crowd of haggard-looking
men and women turned to look at me with such alien ferocity I
thought that should I ever find myself stranded here, I'd blow my
brains out. Now, there's a thought.

FINGAL. So why come at all?

AUDELLE. Well, besides accompanying the Reverend... I came in
search of ghosts, Mr Fingal.

FINGAL. Ghosts?

AUDELLE. Ghosts, Mr Fingal.

HANNAH. Why here?

AUDELLE. Well, Hannah, while the city of London will present the
ghoulish at every corner, a true doorway to the eternal seems to
demand the spiritual quietude and awesomeness as only desolate
places such as Ireland may possess.

HANNAH. The vicar at Ballycliff says the eternal resides in the
everyday things we see.

AUDELLE. Yet few ever seem to hear its song until it's too late!

HANNAH. Perhaps they are deaf.

AUDELLE. But you have heard, have you not? Here in this house?

HANNAH. Not just in the house, here in this very room, sir.

FINGAL. Miss Hannah...

HANNAH. Well, it's true, Fingal.

AUDELLE. Do tell us.

FINGAL. Mr Audelle, I think it would be better were we to take our dram and...

The door opens. MADELEINE *and* GRANDIE *come in with* CLARE, *who lights some candles.* MADELEINE *looks on the company disapprovingly.* FINGAL *and* AUDELLE *rise to their feet guiltily.* BERKELEY *comes in behind her waving a letter.*

BERKELEY. Gather ye! Gather ye! I bring news from beyond the realm.

HANNAH. Oh, Berkeley, please, must you read it?

BERKELEY. Of course I must! I am under strict instructions. It will be read 'before the host who inhabit the child's home,' to quote Lord Ashby directly.

HANNAH. This is outrageous.

MADELEINE. Hannah, we will all watch our manners.

BERKELEY. He assures me it is not long and I have no doubt it is perfectly innocuous. Now, where are my spectacles?

HANNAH. Oh God...

MRS GOULDING *puts her head round the door. She wears her best evening dress. It may be quite old but has a striking amount of gold brocade and ornamentation.*

MRS GOULDING. Have I missed the letter?

MADELEINE. No, you are just in time.

HANNAH. Of course! Come in! Come in! Clare, do take a seat.

MRS GOULDING (*lampooning* HANNAH's *concerns. She is drunk and consequently emotional and energised*). Oh, the drama of it all! You would swear it was your funeral you were heading off to rather than a wedding that would be the envy of any young girl in the world. Will Grandie take a sherry? She will, won't you, Grandie?

BERKELEY. Is that Irish whiskey I spy?

MRS GOULDING. It is. Only freshly bought – and sampled, personally – this morning.

BERKELEY. My throat is... (*Waves his hand in front of his throat.*)

MRS GOULDING. Clare, pour a drop for the Reverend. I will have a drop also, begging your ladyship's grace. Clare, you may have a small sherry, and one for Grandie.

CLARE. Madam?

MADELEINE. Not for me, Clare, pour yourself a sherry.

MRS GOULDING. A small sherry. But pour me a fitting measure of our Lord's tears.

AUDELLE. And I will join you if I may. Fingal?

FINGAL *hands* AUDELLE *his glass.*

REVEREND. Easy, my friend. Mr Audelle has been sipping spirits for that terrible cold he has had this past year and a half.

There is some laughter at this.

MRS GOULDING. Well, as Mr O'Connell said in his speech at Loughferry – 'It will take a strong draught to blow back the veil of confusion!'

Laughter.

AUDELLE. Well said.

BERKELEY. Now, if we are settled… (*Unfolds the letter.*) He has such a fine hand. (*Sniffs the paper.*) And always the best Corinthian ink.

MRS GOULDING. But of course. Clare, settle!

CLARE *looks for a seat.*

FINGAL (*offering* CLARE *a seat*). Clare, please.

MRS GOULDING. Leave her where she is. She is at work.

FINGAL. As are we, Mrs Goulding. Clare, take a seat here.

MADELEINE. Yes, sit here, Clare.

CLARE *goes to* FINGAL*'s seat.*

HANNAH. This is agony.

AUDELLE. There is seldom sport without it.

MRS GOULDING. Just sit somewhere, child, you will spill your drink. Do you think you could have fit any more in that glass? Look at it!

MADELEINE. Hannah! Berkeley, please begin.

BERKELEY. Ahem... 'My dear Miss Hannah, Tonight the wind rages about the eaves and far across our lands the animals huddle for warmth. The house creaks about me, and yet as I sit here long after all have retired and the last embers colden...' Is that a word? (*Squints at it.*) Colden?

MADELEINE. I don't think so.

HANNAH. Oh God...

MRS GOULDING. The word is 'encolden'.

BERKELEY. Is it?

FINGAL. I have never heard that word.

MRS GOULDING. To encolden – to grow cold, or lose warmth.

MADELEINE. You are having us all on now, Mrs Goulding.

MRS GOULDING. Doesn't his lordship use it himself in his letter?

AUDELLE. Perhaps he has partaken of the early dew. (*Helping himself to a drink.*) Fingal?

FINGAL. No, thank you.

BERKELEY. Audelle, may I continue?

AUDELLE. Forgive me. A smallish dram as I have grown just a tad encoldened.

Laughter.

MRS GOULDING. I am also a tad encoldened. (*Brings* AUDELLE *her glass.*)

BERKELEY. Alright, settle down. 'The house creaks about me, and yet as I sit here long after all have retired and the last embers colden, somehow the memory of your visit to our house last Easter is alive in the mind, as though I am staring through the glass wall of time and observing those happy days when you and your beautiful mother dwelt amongst us and lit our house like a tiny sun. I hear you playing the piano. It still echoes through our hallways; a joyous yet saddening music which only reminds us of your absence and your longed-for presence.

That my eldest, and may I say most time-consuming, son should have you as his prospective bride brings a secret joy to my heart and I sing its mysterious melody tonight. I do admit I may have burdened him with the unrealistic expectations of an inexperienced father – burdens I have perhaps never placed on my subsequent sons – and thus he may have struggled in the past to accept his place in the world satisfactorily. But I am filled with confidence now, because I know your companionship will be, for him, both the steady ballast of his moral bearing and a guiding hand on his tiller.' (*Clears his throat.*) Ahem.

'Until you are with us I send you thanks and warm wishes in recognition of the gifts you have already granted us; your grace and your temperate solemnity. I hear the birds calling far away in the forest and I know that dawn is approaching. I will pass this letter to my rock and spiritual advisor, Reverend Berkeley, and should all befall as one may dare to hope, he stands before you reading it now while I languish hundreds of miles away on my own fair isle of England, but my words are now among you and blessed to be so. My friends, I remain yours, George, 16th Earl of Loughborough and Northampton, humble servant of the King and our Lord God Almighty.'

He lowers the letter.

MRS GOULDING. Well, now, that's what I call a letter!

BERKELEY. I am not in the least surprised. His lordship is a thoughtful creature. He has worried so about his boys since the departure of their dear mother, and he longs to see them settled. He is an especially intuitive soul and I believe he has spotted in Hannah a unique aspect I myself have often wondered about.

GRANDIE. The dog is at the door.

MRS GOULDING. Shush now, Grandie, and drink your sherry.

BERKELEY. Those of a spiritual bent can see that someone of Hannah's beauty must be in touch with something *elemental*. In my numerous and varied travels on the British Isles, I have encountered a great many people in a great many places and please hear me without prejudice when I say that certain persons have a strange energetic effect on the very nature of time itself. His lordship has apprehended this. Hear the passion with which he addresses Hannah as though she is still in his house, one can almost sense his terror he will not be close to her unique atunement again.

MADELEINE. Berkeley, you will frighten the girl...

BERKELEY. Oh, come. (*With sudden unexpected seriousness*.) We all know that Hannah hears echoes of a past none else can hear.

MADELEINE (*straining to be jovial*). I must forbid this conversation. Such seriousness! That letter has quite unsettled me. Clare, tidy up.

MRS GOULDING. Madam, the Reverend is correct. Do not be unsettled by that letter and under no circumstances reconsider your plans. The girl must go to England. Look at the creatures who inhabit this place around us. If she stays here, what will she inherit? The ingratitude of the wretches who skulk about this island? Who are these people? The wildness in them. And the badness in them. They are only filthy tinkers the half of them. I grew up in Jamestown, Reverend. My people had a decent shop. We were schooled until we were eleven years of age. The women out here would thieve anything. And when we serve them soup all out in the back there. All in the yard, the tables lined up, eight gallons of water, onions, turnips, the four legs of a lamb, mind you...

FINGAL. Now, Mrs Goulding, you are too exercised...

MRS GOULDING. Bags of rice in the stew, bags of meal. All out there this year and in 1821 as well. The thieving red-haired look they'd give you, as they hunch over carrying it all out in under the trees out there so as not to share it with each other. The suspicion! They are in league with the devil the half of them. Clare, replenish me.

She holds her glass out to CLARE, *who takes it to get her a drink of whiskey.*

MADELEINE. You can scarcely believe such a thing, Mrs Goulding.

MRS GOULDING. I don't have to believe it, madam! It's just true! Take Mistress Hannah to England, and if you must go yourself, then go. Grandie will be happy with me here. There is less magic in England, and more good sense. The glow that comes off Hannah will bring her good luck there. Here it will only darken all her evenings. The fairies are jealous of her.

FINGAL. Mrs Goulding... For Jaysus' sake!

MRS GOULDING. Do not dare presume to lecture me, sir! You are lost in your own squalor. Sure wasn't my own son nearly taken from us by a fairy woman?

MADELEINE. Mrs Goulding...

MRS GOULDING. He was only sixteen and came back down from working on the boats out at McKenna Island, Reverend. On Christmas Eve he was dressing up in a new shirt and collar. I hardly saw him he was gone so much over the holiday – to meet with a woman he'd met on the road, no less, standing in a hedge! I knew it was no good. Night after night he left to meet her, hurling abuse at me when I tried to stop him. The colour in his face was like the ashes in the fire. He was sick in his heart. He near faded away before my eyes over the days. Till I got the priest to come and bless him while he lay asleep one morning, stretched out in front of the hearth. When he came to he cried his eyes out. He saw that I had saved him. And I had. Yes.

Pause.

MADELEINE. Yes, well…

AUDELLE. I believe you, Mrs Goulding. Your son was lucky to have you to dispel this sapping spirit. I myself had no such good luck until I met our esteemed Reverend. Once, in Spitalfields, I went into a tent to see an exhibit – a monster so they claimed. Of course, the pitiful creature was no more than a misshapen dwarf who was clearly a halfwit. But I saw a monster there all the same. It lurked behind the pain in his eyes. Such a look will always haunt me. And for tuppence I was implicit in heaping further grief upon his soul. The glance he darted at me held such a longing for release and understanding while his keeper barked and hit him. Yes, a monster surely followed among the dirty hoard I kept company with that night as we crawled up the dock wall looking for any dim lantern in a laneway. An elemental darkness is already inside each of us, how we explain it to ourselves is for each of us to bear. Anyone with a gift such as Hannah's is like a beacon in the dark.

BERKELEY. That's right.

MADELEINE. Oh, give me a drink, someone.

MRS GOULDING. Clare…

CLARE *gets a drink for* MADELEINE.

HANNAH. Mother…?

MADELEINE. A small sherry.

MRS GOULDING. A small sherry for Miss Hannah, Clare.

CLARE. Yes, ma'am.

GRANDIE. The old man wipes his feet and says, 'We're home from the fields!'

MRS GOULDING. And for Grandie. Yes, Grandie.

HANNAH. Mama saw a ghost when she was a girl.

MADELEINE. Hannah...

HANNAH. You did.

MADELEINE. I didn't. I have never seen a ghost.

HANNAH. You told us you saw one when you were sixteen in a hotel in London.

MADELEINE. It wasn't in a hotel and I told you it was just a dream.

BERKELEY. Where was it, Madeleine?

MADELEINE. This is ridiculous. I didn't see a ghost, Berkeley. I had a nightmare while I was staying at Great-Uncle Cyril's house in Holborn.

AUDELLE. Oh, do tell us.

MADELEINE. There is nothing to tell. I had eaten too many Belgian sausages before retiring. And not being used to it, I'd had two or even three glasses of white wine. When I went to bed, it being a strange house, I had trouble sleeping. I woke up, wrapped in a knot of blankets and I... I... dreamt I saw a young man standing just inside the door.

AUDELLE. Oh my word.

BERKELEY. They all have the gift.

MADELEINE. It was a dream, Berkeley. And Hannah knows she is making mischief to bring it up.

AUDELLE. Did he say anything?

MADELEINE. Who?

AUDELLE. The young man in your bedroom.

MADELEINE. Oh, I, you know how it is, for a moment I presumed he was real and I said, 'What do you want?' And he told me that...

HANNAH. That he had been murdered...

MADELEINE. Thank you, Hannah. He said he had been murdered in this room many years before. He raised his arm and pointed across the floor. I followed his gaze and… there was his body, lying on the mat under the window, as though it had been severely beaten. With that I let out a scream which brought my aunt and cousin running to my aid. You may imagine my embarrassment as I tried to explain I had merely been experiencing a heavy bout of indigestion.

BERKELEY. Or a visit from the beyond…

MADELEINE. I don't think so, Berkeley. A child will dream.

BEREKELY (*agreeing with her as though she has made his point for him*). Yes. A child will dream. There has always been something here, Madeleine. I have always felt it. In the earth, in the trees, and in the very wind that we hear tonight.

MADELEINE. That's just your memories and a decidedly childhood association with this place, Berkeley. You are a romantic.

BERKELEY. But Hannah has heard it. (*Short pause.*) I believe people get trapped here, Madeleine. Even those we love…

Pause.

MRS GOULDING. Clare, you are excused.

BERKELEY. Let her stay.

MRS GOULDING. She's terrified, look at her.

FINGAL. Are you?

CLARE *shakes her head.*

AUDELLE. She's more terrified of walking all the way down to the scullery on her own in the dark.

FINGAL. Let her be, Mrs Goulding.

BERKELEY. There is something here, Madeleine, Hannah has heard it.

Pause.

MADELEINE. No.

BERKELEY (*to* HANNAH). Have you not?

MRS GOULDING. Holy Mary, Mother of God, pray for us sinners, now and at the hour of death, amen.

BERKELEY. There is no cause for alarm. I have prayed for souls who were trapped in Nottingham, Gateshead…

AUDELLE. Isle of Man.

BERKELEY. Isle of Man.

MADELEINE. Berkeley, I forbid this.

BERKELEY. While the light of so many living souls are gathered together here, we should not lose our opportunity to pray. Will you not pray with us, Madeleine? A prayer before bed, nothing more. I assure you...

MADELEINE. Hannah is a young girl, Berkeley.

BERKELEY. She is a woman who is to be married.

MADELEINE. She was always a dreamer.

MRS GOULDING. Do not stick a blade in the hornet's nest, Reverend.

MADELEINE. Hannah has always loved stories. Her head is always in a book. She didn't hear anything.

HANNAH. But I did.

MADELEINE. Berkeley...

HANNAH. I did hear it. Someone shouted at me here in this room. They screamed right in my ear and if there's no one who believes me I still don't care.

BERKELEY. Shh... shhh... my child...

FINGAL. You are scaring the women, sir.

BERKELEY. No, no. There is no reason for fear. We are modern people now. And as such, we know that the spirit realm resides outside of time. As human animals with material bodies we are unfortunately trapped always in this moment and we don't know how to escape it. We cannot measure the past because it is gone. We cannot measure the future because it has yet to occur and we cannot measure the present because it slips away the instant we try to grasp it. Yet a spirit, a spirit exists in God's time where all moments are one eternal moment and all time is now. Yet man is, consider ye, both spirit and matter. Our spirit longs to commune with the eternal yet is all the while trapped within the prison of time itself, longing to be free. Those who have seen a ghost will say it is shadowy and transparent, often only glimpsed on the edge of sleep – why? Because we have not seen it with our physical eye, rather it is an imprint upon the imagination where our spirit apprehends the infinite. A spirit has spoken with Hannah. No more, no less. (*Gives a little laugh*.) There is nothing to fear! Now, before we retire for the evening, let us pray...

MADELEINE. Berkeley.

BERKELEY. No, no, just a bedtime prayer before we retire. That's all. (*Joins his hands and closes his eyes*.) Dear Lord, we beseech thee, deliver the lost and restless wanderer from the nightmare of darkness that engulfs us. Tell us, traveller, what do you want here? What is the nature of your plight? Tell us, in the name of Almighty God, what time are you lost in? (*Pause*.) Who is here? (*Pause*.) Who is here?

Pause.

MADELEINE. Berkeley...

BERKELEY. Who is here? (*Louder*.) WHO IS HERE? (*Louder again*.) WHO IS HERE??!

Pause. There is a sudden deafening bang like a gunshot over their heads. It seems to blow the room apart with its sonic impact. Their drinks go flying, cups are dropped. Each instinctively cries out and cowers...

MRS GOULDING. Dear God, dear God...

FINGAL (*getting up and looking around the room*). What was that? (*Opens the door to look out into the hallway.*)

MADELEINE (*to* BERKELEY). What did you do? (*Pause*.) What did you do?

BERKELEY. I... I don't know... I...

MADELEINE. How dare you? I asked you! In my house!

FINGAL *wanders back in.*

AUDELLE. There is a spirit here.

MADELEINE. You will be quiet, sir! You are a guest here, Mr Audelle, and I will kindly ask you to mind your manners. Berkeley, you will have nothing more to drink. Mrs Goulding, take Clare down and put the kettle on. Hannah, you will retire.

HANNAH. Mama, I...

MADEINE. You will retire!

HANNAH. Yes, Mama.

MRS GOULDING. Come, Clare... Help me with Grandie.

GRANDIE *pulls away from* MRS GOULDING.

MADELEINE. Leave her be, Mrs Goulding. Go and warm some water.

MRS GOULDING. Yes, madam.

MRS GOULDING *signals furiously to* CLARE *to help her and they start tidying up.*

BERKELEY. Madeleine. I am only trying to help.

MADELEINE. Well, you are lost in the clouds, Berkeley, you always were. We will discuss this in the morning.

There is a loud knocking at the front door. They all fall silent.

MRS GOULDING. Oh my Lord...

FINGAL *goes.*

MADELEINE. It is probably James Furay come to see what commotion we have made. What kind of example can we be setting for the boy?

AUDELLE. But what was it? What was that report?

MADELEINE. Well, it was... it was...

Silence. FINGAL *steps into the room.*

FINGAL. Madam, there is a constable outside.

MADELEINE. A constable?

FINGAL. Yes there has been a...

MADELEINE. Yes? (*Pause.*) What is it, Mr Fingal?

FINGAL. A terrace of houses in Jamestown that belong to this estate has collapsed.

MRS GOULDING. Oh, madam.

FINGAL. A number of families were trapped inside...

MADELEINE. I see.

MRS GOULDING. Oh no...

FINGAL. The constable has ridden out to inform you.

Pause.

MADELEINE. Yes, well, bring him in and see if he wants some soup. Mrs Goulding.

MRS GOULDING. Take him downstairs, Clare.

CLARE. Yes, madam.

CLARE *goes. Pause.*

MADELEINE. Where is he?

FINGAL. He is in the parlour.

MADELEINE *looks at* BERKELEY.

BERKELEY. Come, we will go to him.

BERKELEY *and* MADELEINE *leave. The others stand or sit in a state of numb distress.*

MRS GOULDING. What have we done?

The light changes to afternoon. Sunlight falls in through the foliage outside. It is two days later, Tuesday May 21st, around 3 p.m. HANNAH *sits near the window, writing.* GRANDIE *sits near the fireplace on a stool.* AUDELLE *comes in.*

AUDELLE. Where is everybody?

HANNAH. They are gone to Jamestown with Colonel Bennett to see the ruins of the terrace.

AUDELLE. Oh.

HANNAH. Were you asleep?

AUDELLE. I must have been. Is that tea?

HANNAH. Yes, Clare just brought it. For the first time I am glad that the Reverend was here.

AUDELLE *gets himself some tea.*

AUDELLE. I am gratified to hear that.

HANNAH. Everyone hates us, Mr Audelle.

AUDELLE *takes some tea.*

Mr Audelle.

Pause.

AUDELLE. Yes.

HANNAH. What happened in here the night before last.

AUDELLE. Yes.

HANNAH. Do you think it had something to do with what has happened in Jamestown?

AUDELLE. Absolutely.

HANNAH. Does it not bother you?

AUDELLE. Why would it bother me?

HANNAH. Because people have died, Mr Audelle, children have died, in property we owned and we heard something like a thunderclap here while we were... we were... Well... whatever we were doing, I haven't slept since. Are you only outwardly calm, or are you truly calm because you have no investment in this place and couldn't care less who lives or dies?

AUDELLE. Quite the reverse.

HANNAH. Your hands are remarkably steady then, sir. I can barely raise a cup.

AUDELLE. I administered ten drops of laudanum to myself at noon.

HANNAH. Does it work?

AUDELLE. Oh yes, it works – and I might say the local brew is thankfully intense. You see, I have always been susceptible to a kind of spiritual... distress, in certain places. Though I have never actually apprehended a spirit. Unlike you.

Short pause.

HANNAH *thinks about this and returns to her letter.*

HANNAH. You will excuse me, I hope, I am trying to finish a letter I promised to send by today.

AUDELLE *drinks some tea and looks at* GRANDIE.

GRANDIE. And may I ask you, sir; I don't know did you ever see a king around these parts that has mirrors where his eyes should be?

AUDELLE. A... king?

GRANDIE. Yes, he seems to be a kind of a king, with regal bearing, you understand, but he has mirrors instead of eyes. You see yourself when he looks at you! He's out under the trees there sometimes. Did you know about St Patrick?

AUDELLE. St Patrick?

GRANDIE. Yes, St Patrick.

AUDELLE. I... think I know about him.

GRANDIE. Well, he told me who St Patrick really was. St Patrick was a gold prospector! Did you know that? I didn't. They found gold all up in the hills around Cavan and Monaghan. St Patrick came with the good book all about Jesus Christ. That's how they always come, you see, and he said to everyone, 'These gods you have are no good,' apparently. He said he'd tell them all about this better God he knew all about – a very meek God you see, and while they were all busy praying to this terribly meek God, called Jesus Christ who was dreadfully meek, St Patrick took all the gold away! Yes, he told me all about St Patrick.

AUDELLE. I see. Well, thank you for telling me that.

GRANDIE. Yes.

Pause.

AUDELLE (*turning away from* GRANDIE). Do you have any friends who live nearby, Hannah?

HANNAH. When we were younger I used to play with James Furay, a boy my mother took in. But he lives down in the gate lodge with Mr Fingal now. I sense he has been encouraged not to speak with me.

AUDELLE. I am sorry.

HANNAH (*writing*). I had another friend, Elizabeth Argyle who lived at Drumsna. We used to share a tutor here but she got married last year and now lives in County Cavan.

AUDELLE. Is she happy?

HANNAH. She has a baby who has made her happy.

AUDELLE. You will be loved when you are married, Hannah.

HANNAH (*finishes her letter, lifting the paper to dry the ink*). We do not all pine for the love of a protector, Mr Audelle. Lord Ashby's estate is vast. We will have our own house. Clean linen at breakfast, as much hot water as a person may want. I am to receive an allowance and have a carriage at my personal disposal along with weekly French lessons.

AUDELLE. I'm sure your material circumstances will improve, Miss Lambroke, indeed I believe you will rule your domain just as you do here.

HANNAH. You think so?

AUDELLE. I know so. But I do not believe you expect such things will make you happy.

HANNAH. You are very frank, Mr Audelle.

AUDELLE *shrugs and goes to pour himself some tea.* HANNAH *watches him.*

Do you know anything of my fiancé?

AUDELLE. I know. That he made the Duke of Wellborough's widow pregnant and that both she and the child perished before she could bring it forth, thus freeing him conveniently of his obligations? (*Beat.*) Thus freeing him to marry?

HANNAH. He was under her spell.

AUDELLE. Well, of course he was. And now he isn't.

Pause.

HANNAH. You know, Elizabeth Argyle heard a great deal about you when we learned you were lodging with my cousin.

AUDELLE. Really?

HANNAH. Yes. And none of it encouraging. (*Pause.*) Is it true you abandoned your wife?

AUDELLE. It is.

HANNAH. And your child?

Pause.

AUDELLE. When I met my wife I was not much older than you.

HANNAH. What's that supposed to mean?

AUDELLE. Just that you… You might think me naive, but when I looked into her face – her grey eyes were so disarming I had always felt as though I was looking *through* her eyes into something so meaningful that I swore that somehow I could behold God there. And thus every moment was a moment of adoration.

HANNAH. How nice for her.

AUDELLE. Her father had lent us a remote cottage while I tried to write. The weather had been particularly bad. We hid inside from the continuous deluge. The child was sick and crying. My wife was sick. And then I was sick. Very sick. And one morning I looked into my wife's face at breakfast and I realised I could no longer see into the eternal. It was as though a shutter had come down and God had absented himself. And I… accepted that and I tried to… I tried to… but then, while attending Sunday service one morning in March, I thought I spied God again, peering at me from the eyes of another – two others – sisters.

HANNAH. I had scarcely believed it could be true.

AUDELLE. Yes, emboldened by fortifying my brandy with laudanum, I embarked on what I can only describe as sordid interior escapades at their cottage for days on end.

HANNAH. Is it true you turned your wife away with your dead child in her arms?

AUDELLE. No, that's not true. She had walked several miles in the rain with the child to find me one night and… (*Short pause.*) But you must understand how insensible I was. I thought I had heard her voice below the window while I lay deep beneath the blankets. But I… I was… The facts are that the child passed some days afterward – not that night. (*Short pause.*) I endeavoured to take my own life some several times afterwards and I ended up living in London's parks. If not for your cousin, the Reverend – I would have probably died in the madhouse.

HANNAH. Perhaps I can never understand your actions concerning your family, Mr Audelle, and I know they are unforgivable, but I do know what it is to feel… Last week I sliced an apple knife into my hand.

AUDELLE. Why?

HANNAH. So I might experience a pain I actually understand. You see, I know now there is something real, something waiting for me, calling for me to do what my father did. And I know that belief cannot save me and I suspect that even death cannot save me, because when you are in hell you know only one thing – that only nothingness is holy. (*Pause. Composes herself.*) Will you give me some laudanum?

Pause.

AUDELLE. If you like.

HANNAH. Where is it?

AUDELLE. In my pocket.

HANNAH. How do you take it?

AUDELLE. It is best poured in a little drop of brandy.

HANNAH. Will you pour me some?

> AUDELLE *goes to the drinks and pours her a brandy. He hands her the glass, then takes a small bottle from his inside jacket pocket. She holds out her glass.*

AUDELLE. The old stones up at the top of the hill…

HANNAH. The Queen's Tomb?

AUDELLE. Yes. Will you take me up there for a look?

HANNAH. What for?

AUDELLE. To just behold their magic.

> HANNAH *shrugs.*

HANNAH. If you like.

AUDELLE. Thank you.

> *He takes the top from the bottle of laudanum and goes to pour some into* HANNAH's *glass.*

> *The lights fade.*

> *End of Act One.*

ACT TWO

Night, around midnight on Thursday May 23rd. GRANDIE *is sitting quietly near the fireplace as the fire dies. A wind is picking up outside.* HANNAH *slowly plays a single note over and over on the piano. There is a knock. The door to the hallway opens and* BERKELEY *and* AUDELLE *enter. They stand near the door, wrapped up in their coats.*

BERKELEY. Ah, some nighthawks! We didn't expect anyone to still be up.

HANNAH (*rises*). Sometimes Grandie gets up. She never knows when it's night-time.

BERKELEY. Well, we had a lovely moonlight stroll. To walk off our dinner. Are we alone?

HANNAH. Everyone was in bed.

BERKELEY. Of course. Will we join you for a moment?

BERKELEY *and* AUDELLE *come further into the room.*

HANNAH. What time is it?

BERKELEY. It's after midnight! Goodnight, Grandie. How fares the world? You know, I was only saying to Mr Audelle, Thursday was always my favourite day of the week when I was a little boy. It was the one day I was permitted out of the nursery and could sit all afternoon with my mother while my father wrote his lectures. I keenly remember the fascination and privilege I felt in their company. Every Thursday.

AUDELLE. I used to watch my father writing his sermons.

BERKELEY. I saw him preach. He was a great believer in the corrective terror of hell and damnation which lent his oratory an extra impassioned forcefulness, I remember! (*Laughs. Pause.*) You look tired, Hannah.

GRANDIE *looks at him blankly then gives a slight smile of acknowledgement, turning her face back to the fire.*

HANNAH. Well, yes I am, rather.

BERKELEY. Mr Audelle tells me you were kind enough to bring him up to the Queen's Tomb yesterday.

HANNAH. Yes.

BERKELEY. But you didn't stay long.

Short pause.

HANNAH. Yes, well, the weather was inclement.

AUDELLE. I was just telling the Reverend, for myself, laying my hand upon those prehistoric stones induced a sense of connectedness to the mysterious ancestors of this place, the sheer... force of which I had never experienced before.

BERKELEY. Oh, yes. I have always found it to be a place of dark enchantment. And you, Hannah? Did you experience a... sense of connectedness?

HANNAH. Well, I... I did not remain there for long, so...

Pause.

BERKELEY. You know, I often think of your poor father on nights such as this, Hannah.

HANNAH. I think of him regardless of the day or night.

BERKELEY. He is in your prayers.

HANNAH. With all of my family.

BERKELEY. With all of us. My dear Alice is still alive – in my mind, her fragile bones still shining beneath her transparent skin, just as poor old Edward still lives in yours. He is so strong there. So... real. In which case, how can anyone say he doesn't exist? Of course he still exists! These recent times weigh hard on you, I suspect, Hannah.

HANNAH. Well. I have many blessings. I shouldn't complain.

BERKELEY. Yes, but even good news can bring its difficulties, especially when set against a tragedy so terrible as the one we have witnessed in Jamestown.

HANNAH. Especially when it occurred on the very evening you sought to summon the spirits of the dead.

BERKELEY (*laughs, almost delighted she has risen to the bait*). 'The dead'! We didn't cause those buildings to fall down. Hasn't the Colonel himself said as much. Now, I hope you don't mind, but you will be aware I have learned something of your recent experiences, Hannah.

HANNAH. Yes, well, I don't want to discuss that.

BERKELEY. And I will come straight out with it and say it's a pity you consider the specialness of your gift a burden – when rightly it should be something you ought to cherish. And be grateful for.

HANNAH. I just want to stop it now, so...

BERKELEY. Stop it?! Well, it's my belief that would be a dreadful shame. What you really need is to *understand* it. Yes. You can take the sting of its unknowability away, and we would like to help you.

Pause.

HANNAH. How can you help me?

BERKELEY. Do you know what a... seance is, Hannah?

HANNAH. I have heard of it.

BERKELEY. Yes, on the Continent one hears a lot of rubbish about these matters, I'm afraid. The facts are quite simple. I can explain precisely why you are in your predicament, Audelle?

AUDELLE. It's really quite straightforward.

BERKELEY. Dear me, that's quite a draught. Is that door closed, Audelle?

AUDELLE goes and shuts the door quietly.

You see, Hannah, there is only God. (*Pause.*) Nature comes from God. It is a part of God. And man is part of nature. But we are a very special part, because only the human being can know itself and think for itself. Consider a fish or a dog. They are prisoners of their instinct, slaves to nature, where man is free.

HANNAH. No. A dog is freer than a man, if you ask me.

AUDELLE. But a dog cannot choose. No animal can. When it's hungry it will eat, when it's tired it must sleep. Thus it has no choice, correct? But man – a man may *deny* his instinct, *suppress* his appetite and decide for himself what is right or wrong. He is even free to destroy himself!

BERKELEY. Can a dog do that?

AUDELLE. Being conscious means man is both part of nature and yet free of it – all at once.

BERKELEY. You see, it has recently been proven, Hannah, beyond logical denial –

HANNAH *goes to interrupt.*

Beyond logical denial, that with the emergence of the human subject there is finally a part of nature which *knows* itself! Do you understand? All of this, everything around us, and you and I and Audelle –

AUDELLE. And Grandie –

BERKELEY. And Grandie and everything else – this is all… the mind of God awakening and coming to know itself. And when we look at each other, just as I am looking at you now, it is as though God is looking at Himself in a mirror. And each eye, the beholder and the beheld, reflect the other back and forth as mirrors do, into a kind of genuine infinity. The infinity of God. You see? We *are* God… Isn't that wonderful? Now, knowing that we are God is of course a great responsibility but it's not something we want to bandy about!

AUDELLE. Of course not.

BERKELEY. For so long we have all felt cut away from God, somehow seeking 'forgiveness' in order to be reunited. But we were never separate from Him! So you need not feel any guilt, Hannah. Your feelings are holy! And just as in any walk of life we meet people with great gifts, this one a great carpenter, that one a great musician, so you have a great talent, Hannah.

HANNAH. You call it a gift.

AUDELLE. Hannah, your gift is simply consciousness itself. That's right. And so profound is your talent in this case, so acute its perceptiveness, you are capable of beholding not just what is here in this moment, but what is beyond and before time.

BERKELEY. That's all it is! Nothing more! (*Laughs.*) And certainly nothing to fear. So in order to dispel the terror visited upon you by the voices you have perceived here in this house, I want to invite you now, through the medium of a seance, to reconsider them in this light: and thereby uncover the divine within yourself. Here. With us. Now. Tonight. We are here to support you and to help you. Why, even Grandie can take part! All humankind is welcome here! (*Laughs.*)

AUDELLE. A seance is merely a mindful contemplation, Hannah. We… sit together and reflect. That is all.

HANNAH. Will it stop me hearing things?

BERKELEY. I cannot say it will. Indeed I hope it will not! But I will stake my life on it that it will take the fear away. My life!

Pause.

HANNAH. What happens?

BERKELEY. What happens? Why nothing more than were we to open a book and read a story. The book we open is the book of time. The story is the unfolding revelation of God's presence in all things. No more. Thus we may understand who or what has been drawn to this place to seek you out. And armed with this knowledge, it is my firm belief you will progress into your new life with a hitherto unforeseen freedom, for ever.

Pause. HANNAH *is thinking about it.*

AUDELLE. Do not waste your youth as I have, hemmed in on either side by an abyss of fear.

BERKELEY. Release yourself. Permit yourself.

AUDELLE. Forgive yourself.

BERKERLEY. And trust me. Won't you trust me?

HANNAH *coughs.*

Yes, we are all getting that cold!

AUDELLE. Allow me. (*Approaches the drinks.*) Berkeley?

BERKELEY. Water for me, Audelle. Thank you. Look at you, Grandie. So well I remember your charms when you sang before the assembled throng here at Mount Prospect. Your wit. Your gameful eyes so animated with shy promise. Then, as now. Yes, I remember you, Grandie.

AUDELLE *brings a drink of brandy to* HANNAH.

AUDELLE. Sip this, Miss Hannah.

BERKELEY. Yes, a sip to clear the lungs. Well done, Audelle.

HANNAH *drinks while* AUDELLE *takes his bottle of laudanum from his pocket. He thumps his chest.*

AUDELLE. I think I need to loosen my…

Coughs lightly and indicates the bottle to HANNAH. *She holds out her glass, he pours some laudanum into her brandy and she drinks it.*

BERKELEY. Yes, Grandie. (*Holds out his hand to her.*) How you would dance the young men to a defeated collapse!

GRANDIE *reaches towards* BERKELEY *uncertainly, but then withdraws her hand.*

Yes, long ago… (*Takes a cord with a crucifix, some feathers and stones strung along it, placing it round his neck like a necklace.*) How silent is the darkness tonight. You may take my hand, Grandie. Take her hand, Hannah. She is your anchor. There is great love there still. (*Pause.*) Do not be afraid. Who else has ever offered to help you as we do? Take her hand, she loves you.

HANNAH *takes* GRANDIE'*s hand.* GRANDIE *gives her other hand to* BERKELEY. AUDELLE *takes* BERKELEY'*s hand.*

Let us pray. (*With pained concentration.*) Lord God, unknowable father, while we struggle oftbetimes to comprehend thy wishes, forgive us – sinners as we are – as we fulsomely seek to know thy bidding. Bless us here tonight. Protect us as darkness falls through the world and we gather in Your name to wish our daughter Hannah a peaceful existence, replete with spiritual calm. We are beset at every turn with temptations, with dire puzzles which would draw us from Your path and hide the light that might show us to Your dwelling where our true home awaits. Lord, shield us with the blanket of Your forgiveness, Lord…

Sound of a window rattling in the house somewhere.

GRANDIE *takes her hand from* BERKELEY'*s.*

(*Firmly.*) Grandie… (*More gently.*) Grandie. Let us say our bedtime prayers, come on now. That's it…

HANNAH. Perhaps we have done enough for now, Berkeley.

BERKELEY. We are merely saying a prayer, Hannah. Let us pray. Let us pray.

GRANDIE *looks at* HANNAH. HANNAH *returns her gaze.* BERKELEY *takes* GRANDIE'*s hand.*

Lord, as you peer into the rags of our pitiful souls, grant us safety here, to cleanse our house. To liberate the daughter of our house.

(*Pause*.) To all else who lurk here, I say unto you now – in the name of God – reveal yourselves and submit to our instruction to quit this place. No longer disturb this girl. She may hear you while all else fall deaf to your pleas, but we shall not brook that you harass her with your infernal concerns!

They hear something move, like furniture being dragged across a room above them.

Ignore it! (*Bellows*.) In the name of Our Lord, Jesus Christ…

AUDELLE. Quieter, Berkeley…

BERKELEY. I'm sorry. (*Lowers his volume*.) In the name of Our Lord, Jesus Christ, our saviour, the one true God who became man to know death as man knows it, for love of His children, I command thee – come forward and go. (*Pause*.) Come forward and show yourself!

Again something moves somewhere, a dull thud.

Ignore it. I command thee, cold spirit. Show thyself. Submit thyself. *Credo. Credo. Credo. Credo in Unum Deum, Patrem omnipotentem, factorem caeli et terrae, visibilium omnium et invisibilium.*

HANNAH *coughs.*

Deus meus ex toto corde paenitet me morum peccatorum…

HANNAH'*s body shudders.*

Credo… Credo… Credo…

HANNAH (*suddenly starts singing in a strident voice while her eyes are closed*). Oh, the green moss grows upon the heather where the briar grows upon the wood…

BERKELEY *falls silent.* AUDELLE *and* BERKELEY *look at each other.*

BERKELEY. *Non solum poenas a te juste statutes promeritus sum…*

HANNAH (*sings*). My love is sleeping in the bower where a lonely graveyard stood. She sings of an ancient flower… She sings of an ancient flower…

BERKELEY.…*Adiuvante gratia tua, de cetero me no peccaridique occasiones proximas fugiturum…*

HANNAH (*sings*). She sings… (*Her song peters out.*)

GRANDIE (*casually*). He knew my name.

BERKELEY. Shh… Grandie.

> HANNAH *looks at* BERKELEY. *She speaks gently and calmly, her eyes seeing beyond him into somewhere else.*

HANNAH. Have you seen it?

Pause.

BERKELEY. Have we seen what?

HANNAH (*gently*). The infant.

BERKELEY. What infant?

HANNAH. The baby… that was here.

Pause.

AUDELLE. Berkeley…

BERKELEY. Yes, yes… (*To* HANNAH.) Who speaks? (*Pause.*) Who speaks?

HANNAH.…Shh! Listen… (*Pause.*) Where is it!?

BERKELEY. Where is what? (*Short pause.*) We hear nothing.

HANNAH. Sh… (*Pause.*) Listen…

> HANNAH *suddenly stands up. She looks at the others.*

BERKELEY. Who are you that speaks through this girl?

HANNAH. You can't hear it.

BERKELEY. Are you Edward come to us?

HANNAH. I can hear her.

She looks round the room.

BERKELEY. Do you hear your daughter, Edward? (*Pause.*) Are you Edward? (*Pause.*) You know you must leave here. You must quit this place. You can no longer remain.

HANNAH. But how can I leave?

BERKELEY. You are called to join your Creator. You died here, Edward. You cannot stay.

HANNAH. I cannot go. I will see my child.

BERKELEY. You can no longer see your child, Edward, because you died here. (*Pause*.) You died here.

HANNAH. It was a girl, wasn't it?

She walks round the room, as though looking for something.

BERKELEY. Who was a girl? (*Pause*.) Speak!

HANNAH. I can hear her crying!

Pause.

BERKELEY. Are you Edward Lambroke? Are you he that took his life in this room?

HANNAH. They've locked me in! They've locked me in!

BERKELEY. Well, you must leave in the name of God.

HANNAH. This is a dream. This must be a dream.

She looks desperately round the room. BERKELEY *follows her.*

BERKELEY. We abide only in the dream of our great Creator, in whose name I command you now to go.

HANNAH. No! They must show me my child.

BERKELEY. You must leave this house in the name of Jesus Christ.

HANNAH. Can you not hear it? Are you made of stone? (*Shouts*.) Can you not hear her?!

AUDELLE. Berkeley…!

BERKELEY (*holding her*). Listen no, no, no, listen, Edward. Are you Edward? You are Edward.

HANNAH. I am Hannah.

BERKELEY. No, you are not. Not Hannah.

GRANDIE. She is Hannah.

HANNAH. I am Hannah Lambroke, and I will not be told I cannot see my child!!

BERKELEY. Shhh…

AUDELLE. She will wake the house!

HANNAH goes towards the conservatory door and tries the handle. BERKELEY *blocks her way, she pushes against him.*

BERKELEY. I command whoever torments this girl to leave.

HANNAH. Unlock this door. I demand to see my child.

BERKELEY. Shh… Shh… Hannah, it's alright. Some help please here, Audelle.

AUDELLE goes to assist BERKELEY, restraining HANNAH.

HANNAH. I will see my child! I will hold my child!

GRANDIE is agitated by the disruption. She lets out a cry and moves towards the hallway door.

AUDELLE. Get her out of it, Berkeley! Get her out of it!

HANNAH. Are you mad?! Are you people mad!?

She turns and thumps AUDELLE around the head and chest until he releases her. He tumbles backwards into the furniture and on to the floor.

What kind of people are you that you would do such a thing?

She stands glaring at them.

BERKELEY. Hannah. Hannah. It's me. It's Berkeley. Why, we were just praying… ha ha ha… Let's have a little prayer.

HANNAH. I will not pray with you.

BERKELEY. Well, that's alright. That's alright. You just got a fright, that's all. No need for alarm. That's it. We were just…

HANNAH. Don't touch me.

BERKELEY. No, no. I won't… Here, take a drink of water, now shush…

AUDELLE has backed away towards the hall door near GRANDIE. HANNAH goes to the fireplace, her head on her hands on the mantel. BERKELEY tries to cajole her with a glass of water. He has his back to AUDELLE as the door opens. AUDELLE turns to face the music, expecting to see MADELEINE, but a very small CHILD with a pale face and dark eyes stands looking at AUDELLE for a moment before turning and leaving in the gloom. AUDELLE stands frozen, looking at the empty doorway. GRANDIE is watching AUDELLE. BERKELEY, preoccupied with HANNAH, sees nothing.

That's it. That's alright. Sit down…

HANNAH *sits down, her head in her hands.*

AUDELLE *looks at* GRANDIE *who is staring at* AUDELLE. *She suddenly opens her mouth wide and starts screaming at* AUDELLE. AUDELLE *flinches.* GRANDIE *laughs at him, opening her mouth and screaming at him, terrifying him, as though she knows he has just seen a ghost and is mocking him. She hits him with a stick.*

Grandie, shush! Grandie... now... Grandie! What did you do to her?

AUDELLE. What? I... I...

GRANDIE *screams at* AUDELLE *as* MADELEINE *rushes in carrying a candle.*

Pause.

MADELEINE. What in the name of God is happening in here?

BERKELEY. Grandie has... become a little overwrought.

Pause.

MADELEINE. Grandie. That's enough. Hannah. What happened?

BERKELEY (*quickly removing his necklace*). She's just exhausted. We all are. This last week has taken such a considerable toll on all of us.

MADELEINE. What are you talking about?

MRS GOULDING *appears in her nightdress.*

MRS GOULDING. Was someone at the door?

MADELEINE. No, Mrs Goulding. Kindly take Grandie to bed. It's time everyone retired.

MRS GOULDING. Come, Grandie.

GRANDIE *goes to* AUDELLE *and pinches his cheek.*

AUDELLE. Get off me!

MADELEINE. Grandie! Go to bed!

GRANDIE *leaves, followed by* MRS GOULDING.

MRS GOULDING. Grandie, wait for the candle!

Pause.

MADELEINE. What happened?

BERKELEY. Why, nothing! (*Short pause.*) Ha, ha, ha…

MADELEINE. What were you doing?

BERKELEY. Nothing! We were all just discussing the… horrific events of the past few days. And how upsetting it's been… and Grandie just…

MADELEINE. Hannah?

HANNAH. I need to lie down.

MADELEINE. Well, get yourself to bed.

HANNAH. Yes, Mama.

MADELEINE. You're shaking.

BERKELEY. That's a dreadful cold that's been going round.

> HANNAH *readies herself to leave. She looks at* BERKELEY *and* AUDELLE. *Behind* MADELEINE*'s back,* BERKELEY *puts his finger to his lips, begging* HANNAH*'s silence.*

We will all talk in the morning.

Pause.

MADELEINE. You will pack your bags tomorrow. There will be too little time on Saturday.

BERKELEY. Yes. We will all pack tomorrow. (*Pause.*) Yes.

> HANNAH *leaves.*

> MADELEINE *looks at* BERKELEY. *He gives her a little smile.*

What can I say? Goodnight, Madeleine.

She looks at AUDELLE.

MADELEINE. And what's the matter with you now, Mr Audelle? Too much or too little brandy?

She leaves. Pause.

BERKELEY. Well! Intriguing! (*Wipes his brow with a handkerchief.*) What did you make of that?! Are you alright, Audelle? You look ghastly.

AUDELLE. Yes, I'm… I'm fine.

BERKELEY. She was… I mean, we were really in the presence of something, weren't we?

AUDELLE. Yes.

BERKELEY. My word. The very air crackles. What did we unleash?

AUDELLE *doesn't answer.*

Come, we must abed. I would not anger our hostess a moment more.

AUDELLE. I will follow you.

BERKELEY *pauses.*

Please, Berkeley. I need a moment.

BERKELEY. Alright, well… Do not stay too late.

AUDELLE. No.

BERKELEY. And no more brandy. Or medicine. Come now. Directly.

BERKELEY *takes a candle and leaves.* AUDELLE *sits on the arm of a chair looking at the spot where he saw the* CHILD.

The lights darken and he leaves as the room brightens again, bringing us to the next day, Friday May 24th. It is late afternoon, between 5 and 6 p.m. The first bare fade of dusk is in the sky. CLARE *is changing candles and lighting new ones. She throws the old stubs in a cloth bag to be reused downstairs.* FINGAL *comes in through the conservatory. He opens the tall double doors and trips, almost falling into the room, dropping the rifle he carries and startling* CLARE. *He has a swollen black eye.*

CLARE. Mr Fingal!

FINGAL (*drunkenly putting a finger to his lips*). Aye aye aye… (*Looking at where he lost his footing.*) Someone needs to fix those floorboards.

CLARE (*resuming her work*). There's nothing wrong with the floorboards.

FINGAL *props his rifle against a wall and stands in the room seemingly devoid of purpose, drink having reduced his worries to an unreachable drone within his head.*

FINGAL. Miss me?

CLARE. Why would I miss you?

FINGAL. Because... I've been gone.

CLARE. You always turn up. Where were you? Down in Jamestown, I suppose?

FINGAL. And if I was?

CLARE. Look at you. What happened to your eye?

FINGAL. A bat flew into it.

CLARE. A bat?

FINGAL. I was... coming up, down the road, up out of Jamestown and – kablammo! Right in the kisser.

CLARE. Yes, well wait until the others see you.

FINGAL. Nobody can see me, Clare. I'm like a ghost now.

CLARE. You will be a ghost the way you're going.

Pause. He watches her work.

FINGAL. They found another little one this morning. In the rubble. An infant.

CLARE. Yes, I heard.

FINGAL. That's seven little ones.

CLARE. Yes, I heard already, Mr Fingal.

FINGAL. Alright, Jesus Christ! I'm only telling you. Pss.

He goes to pour himself a drink.

A bloody death hole is all it was. Still, roof over your head. (*Gloomily.*) All warm in together. (*Drinks.*) So, look, I'll have my money soon. When the dowry comes in. Thirteen months' wages, I'm owed. What do you think of that? That's when the pressure comes off. (*Pause.*) And given time, perhaps even I will be forgiven.

CLARE. Forgiven what?

FINGAL. Even you'll forgive me.

CLARE. What's to forgive? Except how you would kill your own kindness.

FINGAL. Kindness? What kindness?

CLARE. Don't act the criminal, Mr Fingal. I have seen it.

FINGAL. Where? In those whispers I stuck in your ear, so full of grog and poitín you had to hold me up in the darkness of the laneway?

CLARE. I have seen it.

Pause.

FINGAL. So anyway… Clare… Em… Can you loan me some money?

CLARE. Pardon?

FINGAL. Can you loan me some money, just until… I am in debt.

CLARE. For how much?

FINGAL. Fifty-five guineas.

CLARE. Fifty-five guineas! From playing cards!?

FINGAL. I will sign a promissory letter this very day and endeavour to have you reimbursed within the month, or when the dowry for Miss Hannah arrives, whichever is sooner.

CLARE. I have but two guineas in the world.

FINGAL. Two guineas will suffice for today.

CLARE. I can't.

FINGAL. Why not?

CLARE. It is for my passage to Ontario.

FINGAL (*disparaging*). You're not going to Ontario, Clare…

CLARE. When her ladyship and Hannah move to Northampton I will be left with no employment. What will I do without my passage?

FINGAL. But you will get your money back!

CLARE. No. My father would kill me.

FINGAL. He'll never know!

CLARE. He holds my money for me!

FINGAL. You can get it. Tell him something. What? Would you betray me to him?

CLARE. Of course not, but…

FINGAL. Then it's settled! I will bring you a letter tonight that will ease your mind. It's as good as money, I promise you. When Miss Hannah's dowry arrives, madam will settle her debts, you will have your two guineas, I'll pay the balance of what I owe in Jamestown, and we'll all…

He raises his hands in conclusion. Pause.

CLARE. Would you not… consider going away?

FINGAL. Where? (*Disparaging.*) To Canada? Come on…

CLARE. Or anywhere. Away. Away from the trouble in your nature that drags you down again and again to Jamestown. Away. Imagine a clean country. Your own little place with a fire dying in the hearth and a good meal inside you and the peacefulness maybe of knowing that your… wife or your… your child is soundly asleep nearby.

FINGAL. How can you hold out hope like that? Ha? Even for me?

CLARE. I don't know. I just see it.

FINGAL. You see a dream.

CLARE. If you like.

FINGAL. Yeah, well I don't believe in dreams.

He takes a drink.

CLARE (*sharply*). Well, ask her ladyship to loan you the money then! She likes you personally, isn't that what you're always saying?

FINGAL (*moving to quieten her voice*). Don't be ridiculous!

CLARE. Yeah? Well, I saw her here one morning talking to a soldier just out there on the stairs.

FINGAL. What soldier?

CLARE. Some soldier. At the top of the stairs just before it got bright. She never saw me.

FINGAL. From the garrison?

CLARE. No, he wasn't a rough-looking one at all. He had a fancy uniform.

FINGAL. Well, that's… What are you talking about? Can you see in the dark now?

CLARE. Why? Are you jealous? It's so clear how you think of her.

FINGAL. Don't talk nonsense, girl...

CLARE. You do. And you say you don't believe in dreams! Huh! You dream the most of any of us, Mr Fingal.

FINGAL (*loudly*). Will you shut the hell up, I said! (*Pause.*) I'll give you a dream. Before any of you were awake, the other morning, I beat the boy out in the yard. You didn't see that, did you?

CLARE. Little James Furay?

FINGAL. Yes, little James. You didn't see it because I did it before anybody was up. I woke him in the dark and I said, 'Get down here with me to the stables.' He rose without a question, rubbing his eyes, and I got him in there and I made him wash with cold water from the pail and then I said, 'What do you mean, sir, having two lame horses in your charge?' 'What?' he says. 'Take off your shirt,' says I, 'I'm to whip you for what's happened to her ladyship's horse.'

CLARE. When was this?

FINGAL. The morning after we went to Jamestown to see the ruins. Out there by the stable. And do you know what he did? He just went over to the corner and took off his jacket and his shirt and he stood there before me. This boy who's lived with me in the lodge since he was seven years old. His skinny white body, so small for his age, and his eyes so trusting and innocent and I took a whip and I turned him round and belted him so hard I stripped half the skin off his back and he couldn't get his shirt back on. His hands were too shaky anyway, so I threw his jacket round his shoulders and told him to piss off back down to the lodge.

Pause.

CLARE. Why would you do such a thing?

FINGAL. Because her ladyship told me to.

CLARE. She told you to do that to him?

FINGAL. She told me to get to the bottom of what happened to the horses.

CLARE. But, Mr Fingal...

FINGAL. I know. I know! Do you think I don't know?! (*Pause.*) I went down to Jamestown and played cards for three days and nights. I ended up in a fight over my debts and curled up in a ditch and prayed for God to punish me. But He knew, you see. He knew it would be worse to leave me alone.

CLARE. Where is the boy?

FINGAL (*shrugs*). In the gate lodge.

CLARE. On his own?

FINGAL. We must make... that assumption. Can you let me have some money tonight, Clare? Anything that I could just bring down to...

The door opens. MADELEINE *comes in with* GRANDIE. CLARE *resumes her work and* FINGAL *puts down his drink.*

MADELEINE. Clare, will you please go and see if Hannah is still in the chapel? She has a cold and I want her to come in.

CLARE. Yes, madam.

MADELEINE. And come straight back as Mrs Goulding will need you.

CLARE. Yes, madam.

CLARE *goes.*

MADELEINE. Mr Fingal.

FINGAL. Madam.

MADELEINE. What happened to your face?

FINGAL. An altercation regarding a personal matter which has not nor will not interfere with my professional duties.

MADELEINE. You have been in Jamestown, I take it?

FINGAL. Yes.

Pause.

MADELEINE. What say folk?

FINGAL. Regarding...?

MADELEINE. Regarding the collapse of my properties.

FINGAL. They say such is the lot of the poor.

MADELEINE. To suffer the rich.

FINGAL. They suffer themselves. They should better themselves.

MADELEINE. As you have bettered yourself.

FINGAL. As you see.

There is a short pause, and he starts to leave, forgetting his rifle.

Well, good evening.

MADELEINE. We are gathering to say farewell to the Reverend and Mr Audelle. And to wish Hannah a good journey. You may join us, Mr Fingal, should you feel up to it.

FINGAL. Thank you, madam.

MADELEINE. But may I suggest you go to the kitchen and tidy yourself up.

FINGAL. Yes, madam.

MADELEINE. And drink some tea.

FINGAL. Yes, madam.

MADELEINE. Oh, and Mr Fingal.

He halts.

Where is the boy? (*Pause.*) Where is James Furay?

BERKELEY *comes in.*

BERKELEY. Ah, Fingal! The very man. Oh dear me, that is a shiner! What happened? Are you alright?

FINGAL. A hunting accident, sir.

BERKELEY. Oh dear, well, actually, I was going to ask you. We leave tomorrow around noon, but say if I were up at five or so, could I get a pony to go down in the glen to see if I can bag a wood pigeon or two?

FINGAL. Yes, sir.

BERKELEY. I heard there were a few about.

FINGAL. Yes, sir, I'll see about a pony.

BERKELEY. Only if it's no trouble.

FINGAL. No, sir, I'll see to it personally.

BERKELEY. Thanks, Fingal.

FINGAL. Yes, sir.

BERKELEY. And don't let me go without giving you a little... eh... (*Signals a monetary tip.*)

FINGAL *nods uncomfortably and leaves.*

Poor old Fingal. Fond of the drop, I take it.

MADELEINE. No more so than the rest of his family.

BERKELEY. Mmm. Well, Grandie! We gather to say farewell – until Northampton.

GRANDIE *just returns his gaze steadily, giving him the slightest of smiles.*

MADELEINE. Yes.

BERKELEY. Madeleine. I am sorry if I disturbed you when I entered your chamber this morning. I could never have forgiven myself had I awoken to hear sobbing and had done nothing to at least to investigate.

MADELEINE. I was quite alright, thank you. It was just a bad dream.

BERKELEY. Well, it must have been very bad. May I?

He goes to the drinks.

MADELEINE. Not for me

GRANDIE. Good morning, McMickins.

MADELEINE. But a small drop for Grandie if you don't mind.

BERKELEY. Grandie, of course... I know these have been such trying days, Madeleine. Do not think I could possibly be unaware of that. My affection for you is unassailable, for you see, to me – perhaps unfortunately for you – you will always be the little child who would follow me about on my summer visits here as a young man.

MADELEINE. Oh, come, I never followed you about.

BERKELEY. No, no, you did. You were probably too young to remember. You showed such delight when we fished for trout in the lake. She was like my little sister, wasn't she, Grandie? And you still are. So when I heard you sobbing down the corridor in the darkness before dawn this morning, how could I not at least venture forth to offer you my comfort in the gloom? However, if you don't mind me saying, that you would refuse my presence with such vehemence and unexpected bad language quite unnerved me. I hardly slept after I crept back to my bed.

MADELEINE. I regret that your feelings were not spared, Berkeley, but I simply have no time for your perceived hardships at present, I'm sorry.

BERKELEY. You are growing old, Madeleine. I am already old. Mark you, even at fifty, one is very old. These years, between now and fifty – settle your affairs, dear.

MADELEINE. I am settling my affairs.

BERKELEY. Yes, your earthly affairs.

MADELEINE. Oh, Berkeley, please, I'm too tired.

BERKELEY. I mean to speak plainly with you, Madeleine, because I love you and I only want what is for the best. A sickness of denial and illusion pervades here in this room, in this very room you so boldly use. But you will not let me help you.

MADELEINE. But I don't want your help!

BERKELEY. Madeleine, I know you can see the things Hannah has experienced here. You deny your gift in order to embrace your delusion that Edward actually departed the night he ended his life here. It is my firm belief he did not depart.

MADELEINE. Berkeley, I swear I will brain you with this poker if you keep on at me, do you hear me? What were you doing in here with Hannah last night?

BERKELEY. I was assisting her, Madeleine! I was helping a girl who has endured the unimaginable strain of being the sole recipient of a communication from the beyond, with no one to believe her or help her to interpret it.

MADELEINE. Oh!

BERKELEY. The spirit realm flows through this place like a river! It always has! This is the very place that piqued my interest in everything that ever led to my downfall and my disgrace, but I don't regret it. Not for a second. Audelle is sensate. And he can feel it. I know him. And I know he can barely keep his mind together, so strong is its current!

MADELEINE. I would contend that Mr Audelle struggles to keep his mind together under the calmest of circumstances! Are you not ashamed to consort with someone with a reputation such as his? Let alone invite him into my house to instruct my daughter?

BERKELEY (*sadly*). Oh, my child…

MADELEINE. I'm not your child, Berkeley. You *are* old, I don't deny it. Age has racked your body, but it is your brain that has suffered most! I hear you speak and I believe you are like a man with an infant's toy box in his head.

GRANDIE. Woah!

BERKELEY (*shocked and angry*). Madeleine!

MADELEINE. Yes! You may say you have always regarded me as your sister, but in truth when I was a child I always thought you were an embarrassing buffoon and I was never anything less than utterly fatigued by your boring theories. I had assumed life's experience might mould you into a more agreeable person; however, I am confounded by your undeniable mental degeneration. In my opinion, mere vanity has convinced you of your holy vocation and I was not in the least part surprised you managed to get yourself defrocked! To say nothing of the unspeakable strain it must have caused your poor Alice! And while we are speaking plainly, may I say I find the fact that you are still one of Lord Ashby's spiritual advisors only makes me wonder should I worry more for his soul or his sanity!

BERKELEY. I see.

MADELEINE. None of this means I don't love you, Berkeley. And I am grateful for your introduction to Lord Ashby, but the sooner we deliver Hannah from your orbit and into the shelter of her new life in Northampton, the happier I will be.

BERKELEY. We will all be in the same orbit in Northampton, Madeleine, supping from the same well.

MADELEINE. You will not get past me again, Berkeley. And I will outlast you.

BERKELEY. Yes, perhaps I stand on the threshold of forever's mysterious twilight while you still reside in life's bright room of vitality where all appears commodious, but you cannot fool a fool. I have heard you – crying in the night, while you push away the hand that would help you.

MADELEINE. I cried while I slept! I was dreaming about those poor souls who lost their lives crowded into a dreadful terrace in Jamestown I had scarcely ever thought about! I cried at my own powerlessness and selfishness seeing how they had lived and died! What do you want me to say?

BERKELEY. Madeleine, we all heard it.

MADELEINE. Heard what?

BERKELEY. The great clap of thunder here – in this room – the night those wretches perished. Their pain was manifest here in that moment, surely to God, and yet you deny it. You see it all, Madeleine, I know you do. You, Grandie, your poor mother, Hannah, all of you have a shared capacity to apprehend the beyond. And you perhaps more than any of them have the darkest instinct for second sight.

MADELEINE. No, Berkeley.

BERKELEY. Do not lie! What is it about this place that it is such a conduit for desperate souls? Don't you care to know!?

MADELEINE. No I don't! Because there was always pain here at Mount Prospect! It was here before us and will be here after we are gone!

BERKELEY. But Hannah cannot endure it, can she? Nor could Edward. Yet while he sought the sweet embrace of the final escape, he never got out, did he!

MADELEINE. Oh, he got out. And yet he lives. And he will live wherever I live as long as I am alive. But not because he is trapped. What lives is my knowledge that what happened to him was all a stupid mistake. It was a mistake, but every single I day I believe I might somehow reach out and correct it – but I can't! Don't you see that? I can't!

There is a knock at the door.

Yes?

CLARE *appears at the door.*

CLARE. Excuse me, madam, Mrs Goulding has asked may we bring up the hot punch and scones?

BERKELEY. Thank you, Clare.

CLARE *leaves.* MADELEINE *crumples, taking a moment to compose herself.* BERKELEY *looks on uncertainly.*

Madeleine, I… I had no idea that you – (*Short pause.*) Well, I… Don't cry.

MRS GOULDING *rings a bell in the hallway.*

MADELEINE. Mrs Goulding is bringing the refreshments. I insist Hannah's last evening here be an easy and gay affair. It's the least she deserves.

BERKELEY. Well, of course.

MADELEINE. I'm warning you, Berkeley.

BERKELEY. I am the soul of joviality.

The door is opened by MRS GOULDING. CLARE *carries a large tray and* FINGAL *carries a bowl of hot punch, using napkins to protect his hands from the heat. Dusk is gathering and this scene gradually darkens.* FINGAL *is unsteady and spills some punch.* CLARE *goes to wipe it.*

Mrs Goulding's hot punch.

MRS GOULDING. Most certainly. Mr Fingal! I have it, I have it. (*Wipes up the drops.*) Scones on the mat, hot punch on the trivet, Mr Fingal.

BERKELEY. I trust you have been as moderate as ever with the rum?

MRS GOULDING. I would say I have been judicious.

BERKELEY. In that case, a measure for our generous hostess, quickly, Clare.

MADELEINE. Please, tend to yourselves first.

BERKELEY. No, no, a dram, Madeleine. Let us dispel the evening gloom. Thank you, Clare. That's right.

CLARE *helps* MRS GOULDING *fetch drinks for* MADELEINE *and* GRANDIE.

MADELEINE. Clare. Did you find Hannah?

CLARE. Yes, madam. She is changing in her room.

MADELEINE. Will you tell her we are waiting for her to come down, please?

CLARE. Yes, madam.

MADELEINE. Thank you, Clare.

As CLARE *goes,* AUDELLE *enters.*

BERKELEY. Ah, Mr Audelle's nose for impending hospitality remains impeccable.

AUDELLE. Yes, well, good evening. It's a lucky thing you rang that bell, Mrs Goulding. I was positively pole-axed up there in my room. Is that tea.

BERKELEY. Well, this will wake you up.

FINGAL *brings a drink for* AUDELLE.

AUDELLE. Oh, thank you.

MRS GOULDING. This hot rum punch was a recipe given me by my grandmother and has been the requisite post-hunting libation here at Mount Prospect for at least fifty years or more.

BERKELEY. You get a sniff of that, Audelle? It's not the gut-rot that you quaff by the pint in Chapelgate.

MRS GOULDING. On one famous occasion in 1797, a shout went up while sixty waited to dine: 'Forgo the meal,' they cried, having downed a barrel of this grog, 'Our thirst has eclipsed our appetite!' And nothing would do only except for me to go back down in the scullery – somewhat unsteadily myself – to mount a fresh barrel upon the fire.

BERKELEY. In the golden days here at Mount Prospect. The Earl in all his splendour yet. Grandie in gracious repose. The stories the Earl would regale us with – how his great-grandfather survived to see his one hundred and six living descendants, borne of four wives…

MRS GOULDING. 'And each uglier than the last.'

BERKELEY (*simultaneously*). 'And each more ugly than the last!'

HANNAH *enters with* CLARE.

MRS GOULDING. Miss Hannah may be glad her mother's line is in a straight descent from the early batch!

BERKELEY. The fresh flowers!

MADELEINE. You speak of my family, Mrs Goulding.

MRS GOULDING. Psh! They are practically my family too, madam, may I be so bold.

BERKELEY. Yes, where would Mount Prospect be without good old Mrs Goulding?

MRS GOULDING. I wonder!

BERKELEY. And Mr Fingal, of course. Remember, Fingal, those endless afternoons on the lawn, you were but a garsoon – and two or three summers in a row, if I'm not mistaken. When you were only ten or eleven. You followed that girl round and round.

MRS GOULDING. Oh yes!

BERKELEY. We talked of it so much and laughed so often! Your little moon-face behind her – her nut-brown hair always tied up in a white ribbon. Remember? She was perhaps a year or two older than you – who was she?

MRS GOULDING. She was the daughter of old Mr McElligot who used run the stables back then.

BERKELEY. Oh yes! Kate McElligot! And Fingal would follow behind her, follow her, follow her, while we all dined on blankets on the lawn. A hundred guests or more – until one day she finally turned round, in front of all of us and said, 'Will you leave me be, Fingal, or I'll break your feet to halt you!'

MRS GOULDING (*simultaneously*). '...I'll break your feet to halt you!' Yes...

They laugh.

BERKELEY. Do you remember? We were all in earshot and everybody laughed! Whatever happened to her?

Short pause.

FINGAL. She married my brother.

BERKELEY. Oh, yes. (*Beat.*) Yes... Yes. A lovely girl. (*Pause.*) Who will give us a song? Hannah?

HANNAH. I have a cold, Berkeley.

BERKELEY. A quiet song?

HANNAH shakes her head.

Oh, who will sing? Mrs Goulding?

MRS GOULDING. Oh dear me, no – it's far too early for me. Clare will sing.

BERKELEY. Do you sing, Clare?

MADELEINE. She has a sweet voice.

CLARE. Oh, I don't know!

BERKELEY. Oh, please do!

MRS GOULDING. Here, get yourself another dram of punch and Miss Hannah might play the piano for you?

BERKELEY. Oh, say you will. She will! I will pour you a dram. (*He takes* CLARE*'s glass.*) Hannah, please play for her.

CLARE. I have not sang for so long.

BERKELEY. No matter! No matter! What better reason not to refuse? Here, drink this. Hannah, what will you play?

MRS GOULDING. 'As I Roved Out'?

BERKELEY. Oh yes, so beautiful. Come listen to this, Audelle.

CLARE *and* HANNAH *look at each other in silent agreement.* CLARE *takes a drink and* HANNAH *goes to the piano and starts to play a simple accompaniment. She looks round at* CLARE.

CLARE. Oh my God…!

She laughs nervously and presently begins singing a plaintive rendition of an old ballad.

(*Sings.*)
    I dreamed I roamed on a bright May morning
    To view the meadows and flowers gay
    Whom should I spy but my own true lover
    As she sat under yon willow tree
    I took off my hat and I did salute her
    I did salute her most courageously
    When she turned around, well the tears fell from her
    Saying 'False young man you have deluded me…'
    At night I wake in my bed of slumber
    Thoughts of my love running in my mind
    As I turn around to embrace my darling
    Only darkness and grief do I find
    And I wish the Queen would call home her army
    From the West Indies, Amerikay and Spain
    And every man to his wedded woman
    In hope that you and I will meet again.

As the song ends, she is crying, as is MRS GOULDING.

HANNAH *sits quietly at the piano.* FINGAL *looks at the floor.* GRANDIE *leads the applause.*

MRS GOULDING. Isn't that lovely?

BERKELEY. Dear me. I am quite overcome now! Well done, Clare.

CLARE. I'm sorry, I... (*Dabs at her eyes.*)

BERKELEY. No, no. Such depth of emotion is only appropriate.

MADELEINE. That was beautiful, Clare.

CLARE. I'm sorry, madam.

MADELEINE *smiles reassuringly.*

BERKELEY. Has anyone lighter fare? Hannah?

HANNAH *shakes her head.*

One more song in your parlour?

HANNAH. I can't, no, I'm sorry.

GRANDIE (*suddenly sings with confidence*).
　　While the green moss grows upon the heather,
　　The briar grows upon the wood,
　　My love lies sleeping in a bower,
　　Where a lonely graveyard stood...

She applauds herself. The others clap.

BERKELEY. Thank you, Grandie.

MRS GOULDING. Very nice, Grandie.

HANNAH. Em... I just wanted to... em...

BERKELEY. Hannah...

HANNAH. Firstly, I wanted to thank everyone for all your efforts in the last few days. And thank Berkeley and Mr Audelle for travelling all this way to chaperone me and Mrs Goulding for making so many arrangements for my departure. And thank you, Mother, for putting my future so firmly at the centre of your concerns. However, something has happened to convince me that... I... I have decided... that I cannot go.

Pause.

BERKELEY (*with a slightly sickened laugh*). Hannah...

HANNAH. I am sorry and I want to apologise to everyone, but my mind has been made up and I feel unable to fulfil my commitment. I'm sorry.

She looks at MADELEINE. MADELEINE *looks down. All is silent.*

FINGAL. But she has to.

MRS GOULDING. Mr Fingal...

Pause.

FINGAL. She has to!

BERKELEY. Alright, Fingal...

FINGAL. Everything is arranged! This is... I mean... (*Laughs as though this just can't be happening.*) What are we going to do?

MADELEINE. Mr Fingal, we can discuss this later.

FINGAL (*points at* AUDELLE). No. No, hold on a minute. This is him. Isn't it? Yes, you.

AUDELLE. I beg your pardon?

FINGAL. They were supposed to escort her to her new home and settle the advancement of the estate, but they brought the undoing of the whole venture within them.

MADELEINE. Not now, Mr Fingal...

FINGAL. What?

MADELEINE. Not now!

CLARE. Willie...

FINGAL. Don't you 'not now' me, madam, now, not now, not now! (*To* AUDELLE.) Yous were seen. They were seen! You think we know nothing of your reputation, Mr Audelle? You come here with the Reverend, your heads bowed and your hands clasped together, but nothing is holy. I've heard all about you down in Jamestown, ha? Ha? What were they doing up at the Queen's Tomb?

MADELEINE. What?

FINGAL. Ask them that!

MADELEINE. When?

FINGAL. The other evening. When they were abroad on one of their nature walks.

AUDELLE. I may assure you, sir…!

FINGAL. No. You can't assure me. You were seen, sir. You were seen.

BERKELEY. What was seen? What are you talking about?

FINGAL. Miss Hannah was seen, running, and tears streaming down her face, all down the hill from the Queen's Tomb and your man here chasing after her and pursuing her down into the trees! Yes!

AUDELLE. No!

FINGAL. Where God knows what happened.

AUDELLE. No!

FINGAL. You were seen!

AUDELLE. I swear to you. I swear before you all…

FINGAL *grabs his rifle and points it at* AUDELLE.

FINGAL. What? Ha? What?

BERKELEY. Fingal!

MRS GOULDING. Mr Fingal, how dare you?

FINGAL. Ah, ah. Now, nobody leaves till we get some answers.

MADELEINE. Mr Fingal…

FINGAL (*attaining a semblance of responsibility through his drunken fog*). You have nothing to fear, madam. I know this type. We will have an answer.

MADELEINE. Put the gun down, Mr Fingal, this instant.

FINGAL. No, do not presume to order me about! I haven't been paid in over a year, so I may as well take his brains with me on my way out. What have I got left anyhow? I don't care. You deflowered her, sir, didn't you?

AUDELLE. I did not.

FINGAL. You defiled her!

AUDELLE. I did not.

FINGAL. You have rendered her worthless.

AUDELLE. No, sir.

FINGAL. Well, I will shoot you dead, sir.

He points the barrel at AUDELLE*'s head.*

MRS GOULDING (*shouts*). Mr Fingal!

FINGAL. What?

Short pause.

MRS GOULDING. You are not well!

FINGAL. I am well enough.

BERKELEY *puts himself between* FINGAL *and* AUDELLE.

BERKELEY. Surely to God this is a misunderstanding!

Hannah…

HANNAH. That's not what happened, Mr Fingal.

FINGAL. Do not be afraid, Miss Hannah. There is no need for any lies now. This man does not deserve your protection.

AUDELLE. Hannah, please… Tell him…

HANNAH. Mr Fingal, I don't know who saw us, but they have misinterpreted what they saw.

FINGAL. You say I am a liar?

HANNAH. No!

FINGAL. But you say none of it happened?

HANNAH. Not in that way.

FINGAL. Then in what way? What way?

HANNAH. Mr Audelle asked if I might show him the Queen's Tomb. There was still just enough light so we walked up the path, up out of the glen and on up the side of Knockmullen…

Short pause.

FINGAL. Go on.

HANNAH. Mr Audelle went on ahead of me as I was fatigued. When I reached the tomb I sat alone. After he had been out of sight for some minutes I realised there was someone sheltering within the mouth of the tomb, a man and a woman who were watching me. I called out for Mr Audelle to show them I wasn't alone. On hearing my voice, the figures in the tomb stumbled out. And as they lurched towards me I realised I was somehow seeing... myself and Mr Audelle! It was us but... our corpses... walking. And I... I turned and ran. I slipped and slid all the way back down to the road at Knockmullen, until Mr Audelle caught up to me. I was unable to tell him what had happened, as I scarcely know myself, but that is the truth, Mr Fingal, and that is the event which must have been witnessed and of which you have heard. For myself, I said nothing.

MADELEINE. Oh, Hannah...

HANNAH. What could I say? I am so tired of all the trouble I keep bringing on this house!

MADELEINE. You don't. You never do.

BERKELEY. The child saw some hungry souls sheltering in the hollow. The gloaming and her imagination did the rest. Indeed we are maybe thankful Mr Audelle was on hand, we should thank him.

Pause.

FINGAL. You gave her that laudanum to drink, didn't you?

AUDELLE. No, I... I... (*Laughs.*)

MADELEINE. Laudanum?

FINGAL. Laudanum. And it has unbalanced the child.

MRS GOULDING. No, sir!

AUDELLE. No, no... It's merely a tincture I use as a cough suppressant.

MRS GOULDING. I know what laudanum is, Mr Audelle. You were trying to get Clare to procure it for you in Jamestown and I forbade it!

FINGAL. And me, like a bloody fool getting it for you.

MRS GOULDING. You got it for him?!

FINGAL. I didn't know the devil was going to give it to a child! A child!

AUDELLE. No! I meant no harm...

FINGAL. No harm? Look at her! Look at her!

BERKELEY. I'm sure Mr Audelle only wanted to help Hannah suppress her cough.

FINGAL (*disparaging*). Ah! Rather he wanted to render her senseless and have his way. I know that game!

HANNAH. No. I asked him for it. Yes, I took it, but I asked him for it!

MADELEINE. Oh, Hannah! Why?

HANNAH. Because I needed to see the future. And I did. I saw it. We performed a rite and I saw it!

MADELEINE. You performed a what?

BERKELEY. No, no… Not a rite.

HANNAH. We performed a rite in here. And I saw it.

MADELEINE. What do you mean, 'a rite'?

BERKELEY. No, no, no, no, no, no, no, not a rite. Some prayers merely, a few words in order to…

FINGAL. Why don't you shut up, Reverend? I'm tired of hearing your interminable voice, and I don't want to hear another damn word out of you. I am in charge here tonight so you can just shut up. And you too, Mrs Goulding.

MRS GOULDING. I never said a word!

FINGAL. Yes, well, don't.

MRS GOULDING. Yes, well, I didn't.

FINGAL. Yes, well, don't.

MRS GOULDING. Well, you have said enough. You gobaloon.

GRANDIE. Let her sing!

MRS GOULDING. Yes, shush, Grandie, shush now.

MADELEINE. Berkeley, you better tell me what you did or I'll take this gun and shoot you myself.

HANNAH. No. I needed to understand what was happening to me, Mama. But I know now I was seeing and hearing what is yet to be! Not the past! I have never seen the past. I saw that the child I have heard crying here is my child, the child I will never know because I will perish bringing it into the world.

MADELEINE. No!

HANNAH. After I go to Northampton. Yes.

MADELEINE. Hannah, no…

HANNAH. Yes! And I saw that I would forever wander looking for my baby. I have seen what eternity holds for me.

MADELEINE. No! This is preposterous!

HANNAH. I will be locked in a room. And that room is death and there is no door from which to leave. I saw it all!

MADELEINE. No!

FINGAL. Right. (*To* AUDELLE.) You see what yous have done? You see it? You put the girl in a state like that, and you drive her insane? What possible purpose can you have? You have no purpose. No purpose but to defile and destroy and degrade. (*Aims the rifle to shoot* AUDELLE.) What conceivable good can your presence bring in the world?

BERKELEY. Wait, Fingal…

MADELEINE. Mr Fingal…

AUDELLE. No purpose.

Pause.

FINGAL. You brought this on yourself, Mr Audelle, for none can make sense of your actions.

HANNAH. Or your actions, Mr Fingal!

FINGAL. Ha?

HANNAH. I say what of your actions?

FINGAL. My actions?

HANNAH. You skulk in here and sit in judgement on all of us like the coward who can only hold his head up when he has a weapon. What do you know about fairness or rightness, you ignorant lout?

FINGAL. You dare to speak to me like that? You were always mad. All of yous always were. Look at your Grandie. She's never had a bloody clue what in the name of Jaysus is going on! Or your father? Who brought this whole place to its knees before hanging himself in front of his own child practically! Your cold-hearted mother there, hardly even of this earth so remote and incomprehensible are her secret wishes!

MADELEINE. You are drunk, Mr Fingal.

FINGAL. I'm not drunk. Nor was I drunk all those nights I was fetched up here to lock that mad bastard in a room upstairs while you and I sat here with the long hours ticking by.

MADELEINE. You are drunk, sir, and you will put that gun down this instant.

She goes to grab him. He pushes her away roughly.

BERKELEY. Fingal!

FINGAL. I don't care, do you hear me?! I've had it up to here with all of you. No longer will I walk out of this bloody house, ignorant of the forces that keep me perpetually on my knees! No longer!

MADELEINE. No, sir! You are drunk, sir! What ever will you think when you have come to your senses?

FINGAL. I am in my senses.

MADELEINE. Well, what do you want? What are you asking of us?

FINGAL (*drunkenly*). What?

HANNAH. Mr Fingal cannot bear to come to his senses for then he must face what he has done.

FINGAL. I'm in my senses, don't you worry about that.

HANNAH. Oh yes, and were you in your senses when you did what you did and went and beat James Furay? Have you seen him? (*Pause.*) Have you?!

MRS GOULDING. What happened to James Furay?

HANNAH. Tell them what you did.

Pause.

MADELEINE. What did he do?

FINGAL. No... I...

MRS GOULDING. Is he alright?

HANNAH. I have seen him, Mr Fingal. I went to say goodbye to him today. And I found him in the gate lodge. Yes. With no fire lit. No candle burning. I found him curled up in the cold of the loft, Mr Fingal, lying in his own mess of congealed blood and pus.

Pause.

FINGAL. Yes... well...

MRS GOULDING. What happened to him?

Pause.

What happened to him?

FINGAL (*quietly*). I beat him.

MRS GOULDING. What?

FINGAL. I beat him! I beat him!

MRS GOULDING. What did you beat him for?

FINGAL. I had to.

HANNAH. You had to? He couldn't get down the ladder from his bed by himself. He couldn't even look at me. He forbade me to fetch the doctor. He begged me not to tell anyone. I bathed his wounds which are so deep and vicious he will surely be marked for the rest of his life. I couldn't even bandage him for fear the cloth would only stick into his wounds causing him greater agony – and I knew I was supposed to be leaving here tomorrow!? We both wept there, Mr Fingal, each of us hiding their tears from the other. I, for the misery I was about to leave him in. But do you know why he wept? Out of shame, sir! For shame! That boy who was brought up as my brother, and was almost as much as your son! But you are not worthy of him, Mr Fingal. How can I go and marry a man I hardly know when I am unable to provide affection for those I truly love?! You have caused me to stay, Mr Fingal. Not Mr Audelle, not Berkeley or my mother, but you, sir! So do what you will and go home.

FINGAL *looks at them all.*

MADELEINE. Mr Fingal. Why would you do such a thing?

Pause.

FINGAL. For you.

MADELEINE. For me?

FINGAL. I wanted to show you I can be strong. I wanted to show you I can bring discipline to this place, and I'm not just some... joke.

MADELEINE. But, Mr Fingal...

FINGAL. You were so angry about the horses! You told me to put the boy before his responsibilities!

MADELEINE. But I would never have wanted you to beat him,
Mr Fingal!

FINGAL. It was the morning after all the buildings collapsed! I'd been
up the whole night, sitting up on my own, knowing how bad things
were going to get now. You never think how hard it is for me. To
have to show my face in Jamestown! Even my own family are
ashamed of me! They hate me all round the country all around here
because of my loyalty to you. No one respects me. But I stay. I stay.
And I stay because I am faithful to you – (*Short pause, he looks at
the floor.*) and because I've always loved you! I can't help it! You
don't know how hard I've tried to ignore it. To banish it! But then
once again your eyes fall on me and my heart submits. It's never
stopped. It's beyond my abilities. I walk around with no money in
my pockets, it doesn't matter, the locals and their keepers laugh at
me, it doesn't matter. I see your face in my mind and it just doesn't
matter because I know I would live in a moment forever if you
might just deign to put out your hand to me. Even if it were my last
moment on this earth. Don't you see that? Of course you do. You
have seen it. You know it. But what do you do? You use it. You use
it to keep me, and use me. And you know what? I don't care, do you
see? I don't care because I still love you! (*Pause. Looks at them all.*)
It's all just a big trick though, really, I suppose, isn't it? It's just a big
joke that keeps us all running around in God's playground for his
amusement. And we all think it's so real…

Pause. FINGAL *is drowning in his own confusion. He has ended
up on the floor near* MADELEINE. *She reaches out, touches his
face tenderly then brings her lips to his. They kiss for a moment
and then lay their heads together, their foreheads touching.*

BERKELEY. Well… There now, my good man. That's alright.

BERKELEY *goes to* FINGAL *and takes the gun from him gently.*

We are all overwrought. Yes. That's alright. A little drink of water.

He hands the gun to CLARE *behind* FINGAL*'s back. She takes it
out to the hall quietly and comes back to stand in the doorway.*

Mrs Goulding.

MRS GOULDING. Yes, of course.

She pours some water to bring to BEREKLEY.

BERKELEY. There's a good man. Let us walk out to the steps and
get us some fresh air, shall we? Yes…

BERKELEY *signals for* MRS GOULDING *to open the doors to the conservatory, which she does.* BERKELEY *leads* FINGAL *towards the conservatory.* FINGAL *turns to the room.*

FINGAL. I'm... I'm sorry.

BERKELEY. That's alright. Come on now, there's a good man.

BERKELEY *brings* FINGAL *out through the conservatory.*

MADELEINE. Are you alright, Mr Audelle?

AUDELLE. Yes.

MRS GOULDING. I don't know what has come over him. He has lost his mind completely. Here, Mr Audelle, sit down, take a drink.

AUDELLE. Thank you.

MRS GOULDING. And Grandie. Poor Grandie.

AUDELLE. Is she alright?

MADELEINE. She'll be fine.

MRS GOULDING *gets them some drinks.*

Are you alright, Clare?

CLARE. Yes, ma'am.

MADELEINE. You are gone quite pale. Will you sit by the fire?

CLARE. No thank you, ma'am.

MADELEINE. Are you sure?

CLARE. Yes, ma'am.

Pause.

MRS GOULDING. Yes, well. I will make a bread poultice to bring down to James Furay.

MADELEINE. But bring him up to stay here tonight, please, Mrs Goulding.

MRS GOULDING. Yes, madam.

MADELEINE. Can we light some more candles please?

MRS GOULDING. We will, of course. Clare, come and help me light the house.

CLARE. Yes, ma'am.

MRS GOULDING *and* CLARE *leave. Pause.*

HANNAH. I'm sorry, Mama.

MADELEINE. No.

AUDELLE. Do not fear your future, Miss Hannah. A child you cannot save, being locked in a room from which you cannot escape. That is not your future, I can assure you.

HANNAH. How so?

AUDELLE. Because you saw my present, not your future. The locked room is this moment I may never escape from. The child you hear crying is the ever waking dream child whose sobs I dose myself to quiet. She is the child I abandoned. Such is your gift, you saw Hell, Miss Hannah. But it was my hell. The nightmare unto which each morning delivers me and each evening awakens me to contemplate. Do not fear your future. It is as open as the sky. I must ask you ladies to forgive me. I must administer my medicine.

AUDELLE *bows to them and goes out.*

GRANDIE (*listening*). The old dog.

MADELEINE. Are you alright, Grandie?

GRANDIE. The blind old dog used live here long ago.

MADELEINE. What of him?

GRANDIE. Can you hear him? Barking?

Pause. There is a sudden deafening bang in the hallway which shakes the whole house. They are startled into silence.

MADELEINE. What is it?

HANNAH *steps towards the hallway door.* BERKELEY *comes in through the conservatory doors holding a candle, as smoke drifts in from the hallway.*

BERKELEY. Did you hear it? Did you hear it again?

Offstage, we hear CLARE *scream and run down the stairs.* HANNAH *stands looking into the hallway, her hands up to her face.* CLARE *comes in.*

CLARE. It's Mr Audelle! (*Short pause.*) He got the rifle!

BERKELEY. Where is he?

CLARE. He's in the hallway! (*Turns and goes out.*) Oh, Mrs Goulding! Mrs Goulding!

The lights change as everyone but GRANDIE *drifts out to the hallway. An afternoon materialises around* GRANDIE *as she sits there. It is two weeks later, Friday June 7th.* FINGAL *comes in, puts some hardbacked ledgers on the table and stands waiting, much as he did in the first scene of the play. He wears a new dark coat with brass buttons. His hair is brushed across his head and his black eye is healed.* MRS GOULDING *comes into the room with a shawl round her shoulders.*

MRS GOULDING. Well, Mr Fingal.

FINGAL. Mrs Goulding.

MRS GOULDING. Your arrangements are all made?

FINGAL. Yes. We leave tonight.

MRS GOULDING. Yes?

FINGAL. We'll be married in Swords in County Dublin and sail for Liverpool next Tuesday morning.

MRS GOULDING. When do you leave for Canada?

FINGAL. In the following week. Clare's sister will house us.

MRS GOULDING. Very good. Clare is a clever girl.

FINGAL. I know.

MRS GOULDING. Well, look after her. (*Pause.*) She is your salvation, Mr Fingal.

FINGAL. I have left a copy of the accounts here for madam.

MRS GOULDING. Yes, she will be into you herself in a moment. The Colonel is delayed. You heard he shot at some intruders last night.

FINGAL. Yes, I heard. (*Short pause.*) Is it true you will be kept on?

MRS GOULDING. Yes, the Colonel has asked me personally to keep the house for his daughter. James Furay will remain in the gate lodge and act as groundsman to the estate.

FINGAL. Well, that's… He'll make an excellent groundsman.

Pause.

MRS GOULDING. Yes, well, I wish you luck, sir.

FINGAL. Thank you.

She shakes his hand. MADELEINE *comes in.*

MRS GOULDING. Would Grandie like some tea? I think she would. Are you warm enough there, Grandie?

She goes and settles some cushions around GRANDIE.

I'll bring us up some nice soup, will I?

MADELEINE. Thank you, Mrs Goulding.

MRS GOULDING. Yes, not at all.

She leaves.

MADELEINE. Are these the accounts?

FINGAL. Yes, madam, in order of year, most recent on top.

MADELEINE. Grim reading no doubt. Have you received your money?

FINGAL. Yes. Thank you. (*Hands her a small bag with some coins in it.*) I wondered if I might give you this to pass on to James Furay for me. I haven't had a chance to… to see him.

MADELEINE. That's very generous. I'm sure he will be most grateful. You have enough for your passage?

FINGAL. Yes, we'll be fine.

MADELEINE. Well, congratulations.

FINGAL. Thank you.

MADELEINE. When is the wedding?

FINGAL. Next Monday. In Swords, in County Dublin. A relative of Clare's knows the curate there. We sail for Liverpool on Tuesday.

MADELEINE. I'm very pleased for you both.

Pause.

FINGAL. I trust Miss Hannah is in good health.

MADELEINE. Yes, I had a letter from her just this morning. She is arrived in Northampton. All is well. As soon as I have settled my affairs here with Colonel Bennett, myself and Grandie shall join her.

FINGAL. Well, please send her my congratulations and I wish you all the very best.

MADELEINE. Thank you.

FINGAL. Right, well. (*Gathers himself to leave but halts near the door.*) Madeleine.

MRS GOULDING *returns.*

MRS GOULDING. Madam, a boy came to the door and says the Colonel will be here in thirty minutes. They are inspecting the back gate.

MADAM. Thank you, Mrs Goulding.

MRS GOULDING. Is it chilly? Will I light the fire?

MRS GOULDING *goes to the fireplace and rakes it with the poker.*

MADELEINE. Light it for Grandie. I don't particularly want to encourage the Colonel to stay. Bring some tea for him in the small parlour and we may conduct our business in there.

MRS GOULDING. Very good. I haven't forgotten you, Grandie. Wrap up there, we'll light this for you in a minute and I'll be back with hot soup in the flea's time.

FINGAL. Right. Well, I'll... Goodbye.

MADELEINE. Goodbye, Mr Fingal. Thank you.

FINGAL. Goodbye.

MRS GOULDING. Goodbye, Mr Fingal.

FINGAL. Goodbye.

He leaves. Pause.

MRS GOULDING. Right.

MADELEINE. Thank you, Mrs Goulding.

MRS GOULDING (*tone of 'That's that...'*). Now...

She leaves.

MADELEINE *looks out the window then starts to peruse the ledgers.*

GRANDIE. A boy once proposed to me who was from Northampton, but Daddy wouldn't brook it. He had a kind face. He wasn't good-looking but he was kind. Yes. He said he thought his feelings might kill him.

MADELIENE. Who did?

GRANDIE. He said he hadn't slept for three weeks.

MADELEINE. Oh dear.

GRANDIE. He was very tired.

MADELEINE. Yes, well, he must have been.

GRANDIE. Well. He married in the end. And I married.

MADELEINE. Yes.

GRANDIE. He wasn't good-looking but… he was… You always look after me so well, Madeleine. Don't think I don't know.

MADELEINE. What's that?

GRANDIE. I say even when I don't know who is here or how old I am, I always feel safe when I see you. And you know that love is a gift from God.

MADELEINE. Well, that's good, isn't it?

GRANDIE. Yes. You are a good mother, Madeleine.

MADELEINE. Am I?

GRANDIE. You don't mind?

MADELEINE (*smiles*). How could I mind?

GRANDIE *shrugs*.

Of course I don't mind!

BERKELEY *comes in. He looks a bit sleepy. He wears a woollen cardigan.*

Oh, hello, did you have a good sleep?

BERKELEY. Yes. Too good. Have I missed the Colonel?

MADELEINE. No, he was delayed. Did you hear he shot at some intruders on his estate last night?

BERKELEY. No!

MADELEINE. Yes, well, he's on his way.

BERKELEY. Intruders!

MADELEINE. Yes.

BERKELEY. Right. Oh dear, well… I thought I should say hello.

MADELEINE. We received a letter from Northampton this morning. Hannah has arrived.

BERKELEY. Oh, that is good news. And… she is well?

MADELEINE. She slept soundly, remarking on the peculiar silence of the estate.

BERKELEY (*concurring*). Yes.

MADELEINE *brings him the letter*.

MADELEINE. Lord Ashby sends you his personal condolences about Mr Audelle.

MADELEINE *goes back to her work*.

BERKELEY. How kind. (*Glancing over the letter*.) I had the strangest dreams. I woke up feeling quite anxious, I must say. You do think we are doing the right thing, Madeleine? Leaving Audelle here? When we go to Northampton?

MADELEINE. Oh yes. I should think he likes it here, Berkeley. The graveyard is so quiet and such a peaceful place to rest. And I know the Colonel would never mind you paying your respects when we return on a visit. Leave him here, Berkeley.

BERKELEY. Yes, I know. You are right. I just… I mean, I was his family.

MADELEINE. Of course. And you were very good to him, Berkeley. (*Short pause*.) Now, Mrs Goulding is bringing some soup up for Grandie. Will you have some? You will.

BERKELEY. Yes, Madeleine. Thank you.

MADELEINE. Good. (*Looks out the window*.) Oh. Will you sit with Grandie for a few minutes, Berkeley?

BERKELEY. Of course I will.

MADELEINE *picks up the ledgers and makes to leave*.

Good luck.

MADELEINE. Thanks.

BERKELEY. I know you will charm a price way over the odds from him.

MADELEINE. Oh, stop it now.

BERKELEY. Will you tell the Colonel I must say hello before he goes?

MADELEINE. I will.

BERKELEY. Madeleine?

She halts at the door.

I… appreciate your… understanding.

MADELEINE. What's to understand?

She leaves. BERKELEY *opens the letter and brings it to the window for better light.*

BERKELEY. Well, Grandie, we'll all be going soon now, won't we?

GRANDIE. Yes.

BERKELEY. We'll all ride a cock horse to Banbury Cross. And delicious soup on the way. We are such lucky souls are we not?

GRANDIE. We are, yes!

GRANDIE *sings softly, almost silently, to herself while she goes to the mantelpiece. She gently touches some of the ornaments there, glancing at herself in the mirror.* MRS GOULDING *brings in a tray with some bowls, and lays the table for their lunch, then leaves to fetch the food.* BERKELEY *stands in the window, absorbed in the letter with his hand to his face.* GRANDIE*'s singing fades to silence while she stands looking high into the mirror.* BERKELEY*'s attention is drawn from his letter. He observes* GRANDIE *as the lights gradually fade.*

End.

THE DANCE OF DEATH

After August Strindberg

This version of *The Dance of Death* was first performed at the Trafalgar Studios, London, as part of the Donmar Trafalgar season, on 13 December 2012. The cast was as follows:

KURT	Daniel Lapaine
THE CAPTAIN	Kevin R. McNally
ALICE	Indira Varma
Director	Titas Halder
Designer	Richard Kent
Lighting Designer	Richard Howell
Composer and Sound Designer	Alex Baranowski
Movement Director	Laïla Diallo

Characters

THE CAPTAIN, *at a coastal artillery fortress,*
    late fifties/sixties
ALICE, *his wife, forties*
KURT, *newly appointed Master of Quarantine, forties*

Setting

An island near a port in Sweden, 1900.

ACT ONE

The interior of a round fortress tower built of granite.

Upstage are a large pair of doors with glass windowpanes, through which can be seen the sky at dusk and a distant shoreline with some lights. To the side of each door is a window.

There is a dresser with some framed pictures and books; a piano; a table with some chairs; an armchair; a mounted mercurial barometer and a desk with a telegraph machine. There is also a kind of 'bar' – a high table against one wall – with glasses and bottles of liquor with a mirror above it. There are a few rugs, but the walls are bare granite and nothing can take away a feeling of foreboding – this building used to be a jailhouse. On one wall hangs a portrait of ALICE *in costume on stage in a production twenty-five years ago.*

There is a lamp suspended from the ceiling. A heavy door, stage right, leads to steps going down to the kitchen, and beside this is a large free-standing hat stand on which hang coats, pieces of military equipment: gloves, helmets and swords.

It is a mild autumn evening. The doors are open. The sea is dark and still.

ALICE, *an attractive woman in her forties, sits at the table listlessly staring into space.*

The CAPTAIN, *a well-built but tired-looking man in his sixties, is sitting in the armchair, fingering an unlit cigar. He is dressed in a worn dress uniform with riding boots and spurs. A discarded newspaper lies on his lap. In the distance they can hear snatches of a military band drifting in on the wind.*

CAPTAIN. Play something?

ALICE. Play what?

CAPTAIN. Whatever you like.

ALICE. You never like what I play.

CAPTAIN. Well, you never like what I play.

ALICE. Edgar, you can't play. Do you want the doors left open?

CAPTAIN. I don't mind.

ALICE. Well, are you going to smoke that cigar?

CAPTAIN. You know, I'm not sure strong tobacco agrees with me any more.

ALICE. You should take up a pipe.

CAPTAIN. A *pipe*?!

ALICE. Why not? Why deny yourself your 'only pleasure', as you call it.

CAPTAIN. Pleasure? Hmph, I've forgotten what that is!

ALICE. Well, don't ask me to describe it for you! Have a glass of whiskey.

CAPTAIN (*shudders at the idea*). Better not. What's for dinner?

ALICE. How would I know? Go down and ask Christine.

CAPTAIN. Isn't this the time of year for mackerel? Autumn?

ALICE. I suppose so.

CAPTAIN. Yes, it's autumn – outside and in. You see, what you do is, you take a mackerel, grill it, drizzle a little lemon on it, serve it up with a huge glass of white Zinfandel – and one doesn't feel quite like blowing one's brains out any more, does one?

ALICE. You're asking the wrong person.

CAPTAIN (*smacking his lips*). Have we any of that Zinfandel left, chilling away down there in the wine cellar?

ALICE. We don't have a wine cellar.

CAPTAIN. What happened to our wine cellar?

ALICE. You mean the laundry room?

CAPTAIN. I mean the wine cellar, where we keep the wine.

ALICE. There is no wine.

CAPTAIN. Well, this is not good enough. We have to stock up for our silver wedding celebrations.

ALICE. You really want to celebrate that?

CAPTAIN. Well, of course I do. Don't you?

ALICE. I thought we might show more decorum by keeping our long miserable mistake to ourselves.

CAPTAIN. Oh come, Alice! We've had fun. (*Beat.*) Now and then. And soon it will be all over. We'll be dead, and all that's left is your rotten carcass. And all it's good for is to fertilise the cabbages.

ALICE. So we go through all of this just for the sake of the cabbages?

CAPTAIN (*picking his paper up*). Listen, I don't make the rules.

ALICE. Well, it seems like a stupid waste if you ask me. Was there any post?

CAPTAIN (*affirmatively, while he reads*). Mm-hm.

ALICE. The butcher's bill?

CAPTAIN. Mm-hm.

ALICE. And?

CAPTAIN (*still reading, he takes the bill from his pocket and holds it out to her*). I can't read his writing.

ALICE (*coming to take it*). That's old age, you know.

CAPTAIN. What?

ALICE. Your eyes.

CAPTAIN. Rubbish!

ALICE. Well, I can read it.

CAPTAIN. Your scrawl is worse than his.

ALICE (*reading*). Oh my God! Can we pay this?

CAPTAIN. Of course we can. Just not at the moment.

ALICE. Then when? In a year's time when your miniscule pension kicks in? Which won't even be enough for the doctor's bills when you're sick.

CAPTAIN. Sick? How dare you? I've never been sick. Not one day in forty-four years of military service!

ALICE. That's not what the doctor says.

CAPTAIN (*dismissively*). 'The doctor'… What does he know?

ALICE. Well, who else would know?

CAPTAIN. Now, you listen to me. There's nothing wrong with me and there never has been. Real soldiers don't get sick. They just drop dead where they stand, in their boots. Bang! Just like that. And I have twenty good years left in me, you know…

ALICE (*simultaneously with him*). 'Twenty good years left in me…' Yes, well you're half-deaf already. You probably can't hear that music is coming from the doctor's house. You do know he's throwing a party for the entire command this evening.

CAPTAIN. Yes, I do know actually, and do you want to know why I wasn't invited? Shall I tell you? Because I refuse to mix with that scum – and because they all know I'm not afraid to speak my mind, that's why.

ALICE. You think everyone is scum.

CAPTAIN. They *are* scum!

ALICE. Except you.

CAPTAIN. Hey, I have always behaved in a decent, civilised manner, no matter what life has ever thrown in my path. You know I am not scum! (*Beat.*) Alice.

Pause.

ALICE. Do you want a game of cards?

CAPTAIN. Not if you're going to cheat, I don't.

ALICE. I won't!

ALICE *gets the cards and starts dealing.*

Yes, well, apparently it's the first time the regimental band has ever been given permission to perform at a private party.

CAPTAIN. Well, if I spent the bulk of *my* working life creeping round the garrison, sucking up to the Colonel all day, I could have the regimental band in here while I ate my bloody breakfast if I wanted! But I don't. (*Takes up his cards.*) That doctor was always a little dirtbag.

ALICE. There was a time I used to be quite friendly with Gerda. Until I found out she was backbiting me.

CAPTAIN. They're all backbiters! What's trumps?

ALICE. Where are your glasses?

CAPTAIN. They don't work. They've never worked, just tell me.

ALICE. Spades.

CAPTAIN. Spades! Typical...

ALICE (*playing*). None of the new officers' wives ever speak to me.

CAPTAIN. Who cares? We're better off. I don't even like parties.

ALICE. Well, that's alright for you – and even for me, but what about the children? They have no friends.

She reaches to take a trick.

CAPTAIN. I'll take that, thank you.

He takes the trick.

ALICE. What are you doing?

CAPTAIN. Six and eight – fifteen.

ALICE. Six and eight are only fourteen.

CAPTAIN (*bluffing*). Yes, six and eight, fourteen, and two, sixteen, it's your trick. That's what I said. Take it.

ALICE. What are you talking about? You should go to bed.

CAPTAIN. No, no. Deal.

He gets up and wanders to the window, listening to music in the distance, a rousing military march with drums pounding.

Listen. That's the full band! You can hear it all the way over here! Can you imagine how loud it must be in his little house? What an idiot.

ALICE (*dealing cards*). Do you think Kurt has been invited?

CAPTAIN (*as though sick of talking about Kurt*). Kurt! Kurt, Kurt, Kurt, Kurt, Kurt, Kurt! (*Short pause.*) My spies tell me he arrived on the seven o'clock train this morning so he'll have had plenty of time to get his glad rags on. Although I notice he hasn't managed to drag himself up here to say hello!

ALICE. It's quite an honour when you think about it. My cousin being appointed the Quarantine Master.

CAPTAIN. Sharing your family name is no honour, darling.

ALICE (*with sudden anger*). Now you listen to me, if you want to start dragging families into it, I'm happy to do that all night!

CAPTAIN. Alright, alright…

ALICE. We've agreed to stop doing that!

CAPTAIN. Alright, calm down, let's not start all that nonsense all over again. It was just a joke. (*Pause.*) All the same. Quarantine Master. He'll have a lot of clout.

ALICE. Really?

CAPTAIN. Oh, yes. They'll all bow and scrape before him. You know what they're like.

ALICE. Will he be a kind of doctor?

CAPTAIN (*disparagingly*). Of course not! Can you imagine a lunatic like him knuckling down to medical studies? No. He'll just be another overpaid pen-pusher, that's all.

ALICE. Well, I'm glad things have come right for him. He's never had it easy.

CAPTAIN. He cost me a bloody fortune, Alice! Leaving his wife and children in the gutter, chasing round after some whore! He's a disgrace!

ALICE. How can we know what goes on in any marriage, Edgar? Let's give him the benefit.

CAPTAIN. Oh, please. Gallivanting about in America ever since! And it's a shame, because even though he was such a loose cannon, he always managed to be such an absorbing philosopher, debating with me, far into the night!

ALICE. You only say that because he always gave in to you.

CAPTAIN. Gave in? He was invariably crushed by the weight of my superior logic – that's all! There's no point even beginning a philosophical discussion with half the dimwits on this island. Was ever a greater horde of imbeciles crowded into so small a space? I doubt it.

ALICE. Do you think it's just a coincidence?

CAPTAIN. What?

ALICE. That Kurt should arrive just in time for our silver wedding anniversary?

CAPTAIN. Well, I hope it's a coincidence! You think he'd come all this way just to witness the dregs of his handiwork? What a terrifying idea!

ALICE. Well, he did bring us together.

CAPTAIN. He certainly did! And what a match!

ALICE *laughs*.

You may laugh. It's me that's had to live with it!

ALICE. And me!

CAPTAIN. I mean you too. I mean us both.

He laughs ruefully. For a moment they are linked by their pain.

ALICE. Oh, Edgar, just think, if I had stayed in the theatre…!

CAPTAIN. Oh, here we go!

ALICE. Everyone I started out with is a celebrated artist now!

CAPTAIN. I think I will have that drink.

He goes to pour himself a large whiskey at his 'bar'.

ALICE. They're all such big stars!

CAPTAIN. You know what we need here? A low rail along here, see? So you can lean your boot up here and perch on the bar. Pretend you're having an evening drink at the American Club in Copenhagen.

ALICE. That's a good idea! (*Joins him.*) We can stand here and pretend we're in Copenhagen when we were happy.

He pours her a drink.

CAPTAIN. Do you remember? The late-night lamb stew upstairs in Nimb's? Eh? God, my mouth is watering just thinking about it.

ALICE. The concerts at the Tivoli. And the plays.

CAPTAIN. The plays! You see, that's what it is – your taste was always just that little bit too…

ALICE. Too what?

CAPTAIN. Refined. That's what makes you so unhappy.

ALICE. You should be proud to have a wife with refined taste!

CAPTAIN. No, I mean, I am, but…

ALICE. I've heard you – on more than one occasion – bragging about how, when you first clapped eyes on me… on stage at the St John Playhouse…

CAPTAIN (*looking out of the window at the darkening sky*). Listen to that.

ALICE.…When you've had enough whiskey, of course…

CAPTAIN. It's time for dancing. They've gone into three-four time.

ALICE (*listens*). It's the Alcazar Waltz. (*Lost in thought.*) I used to believe I could dance all evening to the Alcazar waltz.

CAPTAIN. Do you think you still could?

ALICE. Of course I could. What do you mean, do I think I still could?

CAPTAIN. Well, I mean…

ALICE. I'm fifteen years younger than you!

CAPTAIN. That makes us the same age though.

ALICE. How do you deduce that?

CAPTAIN. Because the woman is supposed to be younger.

ALICE. How pathetic, Edgar. Just face it – you're an old man. And I'm still young.

CAPTAIN. Well, flirt away to your heart's content then, Alice.

ALICE. I never flirt!

CAPTAIN. Well, you should, shouldn't you?

They look at each other for a moment.

ALICE. Do you think we should light the lamp?

CAPTAIN. I suppose so.

ALICE. Will you call Christine?

She goes and gazes out at the sea.

CAPTAIN. Well, of course.

The CAPTAIN *goes to a speaking tube by the wall and blows the whistle. He listens for a moment then speaks into it.*

Oh, Christine? Hello, how are you, my dear? (*Listens, then speaks into it again.*) Oh. Oh, I see. Oh well, no, because we were just remarking it looks as though may be nearing twilight now so, if you had a spare moment, we were wondering if you might be able to make your way up to us.

ALICE *glares at him, irritated by his deference to the maid. The* CAPTAIN *listens and speaks into the tube again.*

Well, you see, because it would be very nice if we might have the lamp lit! Ha ha ha. (*Listens.*) Oh. Oh, I see, well, in that case...

ALICE. Oh, for God's sake!

ALICE *goes to the tube and pushes the* CAPTAIN *away.*

Christine, get up here and light the lamp. Straight away! (*Listens.*) What's that got to do with it? (*Listens.*) What did you say? How dare you speak to me like that when I ask you a question?

CAPTAIN. Now, Alice, just...

ALICE (*into the tube*). You are an impudent brat and you are lucky I don't come straight down there and thrash you with the Captain's belt! What's that?

CAPTAIN (*trying to get the tube*). Alice!

ALICE (*holds the* CAPTAIN *at bay, listening to the tube, then replies to Christine*). Yes, well, pack your bags then, I don't care. Go on then!

ALICE *slams the tube back in its holder.*

CAPTAIN. Oh, Alice...

ALICE. Do you think she'll go?

CAPTAIN. Well, I wouldn't be surprised after that! We'll be in a right fix then!

ALICE. It's your fault, you know!

CAPTAIN. How is it my fault?

ALICE. You always mollycoddle the servants!

CAPTAIN. Rubbish!

ALICE. You ruin them so they're no good!

CAPTAIN. What are you talking about? They're always perfectly polite with me.

ALICE. That's because for some perverse reason you always ingratiate yourself with your inferiors, and then you look down your nose at your superiors – and you wonder why you've never risen up the ranks!

CAPTAIN. Oh, you know all about the army now, do you?

ALICE. I know they can spot a bully and a coward!

CAPTAIN. Oh, shut up!

ALICE. Yes! And a tinpot tyrant when they see one!

CAPTAIN. Yes, you'd know all about that.

ALICE. Do you really think she'll go?

CAPTAIN. Just go down quickly and apologise, say you have a migraine.

ALICE. You do it.

CAPTAIN. What? And have you on at me all night for flirting with the maid? No fear.

ALICE. Look at my hands. If she leaves they'll be ruined doing the housework.

CAPTAIN. And I'll tell you one thing – we won't get another one to come out here. That new lot who work the ferry can't keep their hands off a young girl. And even if she made it here for an interview, our sentries would never stop trying to maul her.

ALICE. Yes, you really manage to keep your sentries in line, too, don't you? Every time I go down in the kitchen, they're either chasing Christine round the kitchen table or else they're helping themselves to the last of our bread and butter and you never say a word!

CAPTAIN (*involuntarily sotto*). Listen, if I spoke to them like that, they'd clear off to the mainland. Then we'd have no troop, no commission, and no function – we'd be kicked out!

ALICE. We can't afford to feed them, Edgar! We have nothing for ourselves!

CAPTAIN. That's why I'm encouraging the high command to sign my letter – petitioning the King.

Pause.

ALICE. The King?

CAPTAIN. Yes. For a special allowance.

ALICE. For us?

CAPTAIN. No, for the sentries.

ALICE. For the sentries?!

CAPTAIN. Well, of course.

ALICE (*laughs*). Have you really written to the King?

CAPTAIN. I haven't sent it yet, but...

She laughs.

Go on, have a laugh. This one's on me.

ALICE. I thought I'd forgotten how to laugh.

Silence. The CAPTAIN *gazes out of the window and* ALICE *wanders to the table. They hear snatches of music and laughter from the party.*

Do you want another game?

CAPTAIN. No, put them away.

ALICE. Well, I'm pleased for Kurt. The only thing that bothers me is that my own cousin gets a plum job – Quarantine Master – and he runs off to cavort with our enemies before he even drops in so much as a card.

CAPTAIN. Oh, who cares?

ALICE. And did you see in the paper? He's described as 'a man of independent means'. I wonder how he got rich.

CAPTAIN. I know. A rich relative. That'll be a first.

ALICE. Maybe in *your* family...

CAPTAIN. Well, I don't care. Rich people don't impress me. I mean, what's money at the end of the day? I mean, what is it?

ALICE *just looks at him incredulously. The telegraph machine starts tapping.*

ALICE. Who is it?

CAPTAIN. Sh!

ALICE. What does it say?

CAPTAIN. I'm trying to listen!

He goes to the machine, holding his hand up for ALICE *to remain quiet, while a ribbon of white paper emerges.*

It's Sergeant Alfredsen, the children are with him over at the guardhouse in the harbour. They can see our light.

ALICE. Well, where else would we be?

CAPTAIN. He says Judith is sick.

ALICE. Ask him what's wrong with her?

CAPTAIN. She's not going to classes this week.

ALICE. Of course!

The CAPTAIN *starts tapping a reply.*

What are you saying? (*Pause.*) What are you saying?

CAPTAIN. He says she needs money for books.

ALICE. More books?!

CAPTAIN. He says she's going to fail her exam if she doesn't get them.

ALICE. Tell him to tell her she'll just have to take the exam next year.

CAPTAIN. Yes, you try telling her that!

ALICE. You're her father!

CAPTAIN (*angrily*). Do you think I haven't tried telling her what to do? I'm blue in the face trying to tell both of them what to do! I'm sick of it!

ALICE. That's how you've raised them!

The CAPTAIN *turns in exasperation and walks away from* ALICE. *He raises his head to the sky and lets out a long groan.*

Is that all you have to say?

CAPTAIN. Alice. There's plenty I could say, like, 'Yes, well, they're your children too,' or 'Why don't you just shut your stupid face,' or 'Let's just get a divorce,' or any of the other regulars from the old bag of crap. I could say any or all of them if you like, but you know what? Just take your pick, because I'm too tired.

ALICE. What's got you in such a bad mood all of a sudden?

CAPTAIN. Oh, I don't know. You think Christine will bring up some dinner?

ALICE. I doubt it. (*Short pause.*) The doctor has ordered supper from the Grand Hotel.

CAPTAIN. The Grand Hotel? (*Whistles, impressed.*) They'll all be having grouse then. There is no finer bird than a grouse that's just been blasted out of the sky – freshly delivered to its master from the salivating jaws of a hungry dog.

ALICE. Edgar! You'll make me sick.

CAPTAIN. But whatever you do – you must never ever *ever* stuff a grouse with pickled peanuts. It's utter insanity!

ALICE. Well, I'm sure most people would agree.

CAPTAIN. You'd be surprised! Those ignoramuses over there won't even know what wine to drink with it. You know, one almost feels sorry for them really.

ALICE *has wandered to the piano without much enthusiasm.*

ALICE. What'll I play?

CAPTAIN. You can play whatever you like as long as it's major keys only please. As soon as you drift into the minor I hear all your true feelings seeping out: 'I wish I was dead.' 'I wish my husband was dead.' 'I wonder if we're actually dead.'

ALICE *gently plays a few sad notes.*

I'll tell you what. Sod the lot of them. Let's break out that bottle of champagne!

ALICE. No, it's mine. I'm saving it for a special occasion.

CAPTAIN. Oh, don't be such a miser!

ALICE. Look who's talking!

CAPTAIN. I'll dance for you.

ALICE. No thanks. I wouldn't want you to do yourself an injury.

CAPTAIN (*with circumspection*). You know, I *was* going to suggest... that perhaps, some evening, we might, eh... well, invite a female companion up for a... for an evening. You know.

ALICE *stops playing. Pause.*

ALICE. I'd prefer we invited a male friend.

CAPTAIN. Right. Well… I'm not sure that worked out too well the
last time. I mean, it is a while ago and it was certainly interesting.
I'm not saying no, but, my God…

ALICE. Yes I know, afterwards was…

CAPTAIN. Yes, the aftermath was…

There is a sharp knock at the door, which makes them both jump.

ALICE. Who is it?

There is no answer.

Who can that be? Christine never knocks.

CAPTAIN. I don't know.

ALICE. Well, open it!

The CAPTAIN *approaches the door and opens it with
apprehension. There is nobody there. He sees two cards on the
floor outside the door and picks them up.*

CAPTAIN. Two cards.

ALICE. Who from?

CAPTAIN (*reading the first card*). Christine. She's gone.

ALICE. Oh no!

CAPTAIN. Well, you've done it now, haven't you?

ALICE. You'll just have to use your authority and march down there
and tell one of your men you're assigning him to our kitchen and
that's all about it.

CAPTAIN. Are you mad?!

ALICE. Can't you give an order?

CAPTAIN. Well, yes, but not without… not without…

ALICE. Without what?!

CAPTAIN. I mean, it's a chain of command…

ALICE. Oh, for God's sake! Who sent the other card?

CAPTAIN. What?

ALICE. The other card?!

CAPTAIN. Oh. (*Peers at the second card.*) I can't read it.

ALICE. Oh, give it to me. (*Takes it and reads.*) It's Kurt!

CAPTAIN. What?

ALICE. It's Kurt! It's Kurt! Go down to him!

CAPTAIN. Why didn't Christine bring him up?

> *The* CAPTAIN *hurries out.* ALICE *immediately goes to the mirror, fixes her hair and smoothes her eyebrows. She quickly does a circuit of the room, tidying up and lighting candles, then faces the door, expectantly, almost a new person. The* CAPTAIN *returns with* KURT, *a haunted-looking man in his forties.*

Here he is, the old rogue! Well, come in, come in, we don't stand on ceremony round here!

ALICE. Kurt. You are welcome.

KURT. Thank you. It's been too long.

CAPTAIN. What are we talking about, fifteen, sixteen years? Look how old we've all gotten! Ha ha ha!

ALICE. Kurt hasn't changed at all.

> *A beat while* KURT *and* ALICE *take each other in.*

CAPTAIN. Right, well, don't just stand there, give me your coat, that's right. Sit down. Now, tell me, what are your plans for the evening?

KURT. Well, I've been asked to drop up to the doctor's big bash...

ALICE. Oh, no, no, no. You'll dine with us, Kurt, you're here now, so...

KURT. I'd like to, of course, but the doctor is my superior, so I better at least... I mean...

CAPTAIN. What are you talking about? He's an idiot! Drop by on Monday, it's time enough!

KURT. He knows I'm here...

CAPTAIN. Now you listen to me. This island is a snake pit! Don't get off on the wrong foot – show him who's boss, and Alice will tell you – when I've got your back you are invincible. Alice?

ALICE. Oh, shush, Edgar! The doctor will understand you had to see your relatives, Kurt. Stay here with us. Anything else would be improper.

KURT. Of course. You are right, Alice. You make me feel so welcome!

CAPTAIN. Why wouldn't you be welcome? There's no problem. I mean, I don't have a problem, and you don't have a problem...

KURT. No!

CAPTAIN. There's no problem! Alright, there was a time you were a bit all over the place. But you were just extremely immature and now you're older. And I've forgotten all about it. I don't bear grudges, Kurt. Alice?

ALICE (*ignoring the* CAPTAIN). I want to hear all about your travels, Kurt.

KURT. My wanderings more like!

CAPTAIN. Yes, your wanderings which have led you straight back to the man and woman you stitched together twenty-five years ago.

KURT. Oh, I can't take credit for that! But it's certainly gratifying to see you both still so happy after all that time.

CAPTAIN. I won't lie, Kurt. We've had our ups and downs! Ha ha ha... But yes, as you see. Here we are. Still together. The money that flowed in from my writing has certainly helped.

KURT. Your writing?

CAPTAIN. Oh yes, you'll hear my name quite a lot in the military tactical sphere.

KURT. Oh, of course! I remember – they asked you to write that manual for their new rifle!

CAPTAIN. Absolutely, yes, and it's still very sought after. Those particular rifles have been decommissioned now, of course. But my manual is still... you know... it's still right there. On the shelf. In the library. At the old academy.

Pause.

KURT. Well, that's... and you've been abroad, I believe?

CAPTAIN. Yes. Five times!

KURT. Five times?

CAPTAIN. Yes. And each time – to Copenhagen!

KURT. Each time?

CAPTAIN. Each and every time, to Copenhagen. You see, Kurt, when I rescued Alice from the theatre…

ALICE. Rescued me?

CAPTAIN. Yes, dear, rescued.

ALICE. Well, now…

CAPTAIN. I mean the *types* who hung around that laneway leading down to the stage door, Kurt. You could smell the cheap schnapps on their breath from up on the street! But, of course, what thanks do I get? Why, the endless drill of reiteration about how I ruined her career. Her *career*, no less! So five times, I've had to take her back to make amends. I ask you! You know Copenhagen?

KURT. Not very well. I've been in America all these years.

CAPTAIN. How can anyone live in America? No tradition, no honour?

KURT. Well, it's… it presents great opportunity.

CAPTAIN. Great what?

ALICE. Did you ever get to see your children in all that time, Kurt?

KURT. No.

ALICE. I don't know how anyone could bear to stay away from their children for so long – if you don't mind me saying.

KURT. I had no choice. The court took away my rights.

CAPTAIN. Oh, let's not get into the whys and the wherefores. Alice. The past is gone!

Pause.

KURT. Yes. Well. And your children are doing well?

ALICE. Oh yes. Fifteen and sixteen now.

KURT. My word!

ALICE. Oh yes. They attend the school in town. They board there.

CAPTAIN. Both like me. Very bright. The boy is brilliant. Officer class – already a dazzling strategist.

ALICE. If the academy takes him.

CAPTAIN (*with sudden fury*). What are you talking about? 'If the academy takes him'?! Of course they'll take him! They'll be lucky to have him! (*Pause.*) Ha, ha, ha…

An awkward pause.

KURT. So! I've been ordered to set up a quarantine station for cholera. I'll have to report to the doctor mainly. Is he a nice man?

CAPTAIN. He's neither nice, nor a man.

KURT. Well, that doesn't sound so good!

ALICE. Well, he's not the worst, but he's somewhat…

KURT. Yes?

ALICE. Well, sort of calculating.

CAPTAIN. He's just another career scumbag is what he is. Him and all his cronies; the postmaster, the excise officer, the chief of police, and the biggest crook of the lot, what's the new name they made up for him?

ALICE. The Alderman.

CAPTAIN. Oh yes, 'the Alderman' if you don't mind. Who wears a silver *chain*, if you please, like this, all down to here.

KURT. Don't you get on with any of them?

CAPTAIN. No.

ALICE. They're really not nice people, Kurt, I'm sorry to say.

CAPTAIN. You see, what they did was, they rounded up every power-mad jobsworth in the country and posted them all them right here.

ALICE. Yes, all of them!

CAPTAIN. Oh, you're referring to me? Listen, I've never been a dictator. Not in here at any rate!

ALICE. No, well, I'd like to see you try!

CAPTAIN. Yes! Ha, ha, ha… Don't listen to her, Kurt. We joke back and forth like this all the time. You won't find a more united husband or wife. Now, please, have a whiskey.

KURT. Oh, not for the moment, thanks.

CAPTAIN. Oh God, don't tell me you've become a… a…

KURT. I haven't become anything. I just don't drink.

CAPTAIN. What is that? An American thing?

KURT. Perhaps.

CAPTAIN. Well, I find that incomprehensible. A man should be able to hold his liquor. At all times.

The CAPTAIN *gets himself a drink.*

KURT. I may have to, if our neighbours are all as bad as you make out!

ALICE. Just do your best, dear, you'll always have us to return to.

KURT. You must find it hard going!

ALICE. Well, it's not a lot of laughs, let's put it that way.

CAPTAIN. It's not hard going at all! Your enemies give you something to push against! They make you stronger and develop your guile. And on the day I die, I'll be able to stand up and say I never got something for nothing in this life, my friend! I earned all my achievements.

ALICE. Yes, I think it's safe to say Edgar's particular path hasn't been strewn with rose petals.

CAPTAIN. No, in fact, it's the opposite. You wouldn't believe the obstacles I've had to surmount. But one man's strength can bulldoze a fortress.

KURT. Mm, I wonder.

CAPTAIN. Yes, and that's why you're so pathetic.

The wind has started to make one of the upstage doors bang open and closed. The CAPTAIN *goes to close it.*

ALICE. Edgar!

CAPTAIN. We used to have a name for people like you in our regiment, Kurt. You are a nincompoop.

KURT. A nincompoop?

CAPTAIN. Yes, a man who can neither fight nor shite!

KURT *bursts out laughing*.

You think it's funny now, but you should heed my philosophy before it's too late, I mean it. There it is – that wind has come right up. I knew it would, I said so earlier.

ALICE. Kurt, say you'll stay for supper.

KURT. Well, only if I'm not imposing.

ALICE. Oh no. It may only be a cold plate. We're between maids, I'm afraid.

KURT. A cold plate is just what I'd like.

ALICE. Oh, Kurt. Always so accommodating!

She takes KURT*'s hand with affection. The* CAPTAIN *taps the barometer and looks at his watch.*

CAPTAIN. Storm's coming.

ALICE (*aside to* KURT). You make him so nervous!

CAPTAIN. Oughtn't you be making us something to eat, dear?

ALICE. Yes, I'm going! You can philosophise to your heart's content. Only, whatever you do, Kurt, don't contradict Socrates here or he'll have a convulsion. And he wonders why they never made him a major.

She starts to leave, looking at the CAPTAIN *who glares at her.*

CAPTAIN. You just make sure you bring us a decent meal, woman.

ALICE. You give me the money and you can have whatever you like!

She leaves.

CAPTAIN (*calling after her*). I've given you everything I have! (*To* KURT.) Money. It's all she ever bangs on about. You've been there…

KURT. Well…

CAPTAIN. I know you have. Your wife was unbelievable!

KURT. Well, that's all over now.

CAPTAIN. She was a right tulip! In fairness to Alice – she was never a dunce.

KURT. No.

CAPTAIN. In fact, you know, on the whole, she's actually not a bad wife.

KURT. Well, of course not!

CAPTAIN. She's certainly not the worst. If she could just...

KURT. What?

CAPTAIN. Well, keep that damned temper of hers under control, she'd actually be quite a pleasant person. Although there were times, I have to admit, I cursed your guts for tricking me into marrying her.

KURT. Well now, hold on there, my friend...

CAPTAIN. Yah, yah, yah, yah, yah, you always talk gobbledegook when you know you're in the wrong. I'm a commander of men. I know a man's mettle, so don't take it personally, it's just my job...

KURT. But just a minute, Edgar, as I remember, it was you who begged me to introduce you...

CAPTAIN (*ignoring* KURT, *loudly*). Life! It's a funny old thing though all the same, isn't it?

KURT. It certainly is!

CAPTAIN. And growing old – it's horrible. But it is interesting – I'd imagine. I mean, I'm obviously very far from being old, but it's just... when you start to notice that all your friends have died, I mean, you start to feel dreadfully alone.

KURT. Well, any man who has a nice wife to grow old with is very lucky. Take it from me.

CAPTAIN. Yes, you have to cling on to the wife because even the children piss off. And to think you abandoned yours!

KURT (*angrily*). My children were taken away from me, Edgar!

CAPTAIN. Well, don't get angry with me about it!

KURT. Well, it wasn't like that! Alright?

CAPTAIN. Alright! Take it easy! Jesus Christ! Who cares what it was like? The upshot is you are completely alone!

KURT. Yes, well. There are worse things.

CAPTAIN. Really? You really think that?

KURT. Yes, I do.

Pause. The CAPTAIN *goes to fill his glass.*

CAPTAIN. Anyway, good to see you, Kurt. Tell me, what have you been doing with yourself – these past fifteen years?

KURT. God, what a question! So many things have happened. Let me see… When I left here, my plan was to spend a year in Paris, but then…

CAPTAIN. Kurt, I'll come straight to the point. I hear you've gotten rich.

KURT. Well, not rich exactly.

CAPTAIN. It's alright, I'm not going to ask you for a loan.

KURT. If you were, I'd be more than happy to. I mean it.

CAPTAIN. Take it easy. The truth is I have too much money.

KURT. How so?

CAPTAIN. The bank tell me I have too much in my account. They're on at me all the time to become an investor. But I've no time for that. You see, I'm a soldier! But thank God I do have a massive bank account, because – (*Sotto.*) the day I don't? (*Indicates the door.*) She'll be gone. Like that. (*Snaps his fingers.*)

KURT. Oh, come now…

CAPTAIN. I'm serious. Nothing gives that woman more pleasure than watching me squirm when we can't pay a bill.

KURT. I thought you just said you had a massive bank account.

CAPTAIN. I know. I do.

KURT. But if you can't pay your bills, it can't be that massive, I mean, as the term is commonly defined.

CAPTAIN. Oh no, it is, it is. It's just…

KURT. What?

CAPTAIN. Well, it's just, it's never *enough*, is it?

KURT. I'm sorry, but I don't…

CAPTAIN (*with sudden volume*). Life! My God, life is a strange thing, don't you think? You see? Oh, how I've missed our philosophical conversations!

The CAPTAIN *drains his glass and stands looking at* KURT. *The telegraph machine starts tapping.*

KURT. Good Lord, what is that?

CAPTAIN. It's our telegraph – the guardhouse at the harbour sending me the evening report. Storm's coming up.

KURT. Don't you have a phone?

CAPTAIN. No. (*Getting himself another whiskey.*) We got rid of it because the girls at the exchange were listening in and reporting all my business to the postmaster who passed it to the Colonel.

KURT. That's terrible!

CAPTAIN. That's life, Kurt. Life is terrible. I could never understand people like you. People who actually want more life, some in eternal hereafter. More life! Why?

KURT. Well, I'm not so naive as to think it will be all plain sailing, but the older I get the more convinced I am that one day we will meet our Creator, and we will all have to account for...

CAPTAIN. What balls! When I die – just annihilate me. Body and soul!

KURT. How can you be sure such annihilation would be painless?

CAPTAIN. Listen, when I drop dead, I'll just go – bang – without any pain.

KURT. Oh, and you know that, do you?

CAPTAIN. Yes, I do know that, as a matter of fact. Bang. There you go. You're gone.

Pause.

KURT. Right... You don't seem very happy with your lot, Edgar.

CAPTAIN. Happy? I'll be happy the day I drop dead, Kurt, and that's all.

KURT (*gets up*). It's this house, isn't it? What is it? Is it even a house?

CAPTAIN. Well, it was the old jail, before they built the new one. They used to hang prisoners downstairs.

KURT. I knew it! Can't you see what it must be doing to you? One can almost feel the suffering and the hatred – the corpses screaming in the walls. (*Pause.*) I'm sorry. I shouldn't have said that. I'm just so tired. It's been a very long journey and I... (*Pause.*) Edgar?

The CAPTAIN *stares into space.*

Edgar? Edgar? Are you alright? (*Shakes the* CAPTAIN's *shoulder.*) Edgar?

The CAPTAIN *stirs as though coming out of a deep sleep. He looks around him trying to figure out where he is.*

CAPTAIN. Alice? (*Looks at* KURT.) Oh. I thought you were Alice. (*Sinks into a chair and stares into space again.*)

KURT. Edgar.

KURT *goes to the door and calls out.*

Alice! Alice! Quickly! Come at once!

ALICE (*off*). What is it?

KURT. It's Edgar!

ALICE *comes in wearing an apron, holding a limp old cabbage.*

ALICE. What's wrong?

KURT. I don't know. Look!

ALICE (*calmly*). Oh. Yes, he goes off like that sometimes. If I play, he'll come round. Hold on.

She goes to the piano and plays.

KURT. Can he see us?

ALICE. No.

KURT. It doesn't bother you?

ALICE. Hm?

ALICE *plays while* KURT *stands looking at the bizarre scene.*

KURT. Alice. What's happening in this house?

ALICE. Don't ask me – ask that.

KURT. 'That'? He's your husband.

ALICE. That man is a stranger to me, Kurt. He's as much a stranger now as he was when I married him twenty-five years ago. I know nothing about him, and I don't care to either.

KURT. Alice! He'll hear you.

ALICE. He has no idea what's happening at the moment.

Outside, a trumpet sounds the changing of the guard. ALICE stops playing. The CAPTAIN *suddenly gets to his feet and automatically takes his helmet and his sword.*

CAPTAIN. Gentlemen, you will excuse me, I must inspect the sentries.

He exits through the double doors at back.

KURT. Has he lost his reason?

ALICE. With Edgar, how could one tell?

KURT. I notice he's drinking.

ALICE. He was never able to drink.

She goes and looks out at the purple sky.

KURT. Should I go after him?

ALICE. What good would that do? It's too late. I've allowed myself to be locked in this tower for a whole generation with a man I hate so much that I fear – on the day he dies – I will probably just burst out laughing at the news.

KURT. Why haven't you separated?

ALICE. We were separated – for five years!

KURT. And you reunited?!

ALICE. The mistake we made was that, while we were separated, we both continued to live here.

KURT. Well, that's hardly separated!

ALICE. I know! Finally we had to recognise that we are bound by some evil force. Something only death may dissolve. So we wait for death.

KURT. What are you talking about? Surely your friends or your family – or someone – might have advised you before now?

ALICE. If only! No, Edgar isolated me, you see. You don't even see it happening! First he cut my siblings away. And then he set about my friends, one by one, until he had poisoned them all against me.

KURT. So I assume you did the same to him.

ALICE. I had to!

KURT. Right. And then what's worse is that I walk in and he blames me! Do you know that the first time he ever saw you he came to me and begged me to help him? I actually said no, because I knew only too well how cruel you could be to... to men.

ALICE. Well, thank you very much!

KURT. Oh, you know I'm right, Alice. You played one against the other so often, men were driven insane!

ALICE (*laughs*). Kurt!

KURT. I warned him. But he wouldn't leave me be until I finally wrote him a glowing letter of introduction! Well. Let him blame me then. But I'll tell you one thing – I won't have him or anyone else telling me I abandoned my children. I swear to God I'll punch him in the face if he says that again.

ALICE. Kurt, I know. It's despicable, and the thing is he actually likes you! He always has. But please don't turn your back on us now. You were meant to come to us...

ALICE's *face crumples*. KURT *goes to comfort her.*

KURT. Oh, Alice. Listen, I know! I thought my marriage was rotten, but this is mind-boggling!

ALICE. You can see it's not my fault.

KURT. You know, I don't care whose fault it is. It's just sad. Whatever way you look at it.

ALICE. But will I tell you what he fears most in the world? That if he dies – I'll remarry.

KURT. Well, then he must love you.

ALICE. Oh, perhaps, who knows? But that doesn't stop him hating me.

KURT. Yes, I know that particular emotion – hate and love forged together in the foundry of Hell. You probably still love him too, you know.

ALICE. Oh, I don't know.

She laughs.

KURT. What?

ALICE. No, it's just, sometimes he asks me to play a mindless tune
called 'The Entry of the Boyars' on the piano. He insists on
dancing to it.

KURT. Oh no, don't tell me he still dances!

ALICE. Oh yes! He dances up and down. And he's so proud of
himself and it's so funny that I can never help laughing. And at
times I like that, I sort of marvel at him, and I pity him. But can
you call that love? I don't think so! (*Beat.*) You know that two of
our infants died, Kurt. You know that, don't you?

KURT *nods silently.*

And our other two. I couldn't let them stay here because he turned
them against me!

KURT. So you turned them against him.

ALICE. I had to! You see, being in this family is like a curse.

KURT. Oh, we're all cursed. Since our first sin.

ALICE. Do you think it was a sin?

KURT. I mean our original sin – the fall of man.

ALICE. Oh. I thought you were referring to… when you and I…

KURT. No.

An awkward pause.

ALICE. Oh, Kurt, I was always so terribly mean to you. Can you
forgive the time I invited you to come and see me, just after you
had gotten engaged? I was a beast.

KURT. Let's not speak of it now.

ALICE. I suppose it must give you such pleasure to see me getting
my just desserts.

KURT. No. I could never feel that way, Alice.

*Pause. They look at each other. Something undeniable passes
between them.* ALICE *breaks the moment.*

ALICE. You have no idea the mood he'll be in now when he comes back. It's the humiliation, you see. Inviting you to dine with us and he has nothing to give you!

KURT. Oh, look, I'll run out and get us something.

ALICE. Kurt, don't you know where you are? You'll find nothing open.

KURT. But isn't there a café or a…

ALICE. No. This island is a fortress. They drink, they don't care about food.

KURT. Well, look, no matter. I'm not hungry. I'll pour him a moderate drink and you can play for us and we'll keep the mood light and gay and we'll…

ALICE. I can't play – my hands are wrecked from all the housework.

KURT. Where are your servants?

ALICE. We can't get anyone decent to come and live on this rock so the truth is we are always without! Oh, Edgar is going to go berserk when he gets back.

KURT. Has he ever hit you, Alice?

ALICE. Well, no, not… I mean he…

They hear the CAPTAIN *calling.*

CAPTAIN (*off*). At ease, men, at ease! You know I don't go in for all that bollocks-ology!

ALICE (*with sudden fury and despair*). Oh, I just wish this house would burn down!

KURT. Is that him?

ALICE. Yes. Look, if you want to leave, Kurt, I understand.

KURT. I won't leave you.

The CAPTAIN *comes in the doors at back and stands looking at* KURT *and* ALICE *without speaking for a few moments.*

You're back!

CAPTAIN. Yes, old Bluebeard is back. I suppose she's been spilling her guts about what a bastard I am.

KURT. Well, of course! What do you expect? Ha ha ha! Actually we were talking about music we like. Alice tells me you enjoy 'The Entry of the Boyars'.

Short pause.

CAPTAIN. You know it?

KURT. Know it? I love it!

CAPTAIN. Well, you're in for a treat. Watch this!

He prepares to dance.

Alice, what in God's name are you doing with that apron on? Play!

ALICE *gets her sheet music while the* CAPTAIN *limbers up.* KURT *goes to the piano to turn the pages for* ALICE. *The* CAPTAIN *stands with his hands on his hips, ready to go.* ALICE *starts playing and the* CAPTAIN *begins to perform a Hungarian folk dance very seriously with vigorous clapping and stamping, enjoying how his spurs ring out.* KURT *watches, dumbfounded, then turns to concentrate on the music with* ALICE. *While she continues to play, the* CAPTAIN *suddenly collapses out of sight behind some furniture. Neither* KURT *nor* ALICE *notices he is gone for some moments.* KURT *looks up and wonders where the* CAPTAIN *is before realising he is lying on the floor.*

KURT. Oh my God!

KURT *rushes to the* CAPTAIN. ALICE *turns round.*

Edgar. Edgar. What happened?

ALICE. Is he dead?

KURT. I don't know. (*Pause.*) No, he's alive.

ALICE (*disappointed*). Oh!

KURT. Come on. That's it, me old sausage.

KURT *helps the* CAPTAIN *to his feet and gets him to a chair. The* CAPTAIN *pushes* KURT *away.*

CAPTAIN. What in God's name are you doing?

KURT. You fell!

CAPTAIN. What are you talking about?

KURT. You collapsed!

CAPTAIN. When?

KURT. Just now! Sit down, Edgar, please.

> The CAPTAIN *suddenly scrunches up his face and puts his hand to his head, sinking into the chair.*

CAPTAIN. Jesus… *Christ*!

ALICE. You're sick! Don't you see that, you stupid old fool!

CAPTAIN. Well, shouting at me won't help! (*Winces, putting his hand to his head again.*) Ah!

KURT. Where's the nearest phone?

ALICE. In the sentry box at the bottom of the steps.

KURT. I'll call the doctor.

> KURT *goes out.*

CAPTAIN. I don't want that damn doctor! If he comes near me, I'll stab him. (*Winces again.*) Ah!

> ALICE *takes off her apron. The* CAPTAIN *watches her.*

Get me some water, will you?

ALICE (*with unconcealed contempt as she pours some water from a jug*). Oh!

CAPTAIN. Well, forgive me for being sick!

ALICE. *Are* you sick?

CAPTAIN. What – do you think a person can fake this kind of pain?!

ALICE. It was you who said real soldiers don't get sick, Edgar. (*Short pause.*) Well, that's it. You're going to have to take great care, aren't you?

CAPTAIN. Well, you're not going to look after me!

ALICE. You've got that right!

CAPTAIN. It's the moment you have longed for all these years.

ALICE (*matter of factly*). And the moment you dreaded.

CAPTAIN. Alice.

ALICE. What.

CAPTAIN. Please don't be cross with me.

Pause. She looks at him. KURT *enters.*

KURT (*breathless*). Well, this is unbelievable!

ALICE. What happened?

KURT. He hung up! As soon as I mentioned your name.

ALICE. Well, this is it – this is what you get, isn't it? You stupid old twit!

CAPTAIN. Oh God, I can't feel my hands!

KURT. Isn't there another doctor?

ALICE. Only in town.

KURT. Can we phone the mainland?

ALICE. No. We have to send a telegraph.

CAPTAIN. And I can't move my arms!

ALICE. Oh, I'll do it.

She goes to the telegraph machine and starts sending a message.

CAPTAIN (*rising*). Now you just hold on one damned second! You mean to tell me you can, in fact, telegraph after all these years?

ALICE. Yes. And I always could.

CAPTAIN. Yes, of course. (*To* KURT.) You see? This is what we're dealing with!

ALICE. Oh, shut up.

She continues to send a telegraph.

CAPTAIN. Kurt. Will you hold my hand?

KURT *goes to him.*

It's like I'm rising up and falling all at once. It's absolutely horrible.

KURT. Has anything like this ever happened before?

CAPTAIN. Never.

ALICE (*in utter disbelief*). What?!

CAPTAIN. She doesn't know what she's talking about.

KURT. Look, we can't wait for someone to come all the way out here on a boat. This is madness! I'll phone the doctor again and I'll... I'll just tell him – this is not good enough. Has he ever treated you before?

CAPTAIN. Well, if you can call it 'treating' me.

KURT (*going*). I mean, for Christ's sake, wouldn't you think the Hippocratic oath might drag him away from his canapés?

CAPTAIN (*calling after him*). Not on this island! (*Short pause.*) Isn't Kurt a good man? It would do you good to see how a man can change.

ALICE. I know. He has assumed a new... I don't know... attractiveness. And now we've dragged him down – straight into our slurry.

CAPTAIN. He'll be a fine ally for us here. It may tip the balance. Although I notice he's reluctant to give us any real detail about what he's been up to.

ALICE. In fairness, I don't remember anyone really asking him.

CAPTAIN. Oh God, Alice, what do you think is wrong with me?

ALICE. You tell me.

CAPTAIN. Well, it's either my heart. Or my head. Or maybe it's my soul. Maybe I should just... let it out.

ALICE. Do you think you could eat something?

CAPTAIN. Well, of course I could! I'm bloody ravenous – as usual! Nothing can change that! And here we are with not a sausage in the larder, and Kurt walks back in the door. It's just so humiliating!

The telegraph starts clicking. They listen.

You hear that? An accident at the shipyard. No one can be spared. Absolutely bloody typical. And aren't you the one? How much of my life have I wasted decoding that blasted machine for you, and you bloody well knew what it was saying all along!

They laugh.

ALICE. And all the times you lied to me about what it said.

The CAPTAIN *stops laughing.*

Well, you've certainly got your comeuppance now, haven't you? You were always such a stingy old squirrel. 'Send me your bill, my good man!' 'Send it to the Quartermaster's office!' Well, they're all on to you now.

CAPTAIN. Oh, shut up, Alice.

ALICE. And I'll tell you another thing. Kurt won't be back either. Phoning the doctor was his ruse – so he could – (*Cocks her thumb and gives a short whistle – meaning 'depart'*.)'The Hippocratic oath…' Did you ever hear such codswallop?

CAPTAIN. I know! He was always a cowardly little bastard. I spotted it the day I first laid eyes on him. He's on his way up to the doctor's now in search of a good feed, the wretched little shit.

KURT *enters*.

KURT. I got him. I told him I'd report him. He wasn't one bit happy!

CAPTAIN. What did he say?

KURT. He said it's your old complaint – calcification of the heart.

CAPTAIN. Calcifi–what–tion?

KURT. Calcification.

ALICE. A stone heart, dear.

KURT. Yes. You can't smoke any more cigars – it's absolutely lethal – and whiskey will kill you, so you have to stop that immediately.

CAPTAIN (*with panic*). This is terrible!

KURT. And he says you have to get straight into bed.

CAPTAIN. Well then, that's it! It's all over! You see, once they tell you to get into bed, that's the end. You never get up! No, no, no – I just need to eat something, that's all.

KURT. He said you can't eat anything for three days, just a glass of milk.

CAPTAIN. I can't drink milk! I hate milk!

KURT. Well, you'll have to learn.

CAPTAIN. I can't learn! What are you talking about? I'm too old to learn!! (*Winces, placing his hand to his head.*) Oh Jesus *Christ*.

The CAPTAIN *lapses into a state of catatonia once more, staring into space*.

ALICE. He's gone.

KURT. The doctor said he could die, Alice.

ALICE. Thank God!

KURT. Alice…

ALICE. What.

KURT. Perhaps you should get him a blanket and a pillow.

ALICE. Oh, so now I'm going to take my orders from you?

KURT. I don't care what you do. I'll get it.

ALICE. I'll get it!

She goes. KURT *takes the water carafe to get a drink for the* CAPTAIN.

KURT. I'll get you some warm water. (*Exhaustedly to himself as he goes out.*) Oh God…

The wind whips up and the doors at back creak open once more. The CAPTAIN *looks round and sees someone come to the door. He is terrified. The audience see nothing.*

CAPTAIN. Who are you? (*Pause.*) Well, that's impossible. (*Pause.*) Well, because… because I'm… Well, I'm just not ready. (*Pause.*) But, my dear lady, that's no concern of mine. (*Pause.*) I don't care what it's like! I told you – I'm not ready!

The CAPTAIN *is distracted by* ALICE *coming back with some blankets. She starts making a bed for the* CAPTAIN. *The* CAPTAIN *goes to the doors and looks out into the night.*

Alice, did you see anyone in here just now?

ALICE. No.

CAPTAIN. You didn't see an old woman?

ALICE. I saw old Maja coming up the steps from the workhouse, but she couldn't have gotten in.

She sees the CAPTAIN *looking at the doors. She goes to close them.*

Why, did you get a fright?

CAPTAIN. A fright? Me? That's a good one!

ALICE. Right. Lie down here.

The CAPTAIN *goes to the bed she has made. He tries to take* ALICE*'s hand.*

Oh, get off me!

KURT *enters with the water carafe.*

CAPTAIN. Kurt, stay with me tonight, won't you?

KURT (*to* ALICE). I'll sit with him.

ALICE *looks at* KURT.

CAPTAIN. Thank you. Well, goodnight, Alice. That will be all.

ALICE (*shoots the* CAPTAIN *a withering look*). Goodnight, Kurt.

She goes.

KURT. Right. (*Pulls a chair over to the sofa.*) Aren't you going to take off your boots, Edgar?

CAPTAIN. No.

KURT. Wouldn't you be more comfortable?

CAPTAIN. No. I never take them off.

KURT. Why?

CAPTAIN. Just in case.

KURT. In case what?

CAPTAIN. You know, you can be quite stupid at times, Kurt.

KURT. Alright.

CAPTAIN. I'm going to say something completely startling, Kurt, are you ready?

KURT. I think so.

CAPTAIN. I've realised, just this evening, you're the only person I really can talk to, isn't that something?

KURT. Well, it's not so unusual for men to have only a few confidants.

CAPTAIN. Hm. If I die, tonight, I mean. I want you to do something for me. I want you to take care of my children. Will you do that for me?

KURT. Well... it's not really my place, is it? I mean, it's a big...

CAPTAIN. Thank you, Kurt. You see, it's nothing personal but the reason you and I could never be friends is simply because I have never believed in the concept.

KURT. The concept?

CAPTAIN. The concept of friendship. I mean, what is it? At the end of the day? 'Friendship', I mean, come on.

KURT. Well... I suppose the question is simply – do you trust me?

Long pause.

CAPTAIN. Kurt?

KURT. Yes?

CAPTAIN. Do you think I'm going to die?

KURT. Yes.

CAPTAIN. Oh God.

KURT. In the sense that we are all going to die.

CAPTAIN. Oh, don't give me a smart-alecky answer at a time like this! What's wrong with you, man?!

KURT. Why? Are you afraid of dying, Edgar?

CAPTAIN. Well, it's just, what if it isn't the end?

KURT. That's why one must be prepared for anything, Edgar.

CAPTAIN. Even Hell?

KURT. Yes. Surely you must believe in Hell, Edgar. You are smack in the middle of it, it seems to me.

CAPTAIN. Oh, that's just a saying, a metaphor – (*Disparagingly.*) 'I'm in Hell...' I'm talking about what if there really *is* a Hell? That's what I'm talking about. Come on, keep up with me.

KURT. Well, maybe this *is* Hell, and part of the agony is that we don't even realise it?

CAPTAIN. Yes! I *am* in agony, Kurt.

KURT. Physical?

CAPTAIN. No.

KURT. Well, then you are in spiritual pain, Edgar, there's no other alternative.

CAPTAIN (*takes* KURT's *hand*). You see the thing is – when you get down to it – I don't want to die!

KURT. But a few moments ago you were talking about how you would relish annihilation!

CAPTAIN. Only if it's absolutely painless, Kurt!

KURT. But it can't be.

CAPTAIN. Is this it?

KURT. It's the beginning of it, yes.

CAPTAIN. Oh God!

The CAPTAIN *sinks back in despair. Pause.*

KURT. Well, goodnight, Edgar.

The CAPTAIN *just looks at* KURT, *then turns away, wrapping himself in the blanket, curling up like a child. Music and lights take us to morning. A pale dawn rises behind the windows and the sea breaks evenly on the shore. Some birds chirp while the* CAPTAIN *lies in the same position and* KURT *sits with him, looking absolutely exhausted.* ALICE *comes to the door. She is munching a piece of fruit.*

ALICE. Is he still asleep?

KURT. I dosed him with morphine.

ALICE. Morphine?

KURT. I had to. He wouldn't stop talking.

ALICE. Do you have morphine?

KURT. Strictly for moments of extreme anxiety.

ALICE. Well, absolutely.

KURT knows she will badger him till he gives her some. He takes out his bottle and puts a few drops on her tongue.

Huh. Look at him. The first time I met him he had no coat, just two shirts against the snow. I thought he was noble! I actually thought he was so brave bearing that ugly face with such resignation.

KURT. Yes, his ugliness was always frightening. Whenever he got angry with me, I used to have nightmares for days.

ALICE. And I married him!

KURT. You saw his good qualities.

ALICE. Well, of course. He can be kind and sensitive. You should hear him talk about Judith, but by God is he a horrible enemy to have. He's so sneaky.

The CAPTAIN *turns round and looks at them.*

CAPTAIN. Thank God! It's the morning.

KURT. How are you feeling?

CAPTAIN. Awful.

KURT. Shall I phone the doctor?

CAPTAIN. No! I want to see my little girl. I want to see Judith.

ALICE. Well, she's not here, is she?

KURT. You know, talking of your children, Edgar, I was thinking it may not be a bad idea to set your affairs in order before too long.

CAPTAIN. Why?

KURT. Well, in case something were to happen.

CAPTAIN. What could happen?

KURT. Only what could happen to anyone.

CAPTAIN. Listen, I'm not going to die just yet, my friend, and not for a long time either, so don't go making plans, Alice.

KURT. I know, and I hope that's the case, but anything can happen to any of us at any time. Imagine if Alice were to be cast out in the street for no better reason than that you wouldn't call a lawyer to pop in for half an hour to just...

The CAPTAIN *winces, putting his hand to his head.*

CAPTAIN. Oh, here it is! Here it is! It's back!

ALICE. Oh, for Christ's sake!

She goes. The CAPTAIN *recovers.*

CAPTAIN. So, Kurt, tell me. This 'quarantine station' of yours, how are you going to set about getting it up and running?

KURT. I'm sure I'll manage.

CAPTAIN (*laughs*). Oh really? You do understand that to all intents
and purposes I'm in charge on this island. I mean, nothing can
really happen without my acquiescence.

KURT. Alright. And you've seen a quarantine station in operation,
have you?

CAPTAIN. Seen one? Listen, mate, I've been seeing quarantine
stations in operation all up and down the continent since before you
were born! Don't you worry about that, and I'll tell you one thing,
never ever *ever* put a quarantine station next nor near the water.

KURT. But we're going to build it right on the shore!

CAPTAIN. Well, there you go! You see how much you know about
it? Bacteria thrive in the water!

KURT. Not in saltwater! In fact – we're building a bathing facility!

CAPTAIN. Kurt, you are an idiot. Now, listen to me, you should
bring your children here.

KURT. It's not up to me to bring them anywhere.

CAPTAIN. Well, you'll just have to persuade them. It doesn't look
good, Kurt. Coming here on your own. Dumping your children…

KURT. Now, hold on a minute, I've already told you…

CAPTAIN. Because people will ask how any man can just abandon
vulnerable little children…

KURT. Edgar!

CAPTAIN. Just so he can traipse off like a ninny, prancing around the
place…

KURT. I told you I was ordered by the court to have nothing to do
with my children!

CAPTAIN. It looks just awful…

KURT. I was stripped of my custodial rights! My wife forbade me
from seeing them! You have no idea what it's done to me! I fought
and I fought to get them back! You have no idea what you're
talking about!

CAPTAIN. Alright, calm down… there's no need to raise your voice,
Kurt, I know how this island works and I'm simply trying to give

you some friendly advice. No need to leap off the handle like some bloody madman.

Pause. KURT *composes himself.*

And I'm not very well at the moment.

KURT. Yes. I know. Can I get you anything?

CAPTAIN. Well, yes, if you don't mind. I'd like a fillet steak, please.

KURT. Don't be ridiculous, Edgar, that'll finish you off!

CAPTAIN. Oh, come on. Is it not enough that I'm ill? You all want me to starve as well?

KURT. You know it's not like that.

CAPTAIN. Do I? I suppose you're all having a good laugh – no drink, no tobacco, 'Let's watch him suffer'…

KURT. Not at all. Death demands sacrifices, otherwise he comes at once.

CAPTAIN. That's supposed to sound clever, is it?

ALICE *enters with several bunches of flowers, telegrams and letters. She throws the flowers on the desk.*

ALICE. These are for you, apparently.

CAPTAIN. For me? From who?

ALICE. From the non-commissioned officers and the sentries.

CAPTAIN (*to* KURT). You see? (*Sorts through the letters, handing them one by one to* KURT.) Aha – this one is from the Colonel's office, if I'm not mistaken. You'll find the Colonel is a gentleman, Kurt, even if he is a duplicitous little shit. And, look, from Judith! I can't read these tiny telegrams, can you read that please? And look at this, that's from Staff Sergeant Alfredsen, the old dog, you'll be getting to know him, Kurt, that's for sure! Look at all of these…

ALICE. I don't understand what's happening. Is everyone writing to congratulate you on becoming ill?

CAPTAIN. You see, Alice, an unfortunate hyena like you that hasn't a friend on the face of the Earth *couldn't* understand an outpouring of warmth such as this, so I won't bother explaining.

KURT (*reading*). Judith says she won't be able to come and see you this weekend because she's promised to help her tutor pick a veil for the harvest parade.

CAPTAIN. Is that it?

KURT. No, she… she…

CAPTAIN. What, what is it?

KURT. She also says… well…

CAPTAIN. What, damn you?

KURT. She begs you to please stop drinking.

Pause.

CAPTAIN. Well, that's… (*Gives a pathetic little laugh.*) That's…

Pause.

And the Colonel? What does the Colonel say?

KURT. You have been relieved of your command.

CAPTAIN. What?! That's impossible! I haven't requested to be relieved of my…

ALICE. I asked him for it.

CAPTAIN. Why?!

ALICE. Because you are unwell.

CAPTAIN. What did you do that for, you stupid woman?! Don't you see what you've done!?

ALICE. Yes, I do.

CAPTAIN. Well, I… I refuse to accept the order. I didn't hear it. You didn't see it.

ALICE. But it has been issued.

CAPTAIN. He's obviously been misled! I'll just have to speak with him. Have a friendly word.

ALICE (*handing the* CAPTAIN *his bunches of flowers*). You see, Kurt? No laws, be they natural, physical or legal may proscribe this man. The universe bends to his every whim.

ALICE *is on her way out of the door.*

CAPTAIN. I suppose you have invited Kurt to breakfast with us?

ALICE. No.

CAPTAIN. Well, I'm inviting him. Two fillet steaks, straight away, please.

ALICE. Two?

CAPTAIN. Yes, I'm also having one.

ALICE. There are in fact three of us.

CAPTAIN. Well, three fillet steaks then, straight away, thank you. That will be all.

ALICE. And where am I supposed to magic three fillet bloody steaks from? Out of my backside?!

CAPTAIN (*to* KURT). You see?

ALICE. You invite Kurt to dinner *and* breakfast and we can't even give him a cup of coffee!

CAPTAIN (*an indulgent laugh*). She's just angry because I didn't die last night.

ALICE (*with fury*). No, I'm angry because you didn't die twenty-five years ago and spare me the degradation of watching you ruin my life before my very eyes!

She weeps into her hands.

CAPTAIN (*a little laugh*). You see, Kurt, this is what happens when you set about matchmaking two people who are simply not of the same class. Now, you will excuse me.

He goes and takes a large artillery helmet with a long plume of feathers on top.

KURT. Where are you going?

The CAPTAIN *takes his sword and cloak and goes to the doors at back.*

CAPTAIN. To attend to my duties. If anyone needs me, tell them I've gone to inspect the battery.

KURT *tries to stop the* CAPTAIN.

KURT. You are not well, Edgar.

The CAPTAIN *pushes* KURT *roughly back into the room.*

CAPTAIN (*with sudden ferocity*). Stay out of my way, you impudent pup!

The CAPTAIN *leaves.* ALICE *rushes to the door and shouts after him.*

ALICE. Yes, that's it! Go on! Walk away! Do what you always do when the fighting gets hot! Run away! Run away, you cowardly drunken liar!

KURT *gapes at* ALICE, *trying to recover his breath.*

This is nothing.

KURT. God, it's all so *awful*!

ALICE (*tone of 'this is what I live with'*). Well...

KURT. Where will he go?

ALICE. Oh, he'll go down and start drinking with the conscripts. He'll put his feet up on the table in the guardroom, malign the officer command for a few hours and then stagger home looking for something to eat.

KURT. You know, the reason I came here was I thought how peaceful it would be!

ALICE. Oh, Kurt, let me get you something to eat, I'll scrounge us up something if you can wait here for an hour.

KURT. No, don't do that. I'll go up to the doctor's house and introduce myself. Maybe he'll give me some breakfast I can bring us down.

ALICE. I'm so ashamed!

KURT. The time for shame has long gone.

KURT *is on his way towards the door.*

Alice, did Edgar have anything to do with me losing custody of my children?

ALICE. Oh, Kurt, it's all so long ago.

KURT. No. Tell me.

Pause.

ALICE. When you sent him to mediate with Martha on your behalf he… well, he began an affair with her. (*Pause*.) And then he… he introduced her to a lawyer to help her gain full custody.

Pause.

KURT. Last night he asked me if I would provide for *his* children should anything ever happen to him.!

ALICE. Please don't avenge yourself on my children.

KURT (*putting on his coat*). No, my vengeance would be to show him I am not like him. That I am capable of keeping my promises.

ALICE. Then you are a better class of person than us, Kurt.

KURT. No, I've just been along a different road. Alright, well, I'll go and see if I can find us some warm bread and some coffee. Will you be alright?

ALICE. Yes. Thank you, Kurt.

KURT. What will you do now?

ALICE. Why, I'll wait for you.

Pause. She goes and kisses him on the mouth. She pulls away and they stand looking at each other. Then KURT *leaves.*

Lights down.

ACT TWO

Early morning. ALICE *sits in a shaft of sunlight looking out of the window.* KURT *enters.*

KURT. Alice?

ALICE *turns to look at him.*

ALICE. Oh, it's you.

KURT. Yes. Your front door was wide open. I hope you don't mind.

They hear a blast from a ship's horn.

There's the ferry.

ALICE. Yes, he'll be home soon.

KURT. I could see him from my little window in the hostel, standing at the prow in his full dress uniform. The sun was glinting on his helmet.

ALICE. Yes, he went to town to see the Colonel – to ensure his continued dominance.

KURT. Over whom?

ALICE. Good question.

She gazes out of the window.

KURT. Alice, what's in your hand?

She looks down at a handful of her hair.

ALICE. Oh, just my hair. It comes out in clumps! My two babies who perished in here died for lack of light. (*Turns and puts a handkerchief away.*)

KURT *realises she has been crying.*

We must steel ourselves now, Kurt.

KURT. Why?

ALICE. Because the Captain's campaign has started in earnest. Against me – and against you.

KURT. Against me?

ALICE. Kurt, as soon as you read that telegram from Judith, I saw it. A darkness I know all too well fell across his brow. You see, he could never harm Judith, so I saw him decide to destroy you.

KURT. Just like that?

ALICE. Oh yes, exactly like that! Why else do you think he was he hanging about, down at your quarantine site, all day yesterday?

KURT. He was offering us his advice.

ALICE. Huh! He was surveying the terrain. What he really wants is to ruin your reputation.

KURT. Yes, well, it's a bit too late to worry about my reputation, I'm afraid.

ALICE. Well, you should worry – because his main goal is to wreck the future for your children.

KURT. My children?!

ALICE. Yes! You see, our boy has inherited Edgar's frenzy for whiskey whilst our daughter, no matter what Edgar thinks, was always just a greedy little tart. To see your children flourish while his own… (*Makes a dismissive gesture.*) well, that's the final dagger in his guts.

KURT. But he couldn't do anything to my chil…!

They hear a door slam and the heavy tread of the CAPTAIN *on the stairs.*

ALICE. Now listen, just be polite, pretend everything is perfect. (*With poise, as though they are above arguing with people.*) When he lies, just humour him. Never rise to his taunts. Our advantage is that we are sober and we can think straight. So just…

ALICE *breaks off while the* CAPTAIN *appears in the doorway stage right, wearing a helmet, a long cloak and white gloves. He looks tired but resolute as he stands there – attempting to conceal that he has been on a night-long bender. He removes his sword and scabbard from his belt and crosses unsteadily to a chair where he sits, holding his sword on his lap. He speaks with a slight drunken slur he labours to correct.*

CAPTAIN. Kurt. There's a pleasant surprise. You will excuse me for being seated in your company, but I'm afraid it's been a very long night over in town.

KURT. Of course!

ALICE. Good morning, Edgar.

CAPTAIN. Good morning, Alice.

KURT. How are you feeling?

CAPTAIN. Good! Feeling no pain! Just very tired!

ALICE. Any news in town?

CAPTAIN. Yes. I visited the doctor over there. And he says – I have another good twenty years in me!

> ALICE *shoots* KURT *an incredulous look.*

ALICE. Well, that is good news.

CAPTAIN. Yes. It is!

> *A silence descends which* KURT *instinctively goes to break, but* ALICE *signals to him to say nothing.*

Now, Kurt...

ALICE (*aside*). Here he goes.

CAPTAIN. I beg your pardon?

ALICE. No. Nothing.

CAPTAIN. Did you want to say something?

ALICE. No, I didn't say anything.

CAPTAIN. Right, well, you see, Kurt. I was in town. As you know. And I was in the company of some fine men from my old regiment and we visited this place, and that place, and whose acquaintance did I make? Only a fine young man, a cadet from the academy, a fine young chap, and as we are always short of cadets over here, I arranged it with the Colonel that he be posted over here with us. And I thought I'd tell you, because this news should give you particular pleasure, Kurt.

KURT. Why me?

CAPTAIN. Because he is your eldest son!

ALICE (*to* KURT). I told you.

CAPTAIN. What?

ALICE. I didn't say anything.

CAPTAIN. Well, stop mumbling then! Myself and Kurt are trying to have a conversation here, what's wrong with you?

ALICE. There's nothing wrong with me. You need to get the wax flushed out of your ears.

CAPTAIN. Oh, be quiet! (*To* KURT.) Hm? What do you make of that? He's grown into a fine, fine young chap, you'll be pleased to hear.

KURT. Yes, well, while any father would be thrilled to see his little boy again, under these particular circumstances I have to say I'm rather displeased, Edgar.

CAPTAIN. I don't understand.

KURT. You don't have to. I don't want him coming here so that's… I forbid it.

CAPTAIN (*laughs*). Oh, you forbid it, do you? Then allow me to inform you that he is already under my command as of this morning! My command!

KURT. Well, then I will make him transfer to another regiment.

CAPTAIN. But, you see, you can't do that because the courts have taken away your rights over your son and you have no legal standing!

KURT. Well, I shall go to his mother.

CAPTAIN. But there's no point in that. (*Beat.*) Kurt.

KURT. Why?

CAPTAIN. Because I have already spoken to her! Yes!

ALICE (*to* KURT). You see?

CAPTAIN. Yes, my dear?

ALICE. I didn't say anything! You're an old man and you're going deaf.

CAPTAIN. Yes, I must be! So come here closer to me till I tell you something just for your ears.

ALICE. No, I prefer a witness for anything you have to say to me.

CAPTAIN. Very well – a witness may be advantageous for us both. First of all, has my will been notarised?

ALICE (*hands him a document*). The regimental lawyer did it yesterday evening.

CAPTAIN (*peers at it*). Everything goes to you. Alright. Fine. (*Tears it up in front of her.*)

ALICE (*to* KURT). Have you ever seen such behaviour?

KURT *shrugs and turns away, sitting down.*

CAPTAIN. Now, I have this to say to you, Alice…

ALICE. Yes?

CAPTAIN. Yes, I'm saying it! Now, in light of your long-expressed desire to bring our unhappy arrangement to an end, and on account of your cruel and uncharitable treatment of your children and your husband and your cavalier attitude regarding the household finances, I have filed a petition for divorce at the town court.

ALICE. I see. On what grounds may I ask?

CAPTAIN. On the grounds I have just… on the aforementioned grounds!

ALICE. Yes, well, good luck with that!

CAPTAIN. And…! And! I have… other grounds of a more personal nature. As ascertained aforthwith, now that it has been appraised of me that I will definitely live for another twenty years or more, I am therefore am obliged to terminate this unhappy union in order to commence one with someone who can show me the requisite devotion, who might bring some longed-for youthfulness into my home, and some yearned-for attractiveness!

ALICE *rips her wedding ring from her hand and throws it at the* CAPTAIN.

ALICE. You conceited prick! You think you can just toss me into the street and shack up with some young… girl in here under my own roof?

CAPTAIN. Yes. Will the witness please take note: the spouse rescinds her wedding ring.

The CAPTAIN *retrieves the ring and puts it in his pocket.*

ALICE. Alright, let's play it that way then! Kurt, you are a witness. This man has attempted to murder me.

KURT. Murder you?

ALICE. Yes, the summer before last, he pushed me into the sea.

CAPTAIN. There are no witnesses.

ALICE. That's a lie – Judith saw what happened.

CAPTAIN. No she didn't.

ALICE. She did, and she can testify!

CAPTAIN. No, she can't, because she's already told me, she didn't see anything of the sort.

ALICE. When did she tell you?

CAPTAIN. Last night. We had a nice supper and we discussed that self-same stormy afternoon; how slippery the pier wall was, and how anyone could have lost their balance, and how, if anything, I *saved* you.

ALICE. Is that how she described it?

CAPTAIN. Yup. In precisely those terms.

ALICE. That little bitch.

CAPTAIN. Yes! Because I thought you might try and pull that old sausage out of the sack! Now! I take it the fortress surrenders. Here is my watch. The time is twenty minutes past eight. I give you, the enemy, ten minutes to withdraw from the field. Ten minutes starting from… oh!

He clutches his heart. ALICE *goes to him.*

ALICE. What's wrong?

CAPTAIN. I… I don't know.

ALICE. Kurt, quick, bring some brandy.

CAPTAIN. No brandy! I don't drink any more! What are you trying to do? Kill me? You saw that, Kurt. Now, ten minutes, you hear me? No quarter will be given. (*Draws his sword.*) Ten minutes.

The CAPTAIN *goes out.*

KURT. Who is this man?

ALICE. He's not a man. He's a devil.

KURT. What does he want with my son?

ALICE. He wants to hold him hostage in order to control you and isolate you, and make you look so bad that you might never hold your head up again. (*Pause*.) Kurt, I haven't been entirely honest with you.

KURT. How so?

ALICE. I lied when I said that Edgar never hit me. He's been beating me, on and off, for nearly twenty years.

Pause.

KURT. You know, when I came here, I had no anger, no grudge. Any slander or humiliation I had suffered in the past – well, I... I forgave him. Because, to be perfectly honest with you, there were times in my past that I... Well, I took things a bit too far when people made me angry so I... Well, I... But now I ... I mean... I...

ALICE. Yes, that's right.

KURT. I hate him.

ALICE. Yes.

KURT. This animal who has separated me from my family...

ALICE. Yes.

KURT. Who beats up his own wife...

ALICE. Yes.

KURT. And holds my son like a ransom demand. My own son who I have not seen for sixteen years!

ALICE. Yes!

KURT. I mean, I... I want to kill him!

ALICE. Yes!

KURT. To think he even went and tracked down my wife to lay his groundwork! Why couldn't that pair have met thirty years ago and spared us all?

ALICE. I know. They're soulmates! But just as he has his allies, so must we exploit his enemies.

KURT. Yes, you're right! Who is his biggest enemy on the island?

ALICE. The Alderman. He hates Edgar. And he has long suspected something I know to be true. Something about Edgar and Staff Sergeant Alfredsen.

KURT. What?

ALICE. Well, a few years back, everyone thought they were heroes because they made a big show of setting up the first ever fund for officers' widows. No one could refuse putting money in, and before long they had a massive bank account. Has he told you about it?

KURT. Yes, I think he...

ALICE. Yes, well, Sergeant Alfredsen has invented two extra 'widows'. He forged papers for them! And guess who they are! Yes! Edgar and Sergeant Alfredsen get all their drink money paid directly into their own pockets every month!

KURT. Oh, that's...! Look, I don't know if I want to do it that way. It's so tawdry! Does anybody even care!?

ALICE. You need the killer blow, Kurt. You must be prepared to strike directly at your enemy's weakest point.

KURT. No, no! (*As though restraining his darker nature, trying to remain calm.*) Life will do it to them.

ALICE. Do what?

KURT (*with restraint*). I just discovered over time, in cases like this, that... life... administers its own justice sooner or later – you'll see.

ALICE. What will I see?

KURT. That justice usually gets done in the end. A kind of... natural... justice.

ALICE. 'Justice'? What are you talking about? There's no such thing as justice! If you want to wait around for justice to come knocking on your door, you're welcome to it, 'cause I won't! Your son is being taken away from you right before your eyes and you wait for someone else to do the dirty work before you lift a finger?! No wonder you lost everything, Kurt. Well, I'm going to dance on his bloody head. I'll do the 'Entry of the Boyars' all over his stupid face for him with my boots on.

KURT *watches her, his eyes blazing.*

KURT. You are a devil too, aren't you, Alice?

ALICE. Yes. I am!

KURT. Yes, you are.

ALICE. You always called me that, remember? When we were younger?

KURT. Yes.

ALICE *lets down her hair.*

ALICE. You see, I'm not old, Kurt. Not like him.

KURT. No.

ALICE. I'm young and I have desires. I'm going to change into something more becoming, pop up to see the Alderman and in two hours I'll be free of that old fart. (*Goes to the mirror and fixes herself a little, opening a few buttons on her blouse.*) I know that shy men often like crude women, Kurt.

KURT. Yes, that's true.

ALICE. And crude women often like shy men.

KURT. Do they?

ALICE. Yes, always. And I know you always liked me, Kurt. (*Pause.*) Now, turn away while I change.

Pause. KURT *does not turn away.*

(*Coyly.*) Kurt. I'm changing my blouse.

KURT *does not turn away.* ALICE *continues to unbutton her blouse revealing her bosom and her bodice.* KURT *is unable to contain himself. He rushes at her and grabs her, lifting her high into the air. Then he bites her throat. She screams.* KURT *throws her on the chaise longue, looking down at her in horror. She holds her hand to a bleeding wound while blood drips down* KURT's *chin from his lips.*

KURT (*breathlessly*). Alice, I... I...

He rushes out of the door stage right. Music plays and the lights gradually change through dusk to evening. ALICE *holds a napkin to her wound and leaves. The* CAPTAIN *enters through the double doors at back, closing them after him. A wind has come up.*

He wears old, worn-looking fatigues. He is hollowed-eyed and exhausted. He lights a half-dozen candles and sits at the table in the semi-darkness, absent-mindedly turning playing cards over. The doors rattle behind him in the wind. He turns and stares at them. There is no one there. He goes to the 'bar' and takes out a whiskey bottle and a glass. He looks at the whiskey for a moment, then takes two more bottles of whiskey out and carries them all to the window. He opens the window. Wind whips into the room. He throws all the bottles out. Then he takes his box of cigars and sniffs them. He brings them to the window and throws them out.

He closes the window, comes into the room and stands there wondering what to do with himself. He sees the painting of ALICE. *He takes it from the wall, puts his fist through her face and rips it apart, before tossing the pieces out of the window. He goes to his bureau, takes a bundle of letters wrapped in a black ribbon, brings them to the stove and burns them. He puts his face in his hands and weeps.*

The windows rattle. The CAPTAIN *is startled. He turns and looks out but sees nothing. He steps out of the double doors and closes them after him, walking off into the evening. The music ends and the door stage right opens.* KURT *peeps in. He leaves and returns with* ALICE *who is dressed in a black outfit.*

Well?

ALICE *raises her hand for* KURT *to kiss.*

ALICE. Thank me.

KURT. What happened?

ALICE *keeps her hand raised.*

ALICE. I asked you to thank me.

KURT *takes her hand and kisses it.*

I have made my deposition and named three witnesses. Two of whom I count as unassailable in a court of law. The prosecutor shall convey his answer here – right into the heart of the fortress – by means of that telegraph.

KURT. So it's done.

ALICE. You bet it's done.

KURT. What's happened to the room?

ALICE. Looks like he's preparing to move me out. I'll say one thing, he better have stored my pictures nicely, because he's the one who's moving. Into a six-by-three cell.

KURT. I'm glad you're finally separating, but surely one must feel pity for an old man who's going to jail. It will be tremendously frightening for him.

ALICE. Pity? Where's the pity for me – who never did anything wrong in my life and gave up my career for that monster?

KURT. I remember your career, Alice. It wasn't all that glorious.

ALICE. How dare you?! Everybody knew who I was and what I was capable of!

KURT. Really?

ALICE. Yes, really! Another year or two and I'd have been the leading actress in Copenhagen.

KURT. If you say so.

ALICE (*aghast*). Don't *you* start in on me now as well!

KURT. I'm not starting in on you. I'm merely pointing out that your career, as you call it, was hardly...

ALICE *suddenly flings herself around* KURT*'s neck and kisses him. He pins her arms by her sides and starts nuzzling her throat.*

ALICE. Oh Kurt! Oh...

KURT (*rapidly, passionately*). Oh, Alice, my God, I want to bite your throat and rip all your blood out like a wolf.

ALICE. No, don't! You'll hurt me!

KURT. You have awakened a part of myself I've tried for years to suppress with deprivation and torture. But now I know – I am the worst of all of us! When I saw you in your ravishing nakedness, passion clouded my vision and everything shone in the full glare of evil all over again. And now, well, I want to cover your mouth and suffocate you with my teeth.

ALICE. Oh, Kurt! Look at my hand! You see the mark of the ring that was there? The mark of my shackles? I suspected only a wild beast could ever break them!

KURT. Yes, I am a beast. And I'm going to bind you down and have you until you are no more.

ALICE (*laughs*). And to think I thought you had found religion!

KURT. Religion?!

ALICE. Yes! When you were banging on about the fall of man!

KURT. That wasn't me.

ALICE. I thought you had come to start preaching to us!

KURT. You listen to me. We're going to go down and get on that ferry and in one hour we'll be in town and we'll lock the door and then you'll see what I am.

ALICE (*pulls away with the energy of a bright idea*). Kurt! Let's go to the theatre tonight!

KURT. The theatre?!

ALICE. Yes! Let's walk in arm in arm and show everybody what a dismal little creature my husband really is.

KURT. Isn't it enough that he's going to prison? You want to rub his face in the dirt?

ALICE. No, it isn't enough!

KURT. Then you will be the prisoner because you'll let hatred rule your life – all the while believing you are free! You see, the difference between you and me comes down to this: while you dream of parading around some stupid theatre house like a giant child – (*With great passion.*) I am thinking about my son!

As KURT *says 'son', ALICE* slaps him across the face.

ALICE. Edgar's right. You're pathetic.

KURT *raises his fist to bash her, but manages to restrain himself.*

Pause.

KURT. I'm sorry.

ALICE. Very nice!

KURT. I'm sorry!

ALICE. Oh no, no no.

KURT. You won't accept my apology?

ALICE. Not like that. On your knees.

Pause. KURT *kneels.*

KURT. I'm sorry.

ALICE. On your face.

KURT. Excuse me?

ALICE. Get down on your face.

KURT. My face?

ALICE. Get down on your face.

> KURT *lowers his face to the floor before her.*

Kiss my boot.

> KURT *moves toward her boot about to kiss it.*

Lick it.

> *As* KURT *goes to do so:*

(*With disgust.*) Don't lick it! And never, ever, do that again. Now get up.

> KURT *gets up and stands there.*

KURT. I don't know who I am any more!

ALICE. Oh, don't give me that. You know.

> KURT *is startled by the sudden appearance of the* CAPTAIN *in the doorway stage right carrying a stick.*

CAPTAIN. Kurt. May I speak with you alone, please?

ALICE. Is it about safe passage for your poor defeated enemy?

CAPTAIN. I just want a moment's peace to speak with Kurt if I may.

ALICE. Oh! Talk of peace! Well, Kurt, you are honoured! Be seated! And bask in the glory and wisdom such as only ripe old age may impart! But please, gentlemen, should a telegram come through, please be so kind as to inform me. I am awaiting some news. Au revoir.

> *She goes out. The* CAPTAIN *sits with his walking stick and considers* KURT.

CAPTAIN. Can you explain how I got here? In my life I mean.

KURT. No more than I can explain mine.

CAPTAIN. Isn't there any meaning?

KURT. I used to think that *was* precisely the meaning. We cannot know, and so we must bow to the mystery.

CAPTAIN. But how can I bow to something I don't know exists?

KURT. You studied mathematics. You find an unknown fixed point by using the ones you do know.

CAPTAIN. I failed mathematics! They only let me graduate because I was so good at throwing.

KURT. You just have to find it.

CAPTAIN. How have you achieved such resolution, Kurt?

KURT. You overestimate me.

CAPTAIN. Well, I'll tell you the art of living – the real trick of life – are you ready?

KURT *shrugs*.

Elimination! You wipe the slate clean and you move on. You take a bag, and you stick all your humiliations in it and you chuck it in the sea and you walk away. It's that simple.

The CAPTAIN *clutches his heart.*

KURT. Are you alright?

CAPTAIN. The doctor in town says I won't live much longer.

KURT. When did he say that?

CAPTAIN. The day before yesterday.

KURT. So it wasn't true?

CAPTAIN. What wasn't true?

KURT. That he said you were going to live for another twenty years?

CAPTAIN. No, that wasn't true, I'm afraid. I just said that to… (*Signals: 'Annoy Alice.'*)

Pause.

KURT. And the rest of it?

CAPTAIN. Of what?

KURT. About my son.

CAPTAIN. What about him?

KURT. About my son joining your regiment.

CAPTAIN. Does your son want to join our regiment?

KURT. You said he already had!

CAPTAIN. That's the first I've heard of it, old chap, I didn't even know he was in the army!

KURT. Yes, your ability to disown your past misdeeds is quite effective. Isn't it?

CAPTAIN. I'm not with you.

KURT. And your divorce?

CAPTAIN. What divorce?

KURT. You just made that all up too?

CAPTAIN (*dismissively*). Oh, we always talk about getting a divorce! We could never get a divorce!

KURT. And your dinner with Judith? When she agreed to say that Alice slipped and fell in the water?

CAPTAIN. Judith? Judith barely speaks to me. She would never invite me to dinner!

KURT. So you're just… what? You're just a casual… liar!

CAPTAIN. I'm not a liar! Liar is such a strong word. Can't you indulge a little…

KURT. What…

CAPTAIN. …Banter? I can't even remember what I said! We all need a little forbearance, Kurt. Even the best and even the worst of us.

KURT. Oh, you've come to see that, have you?

CAPTAIN. Yes, I have. I have come to see that. Please forgive me, won't you, Kurt? Forgive me for everything. If you ever can.

KURT (*gets up*). I'm not sure I am entitled to forgive anyone.

CAPTAIN. Life! Life is so *strange*, don't you find? You see when one is *surrounded* by evil, it's very, very difficult to…

He notices that KURT *is on his feet, looking anxiously at the telegraph machine.*

What's the matter?

KURT. Can this machine be switched off?

CAPTAIN. Not very easily – it's wired directly to the station.

KURT goes to the window and looks out.

Is something coming through?

KURT. No, not yet.

CAPTAIN. Anyway, I was just going to say – life! It's just so awfully…

KURT (*interrupting the* CAPTAIN). There are some men with a lantern down at the pier – climbing out of a boat. Do they normally run boats this late?

CAPTAIN. What colour is the lantern?

KURT. Red.

CAPTAIN. It's what we call a 'welcoming committee'.

KURT. What's that?

CAPTAIN. Some poor wretch is about to be arrested.

KURT. Oh.

CAPTAIN. Mm. A night in irons. And up before a court martial at dawn. Now, tell me, now you've had a bit of time with Alice, what do you make of her? Be honest with me.

KURT. I have no idea! I understand less and less the older I get. Edgar, did you really push her into the sea?

CAPTAIN. I did.

KURT. Why?

CAPTAIN. I don't know. It just seemed so natural! There she was. And there was the fifteen-foot drop to the water. And the angle was just absolutely perfect.

KURT. You didn't regret it?

CAPTAIN. No. Not for a second. It was delicious.

KURT. Didn't you know she'd come for revenge one day?!

CAPTAIN. I fully expected her to! And she's been exacting revenge every day since!

KURT. You're very philosophical about it!

CAPTAIN. Staring death in the face changes you, Kurt. Will you give me your hand, and let us part on good terms?

The CAPTAIN *stands and offers* KURT *his hand.* KURT *considers him and comes to make up. They shake hands. Then the* CAPTAIN *throws an arm around* KURT. KURT *steps into the embrace, burying his head in the* CAPTAIN*'s shoulder, weeping.*

There now, my good man, that's alright.

ALICE *appears in the doorway.* KURT *steps away, composing himself.*

ALICE. Well now, look at this! Sorry to interrupt, but has my telegram come?

KURT. No.

ALICE. My great failing was always my impatience. But then again, perhaps it's a great strength. (*Lifts her parasol like a rifle and aims it at the* CAPTAIN.) So let's get this over with. Now, how do I fire this thing? Oh yes, I remember now – I read that manual you wrote. Myself and three others – the lucky few. FIRE! (*Makes an explosive sound.*) So how's the new wife? The beautiful young one? I haven't seen her around lately. Oh, you don't know? Oh dear. Well, I know how my lover is!

ALICE *puts her arms around* KURT*'s neck.* KURT *pushes her away.*

He's well, he's well. He's a little shy, but he's very well. And he's not the first. You see, your problem was that you were always too big-headed to be jealous, so you never saw all the other times I led you by the nose! Yes! Many times!

The CAPTAIN *draws his sword in a cold fury and advances on* ALICE. *She realises he is serious and she darts away from him.*

Kurt! Help me!

KURT *moves to shield her. The* CAPTAIN *advances on them, hitting the furniture, knocking tables and chairs over. Suddenly he stops, clutching his heart.* ALICE *and* KURT *watch as he sinks to his knees.*

CAPTAIN. Judith...!

The CAPTAIN's *head comes to rest on the seat of a chair and he falls still.*

ALICE. Hooray! He's dead!

The CAPTAIN *sits up.*

Oh...

CAPTAIN. No, not yet. (*Stumbles towards a chair and sits, exhausted.*) Oh, Judith...

ALICE (*to* KURT). Right, let's go.

KURT *does not move.* ALICE *goes to him and grabs him by the arm.*

I said, let's go!

KURT *pushes her to the floor. He goes to the door.*

KURT. Go back to Hell.

ALICE. No, no! Wait! I'm sorry! Wait!

CAPTAIN (*simultaneously*). She'll kill me, Kurt. Don't go! Kurt!

KURT *is gone. Pause.*

ALICE (*with a sudden change in attitude*). Well, that's friends for you! (*She gets up.*) There are no real men any more. At least a woman knows where she is with someone like you.

CAPTAIN. Alice. Come here to me.

ALICE *goes to the* CAPTAIN.

I'm dying.

ALICE. What?

CAPTAIN. The doctor told me.

ALICE. But you said...

CAPTAIN. I was lying! I was drunk! I was lying!

ALICE. What about the rest of what you said?

The CAPTAIN *shakes his head.*

Oh my God! What have I done?

CAPTAIN. We can fix things up. Don't worry.

ALICE. No, you don't understand. This can't be fixed.

CAPTAIN. Of course it can – you just forget and you move on.

ALICE. No, I've blown us to smithereens, Edgar.

CAPTAIN. No you haven't.

ALICE. Why did you have to tell so many lies!?

CAPTAIN. Oh, can't we just forgive each other?

ALICE. Oh God, this is like a horrible dream and I can't wake up!
I'd do anything to change it. If we could just get out of this, I'd…
I'd… I'd…

The telegraph machine starts clicking. ALICE *looks up at the heavens.*

Just let us out of this!

CAPTAIN. Out of what?

ALICE (*shouts*). Don't listen!

CAPTAIN. Alright, calm down.

ALICE *runs to the window and looks out. She runs back to the*
CAPTAIN *and puts her hands over his ears.*

ALICE. Don't listen! Don't listen!

CAPTAIN. I won't. I won't, it's alright… Lisa…

A ribbon of paper comes out of the machine and the clicking stops.
ALICE *stands there, breathlessly with her hands over the*
CAPTAIN'*s ears. Then she goes to the machine and takes the*
paper.

What is it?

ALICE (*reading the message, she laughs with relief*). Oh thank God!
It's the evening report. It's raining over on the mainland and all is
well. (*Goes to the* CAPTAIN *and kisses him on the forehead.*) It's
nothing.

ALICE *goes and sits on a chair, taking out a large handkerchief.*
She covers her face and cries into it.

CAPTAIN. What dreadful secret are you expecting?

ALICE. Please don't ask me.

Pause.

CAPTAIN. You know, when I collapsed that first time, I stepped a
little way over the far side of the grave. And I saw something
there.

ALICE. What was it?

CAPTAIN. Hope – for something better.

ALICE. For us?

CAPTAIN. Yes. It's hard to describe but I... I realised that this might
be our life. I had never thought so before. I always believed we
must be dead, playing out some dreadful penance.

ALICE. With each as the other's tormentor.

CAPTAIN. Yes.

ALICE. Do you think we have tormented each other enough?

CAPTAIN. Yes. And then some!

They laugh mordantly.

Shall we tidy up?

ALICE. If we can.

CAPTAIN. Well, it may take more than this evening.

ALICE. Oh, who cares any more?

CAPTAIN. So. You didn't get away this time.

ALICE. No.

CAPTAIN. But I wasn't taken away to jail either.

ALICE *looks at him.*

Yes, I heard all about your little plan, but the only snag is that
none of the regiment ever put any money into the widow's fund.
They're all too mean! Even if I had wanted to, there was never any
money to embezzle, so your deposition was pointless. (*Pause.*) So!

You have your wish. The angels have heard your prayer and they have whisked you out of your predicament.

ALICE. So I'm supposed to be your nurse now?

Pause.

CAPTAIN. Only if you want to.

Pause.

ALICE. Well, what else would I do?

CAPTAIN. I don't know. (*Pause.*) You know, Alice, I'm not sure if it's the light this evening, but you... you really are a particularly attractive woman.

ALICE. Really?

CAPTAIN. Yes, I mean it. You look, well, positively seductive!

ALICE. Oh, Edgar, please.

CAPTAIN. I mean it.

She looks at him openly. He extends his hand to her. She takes it.

ALICE. And you are still handsome.

CAPTAIN. I was never handsome.

ALICE. To me you were.

They regard each other.

Our eternal torment will return, you know.

CAPTAIN. Yes, but if we can be patient, death will come, and then, perhaps, life begins.

ALICE. If only.

CAPTAIN. You think we're bad? I read in the paper the other day about some old codger who's been married seven times, and then at the age of ninety-eight he goes back and marries the first wife again! Now that's what I call torment! (*Pause.*) Don't be angry with Kurt, Alice. He was always weak. And in three months' time we will celebrate our silver wedding anniversary, and you just watch: Kurt will be our guest of honour. Christine will come back and cook for us, the Alderman will make a speech. The Colonel will lead the toast and even the good doctor himself will come and gatecrash it, knowing him!

ALICE. Mm.

CAPTAIN. What. Tell me.

ALICE. I'm just thinking about the Alfredsens' silver wedding.

CAPTAIN. Oh God...

ALICE. You remember? Evelina had to wear the ring on her right hand because Sergeant Alfredsen had chopped off all the fingers on her left – with a cleaver!

CAPTAIN. I know. I can still see the look on the minister's face! It was awful, I mean, it was sort of hilarious, but... I don't know.

ALICE. Perhaps... we laugh and we cry in equal measure. Perhaps that's just the way life has to be. None of us can say if it's all terribly serious or just some pointless joke. And sometimes the joke is so painful that being serious – gloomy even – brings its own kind of relief.

CAPTAIN. Celebrate our silver wedding with me. (*Pause.*) Oh, say yes. Let them laugh at us. We'll laugh too. Or maybe we'll be terribly serious about it – whichever way it turns out. Who cares?

Pause.

ALICE. Alright.

CAPTAIN (*tenderly, simply.*) Our silver wedding. (*Raises himself up.*) You forget and you keep going. I mean, what can we do? You keep going!

They look at each other.

Lights fade.

Conor McPherson was born in Dublin in 1971. He attended University College Dublin where he began to write and direct. His stage plays include *Rum and Vodka*, *The Good Thief*, *This Lime Tree Bower*, *St. Nicholas*, *The Weir* (Laurence Olivier, Evening Standard and Critics' Circle Awards), *Dublin Carol*, *Port Authority*, *Shining City* (Tony Award nomination for Best Play), *The Seafarer* (Tony, Laurence Olivier and Evening Standard Award nominations for Best New Play), *The Veil* and *The Night Alive* (New York Drama Critics' Circle Best Play Award; Laurence Olivier, Evening Standard and Lucille Lortel Award nominations for Best Play).